It was as though time stood still . . .

The lightning had revealed to her a man she had never seen, a Salvador as wild and primitive as the jungle tempest that raged around them. In the shelter of the fallen tree he stared down at her, his gaze devouring her fine-boned countenance, taking in the dishevelment of her wet ebony tresses curling down about her in disarray—and something more; her lush scarlet mouth, so vulnerably parted and tremulous.

Aurora quivered involuntarily as the violent storm outside paled in the face of this new danger. This was not the polite, icy *caballero* who had always treated her with such courtesy and respect. No, this man was a stranger to her, a savage beast who would take what he wanted.

Her blue eyes wide with apprehension, she began to struggle against him, trying to free herself from his grasp, so she might run back out into the storm and the jungle. They were elements she could fight; she did not know if she could resist this man.

Salvador paid no heed to her pleas for release. Instead he pressed his mouth hotly to her throat. "I have wanted you from the first moment I ever saw you," he murmured. "Do not deny me; I know you felt it too."

"No," she moaned. "No, I don't want you."

But it was not true, and he knew it. With a low growl, he claimed her lips . . .

Also by
REBECCA BRANDEWYNE

No Gentle Love

Forever My Love

Love, Cherish Me

Rose of Rapture

Published by
WARNER BOOKS

And Gold Was Ours

Rebecca Brandewyne

WARNER BOOKS

A Warner Communications Company

Warner Books, Inc.
666 Fifth Avenue
New York, N.Y. 10103

Ⓦ A Warner Communications Company

Printed in the United States of America

First Printing: December, 1984

10 9 8 7 6 5 4 3 2 1

For my own tall dark hero,
my husband,
Gary.
With love.

The Players

In Spain

La Casa de Zaragoza

Don Manuel Vitorio de Zaragoza, Marqués de Llavero

Doña Catalina Aguilar de Rodriquez de Zaragoza, Marquesa de Llavero; wife to Don Manuel; later, Condesa de Fuente

Their son:
Don Juan Rodolfo de Zaragoza y Aguilar, Conde de Aroche; later, Marqués de Llavero

Don Salvador Domingo Marcos Eduardo Valentín Rodriquez y Aguilar, called *La Aguila*—the Eagle; Visconde Poniente; son of Doña Catalina by her first husband, Don Esteban Rodriquez (deceased)

Pancho, valet to Don Salvador

Don Timoteo Yerbabuena, Conde de Fuente; a family friend

La Casa de Montalbán

Doña Gitana de Navarra de Montalbán, dowager Condesa de Quimera

Her son:
Don Felipe Hernando Montalbán y de Navarra, Conde de Quimera

Doña Ynez Torregato de Montalbán, Condesa de Quimera; wife to Don Felipe

Their children:
  Don Basilio Enrique Montalbán y Torregato, Visconde Jerez
  Doña Aurora Leila Gitana María Raquel Montalbán y Torregato
  Don Nicolas Montalbán y Torregato

Doña Francisca de Ubrique de Montalbán, Viscondesa Jerez; wife to Don Basilio
Lupe, maid to Doña Aurora

In Texas

Don Rafael Bautista Delgados y Aguilar, called *El Lobo*—the Wolf; Visconde Torreón; a gunslinger; cousin to Don Salvador
Storm Aimée Lesconflair, wife to El Lobo
Gilberto Huelva, a tailor; former valet to Don Basilio

In Peru

Paul Van Klaas, a planter
Heidi Van Klaas, wife to Paul
Ijada, a *mestiza* woman
Mario Nunes, a *mestizo* trader
Bernardo, friend to Mario
Coronel Xavier de la Palma, head of the military
Mayor Farolero, a military physician

Contents

And Gold Was Ours

Of fine Toledo steel they were,
Those blades that glittered bright,
And bittersweet their death knell
That rang out through the night,
Echoing 'cross the Spanish plains
To an ancient gypsy seer.
She heard them not, for her eyes
    beheld
A vision pure and clear.

A journey did the cards foretell.
In secret one must flee,
As another did before her
To seek his destiny.
And still one more would follow
O'er the ocean green and wide,
To clip the Eagle's wings
And steal away his bride.

Oh, sweet Aurora, as morn dawns
So will awaken your desire.
Will you know your heart by then?
One will set your blood afire.
The other's touch will leave but ice,
So have care the path you wind
Through steaming jungle, savage, lush,
Feverish longing's balm to find.

Now petals bloom like passion flower;
He breathes your fragrant musk,
Before the other, silent, comes,
Like shadows fall at dusk,

To slay the one who takes you,
Where the sugarcane stands high,
Rippling 'neath the silver moon.
The night soughs a warning cry:

Hold fast! Hold fast, love's wild
   embrace,
While still there is yet time
To taste the honey of his lips,
Which kiss away the rime. . . .
Melting, melting, frost to flame—
In sweet *amor* so fierce yet tender
Lies gold that does not dull with age,
But shines with lasting splendor.

BOOK ONE

Journey

Chapter One

The Jungle, Peru, 1548

LEGEND called it *El Dorado*—the Gilded One—a lost city where the forgotten streets were paved with gold, and riches beyond a man's wildest dreams lay waiting to be plundered. Whether or not it truly existed no one knew. But many sought to find it, and many died in the attempt: for life in the dense, steaming jungle of South America was a hard and torturous one, even for those long accustomed to it.

Sweat blinded his eyes as with a machete a man hacked his way through the thick, tangled undergrowth, clearing a path where none had been before; and as though in protest of this violation, the jungle struck back with a furious vengeance.

Poisonous plants, which brought a slow, paralyzing coma ending in an agonizing death, flourished in the odd, uncanny hush that hung heavily in the stifling heat. Angry mosquitoes buzzed and swarmed in hordes to settle on a man's flesh and suck his blood, infecting him with a dreaded tropical fever that alternately burned and chilled, leaving him shuddering with delirium and racked with pain. Dangerous, glowing-eyed cats prowled in the night, stalking their prey—be it man or beast—on softly padding paws that sent a shiver down the jungle's spine. Giant, deceptively colored snakes slithered from the overhanging branches of the trees to strangle the unsuspecting, the unwary. And barklike caimans lay ominously still, like fallen trunks in the dark, murky depths of the rivers and swamps, waiting to tear a man to shreds, should he stumble and rouse the sleeping reptiles.

But man's greed for the riches that legend held the lost city of El Dorado contained was even greater than his fear of death; and so he dared to brave the jungle, in search of the Gilded One, ignoring the warnings of the bleached bones that marked the paths of those who had gone before him.

Don Santiago Roque y Avilés was such a man; but, unlike the others, his quest for gold was born of love, not greed. The handsome heir of a noble but impoverished Spanish family, the young visconde had given his heart gladly to Doña Arabela Madrigal y Tarragona, and just as gladly she had given her heart to him in return. But Arabela's father refused permission for the two lovers to marry. Santiago had no money. The only daughter of the Conde de Quinta could not wed a poor man, no matter how blue his blood might be. Arabela wept and pleaded with her father to change his mind—but to no avail. At last, brokenhearted, she retired to her room and began quite simply to pine away. Alarmed by his daughter's decline, the conde finally relented. In three years' time, if Santiago had regained his family's wealth, he might marry Arabela.

Having heard the legend of the lost city of El Dorado, Santiago set out for South America to make his fortune. He searched long and hard for the Gilded One, and perhaps because he was driven by love and not greed, he found it. On the gold-paved streets of the forgotten city's square, he sank to his knees and thanked God that his prayers had been answered. Though the riches that El Dorado contained were beyond his wildest imaginings, Santiago took only enough to restore his family to their former status and, in triumph, returned home to Spain to claim the heart and hand of his beloved.

He was too late. During his absence Arabela had been stricken with a mortal disease and had died, crying his name.

Grieving, unable to bear the sights of Spain that reminded him so painfully of his beloved, Santiago went back to South America; and there by the Amazon River, in the wild jungle of Peru, he dedicated his life to building a manor house that would stand forever as a monument to his cherished Arabela.

At first people thought him a poor madman, and they left him alone with his sorrow. But gradually, as the great house took shape, and the costliest of furnishings and ornaments were paddled down the Amazon by native Indians in dugout canoes and unloaded at his boat dock, there were those who began to realize that, crazed though he might be, Santiago was indeed wealthy. They wondered why a man of his means would settle so alone in the remote jungle, and the more curious among them started to dig into his background. Little by little they uncovered the tragic story of his past, and in time word that the madman had found the lost city of El Dorado spread. Those who thought the tale of the Gilded One only a legend mocked the rumors of Santiago's discovery and paid them no heed. But there were others, greedy men, who did not laugh. They went to the manor to learn the truth.

They were struck dumb by the sight of Esplendor, as Santiago had named his home. Set upon a small hill, it had been built almost entirely of expensive, imported marble to withstand the ravages of the tropics, and it rose like a shining white jewel in the midst of the verdant tangle and bursts of vivid color that were the jungle. Never before had anyone seen anything like it. Constructed from a blueprint in Santiago's mind, it resembled none of the edifices of the day.

The main house was two massive stories square; at its corners large towers topped by domes like those of the Moors stood, keeping watch over the land. It was flanked by smaller one-story wings at whose corners slender minarets rose but did not reach the heights of the primary spires. At the front of the manor were three graduating steps leading up to a porch whose six tall, graceful pillars supported an intricately worked, black wrought-iron balcony onto which fine French doors opened. Beneath that two stout, ornately carved oak doors barred the entrance; and long, narrow, arched casements with diamond-shaped, lead-glass panes gleamed, like eyes behind the slits of a mask, along the entire front of the manor and wings. On the upper story of the main house, on either side of the balcony's French doors, were neatly set smaller Moorish windows; and a widow's walk ran the length of the main roof. The manor was topped by an onion-shaped cupola with inverted, cordate apertures through which could be seen the huge solid-gold bell that hung within and that was rung once each morning at sunrise and once again each evening at sunset, like an angelus.

It rang with a strange, haunting sound—that bell. It was almost as though it wept and whispered, "*Querida, querida,*" its plaintive sigh breaking the breathless still of the jungle.

Many of those who came to wrest Santiago's riches from his grasp were so awed by the angelus's cry and the great house that they crept away, never to return, certain ill luck would befall them, should they dare to disturb the manor's inhabitant. But there were others who were bolder, and against these Santiago was forced to defend himself and his home with his sword and shield.

After each battle he would sigh and shake his head with pity for those who knew naught but greed. Then wearily he would retire to his study, wherein he kept his dearest memento of Arabela: an intricate little clock that each hour chimed a sad melody that reminded him of his beloved.

And so the years passed, and the stories about the aging, greying madman of Esplendor grew. Some said he had angered the ancient Inca gods by robbing the lost city of El Dorado of its riches and had been cursed for pillaging the Gilded One. Others claimed it was not Santiago who was cursed, but the looted fortune itself. To touch it was to go mad, to die. They said he had buried that which he had stolen, deep beneath the dark earth of his jungle lands, and had hidden a map, describing the location, somewhere in his peculiar manor in hope the gods would someday forget their wrath and allow him to reclaim what he had taken. Still others swore he had buried not the treasure, but a map that told how to find the lost city of El Dorado, to which he periodically returned to replenish his wealth (despite the fact that no one ever saw him leave Esplendor).

The wild, superstitious tales were endless. Eventually they reached the ears of a group of mercenary knights, hardened soldiers of fortune who did battle for any lord who paid them. Temporarily without hire, the wicked knights broke into Santiago's home late one evening, taking him unawares. Though he fought them valiantly, they took him prisoner and beat him unmercifully to discover the truth of his secrets.

"Take what ye want," he told them. "All I have is what ye see about me, relics of the past and an old man's dreams."

But the soldiers did not believe him.

"Tell us the way to the lost city of El Dorado!" they demanded. "Tell us where ye buried the treasure ye stole from the Gilded One!"

"I am an old man," Santiago said, "and 'twas a long time ago. I do not remember the way to El Dorado, and the only treasure I ever buried lies in a tomb in Spain—and here in my aching heart."

"Liar!" the knights spat. "The villagers say ye have at least a map."

"Nay"—Santiago shook his head—"there is no map. Foolish men." He sighed tiredly. "Go home. Ye do not need a map to find the greatest treasure on this earth, a treasure that is the most precious of golds. . . ."

But the soldiers would not listen. They interrogated Santiago until finally he was dead and could tell them nothing more. After that they ravaged the manor, searching for the fortune they were convinced that Santiago had had. They found not even a map. Enraged, they plundered the house of what jewels, plate, and objets d'art they could carry away on their horses, then departed, leaving Santiago's bloody body sprawled in the great hall.

Soon others, learning of the madman's death, came to steal what remained of the furnishings until at last the manor had been stripped of all its contents, and nothing was left, not even the brocade draperies that had hung at the windows. Only the cupola's huge solid-gold bell, dulled now by time, survived the pillaging, it being too heavy for just one or two men to remove. A group of the villagers, thinking it would be just right for their church, did attempt to take it; but its deep, resonant chime pealed forth when they touched the angelus, and the eerie, empty sound so terrified them that they dropped the bell, and it smashed through the roof to the floor below. It lay there undisturbed from that day forward. Yet on a moonless night, though the villagers knew it was not possible, they heard the angelus ringing.

As the centuries passed other men took up residence in the manor, only to die there as horribly as Santiago had. In time Esplendor was forgotten, referred to only, with a frightened glance and a crossing of the breast, as deserted, haunted, and accursed.

Like sentries, the tall towers still stood watch, but no one came. Only the jungle drew nearer, reaching out with sultry, gnarled fingers to reclaim the manor that had dared to defy it. Little by little the unrelenting tangle enveloped the house in a dark snarl of thick brush that grew unchecked, crowding ever forward, choking the broad drive until it was but a ribbon, penetrating crevices in the walls of the manor until they began to crumble and give way.

Inside the house itself spiders spun their webs high in the corners, and dust settled in the long marble corridors that seemed to echo with hollow footfalls, though no man trod within.

None mourned the manor's sad demise, for he who would have wept at its destruction was long dead, and she in whose memory he had built it was colder still.

Now, three hundred years later, in this year of 1848, the great house still stands, desolate, a faded ruin of glory. Yet the spirit of the manor remains unconquered, for Esplendor heeds not the ravages wrought by time. Born of love and legend, it looks out knowingly, secretively, over the savage jungle, as though it is only sleeping, waiting breathlessly, expectantly, to be wakened.

And sometimes still, on a moonless night, one who listens with the heart can hear the angelus bell sounding . . . summoning.

Chapter Two

Madrid, Spain, 1848

RAZOR-SHARP silver steel—the finely tempered metal that had brought Toledo fame—flashed in the candlelight; and the dark eyes of the two men who wielded the blades glittered just as murderously.

On a chair in one corner Doña Catalina Aguilar de Rodriquez de Zaragoza, Marquesa de Llavero, sat, trembling. She held a tightly clenched handkerchief to her mouth to stifle her screams of fear, to muffle her whimpers of agony. In moments either her husband, Don Manuel Vitorio de Zaragoza, Marqués de Llavero, or her son Don Salvador Domingo Rodriquez y Aguilar, Visconde Poniente, would lie dead upon the Oriental carpet spread upon the marble-tiled floor. Even now blood from her son's arm spattered, then dripped slowly, staining the plush, intricately patterned rug. Catalina's husband laughed, teeth flashing wickedly, as swiftly he yanked his rapier free.

"First blood!" the marqués crowed triumphantly.

"It is the last blood that counts, Don Manuel," the

visconde noted coolly as with his black silk cravat he bound the wound while keeping a wary eye on his opponent, the stepfather whom he despised and did not trust.

"Oh, *Santa María*, stop them, Timoteo. Please stop them!" the marquesa begged piteously of the only other occupant of the small salon.

"If only I could, Catalina," the white-haired hidalgo, Don Timoteo Yerbabuena, Conde de Fuente, replied with despair. He leaned stiffly on his cane, one arm about Catalina's shaking shoulders. "But I cannot. It has gone too far. This time, it has gone too far."

"It is all my fault, all my fault," the marquesa moaned softly, defeated.

She had been stupid again, utterly and inexcusably stupid—Manuel had shouted the word at her angrily—*stupid!* She had made a fool of him before their guests, the marqués had told her icily when all but Timoteo had departed. Timoteo loved Catalina, had always loved her, and would have married her, had she been free. But, because of his crippled leg, he was incapable of defending her. Knowing this, Manuel had then struck Catalina viciously, blackening her eye and splitting her lip. When Timoteo had tried futilely to intervene, placing himself in the path of the blows, the marqués had jeered at him and thrown a glass of wine in his face.

"Come, Don Timoteo! Why do you not thrash me with your cane?" Manuel had taunted. "It is what you wish to do, is it not? Perhaps you will kill me, and my wife will be yours—if she isn't already. Are you, Catalina? Do you find it more amusing to spread your legs for this lame old *cabrón* than you do for me?"

Smirking, the marqués had fondled his wife crudely before the helpless conde's outraged eyes. Tormenting

the two would-be lovers was a cruel sport that Manuel
could never resist. The incident would probably have
ended shortly thereafter, as usual, with Timoteo pleading for his beloved's release and the marqués laughing
mockingly in the conde's pain-filled face before yanking
Catalina to her feet and carrying her off to abuse her in
bed. Only this time her son Salvador, who had come to
visit, had walked in unannounced, taken in the scene at
a glance, and coldly challenged his stepfather to the
duel.

"To the death, you *bastardo!*" the visconde had
growled. "You have insulted *mi madre* for the last
time!"

And so it had begun.

Twenty-seven long years of hatred was now unleashed
as the two men battled each other with unrelenting
fury. The marqués was older, more experienced; but
the visconde had many debts to settle, and they gave
him strength.

As Salvador thrust he thought of Don Esteban, the
father he had never known, assassinated in a dark alley
by Manuel's henchmen. As he parried he thought of his
mother, Doña Catalina, forced to marry the vile marqués
and to submit to his sadistic perversions. The visconde
sidestepped a vicious lunge and thought of his half
brother, Don Juan, Conde de Aroche, lording it over
him as though he, Salvador, were a peon—or less!
Reengaging arms, he remembered his *tío*, Don Diego;
his *tía*, Doña Anna María; and his *primero*, Don Rafael—
all banished from Spain years ago because of Manuel's
treachery. Perhaps now they too were dead. As blood
flowed from his wound he thought of his own lands,
milked dry by the marqués's thievery and finally sold,
leaving the visconde nothing but an empty title when

he reached his majority. He gritted his teeth. *Basta!* It was enough! Yes, his stepfather had much to answer for. The wound did not weaken Salvador; it only spurred him on.

Outside in the sky the moon was a hazy halo of silver shimmering down through the branches of the deciduous trees, which rustled gently with the faint whisper of the wind. The night was grey and wet with the soft spring rain that drizzled down and danced on the roof of the townhouse. The multicolored flowers of the gardens stirred as they spread their petals and leaves wide to drink thirstily the droplets of life-giving water that splashed upon them. Somewhere in the darkness a coach rattled past on the slick cobblestone street out front, and a dog howled mournfully.

Inside the small salon the rapiers scraped furiously against each other, thrusting in high carte and parrying in low tierce; and the glass-paned cabinets rang with the clash of the steel. Catalina wept into her handkerchief and prayed the son she loved would prevail over the monster she called her husband. Timoteo stood rigidly by her side, cursing the lameness that kept him there while Salvador risked death to fight the battle that should have been the conde's own. His arm tightened about his beloved's quivering shoulders as he heard her moan.

"Why, Timoteo? Oh, why has Salvador done this mad thing? I have suffered Manuel's insults and blows before—" The marquesa broke off, biting her lip, for she had always taken care to see that her son knew as little as possible of the marqués's ill treatment of her.

"And for far too long, Catalina," Timoteo asserted wrathfully in response. "Salvador should have made an end of that swine long before this . . . *would* have done so, had you not pleaded with him not to duel with his stepfather."

"I—I did not want my son to be killed. Manuel is deadly with his rapier!" she cried in anguish. "See how he moves in dangerously even now!"

"And see how Salvador feints and escapes yet again. Come, Catalina. You know what a fine swordsman your son is! Better than Manuel, in fact. Salvador will win the duel; I'm sure of it."

"Oh, Timoteo, I cannot bear it. If Salvador slays Manuel, he will be forced to flee the country. Juan will go to the queen. And if my husband prevails . . . Oh, *Madre de Dios*, have mercy! It is all my fault."

"No, Catalina!" The conde's voice was sharp. "The blame is Manuel's and his alone. His greed and vindictiveness have been a plague upon us all: the fine old houses of Rodriquez, Delgados, Aguilar—and how many others?—all ruined because the marqués has maneuvered himself into power. Even Yerbabuena is broken by that pig! Let us hope that Salvador butchers him *pronto!*"

"Oh, Timoteo! How can you say such a thing? Do you not understand what will happen? Juan will go to the queen, I tell you! He will have my beloved Salvador arrested and executed for murder."

In Catalina's mind she had only one son, and that was Salvador. She could not accept the fact that Juan had also been born from her womb. He was the product of Manuel's savage rape of her on their wedding night, an evil, malignant tumor that had festered inside of her, then had been delivered to prey upon the world as brutally as his father, the marqués, did. She had taken one look at Juan, had glimpsed his demoniacally slanting eyebrows so like his father's, and had known him for the devil's cub. Afterward Pepita, her maid, had given Catalina something to ensure there would be no more babies born of her husband's terrifying assaults upon her body. It was her one small victory over the marqués, for he had longed to found a dynasty and had been forced to settle for Juan.

"Have no fear, Catalina," Timoteo reassured her. "I shall help Salvador to escape from Spain," he promised, for the conde also had no illusions about Salvador's fate, should he kill his stepfather.

"And then I will never see him again!" the marquesa whimpered, cringing at an especially loud clattering of the rapiers. "Oh, why was I so stupid this evening? I shall never forgive myself. Never!"

"Don't be a fool, Catalina. Salvador fights for himself and his dead father as much as he does for you, and I know he would give his life gladly to see you freed from that boar, Manuel de Zaragoza! Watch now; do not hide your eyes. Salvador will be the victor, I promise you!"

Again and again the blades engaged as both men danced lightly upon booted feet, the muscles rippling in their backs and arms as they lunged, then recovered, cursing each other through clenched teeth.

Expensive satin tapestries hung in shreds on the walls, ripped by the rapiers. Globes of oil lamps lay shattered on the floor. Solid-gold statues, which had been in the family for centuries, had been knocked from their marble pedestals; and plush velvet chairs had been torn and overturned. Still the struggle persisted.

Both men were breathing heavily now; the marqués's brow was beaded with sweat. He was tiring, for the visconde could give him twenty years. Manuel stabbed at his stepson's heart, missed, tripped over a footstool, and fell, his steel scratching sparks along one side of the marble floor. He felt the younger man's blade sear his shoulder, then withdraw; and he knew his life had been spared.

"That was for *mi padre*," Salvador snarled as the marqués quickly snatched off his silk cravat and jammed it hastily beneath his sleeve to staunch the flow of blood.

"Your father was a fool," Manuel jibed as he sprang to his feet. "And his son is an even bigger fool. *En guardia*."

Enraged, Salvador began to press his attack. To escape from him the marqués leaped atop a long table, then turned to slash wildly at his stepson, feverishly trying to beat off the younger man's assault. Manuel's rapier cut a small gash in the visconde's shoulder. Salvador grinned, a tight, hateful smile that did not lighten his dark, murderous eyes.

"*Toque*," he murmured grimly. "It is not often a man scores twice against Don Salvador Domingo Rodriquez y Aguilar. But this I promise you, señor el Marqués: For every wound I suffer you will know two in return."

Then he too leaped to the tabletop. The marqués swore.

"Insolent cur," he hissed. "I shall soon teach you a lesson. What a pity you will not survive to profit from it!"

In response Salvador's steel sliced open Manuel's arm.

"For Tío Diego," the visconde observed with satisfaction.

The marqués began to panic. To be torn to pieces by the point of a blade was not the way he would choose to die, and he was suddenly quite certain he *was* going to die. Once, he had been a master of the rapier, but age and indulgence had taken their toll on him. Salvador, on the other hand, had lived a hard life. It had made him lean and tough. His lithe young body was like a whipcord as he feinted and made yet another hit against his stepfather.

"For Tía Anna María, no doubt." Manuel raised one of his demon eyebrows sarcastically.

"But of course," the visconde mocked.

The steel flew, *whoosh*ing through the air until the blades clanged together once more, locking at their hilts. With a mighty shove Salvador forced the older man from the table. Then, flinging away his rapier, the visconde jumped upon the marqués. Manuel, unprepared for such an attack, lost his grip upon his own steel. His blade bounced to one side as the two men rolled across the floor, attempting to choke each other. Salvador slapped his stepfather's face insultingly several times, then wrenched himself free and deftly recovered his weapon.

"*En guardia*," he warned.

The marqués's eyes narrowed with hate. Filled with ire, he grabbed up his rapier and charged. The visconde sidestepped neatly, scoring another touch during the pass.

"For Rafael," he noted. Then, "And for me," as his steel struck Manuel yet another disabling blow. Almost casually then Salvador stepped back to survey the older man. The visconde's lip curled with disgust at what he saw. Briefly, deliberately, he flexed his blade, then stalked forward purposefully. "And now—now I think we will end this little charade," he informed his stepfather. "For *mi madre!*" Salvador spat, then drove his rapier through the marqués's heart.

Catalina gasped and rose to her feet, her eyes wide with horror.

"Salvador. Oh, no, Salvador!"

The visconde pulled his weapon free and wiped it carefully to remove the blood that dripped from it. A slight smile curved upon his mouth.

"Shall I cut off his head for you, Madre?" he asked. "You can mount it in the trophy room, along with the other beasts."

"Oh, Salvador," she wailed. "This is no time for your jokes! Do you not know what you have done?"

"Certainly. I have killed my stepfather—and high time too." The visconde moved swiftly to his mother's side. "Come, Madre. Why do you weep? Surely you did not love an animal such as Manuel de Zaragoza."

"No, never!"

"Then dry your tears. Don Timoteo, wine. We will celebrate my stepfather's death and drink to your wedding day. I trust you will find a priest tonight, my old friend, before there can be any interference, eh?"

"You may rest assured of that, Salvador," the conde told him. "I might be useless in a duel, but, by God, I am still a man of some power in Madrid."

"Oh, Timoteo! How can you even think of such a thing when my son is in grave danger?" The marquesa dabbed at her eyes with the handkerchief she held in her trembling fingers. "Salvador"—her voice was urgent—"you must flee the country, and quickly, before Juan comes home. He will go to the queen. . . ."

"Sí, what a pity. Perhaps I should wait and slay him too," the visconde mused aloud, not at all appalled by the idea of killing his half brother.

"No, my son!" Catalina cried, stricken with fear for

her beloved Salvador. "Juan has too many important friends at court—"

"Whose influence he won by licking boots like the dog he is," the visconde declared. "But very well, if you insist, Madre, then I shall leave." He set his wine cup down. "Give me a kiss, my pretty rose—for luck."

The marquesa's eyes were shadowed with sorrow as she pressed her lips to his cheek.

"Where—where will you go, Salvador?" she inquired at last, her heart beating erratically in her breast. "Portugal? France?" She hoped it would not be too far away.

"No, Madre." The visconde spoke gently. "I think you know that is impossible. Juan's hirelings would seek me even there, and I would be forced to live a life of constant wariness. No, I am done with the old country forever. I shall go to the New World, as Tío Diego and Tía Anna María did. At least there I will have relatives— if they are still alive; and how I do yearn even now, after all these long years, to see *mi primero*, Rafael, again. He was ever the best of friends to me."

"Wait, Salvador." Catalina placed one hand upon her son's arm, regaining some of her dignity and composure in the face of the tragedy that had befallen them. "You will need money. Manuel's greed for your inheritance has left you little enough of your own." The marquesa left the chamber and returned moments later with a small chest. "Here. I want you to have these," she stated firmly over her son's protests, opening the casket to reveal a fortune in jewels.

The visconde gasped with amazement at the sight of the precious gems, for he had not known his stepfather to be a generous man. Salvador was further astonished that the jewels were not locked up in a vault at the de

Zaragoza estate. The second Carlist war had broken out, and it was dangerous to journey with valuables. The wealthy now wore paste copies of their more expensive pieces, in case they should be robbed.

"Manuel was not afraid of the bandits and rebels who prey upon travelers these days," Catalina explained wryly at her son's surprise. "He liked me to look well for guests, and he enjoyed humiliating me in the process. Every time he—he came to my—my bed—" Her voice cracked, but she mastered it and went on. "He would leave something, as though—as though I were no better than a—than a— Then he would force me to wear them later. . . . Take them! Take them! I never want to see them again! If I have bought you a new life with my misery, then the price was worth it all . . . and more, my son. My only son."

The marquesa pressed Salvador's hand to her face and kissed his palm. Tears flowed down her cheeks. She turned away, trying to regain control of her emotions.

"And this. Take this too," she continued, attempting to smile. She handed him an old and yellowed letter. "It is from Anna, the only word I have ever received from her these twenty long years past. I—I do not know if she is even still alive. . . . I have prayed to God that the silence between us has been only because Manuel kept her letters from me—" She broke off abruptly.

The visconde studied the faded sheets of paper thoughtfully.

"'Santa Rosa, Texas, 1828. My dearest sister, we have arrived safely in the New World. . . .'" His voice trailed off as he remembered Tía Anna María, Tío Diego, and Rafael. "How my aunt loved her roses," he recalled aloud quietly. "And you, Madre. She used to say you were her loveliest bloom. That is why I have always called you my pretty rose."

"*Sí,* I know. Ah, well." Catalina sighed. "It was a long time ago. A long time ago," she repeated sadly, "before *he* destroyed us all."

"We are not destroyed, Madre," Salvador said. "He is dead, and we are alive. Don Timoteo, I give the most beautiful flower in all of Spain into your keeping. Guard her well, my old friend."

"You need have no fear for Catalina, Salvador," Timoteo assured him, pressing a card into his palm. "Take that to my office in Cádiz," he directed. "They will get you safely aboard a ship bound for the New World."

"*Muchas gracias,* Don Timoteo."

The marquesa gave a tiny, ragged cry. With fingers that had begun to quiver again, she clutched her handkerchief to her breast.

"Now you must go, my son," she urged anxiously.

"*Sí.*" Salvador bent, tilted her countenance up to his, and caressed her cheek lovingly. He believed it was the last time he would ever see her. He kissed her tenderly. "Take heart, Madre," he whispered fiercely. "*La Aguila* is free!"

Then he strode to the French doors that opened out onto the terrace and flung them wide.

Outside, the rain was still falling. For a moment the visconde stood silhouetted in the glistening shower, looking like some ancient pagan god as lightning flashed abruptly, illuminating his dark figure. Hands spread wide, palms upturned to the night sky, he flung his head back in exultation, uncaring that the rain beat down upon his face. Indeed, he gloried in it as it splashed down upon him, soaking his hair and skin, for it was as though the water washed him clean of the past; and he was finally free.

The years of bitterness fell away, yes; but curiously no peace came in their stead, for Salvador was not as other men were. Other men were content with their lots in life; and if they were not, they accepted what came, learning to make the best of a bad bargain. But there was a strange restlessness in Salvador's spirit even he did not understand, for it was not born of a desire to leave his mark upon the world. Rather it was a peculiar yearning for something that was beyond his comprehension. It was as though all his life he had been waiting... waiting, but for what he did not know. He had searched ceaselessly for the answer; until he found it he would be but half-complete. But that which he sought had managed always to elude him.

Now, as though he had the knowledge from a life long past, the visconde felt he stood on the threshold of discovery. From this moment on he would rush headlong toward his destiny—and he would not be afraid to face it. He wanted desperately whatever the stars held in store for him, for fate alone would satisfy the unbearable longing in his soul, the ache in his heart.

Catalina watched him silently for an instant, wondering what thoughts were chasing through her son's mind, the mind that had always, despite her love for him, been something of an enigma to her. Then her black lashes swept down, and her lips moved in a quiet prayer to God. When at last she opened her tormented eyes, Salvador was gone.

"*Vaya con Dios,*" she breathed, her heart aching. "*Vaya con Dios*, my son."

Chapter Three

Salvador was not the only young hidalgo fleeing through the narrow, twisting wynds of Madrid that rainy night; but he would have been very surprised to learn his half brother, Juan, was the cause of another flight as well.

Don Basilio Enrique Montalbán y Torregato, Visconde Jerez, had made a grave error in judgment. He had dared to aspire to the hand of Doña Francisca de Ubrique; and—worse yet—she had dared to accept him, rejecting Juan, who had also pressed his suit. That Juan would seek vengeance for their perfidy had not occurred to the two lovers. Unfortunately it had occurred to Juan. No one scorned Don Juan Rodolfo de Zaragoza y Aguilar, Conde de Aroche, and got away with it!

Livid with rage, Juan had gone to the queen, young Isabella, who adored him, and had denounced Basilio as a *Carlista* who sought to overthrow the throne. Queen Isabella, who was somewhat timid and not very bright, had issued a warrant for Basilio's arrest. But, warned in time by his friends, Basilio had escaped, racing away desperately from the Condesa de Hervás's party, where he and Francisca had been celebrating their engagement.

Now, stricken, the two lovers hurriedly made their way to the townhouse of Francisca's father, where they begged Don Pedro to summon a priest to marry them before they fled from their homeland. Spain, they knew, was no longer safe for them. Juan was a man of power and importance at court, and his vengeful arm had a long reach. They must journey to the New World to escape from him.

Such a furtive wedding, coupled with a frantic flight from the country, was not what Don Pedro de Ubrique wished for his only daughter. But his wife, Doña Dorotea, whom he had always believed a sentimental fool (and quite rightly so, it now seemed), wept on his shoulder and declared he would be a monster if he stood in the way of young love. So Pedro reluctantly gave his permission for the marriage to take place and sent for a priest, as well as for Basilio's younger sister, Aurora, whom the bridegroom cherished dearly and wanted present at the wedding.

Then all sat down nervously to wait, their anxious eyes fastened on the clock upon the mantel in the small salon. The ticking of the timepiece sounded loud in the silence; but any moment they expected it would be drowned out by the even more deafening noise of Juan and his henchmen pounding ruthlessly upon the front door, brandishing their ill-gotten warrant for Basilio's arrest and demanding entrance to the de Ubrique townhouse.

OUTSIDE, the spring rain continued to drizzle, but inside the townhouse of Don Felipe Hernando Montalbán y de Navarra, the lamps shone cheerfully, for the household was as yet unaware of the tragedy that had befallen its young heir, Basilio.

Upstairs, in one of the ornately furnished bedrooms, Basilio's younger sister, Aurora, stood at her window, looking down at the square below. The glass felt cold upon her skin, where she had her cheek pressed close against the pane, but she paid no heed to the chill. She was too engrossed in her thoughts, which seemed as sad to her as the tears of rain that trickled down the window.

She was different from other girls her age—she knew she was—and it depressed her a little. It would have been good to have been able to laugh and flirt as gaily as the rest of the young debutantes who, like her, had so recently entered into Spanish society; but this Aurora had not been able to bring herself to do. She told herself it was because she was shy and had felt inhibited, but in her heart she knew this was only partially true. The fact was that she had no real interest in such things. Not one of the gallant *caballeros* who'd placed his name upon her program during the many long evenings past had caught her fancy, and Aurora was beginning to think none ever would.

Why? she wondered.

There were many who'd been young enough, handsome enough, rich enough to turn any girl's head; and still Aurora had felt nothing when she'd gazed at them. Yet she was sure that what many had said of her was untrue: she was not cold, hard-hearted. Deep down inside, her nature was far more passionate and caring than that of any of the girls who'd flocked to the parties and balls of Spanish society. Aurora was like Sleeping Beauty in the fairy tale that her mother had read to her in childhood, waiting . . . waiting to be wakened. But she had not yet met a man who stirred her, for none had been the one she was seeking.

How strange that she should know so surely with no more than a glance at a man that he was not for her. Yet that was how it had been.

Once the initial round of parties and balls that had marked her debut into Spanish society had ended, Aurora had retired to her father's townhouse. She'd found no husband—not even a *novio*—but she had not cared. Let people think what they wished. She would go to no more social affairs unless it was absolutely necessary.

Her family had not pressed her, though she'd realized they were worried about her odd behavior. Aurora had eased their fears for her as best she could, but even she had not been able to explain her peculiar actions. How could she, when she did not understand them herself?

It would have been madness to have spoken of the strange feelings that had sometimes possessed her—in a candlelit hall, a moonlit garden—the sense of *déjà vu* that had crept eerily upon her and made her think: I have been here before; here my love and I did meet. . . . Madness to have told how compelled she had felt to search the crowded parties and balls for a face that was never there, a face that belonged to a past so distant that Aurora often wondered if she had but imagined it. Madness to have said the arms of the *caballeros* who had danced with her were not the arms that had held her once and would hold her yet again.

Ever since her childhood she had had such thoughts, had seen visions of a man she knew she was destined to find someday. She could even remember the first time he had come to her. Slowly she closed her eyes and summoned up the memory, bright and clear, as though it had happened only yesterday.

Aurora was just five years old at the time, but she already knew she was not like other girls. She was content to play quietly with them—but with only half her attention, as though she were listening for someone's arrival. Every time she heard a visitor greeted, she would rush to see who it was; then, upon perceiving the caller's face, her own would fall in disappointment. Everyone—even strangers—noticed and remarked on it.

"It's as though she's expecting someone," her family said upon observing this same scene again and again. Then, puzzled, they asked, "But who could it be?"

No one knew—not even Aurora. She knew only that she was driven obsessively to view each visitor who came to Quimera, her father's estate. Her family did not understand her odd behavior. But, because they loved her dearly, they humored her, deciding that she was simply a curious child. Aurora did nothing to banish this belief. Better to be thought overly inquisitive than crazy, like old Simón, the gardener, who was *loco*.

Today was a special day. Aurora knew it even before *he* came, the caller she had been waiting for.

She had managed to escape from the watchful eyes of her duenna; and now, after standing on tiptoe to lift the latch that barred the iron gate, she moved warily through the beautiful gardens of Quimera, keeping a cautious eye out for old Simón, who, though harmless, frightened her a little. At the back of the courtyard she climbed an orange tree whose branches allowed her to scramble onto the top of the stone wall that enclosed the gardens. From her perch she could see for miles in every direction; and after deftly plucking, peeling, and eating a piece of the sweet fruit, Aurora looked out eagerly over the world.

How vast it seemed, so much larger than that within the boundaries of Quimera. How she longed to explore this world that lay beyond her own! But it was a long way down to the ground from the top of the wall. Aurora eyed the drop thoughtfully for a time, then decided it was too far for her to jump. She might be killed, and then her parents would be as sad as little Benito Mendoza's parents had been when he had drowned and gone to heaven.

Nevertheless, it was cool beneath the shade of the orange tree, whose branches secreted her from the sharp eyes of her duenna; so Aurora remained in the hiding place she had found, reveling in her first taste of freedom.

Soon it was *siesta* time. All was still and quiet, the silence broken only by the tolling of the angelus bell from the tower of a distant cloister. Aurora yawned and rubbed her eyes. How long had she been sitting here? She didn't know. She supposed she really ought to be getting back to the house. No doubt everyone was worried about her. Even now she could hear her duenna calling her.

As Aurora turned to go a sudden dizziness assailed her, as though she had whirled about too quickly. She froze, and a mist swirled up to engulf her. Time seemed to stop, then jerk into motion once more; and as though from nowhere, out of the clearing haze, a striking youth suddenly appeared below.

He was tall and dark, mounted upon a white Arabian stallion and riding like the wind across the land. His head was thrown back in exultation, and he was laughing, his teeth flashing whitely against his swarthy face. Spellbound, Aurora thought he was the most handsome man she had ever seen. He was so beautiful he might have been a god.

He drew near, and her heart began to pound with excitement. He was here at last! The visitor she had been waiting for! How she knew this Aurora could not have said. She knew only that he had come.

The sixteen-year-old youth did not notice her at first, but presently he spied her studying him from above and reined in his mount.

"Buenos días, muñeca pequeña," he greeted her pleasantly. "What are you doing up there?"

Little doll. He had called her a little doll. For some reason Aurora was pleased by the notion. She blushed, her eyes downcast, for she had always been shy with strangers, and she didn't know what to say.

Surreptitiously she gazed at him from beneath her lids. He was dressed so strangely, she thought. He looked like some of the old portraits of her ancestors that hung in the long picture gallery of Quimera. She was so bemused by this it took her a moment to become aware that her own clothing somehow had changed as well. She was startled by the realization. How could that be? Gingerly she touched the stiff, heavy gown she now wore, as though to reassure herself that it was not just a figment of her imagination. It felt real enough. But how did she come to be wearing it?

Aurora would have pondered the mystery further, but she felt the youth was still waiting for her to answer him. How rude he must think her! Taking a deep breath, she managed to gather her wits and find her tongue.

"Hiding from my duenna," she confessed timidly.

"Ah." He smiled. "A most difficult task, I should imagine."

"*Sí*," she said, and then, fearing the youth meant to ride on and not wanting him to go out of her life just yet, she offered, "Would you—would you like an orange?"

The day was hot, and the youth was thirsty. Perhaps the sweet, juicy fruit would help.

"All right," he replied.

Aurora picked an orange from one of the overhanging branches of the tree, then hesitantly held it out to him. After wrapping his reins about the pommel of his saddle, the youth drew the knife at his waist, quartered the fruit, and bit into it. She watched him quietly and cast about anxiously for something else to say.

"I—I wish I could ride like you," she stammered bashfully at last.

"You do, eh?"

The youth tossed away the orange peelings and wiped his juice-drenched hands on his handkerchief. The child intrigued him, although he didn't know why. She couldn't be more than five years old at the most, but she was so beautiful!

"I'll tell you what: It's late now, and I have to be going. But you be here tomorrow, if you can get away, and I'll give you a riding lesson."

Aurora flushed, trembling so with excitement that she could scarcely contain herself.

"Really? You're not just teasing me? You promise?"

"I promise. *Hasta luego, muñeca mía.*"

Then the youth disappeared as suddenly as he had come.

After he'd gone Aurora hugged herself tightly, knowing something momentous had just occurred. She scarcely noticed that her garments again had been trans-

formed, returned to their original state; and since she
had no explanation for this, she simply dismissed it.
Perhaps she had been so excited she had merely imagined it after all. At any rate, it was not important. The
handsome youth was all that mattered. Aurora just had
to find a way to escape from her duenna once more.
Whatever the cost she must be here tomorrow when he
came back!

She was so thrilled by her encounter she barely
heard the shrill scolding she received from her duenna
upon returning to the house.

The next day, during *siesta* time, Aurora pretended
to be asleep. But when her duenna nodded off she
slipped quietly from her bed, dressed herself as well as
she could, and hurried to the gardens. Again she climbed
the orange tree and swung herself from its branches to
settle upon the stone wall. Her eyes anxiously searched
the terrain beyond. What if she were too late? What if
she had already missed the youth? What if he did not
come?

No. Once more, as before, the peculiar mist enveloped
her; and when she opened her eyes there he was,
appearing as suddenly as he had yesterday, again as
though from nowhere. Aurora's heart beat joyously in
her breast. He had kept his word! He had come!

She thought she would burst with happiness as he
greeted her, asked if she were ready, then reached up
to lift her down from the wall onto his high saddle,
which was as strange and unfamiliar as his clothing. She
clutched the pommel tightly, glad of the youth's strong
arm about her waist, holding her close so she wouldn't
fall off. He touched his spurs lightly to the stallion's
sides, and presently they were racing the wind.

"Aurora. Aurora. *Aurora!* Are you deaf? I've been

calling you for the longest time. Why didn't you answer me?"

Startled and bewildered, the child glanced about dazedly as her older brother, Basilio, clambered up the orange tree to sit beside her. Why, what was she doing here, still perched upon the stone wall, when only moments before she had been flying on horseback over the land? It wasn't possible. It didn't make sense. She didn't remember coming back to the courtyard; and where was the handsome youth who had held her so tightly? With a disappointed sob Aurora realized he was gone. How could he have vanished so quickly, as though into thin air?

"Are you all right?" the ten-year-old Basilio questioned curiously, concerned. His sister's face, though naturally pale, seemed much whiter than usual. "*Niña,* is something wrong?"

Her tiny hands caught her brother's frantically, for a terrible thought had suddenly occurred to her.

"'Silio," Aurora whispered, "how long have I been sitting here?"

"Why, ever since I saw you sneaking away from the house and decided to follow you," he responded, puzzled. "Why, what's the matter?"

"Noth—nothing," she stammered tearfully; she dared not tell even Basilio about her "dream."

Why, there wasn't any youth at all! There never had been! She had imagined the whole thing! Or had she? It had all seemed so very real. . . . Sweet *Jesús!* Perhaps she was as mad as old Simón was!

The frightening notion seized the child tightly in its grasp. She was afraid she would be shut away in a dark attic somewhere—a fate that had befallen one of her ancestors—a secret, shameful burden to her family, since, naturally, nobles did not wish it known that they had such relatives. The tale of the demented Linda la Loca had made a vivid impression upon Aurora when she'd learned of it; and so, to this day, she had never told anyone about the images of the youth who, despite her attempts to deny his presence, had continued to appear to her, at each meeting growing older just as she had.

As a child, in order to allay her fears about her sanity, she finally had decided he was her guardian angel, and that was why she alone could see him. Now she was not certain this was so. She had thought for a while that perhaps she had the Sight. After all, she would not be the first of her family gifted—or cursed—with the ancient gypsy talent. But of late she was not even sure of this. The visions seemed to be not of the future, but rather memories of the past, of another time, another Spain. The man was always garbed strangely, in a mode that had been the fashion centuries ago, and when she joined him in the vignettes Aurora was wearing like costume. She did not understand any of it.

Why did such thoughts obsess her? Bits and pieces of an interlude in a distant past only half-remembered—or remembered not at all. Imagined. The fantasies of a girl who was different, a girl who lived in two worlds, a girl who was crazy.

No! Horrified, Aurora pushed the awful thought away, as she had so many times before. She was as sane as anyone. Surely she was. There had to be some other explanation for the man who came to her on the wings of time. There just *had* to be! If only she could find him in the flesh, touch him, and know he was real!

Aurora turned from the window, her mind made up. She could no longer bear the burden of her secret visions alone. She would go at once to her grandmother's room and tell Abuela about the man who haunted her so. Abuela's own grandmother had been a Romany gypsy, and the Sight that had been hers had passed to Abuela. Yes, Aurora would tell Abuela about the images that had appeared to her since childhood. Perhaps Abuela would read the cards for her, would look into the future and tell her fortune; and Aurora would finally discover why a man no one else could see had come to her all these years. She must know, for his hold on her was growing so strong it was beginning to interfere with her real life. Aurora was starting to believe she truly must be mad.

THE head of the old and proud house of Montalbán, Doña Gitana de Navarra de Montalbán, dowager Condesa de Quimera, sat silently at the table in her chamber. She was an elderly woman, but she had aged gracefully. Her bearing was as regal as a queen's. Never had Aurora, who now sat beside her, seen her spine touch the back of a chair. Like a crown, Doña Gitana's shining blue-grey hair was neatly coiled atop her head; not a single strand was out of place, for the grand beldam was meticulous. Her jet-black eyes glittered thoughtfully as she shuffled the deck of cards she had taken earlier from an intricately carved box.

Though Doña Gitana seldom left the townhouse in Madrid, she had a lively interest in life and the affairs of those she loved. So when Aurora had come to her grandmother's room and asked to have her fortune told, Doña Gitana had agreed. After all, the girl was sixteen. It was time they knew what the future held in store for her.

The older woman was troubled a little by the things

her granddaughter had told her earlier, though so much
was now explained. No wonder Aurora was not interested in finding a sweetheart. There was no one who
could compete with the man of her dreams. He had
been her friend, teacher, and protector since childhood.
Now that Aurora was older it was only natural that she
should perceive the man in a new and even more
intimate light.

That the man was Aurora's guardian angel had to be
considered, but this Doña Gitana did but briefly. Such
apparitions usually appeared only in times of severe
distress or sorrow, when guidance was needed; and they
certainly did not laugh and eat oranges and whisk away
on horseback those remanded into their care. No, it
could not be.

Nor did the visions, in Doña Gitana's mind, bespeak
the Sight, that gift—or curse—of prophecy that she
herself had. The images that Aurora had spoken of did
indeed seem drawn from the past, as the girl had
guessed, rather than the future; and certainly that past
was not Aurora's own—at least not in this life.

The elderly dowager crossed herself mentally at the
thought. There were those who believed that the soul
had many lives, but this belief went against the teachings of the Church; and adherence to those teachings,
the Spanish Inquisition had proven, was not to be cast
aside.

Still Doña Gitana did not for an instant believe that
her granddaughter was crazy; and if Aurora's destiny
were bound to some distant past, it must be a strong
force indeed to have spanned the wings of time. Doña
Gitana must discover the link. The stars were, after all,
more powerful than men and could not, like mere
mortals, be crossed.

Thus decided, Doña Gitana finished shuffling the cards, then deftly dealt them out upon the table until they lay arrayed before her in the old gypsy pattern she had learned from her own grandmother. One hand closed over her solid-silver-knobbed cane, and she muttered something under her breath.

"What is it, Abuela? What do you see?" Aurora asked. "Oh, tell me quickly, please!" she begged, her face alive with anticipation.

"*Silencio*, Aurora." Doña Gitana raised one hand warningly. "You chatter like a parrot, *niña*, and disrupt my concentration. The cards cannot be rushed. In time they will tell us what you wish to know."

Obediently Aurora quieted, though she leaned forward eagerly in her chair. Tonight—tonight she would learn what the future held in store for her; and at sixteen, it seemed very important to know.

Her grandmother gave her a speculative, searching glance and sighed. The girl was young yet, but already there was the promise of summer fire beneath her wintry beauty. As Spain's cold, snowy mountains shielded her hot, arid plains, so did Aurora's cool, outward being hide her passionate inner nature.

Her long blue-black hair shone like a midnight sky, contrasting sharply with her pale ivory skin touched with the slightest hint of rose on her high cheekbones. Startling too were the swooping jet brows that arched above the wide, dark blue eyes spiked with dense, sooty lashes. Those eyes gleamed like sapphires now, fathomless, vivid with color and the stars of flame that seemed to flicker in their depths. Beneath her straight, classic nose her lush scarlet lips curved enchantingly on her arresting, oval face.

A pulse beat rapidly where the hollow of her graceful

throat sloped down to the full round breasts that swelled
enticingly above her tight, ruffled basque. Her waist
was the barest wisp; her hips were narrow yet softly
rounded; her long legs tapered into small feet as graceful as her slender-fingered hands.

Her every movement reminded one of a young black
swan floating serenely on the calm waters of a lake; and
the girl was indeed much like a cygnet, shy, unsure of
herself, and as yet untried. To those who did not know
her she seemed haughty and aloof—cold, the insensi-
tive would have said. But Doña Gitana was old and
perceptive, and the years had brought her much wisdom. She had looked deep into Aurora's eyes and had
seen the smoldering passion that glowed like embers
beneath the demure sweep of the girl's half-closed lids.

The beldam scrutinized the card she held. She nodded with satisfaction, mumbling to herself once more.
Sí.... This was the man who would fan the flame that
burned deep inside of Aurora. Doña Gitana laid the
card upon the table, then slowly began to speak.

"I see ... a time long past," she said haltingly, "a time
of love unfinished and thus not forgotten; a love so
great, it yet endures, like a golden bell, echoing through
the eons of time. . . .

"The centuries pass. I see deceit and danger, a
journey across vast waters to escape—"

"A journey! But . . . to where?" Aurora cried, confused, for she could not imagine ever leaving Spain and
could make no sense of her grandmother's cryptic words.

"*Silencio!* You disrupt the cards," Doña Gitana cautioned
again. Then, "It is a time of new beginning in a new
world, a world far different from any you have ever
known. It is dark and twisted, a savage place, a jungle!
Sí, it is a jungle through which winds a muddy river so

wide and long as to seem almost endless. I see a tomb—no. It is a house . . . a strange white manor like none your eyes have ever beheld. There is a man—"

"Oh, tell me! What is he like?" Aurora broke in breathlessly, unable to prevent herself from interrupting once more.

If he were her dream man, she must know.

"He is dark and fierce. His arm embraces a woman tightly, and there is a rapier in his hand."

"Am I the woman? Does he defend me, then, this man?"

"He seeks to hold the woman fast, to protect her from another, a man with a scar upon his face. It is growing colder. There is a mist. It is dark, oh, so dark. It is as though I am blind . . . blind. . . . The air is thin. No, there is no air. *There is no air.*" Doña Gitana suddenly clawed horribly at her throat. "No air! Can't— can't breathe . . ."

"Abuela!" Aurora shrieked and leaped to her feet as her grandmother slumped over the table, cane clattering to the floor. "Abuela!"

Screaming for help, the girl loosened the neckline of her grandmother's gown and searched the pockets frantically for the vial of smelling salts she knew was never far from the dowager's grasp. Aurora found the bottle at last, unstoppered it, and waved it beneath her grandmother's nostrils, praying all the while that someone would come to her aid. Presently, to Aurora's relief, she heard footsteps pounding along the hallway outside, then the door was flung open wide by her father, her mother following close behind.

"Aurora! What is it?" Don Felipe hurried toward his mother's prostrate form while his wife poured some water from a pitcher into a basin, wet her handkerchief, and began to dab at Doña Gitana's face and wrists.

"I—I do not know. She was reading the cards, and all of a sudden she—she couldn't breathe. She gasped and—and—"

"Oh, Felipe, perhaps it is her heart," Doña Ynez said anxiously. "I will summon the physician."

"*Sí*, tell him to come at once!" Felipe shouted after his wife's rapidly retreating figure.

"Oh, Padre, forgive me," Aurora wept as she helped her father move her grandmother to the sofa and plumped up the pillows so the older woman would be more comfortable. "I should not have teased her to tell my fortune—" She broke off, biting her lip, tears of contrition streaking her cheeks.

"There, there, Aurora." Felipe patted his daughter's hand kindly. "Do not cry. You are not to blame. You could not have known this would happen, and it might have occurred at any time. Though she would not admit it, I have known *mi madre* was failing in health for some time now."

"But . . . why did she not tell me?"

"She is stubborn, *tu abuela*. She did not wish you to worry and flutter about her as though she were a helpless invalid. She says you spend too much time with her as it is, you, a young girl, who ought to be attending parties and balls instead of waiting on an old woman."

"But I love Abuela! I love spending time with her!" Aurora protested.

"I know, *niña*, and you are a great joy to her, despite all her grumbling to the contrary," Felipe reassured his daughter. "So often I have seen her eyes light up when you entered a room and spied her smiling fondly to herself when she thought you were not watching."

"Dear Abuela. She is not truly as cross as everyone believes. It's just that her joints are old, and they trouble her, especially when it is damp or raining, as it is tonight. Oh, Padre. Do you think she will be all right?"

"Of course . . . I will." Doña Gitana spoke as she opened her eyes and, with effort, attempted to rise. "I am a de Navarra, and we are a family of fighters."

"Abuela!" Aurora's face brightened.

"Madre. Are you in pain?" Felipe queried quickly as his mother grimaced. "Lie still," he commanded. "We have sent for the physician—"

"That young fool Armando, no doubt," Doña Gitana rasped dryly. "A witch doctor shaking a few gourds over my head would serve me better than *that* poor excuse for a healer. Hand me my cane, and help me up, Felipe. There's nothing wrong with me that a few sips of good Madeira won't remedy."

"Madre, I must insist you rest until Doctor Sanchez arrives."

"I tell you the man's a charlatan," Doña Gitana asserted, pulling herself, with her son's reluctant assistance, to a sitting position.

"Ah, señora la Condesa, feeling better already, I see," Doctor Sanchez observed with wry amusement as he entered the room in time to overhear the beldam's last remark.

He crossed the chamber swiftly and caught the dowager's wrist to check her pulse, though she eyed him fiercely and attempted to yank away. After glancing at his timepiece the physician dropped Doña Gitana's hand lightly into her lap, listened to her chest for a moment, then opened his bag.

"What have you got in there? Your beads and rattles?" Doña Gitana inquired tartly.

"Madre, please!" Felipe looked apologetically at the physician. "I beg your pardon, Doctor Sanchez," he said. "As you can see, *mi madre's* attack has done nothing to sweeten her tongue."

"Or my temper," Doña Gitana declared. "Aurora, fetch me a glass of Madeira before this fool tries to poison me with his gruesome concoctions." She glared at Doctor Sanchez once more.

"Poisons, señora, are used by Italians," the physician stated firmly as he poured into a spoon a small measure of liquid from a bottle in his bag.

"Well, what is that, then, Armando?" the beldam queried. "One of *your* untried potions?"

"Oh, no, señora." Doctor Sanchez's mouth twitched. "This is a very old brew."

"What's it for? My heart?"

"No, your tongue. It will make it temporarily mute," the physician claimed with a wink.

"Hmph!" the dowager snorted, then cackled her wheezing laugh. "Trying to cast a spell on me, are you? Well, I won't have it, do you hear?"

"Of course, señora, since you are practically shouting in my ear. Now be a good girl, and open wide."

"'Girl,' is it?" Doña Gitana complained after she'd swallowed the bitter medicine and downed the contents of the glass that Aurora had handed her to take away the vile taste. "Let me tell you something, Armando: If I *were* a few years younger, you'd be bringing me flowers and begging my favor."

"Indeed I would, señora," Doctor Sanchez agreed. "As it is, I must content myself with these small but pleasant moments."

"Hmph!" the beldam snorted again, but Aurora could tell her grandmother was pleased all the same. "Well, what's wrong with me, Armando? Should I call on old Joaquin and tell him to ready my coffin?"

"Not yet, señora. As far as I can determine you merely suffered an unusually strong fainting spell. Your heart is a little weak . . . but steady. I see no reason why, after a few days of rest, you can't be up and about."

"I'll say one thing for you, Armando: You may be a poor physician, but you're a gallant liar. My heart's done for, and I know it, so don't try to tell me otherwise. Well, I've lived a long time. I'm over eighty years old, and life's been good to me. I've few regrets, which is more than most people can say, so I guess I won't be too sorry when I stand before the Lord. Still, if God's willing and the grapes don't sour, I'll live to be a hundred just to spite you, Armando."

"I certainly hope so, señora."

The physician smiled warmly, for he liked the crotchety old dowager and knew she secretly favored him as well.

"Aurora." Doña Gitana turned to her granddaughter hovering worriedly by the sofa. "Pour me another glass of Madeira and one for the doctor too. We'll drink a toast together . . . to vintage wines and women."

"Doña Gitana!" Ynez gasped, mortified.

"Oh, be quiet, Ynez. Don't you know better than to reprimand someone who's got one foot in the grave?" the beldam questioned as she threw her son's wife a sharp glance. "Armando"—she held out one aged yellow claw—"you may kiss my hand."

"I would be honored, señora."

It was then that Nicolas, Aurora's younger brother, who always seemed to know everything that occurred in Madrid, burst without warning into the room. In his haste to impart the terrible news he had just learned, the eleven-year-old boy tripped and slid across the floor on one of the rich Oriental throw rugs that were scattered about the chamber. He managed to catch himself in time to keep from falling but made a spectacle of himself nevertheless.

"Nicolito," Ynez chided with a gentle click of her tongue and a shake of her head. "How many times must I tell you to enter a room with dignity and grace? People will think you have been raised in the stables."

"Sorry, Madre," he apologized automatically. Then, "Doctor Sanchez. What are you doing here?"

"Nicolito!" Ynez scolded again, frowning at her son's rudeness.

"Your grandmother suffered a fainting spell, Nicolas," the physician explained, not at all offended by the young man's presumptuous question.

"Then—then you've already heard the news?" the boy asked, looking about anxiously.

"News? What news, my son?" Felipe inquired.

"Why, I thought—I thought . . . No, Doctor Sanchez, don't go. We may need your services yet again. It's—it's 'Silio."

"Basilio!" Ynez cried, one hand going to her throat, as though she feared the worst. "What has happened to my son?"

Nicolas's mouth tightened with anger, and his nostrils flared.

"Señor el Conde de Aroche falsely denounced him as a *Carlista* and persuaded the queen to sign a warrant for his arrest. Some of his friends managed to warn him in time for him to escape, for when the soldiers came for him tonight—at the Condesa de Hervás's party—he'd already fled, taking Francisca with him. They're waiting now at Don Pedro's townhouse. They're going

to be married before they leave Spain, and 'Silio wants
Aurora to come and witness the vows."

"No! Oh, no!" Ynez wailed.

Then it was she, not Doña Gitana, who fainted in the
physician's arms.

IT had taken some doing, but Don Felipe had at last
persuaded his wife that she must remain at the townhouse
rather than rushing to her oldest son's aid. The Montalbáns
had no powerful friends at court. There was nothing
they could do to help Basilio, and in trying to assist him
they might well bring down Don Juan's infamous wrath
upon their own heads. No, much as Felipe loved his
firstborn son and heir, the boy was a man now and must
make his own way. Felipe must think of the rest of his
family. Doubtless the Montalbán townhouse was already being watched.

Felipe bitterly cursed the fact that he had spent the
money kept in his vault for emergencies only days
before and had not yet replaced it; and though the
women of his household would have parted willingly
with their many jewels, the majority of the gems were
at Quimera for safekeeping. They had brought only
paste copies to Madrid. Due to Spain's civil war the
hills were teeming with ruthless bandits and rebels,
who preyed mercilessly on travelers, robbing them of
their valuables. Felipe had a few pesetas in his pocket;
that was all.

"You will explain to Basilio about the lack of funds,"
he said anxiously to his daughter as he watched her
drape an old rebozo about her face. "If only we had had
some warning, some time to prepare . . ."

"I understand, Padre," Aurora replied quietly, laying
one hand on her father's arm.

How old and tired he looked all of a sudden! Basilio's plight had been a terrible blow to them all—but Aurora knew her beloved older brother was dearest to her father's heart.

"I must go, Padre," she continued, casting a quick glance outside. "Even now Don Juan and his henchmen may be on their way to Don Pedro's townhouse."

"*Sí, sí.*" Felipe nodded, seeming somewhat disoriented for a moment. Then he took a deep breath and gathered his wits. "Take care, *niña*. I'm afraid for you, going out this way."

Aurora was dressed in her oldest clothes, so she resembled a scullery maid. She would journey alone the short distance to Don Pedro's townhouse. That way, if the Montalbáns *were* being watched, she would not arouse suspicion, for no proper, unmarried lady in Spain ventured forth without her duenna, especially at night. Beneath her light cape she carried a small pistol for protection, although she didn't know if she would be brave enough to use it, should anyone accost her.

"I'll be careful, Padre, I promise."

After hugging her father close Aurora stepped out into the blackness and entered the waiting hackney summoned earlier.

It was dark inside the hired carriage, and as Aurora settled herself on the well-worn springs, she was grateful none could see her. She was certain the frantic pounding of her heart within her breast could be spied beneath her cloak. The hackney lurched into motion, the driver urging his horse forward at a slow, steady pace, as he had been instructed, and following a circuitous route to Don Pedro's townhouse. Though she saw three mean-looking men lurking in the shadows, to Aurora's relief they did not try to stop her. Her ruse had worked. She leaned back and closed her eyes, murmuring a silent prayer of thanks to God.

Even before her lashes once more swept open, she felt the man's presence, smelled the masculine aroma of his spicy fragrance, and knew he would be sitting there, opposite her, to comfort her. He seemed always to know when she needed him.

As the now-familiar mist that always signaled his coming cleared, Aurora gazed into his black eyes; and the frenzied racing of her heart slowed.

"*Muñeca mía.*" He spoke softly. "You are troubled."

"*Sí.*"

He reached out and took her hand in his.

"Do not be afraid," he told her, "for I am with you always."

Then, to Aurora's surprise, he pressed his lips to her palm. The heat of his kiss emanated through her body, warming her. Her heart began once more to flutter erratically. But this time no fear accompanied its beating. Instead it was as though in her dark world a small candle now glowed, and she looked at the man in a different light. Her lips parted to speak, but she could find no words to express the strange emotions that had suddenly possessed her.

"*Querida,*" he whispered—and then disappeared.

Aurora blinked her eyes and shook her head to clear it. Then, as she always did, she glanced at her watch, knowing only a few brief minutes had passed, though it had seemed like hours.

The hired carriage plodded on, its driver unaware that for a fleeting instant the hackney had carried not one passenger, but two. Had Aurora informed him of this, he would have thought her mad, she knew. But her dream man had been there all the same. She could still feel the pressure of his hand, giving her courage.

"Who are you?" she asked aloud in the silence. "And what are you to me that you seem so real?"

But there was no answer. The moment out of time was gone.

THE wedding ceremony was, of necessity, brief, but it was evident that Basilio and Francisca did not mourn the rite's simplicity. Despite the lovers' plight, their faces shone with happiness as they sealed their vows with the traditional kiss, then turned to the others hovering nervously in the small salon of Don Pedro's townhouse.

Though afraid for them, as the rest were, Aurora was deeply touched by the newlyweds. It was evident that between them they shared a love that was all-encompassing. It was so strong that they had given up everything for each other—their families, their homeland, perhaps even their lives—to be together. *Sí*, that was love, Aurora thought, sighing, and love as it was meant to be. No wonder none of the *caballeros* who'd courted her had interested her. They had not had the capacity to love as Basilio and Francisca did—as Aurora yearned to. She wondered what it would be like to love and be loved like that. Some faint, distant memory stirred within her at the thought, then was gone before she could grasp it. Yet the feeling that she too was destined for such a love persisted as she raised her wineglass along with the others in a toast to the couple.

Though they had borne up well, the bride's parents were suddenly overwhelmed by emotion at the thought of their only daughter being torn from them so abruptly. Pedro threw his goblet into the fireplace, where it smashed upon the hearth. Then he embraced Francisca tearfully amid the sounds of splintering glass as his wife and the rest bravely followed his example.

Aurora hugged Basilio tightly, her throat choked with sobs. Despite the difference in their ages, she and her brother had always been close.

"Take care, *niña*," he said. "And tell Padre and Madre I—I love them . . . and I'll write . . . as soon as I can."

"I will, 'Silio. Oh, 'Silio! *Vaya con Dios*, my dear brother!"

Then at Pedro's frantic urging the lovers hastened to their waiting coach. They were nearly too late in leaving, for no sooner had the sound of their carriage's wheels rumbling over the cobblestones died away than came upon the front door the horrible, authoritative pounding that all had been dreading.

Quickly, apparently gifted with more sense than her husband gave her credit for, Doña Dorotea motioned Aurora into the kitchen. There Francisca's mother hurriedly set a pot of tea to boiling. Her hands were shaking so badly the cups rattled upon the saucers as she put them down upon the table, but otherwise she appeared outwardly calm.

"If they question us, Aurora, I will say you are the niece of my old duenna, who has fallen on hard times, and that you only arrived here this evening, looking for work."

"*Sí*, Doña Dorotea," Aurora replied, hoping she looked as composed as Francisca's mother.

They would need every ounce of their backbone and courage if they were to survive this night. Aurora stiffened with tension as she heard in the hallway the clatter of boots that signaled the intrusion of Don Juan's hirelings. Then, remembering the part she was to play, she shrank into a corner, fervently hoping, as any young scullery maid would have done, to escape the notice of her betters.

THE hour was late, for it had taken the Montalbán household a long time to recover from the shock of the tragedy that had befallen its young heir. But now all slept—all except Aurora. She lay awake in her delicately carved and gilded white bed, her wide blue eyes staring up at the arched canopy overhead.

This had been the worst night of her life. The patter of the rain, which she usually found so soothing, only depressed her. Her grandmother's fainting spell had fallen upon her like a blow, and the rest of the evening's events had been agonizing. The endless questioning by Don Juan's henchmen at Don Pedro's townhouse had been a terrible strain, testing Aurora's wits to their utmost.

She would never know how she had managed to lie so convincingly—and without error—in the face of the grueling interrogation she'd suffered. She could only be grateful that Don Juan himself had not deigned to question her, a lowly scullery maid, for surely his piercing eyes would have seen straight through the web of deceit that Aurora had woven.

A tear trickled slowly down her cheek. Much as she refused to accept the fact, she knew the days with her grandmother were numbered; and now, in addition to preparing for this wrenching loss, she realized she might never see her beloved older brother again. Her heart ached at the notion.

Irrationally Aurora thought: And I didn't even get to learn my fortune, for doubtless it was Basilio and

Francisca's journey across the ocean that Abuela saw. Oh, Abuela. Abuela! What is to become of me?

The question echoed unanswered through Aurora's mind until finally, exhausted and overwhelmed by sorrow, she cried herself to sleep. It was an uneasy slumber she drifted into, however, one troubled by a dream that was to haunt her again and again as the months passed.

The dream was never clear, but blurred at the edges like a vignette. It was further clouded by the shadowed images moving by in slow motion; and the sound too was somehow distorted, soft and languid.

In the dream Aurora was lost in an intricate maze, like those that had been popular centuries ago. The puzzle was made even more complicated by the fact that it was wildly overgrown with vegetation. Lush flowers as big as trees twined on thick, gnarled stems that burst like arms from the hedges that formed the maze; and, though beautiful, the blossoms seemed as deadly as belladonna. Their leaves appeared to reach out to Aurora, threatening to strangle her; and the fragrance of their perfume was so intoxicating it overwhelmed her like a drug. Her head spun as she staggered through the passages, struggling desperately to find her way out.

The man was there too. She could see him up ahead, but though she called and called to him, he did not hear her; and the harder she tried to reach him, the more difficult her progress became. She ran and ran, but the faster she tried to go, the slower her legs moved.

At last, breathing heavily, she sank to her knees, sobbing with despair.

When she awakened Aurora was still weeping. A

terrible emptiness, worse than any she had ever experienced, pervaded her being. She wished the man would come to comfort her, but he did not.

She was all alone in the darkness, with her aching heart.

Chapter Four

THE night was as black as a raven's wing, illuminated only by faint moonlight from the misty crescent of shimmering silver that gleamed in the heavens. The spring rain continued to fall, as it had for so many evenings now; and its sound mingled soothingly with the soft *whoosh* of the waves that lapped gently at the hulls of the many ships anchored in Cádiz's harbor.

Neither Basilio nor his bride, Francisca, was calmed by the tranquility of the rain and sea, however. Their flight from Madrid had been too harrowing; and now it seemed as though their troubles must continue, for the captain of the vessel on which they sought passage had quoted a first-class fare that would virtually deplete the purse of gold that Francisca's father had given them. If they paid the captain's price, the newlyweds would be penniless upon arriving in the New World. They must either find a way to retain some of the money—or travel in steerage. Basilio shuddered at this last. The idea of Francisca being packed in the dark, dank, cramped quarters below deck appalled him. No, there must be another way.

A muscle worked in Basilio's jaw as he thought of all his wealth, lying useless in the bank, for to write a draft on his account would be to leave behind a clearly marked trail for Don Juan to follow; in addition to which, the conde had probably already ordered that all of Basilio's property be seized. Not for the first time did the young hidalgo curse Juan and his wicked thirst for revenge. Basilio had not even dared to return to his townhouse before leaving Madrid, certain the conde and his hirelings were already there, waiting to take him prisoner. So even the small sum that Basilio kept in his vault for emergencies had had to be forfeited. For the first time in his life the young hidalgo understood what it meant to be helpless; and, as he looked down at his bride, whose well-being now rested solely in his hands, he wanted more than ever to kill the vile man who had brought them to this terrible pass. Both Basilio and Francisca had been nobly reared. They knew nothing of the hardship they now faced and were sadly unprepared to deal with it. What ought to have been the happiest days of their marriage were instead a nightmare.

Still Francisca smiled bravely at her husband through her tears. In their haste to escape she had left behind her small jewel chest. Though her best gems were, of course, at Ubrique, her father's estate, even the simple contents of the casket at Don Pedro's townhouse would have helped them now. Francisca could have wept with despair at her foolishness. Had it not been for her father thrusting his purse into Basilio's hands as the door of their carriage had swung shut, they would have had nothing at all! As it was, the couple had very little; but, as she gazed up at her husband, Francisca knew she would not have gone back, not even if she could have.

Basilio's impeccably tailored black evening clothes, which he had worn for two days now, were dirty with the stains of travel, and the delicate, frothy lace of his white silk shirt was crushed beyond repair. But to Francisca he was as handsome as ever. And she, with the brilliant plumes that had looked so fine in her hair at the Condesa de Hervás's party now wet and bedraggled and her ball gown soiled and torn, was just as beautiful to Basilio. Had the newlyweds been spoiled, they might have begun to be petulant with each other now in the face of this new adversity. But their upbringing had been one of love and graciousness; so instead they clung closely, reassuringly, to each other as Basilio tried once more to reason with the ship's captain.

"I cannot pay you the sum you have asked for first-class accommodations, sir. It is all the money my wife and I have, and we must have *some* funds upon arriving in the New World."

"Then I am sorry, Señor Montoya," the captain said, addressing Basilio by the false surname he had given earlier, "but you must either travel in steerage—or not at all."

The captain was indeed touched, for he could tell the couple were nobly born and newlyweds as well. They were obviously very much in love. From the tattered condition of their expensive and inappropriate-for-travel garments, he had no doubt they were fleeing from someone besides and were indeed in the dire straits they claimed. He would have liked to help them, for the thought of the lovely Señora Montoya packed in with the rabble that traveled below deck was distasteful to him as well. But rules were rules, and they must be obeyed, despite the fact that many unscrupulous captains did not observe them. Had the captain of the *Santa Cruz* been one of these, he would simply have taken Basilio's offer for first-class passage and then once they were out to sea had him and his wife thrown into steerage anyway, pocketing the difference in fare. After all, to whom could Basilio have complained? But the captain of the *Santa Cruz* was an honest man. Had he owned the vessel he commanded, he would gladly have bent the strict regulations. But, as it was, he was only one of the Conde de Fuente's many captains; and he did not want to lose his post, should Don Timoteo Yerbabuena discover the captain had broken the stringent maxims of the shipping company.

"Oh, please, sir." Francisca spoke up, regretting that she had worn her plainest jewels to the Condesa de Hervás's party. If only Spain were not at war, and the roads were not so unsafe, Francisca would have been bedecked in her finest gems. "I'll—I'll give you my pearls to make up the difference in fare."

She indicated the single strand of globes about her slender throat and the small studs that pierced her ears. At least the jewels were real, not paste copies. She would not have offered them otherwise.

"No, my love." Basilio's arm tightened about her, and his voice was gruff with shame. "You have parted from so much already; I cannot allow it—"

"Please, my husband," Francisca begged softly, then continued to the captain. "The pearls are quite genuine, I assure you, and it will be easier for you to sell them here in Cádiz than it would be for my husband and me to get a fair price for them in the New World, where we know no one."

"I don't know, señora," the captain answered, his

hands spread wide, his tone tinged with uncertainty. "Even so—"

"I will throw in my gold watch as well," Basilio uttered quickly as he saw the captain was wavering in light of Francisca's prettily made plea. "It is my dearest possession, sir, but willingly shall I part with it if it will get us aboard. It is quite valuable, for it is a carillon watch, sir," the young hidalgo explained, withdrawing the timepiece from his pocket and springing the clasp.

As the intricately worked cover of the watch opened, a sad, haunting little melody began to chime, attracting the attention of a dark, handsome man who had stood in the shadows, listening to the entire exchange.

The man was Don Salvador Domingo Rodriquez y Aguilar, Visconde Poniente, late of Madrid and now bound for the New World. He had arrived in Cádiz early this morning, but his preparations today for the journey had taken many long hours; and, not knowing if his half brother's henchmen were already hot on his heels, he'd not dared to board the *Santa Cruz* before dark.

Salvador had had a little time in which to put his affairs in order before leaving, since Juan had not yet known of Don Manuel's death when the visconde had made his escape from Madrid. Salvador had closed his townhouse and dismissed all of his servants but two, his valet, Pancho, and his secretary, Señor Ortega. Pancho had been given instructions to pack his master's wardrobe and set out immediately, in a plain, unremarkable cart, for Cádiz, where he was to meet the visconde at the Red Lion Inn. Señor Ortega had been commanded to liquidate Salvador's few available assets before all of his remaining possessions were seized. What was garnered from the sale was to be given to the visconde's mother.

Salvador himself had painstakingly disguised, with a dark stain, his favorite stallion, Nieblo (whose ghostly white coat would doubtless have called attention to him otherwise), then traveled rapidly by horseback to Cádiz. Today, with the help of Don Timoteo's connections, he had already managed to barter some of Catalina's jewels for a good price. Thus, unlike the newlyweds, he was not destitute. He had already paid for first-class passage and had been about to board the *Santa Cruz* when the couple's plight had caught his interest.

Like the captain, Salvador felt sorry for the newlyweds. Still their difficulties were none of his business, and he could not afford to attract attention to himself by meddling. He had just started up the gangplank when Basilio had opened his watch, and the strange, sorrowful tune had begun to play.

Why the music drew him Salvador could not have said. He knew only that it stirred him and tore at his heart in some fashion he could not explain. It was as though he had heard the song a thousand times before in some age long past; and though the distant memory escaped him, the visconde felt as though it had some important significance for him.

To his surprise he found himself declaring, "I will buy your watch, señor," and striding forward to name a sum that made him think he must be crazed. And yet he did not care. He was for some unfathomable reason suddenly obsessed with obtaining the timepiece.

Basilio stared warily at the man who had accosted him. Why should a total stranger wish to buy the watch—and at such a price?

"Though valuable, my watch is not worth that much, señor," the young hidalgo noted, guardedly pulling Francisca nearer as the man's hawklike face was cast into the light. "I do not understand why you, a stranger, would make me such an offer."

"Believe me when I tell you I do not understand it either, señor," Salvador rejoined lamely, cursing his impetuous action, "for I am at a loss as to how to explain it myself. It was the music that drew me. It was as though somehow I had heard the melody before, though I am certain I have not; and it struck some peculiar chord within me.... Forgive me, señor. I know I must sound mad. Indeed, I thought as much myself moments ago. Nevertheless, I assure you I am not. Allow me to introduce myself. I am known as La Aguila, like yourself, a man who seeks passage aboard this vessel. And you, señor?"

"I am Don Basilio... Montoya," Basilio replied reluctantly, "and this is my wife, Francisca."

"I am honored, señora," Salvador said, then with a graceful flourish swept Francisca a low bow and kissed her hand, courtly fashion.

Basilio did not know whether to be alarmed or relieved by this action that bespoke nobility. The man was obviously well born and had spent time at court. *Sangre de Cristo!* Perhaps he was a friend of the evil Juan! At last, however, Basilio decided that he was jumping at shadows. Since the stranger had introduced himself with such an odd name, he was no doubt simply a black sheep, a man on the fringes of society and unlikely to have been received by anyone of note. Such men often went by assumed names in order to spare their relatives further humiliation and disgrace. The stranger doubtless had been cast out by his family and was not apt to pose any threat to Basilio and Francisca, as he too was journeying to the New World and probably would not see Spain again.

Francisca, clearly captivated by the man's charming manners and address and not sensing any danger, smiled at him shyly.

"For such a price, señor, you must take my pearls as well," she stated, reaching up to unfasten the clasp.

"That is not necessary, señora, I assure you," Salvador responded gallantly, forestalling her action with a wave of his hand. "I could not help but overhear your exchange with the captain, and I understand your circumstances are... not the best. Keep your pearls, señora; you may have need of them. The watch alone will suffice."

"Then it is yours, señor," Basilio announced, "for since it seems you are aware of our situation, I must confess I am glad of the coin."

The exchange was made, each party thinking he had gotten the better of the bargain; and the captain, much relieved that providence had intervened on the newly-weds' behalf, was paid the amount needed for first-class accommodations. All boarded the ship; and after casting off, the vessel moved slowly out of the harbor.

Once alone in his small, private cabin, the faithful Pancho having been sent to fetch his master's bathwater, Salvador removed from the pocket of his well-tailored waistcoat the watch that he had purchased from Basilio. Then, freeing his own timepiece from its gold fob, he securely fastened the new watch in its place. After that he sprung the clasp so the haunting tune began once more to chime.

For a moment, caught up by the melody, searching his memory to recall where he might have heard it previously and why it seemed to mean so much to him, the visconde did not notice the portrait of the young girl set opposite the face of the timepiece. It was only

later, when he drew the lantern near to examine the
ornate craftsmanship of the watch, that his eyes focused
upon the picture.

For a fleeting eternity Salvador's heart stopped, then
started to beat again with slow deep strokes. She was
beautiful! The most beautiful woman he had ever seen.
Her hair was as black as a midnight sky, and her eyes,
which seemed to gaze back at him steadily, were bluer
than sapphires and shone with the same fiery light
possessed by those gems. Her pale, creamy skin glowed
as though touched by moonbeams, and the blush of her
cheeks was as fresh as any rose. Her crimson lips
curved invitingly; and Salvador found himself wondering how it would feel to kiss her mouth, taste the
sweetness it must surely offer. Strangely enough he
could almost swear he knew the answer. But how could
that be? He had never seen the girl before in his life;
he would have remembered one such as she. Yet it was
as though he knew every strand of her hair, every
glance of her eyes, every plane of her face as well as he
did his own. Who was she, this enchanting witch who
had so captivated him with her portrait?

He looked closer at the picture and saw the inscription that had been written there in one corner. *Con
amor, Aurora*. For some reason the words stabbed the
visconde's heart like a sharp knife. What was she to
Basilio Montoya that she had given him her love? Not
his wife, for Salvador had met Francisca, and she was
not the woman in the portrait. A mistress, then? The
thought pierced the visconde anew. No, never! To think
of her lying with another, that smile beckoning her
lover on, nearly drove Salvador insane.

I *am* mad! the visconde thought. I am! Somehow I
have become crazed: for why else am I haunted by that

sad music, seized with jealousy over a girl I don't even know? *Sí*, I am mad. I must be, for I feel she is mine, only mine, always mine, that I know her as well as I know myself. . . . Aurora. Dawn. A strange name for one whose beauty rivals a winter night. I would have called her Bella. . . . *Ay, caramba!* I am indeed losing my mind!

With a sharp little click Salvador snapped the timepiece shut and shook his head as though to clear it.

"Pancho," he said as the valet entered the room, lugging a bucket full of water, "do I seem strange to you?"

"Strange, señor?" Pancho queried, plainly confused by his master's question.

"*Sí*, strange, damn it! As though I have—have gone mad?"

"Why, no, señor," Pancho answered, then shrugged, turning away to fill the bathtub that occupied the center of the cabin.

Don Salvador was a devil, but the valet had never thought him mad. A trifle eccentric perhaps, but mad? No.

"It is all this upheaval in your life, señor," Pancho went on as he worked. "You will feel better after your bath, no?"

"*Sí*, you are right, of course," the visconde stated firmly, resolutely stuffing the watch into his pocket.

It was only a timepiece, nothing more.

Chapter Five

EACH clod of earth that fell upon his father's coffin was like a nail of hatred and burning desire for revenge being hammered into Juan's heart. He would find his father's assassin—that murderous swine Salvador—and Juan would make him pay for the foul crime he had committed against the de Zaragoza household. *Sí*, if it took him a lifetime, Juan would see that Salvador paid for Don Manuel's death.

The new Marqués de Llavero would never forget that horrible night a few days past when he had gone to his father's townhouse after receiving the urgent summons of Manuel's valet. There Juan had found his father's prostrate body upon the floor of the small salon. *Por Dios!* No one had even had the decency to cover the corpse; and Manuel's face had been hideous in death, frozen in a grimace of pain and anger at having been beaten by a man he'd despised.

Juan had not loved his father, for Manuel had scorned emotion as a sign of weakness and had taken great care to see that it had been thoroughly stamped out of his son, leaving Juan as hard and cold and cruel as his father had been. But the younger man had deeply admired the older, had looked up to him almost as though he had been a god, for no one had ever gotten the best of Manuel—until now. *Santa María!* To think he had died at Salvador's hands!

"Well, why are you all standing about like a pack of idiots?" Juan had shouted to the terrified servants cringing in one corner. "Someone get a blanket, and cover my father. Then send for old Joaquin, the mortician. He will know what to do. Where is my mother? Why isn't she here at my father's side, where she belongs? Well, speak up! Where is Doña Catalina?"

"She—she has gone, señor el Marqués," Manuel's valet, Alberto, had stammered, petrified by the young master's wrath.

It's unnatural, Alberto had thought. There should be grief in Don Juan for his father, as well as anger. But then perhaps the young master's attitude is not so incomprehensible after all. Don Manuel was not a man to inspire love in the hearts of those who surrounded him.

"Gone? Gone where?" Juan had questioned sharply, lifting one of his demoniac eyebrows wickedly, reminding the servants eerily of their dead master.

"I—I do not know, señor el Marqués," the valet had stuttered nervously. "She—she departed nearly three hours ago with—with señor el Conde de Fuente."

"Yerbabuena, the goat!" Juan had spat. "I should have known."

Red-faced and shaking with anger, the marqués had gnashed his teeth and torn his hair like a madman. It had been the worst night of his life. Francisca de Ubrique had sneered at his advances and rejected his suit. Then Basilio Montalbán y Torregato had managed to escape from Juan's hirelings, taking Francisca with him. While the marqués had been out searching for the fleeing lovers, Salvador had been here at the de Zaragoza townhouse, murdering Juan's father. After that, that stupid bitch Catalina had run away with Don Timoteo. Well, Juan would waste no time on her. She would be easy enough to find and deal with. Besides, she deserved that *cabrón* she'd sneaked off with—the foolish old goat with a crippled leg. No doubt she had spread her thighs for him while Manuel's body had yet been warm. Juan had clenched his fists with impotent ire at the thought. Well, she would pay too. In the end she would pay. Juan would ferret out her son Salvador—the only son she claimed—and kill him. It would break Catalina's heart, as her son had broken Manuel.

"Fetch my hat and gloves," Juan had curtly ordered his father's valet. "I have much to do this night!"

Then the marqués had swept from the townhouse, leaving the stench of fear and a strong odor of oil of Macassar in his wake.

Now, standing at his father's graveside, Juan vowed his vengeance on all those who had dared to do him harm: Francisca de Ubrique, Basilio Montalbán y Torregato, Timoteo Yerbabuena, Catalina Aguilar de Rodriquez de Zaragoza, and Salvador Rodriquez y Aguilar—most of all Salvador, the half brother who had been the worm in Juan's apple for as long as he could remember. *Sí*, one by one, he would punish them all!

He glanced across the hole in the earth wherein his father's coffin lay, to where his mother and her new husband stood silently. Beneath her black veil Doña Catalina's face was pale, and her large dark eyes, though defiant, were tinged with apprehension. But Don Timoteo's visage bore a grim smile of satisfaction that

Juan longed to wipe from the old man's face. How dared they come here, that shameless, disrespectful hussy and her stupid, lame lover? They did not mourn Don Manuel but joyed in his passing instead. No doubt they had come only to be certain he was truly dead and buried and would not, like the devil they had claimed he was, rise up from his grave to seek revenge upon them for their perfidy. Well, despite Manuel's death, they would not go unpunished for their crimes. They would not!

His black eyes flashing, Juan strode toward the two lovers, smiling mockingly as Timoteo's arm tightened protectively around Catalina's waist.

"You fool!" Juan sneered to the conde, his voice low and filled with fury. "Do you really think you can shield her from me? You cannot hide from me. I have but to whisper the command, and your lives are nothing. *Nothing!*" he spat, snapping his fingers for emphasis and causing Catalina to start nervously. "Do you hear? As my father did, however, I intend to let you live—and suffer. I shall torch your lands, attack your ships, see that you are separated once more from one another—"

"Do you truly think that will hurt us?" Timoteo asked quietly, his dignity contrasting sharply with Juan's derision. "Your father did as much, and yet we have survived," the conde uttered with pride. "It is *you* who are the fool, señor el Marqués: for no matter what you do you cannot destroy that which is most precious to us—our love for each other. It is strong, our love. It will endure whatever evil you seek to wreak upon us; and in the end we will prevail over your wickedness, just as we triumphed over your father's cruelty."

"You think so, eh?" Juan taunted insultingly. "Well, we shall see. We shall see indeed just how strong your love is when I deliver the coup de grace—Salvador's head on a platter!"

Catalina gasped, but Timoteo only smiled.

"You are an even bigger fool than I thought, señor el Marqués," he said, "for it is Salvador who will best you, just as he bested your father. How many times do you think that Don Manuel attempted to murder Salvador, and how many times do you think that Salvador eluded his clutches, just as he has escaped from you?"

"He has escaped, *sí*," Juan agreed silkily, threateningly, "but only for now. For I shall search the ends of the world until I find him, and when I do I shall kill him!"

Then, ignoring the many people who out of fear of Juan's reprisals against them otherwise had attended Manuel's funeral, the marqués rudely turned his back on the lovers and left the cemetery, whipping his horses with a brutality that made even the harshest of those present shudder.

JUAN frowned with annoyance at the account books and numerous papers arrayed before him. His father had been a man of importance and wealth, but his rank and riches had been dishonorably achieved—and they had cost dearly. Thus Don Manuel's estate was not as great as Juan had hoped.

Naturally, maintaining a household as lavish as his father's had been had required a substantial amount of money, but surely some of the expenses that Juan saw recorded in neat columns might have been curtailed. Manuel's secret ledger alone, which contained a list of all his illegal bribes and payoffs, was enough to make Juan blanch, for even he found it difficult to comprehend the sizable sums entered therein. His father had owned half the men in Spain, but their prices had been high indeed. Well, that couldn't be helped, Juan supposed. After all, business was business.

But Doña Catalina's gowns and jewels! Why had Manuel wasted his gold on that whore? She ought to have been garbed in rags and adorned with ashes! Well, at least Juan could sell the slut's clothes—she'd left them all behind—but the gems, which were worth a fortune, were gone. Once more the marqués gritted his teeth at the thought. If he saw the bitch wearing any of them, he would rip them from her throat! She'd had no right to take them; many were de Zaragoza heirlooms. He would demand the return of those, though he doubted that Catalina would give them back. No doubt she would claim ignorance of their disappearance, and he could hardly have his mother arrested for thievery. The queen, who adored her own mother, would not look favorably on that; and he must at all costs retain Isabella's goodwill.

As though all this weren't bad enough Juan had discovered that, in addition to the de Zaragoza household, his father had supported several bastard children and no less than five mistresses. The marqués had no use for any of these, except perhaps Doña Doloros, a pretty young thing who could no doubt be easily coerced into seeing the advantages of allowing Juan to take Manuel's place in her bed. The rest would be cut off at once.

Of Salvador's estate, Poniente, there was nothing left. Manuel had long since run through its profits and finally sold it. Juan had known this, but still he had hoped there might be something remaining. The thought of snatching the last of Salvador's inheritance from him had given Juan great pleasure. It was a pity that Salvador had owned nothing but his townhouse, its furnishings, and a few excellent horses. Briefly the marqués wondered how his half brother had managed even this semblance of prosperity; then he remembered Salvador's luck at the gaming tables and had his answer. Well, at least Juan would gain possession of Nieblo, his half brother's beautiful white Arabian stallion, which the marqués had long coveted.

He smiled grimly to himself at the thought, then frowned again with irritation as his silent musings were interrupted by a knock on the door of his father's study.

"*Venga*," he called and looked up to see his secretary, Señor Valdez, entering the room, along with Manuel's secretary, Señor Balboa. "Well, what is it?" he asked impatiently when the two men made no move to speak.

"Begging your pardon for interrupting you, señor el Marqués," Señor Valdez said, "but I thought you would like to know the men have combed the city, and neither Don Salvador nor Don Basilio and Doña Francisca have been found. Further, Don Salvador's townhouse has been closed; its servants have been dismissed; and its furnishings have been sold."

"By whose authority?" Juan inquired icily, a muscle working tensely in his jaw. "Don Salvador has been named a murderer—and a traitor to the queen as well. As such, all his possessions are forfeit to the Crown."

"I am aware of that, señor el Marqués, but unfortunately Don Salvador must have suspected, before fleeing, that he would be accused as such; and he empowered his secretary, Señor Ortega, to liquidate all his assets before they could be seized. This Señor Ortega somehow managed to accomplish."

"Goddamn him!" Juan spat, his rage renewed upon hearing this information; but whether he cursed his half brother or Salvador's secretary the two men could not tell.

Señor Balboa glanced at the younger secretary questioningly, but Señor Valdez only shook his head. Thus engrossed, both men jumped nervously when Juan suddenly banged his fist down upon the desk. Señor Balboa was startled but not alarmed. Señor Valdez, however, feared his master might strike one or both of them. As surreptitiously as possible he tugged on the older secretary's coat and, much to Señor Balboa's surprise, discreetly pulled him out of Juan's immediate vicinity. Although Señor Valdez was long accustomed to his master's ire, Señor Balboa believed the son could be no worse than the father and saw no reason to be afraid. He was therefore faintly contemptuous of his younger counterpart's apprehension and privately thought Señor Valdez a sniveling twit.

In this, however, Manuel's secretary erred gravely. Although his late master had been cruel and vindictive, he had also always kept his wits about him, never needlessly making an enemy. Juan's fits of wrath, on the other hand, were often uncontrollable. He was as apt to lash out at an innocent bystander as he was at the offending party. This trait was, in his late father's opinion, not only stupid but dangerous.

"You will be murdered in your bed by your valet someday, Juan," Manuel had noted dryly to his son once when, after having been spattered by mud from a passing vehicle, Juan had returned home and beaten his innocent personal servant, Carlos, for the mishap. "The accident wasn't Carlos's fault. For Christ's sake! He wasn't even present when it happened! It was the careless driver of the carriage who deserved to feel the sting of your whip. Instead you have wrongfully punished your valet, giving him good reason to resent you. Now whenever you reprimand Carlos for some error, he will believe it to be unjustified, and his resentment toward you will grow until at last he feels nothing for you but hatred. Then, should one of your enemies approach him, offering him a purseful of gold to stab you while you sleep, what do you think your valet will do, eh?"

"If he knows what's good for him, he'll tell me at once," Juan had replied tersely, smarting under his father's coolly raised eyebrows and mocking smile.

"Ah, but sometimes a man's hatred and greed far outweigh his common sense, Juan. Remember that, and you will prosper as I have."

Until you forgot your own advice, and Salvador killed you, Juan thought as he recalled the conversation from the past. For if anyone hated you, it was Salvador, the *bastardo!* And now—now the *hijo de la chingarra* thinks he can best me as well!

The thought galled Juan no end. It was therefore with great difficulty that, remembering his father's words, he restrained himself from striking the two secretaries who had merely delivered the report of Salvador's activities.

"And what of my half brother's horses?" he queried, taking several deep breaths and deliberately forcing his voice to remain calm as he tried to regain his composure.

Señor Balboa, unaware of the violence that had almost been directed at him, spoke up.

"They have all been sold except for one, señor el Marqués. The stallion Nieblo, which most interested you, has not been located. Presumably Don Salvador took it with him."

Once more Juan's fists clenched tightly, and again,

with considerable effort, he prevented himself from boxing both men's ears at the news.

"A most regrettable occurrence," he observed, "since I desired the horse for my own stables, but a misfortune that may, in the long run, prove of benefit to us. The stallion is a white Arabian and most remarkable. If Don Salvador is indeed mounted upon it, he doubtless will be recalled by witnesses. Inform the men that they should begin searching the port cities, as their combing of Madrid has proven fruitless, and tell them to be especially certain to mention the horse in their inquiries."

"I have already taken the liberty of doing so, señor el Marqués," Señor Balboa answered smugly. "Aware that you are, as the late Don Manuel was, an efficient man, I believed you would want as little time as possible wasted in the matter."

"I see that my father was most fortunate to have you in his employ, Señor Balboa," Juan noted somewhat sharply. The man was clever, perhaps too clever. Despite wishing it were otherwise, Juan would have to keep him around—at least for now. The secretary knew too much about Manuel and the late marqués's business dealings to be turned loose upon the city to divulge such information. More pleasantly therefore Juan went on. "I would be pleased if you would continue to serve me as you served my father, Señor Balboa. Tomás has too many duties as it is"—Juan indicated, with an arrogant wave of one hand, Señor Valdez—"and I see no reason why I should not have two secretaries if I desire."

"I would be happy to accept your offer, señor el Marqués," Señor Balboa stated, giving Tomás a small bland smile, causing the younger secretary to wish he had not been so quick earlier in withdrawing his older counterpart from Don Juan's punching range. "It is perhaps the best way, as since Don Manuel's death was so untimely, his affairs are in some disorder."

"So I see ... León, isn't it?" Juan asked.

"Sí, señor el Marqués," Señor Balboa responded as Tomás grimaced sourly.

Obviously he was going to have to get busy, or León would soon oust him entirely from Don Juan's household. Tomás was not particularly enamored of his master; he was simply bright enough to know positions such as his were not easily come by, especially as he might be turned out without a reference—or, worst yet, murdered in some dark alley! He must get on his master's good side—if Don Juan possessed such a thing—at once.

"Señor el Marqués, perhaps it would expedite matters if León assisted you with your father's affairs, and I continued with the search for Don Salvador, as well as for Don Basilio and Doña Francisca," Tomás suggested. "Unlike Don Salvador, I do not think that Don Basilio and Doña Francisca can have gotten very far. Don Basilio did not return to his townhouse before fleeing, and no draft has been drawn upon his bank account. His funds must therefore be limited."

"Quite right, Tomás," Juan agreed, as pleased as León was annoyed by the younger secretary's observation.

"Very well. León, you may assist me here, as I can see that it is indeed going to take some time to put my father's affairs in order. I had not realized he had disbursed his riches quite so ... freely, and I'm afraid I was counting on his money to subsidize the expense of my search for Don Salvador and Don Basilio and Doña Francisca. It is proving to be a personally costly undertaking, as the queen's budget has already been overtaxed by the burden of subduing these rebel *Carlistas*. Nevertheless, for my own reasons I want these three found and punished, and I am thus willing to bear the price of bringing about their capture.

"Tomás, you are dismissed to carry on with the search for Don Salvador, Don Basilio, and Doña Francisca. I'm sure I do not need to remind you they are to be taken alive if at all possible, as I want to personally interrogate them about their . . . treasonable activities."

"*Sí*, señor el Marqués," Tomás said, shuddering involuntarily as he turned away from his master's cold hard eyes and hurried from the room.

The young secretary would not have wanted to be in the three refugees' shoes for anything in the world.

Chapter Six

Aurora closed the door to her father's study quietly, her heart aching as she thought of how tired and worried he had looked. Though only three months had passed, it seemed eons since Basilio's flight from Spain—and they had yet to receive any word from him. For all they knew he and Francisca were dead.

Oh, how Aurora cursed the name Don Juan Rodolfo de Zaragoza y Aguilar! It was he who had wrought this evil upon the fine old house of Montalbán; and though at first they had thought that Basilio's escape was the end of the matter, now it seemed as though it were only the beginning.

Today, after many long weeks of ceaseless, disastrous business setbacks ending in bankruptcy and personal losses that were devastating, her sister-in-law Francisca's grief-stricken father, Don Pedro de Ubrique, had killed himself. Aurora knew that in some way Don Juan was to blame for all the terrible incidents leading up to Don Pedro's suicide; and she trembled to think that now the marqués's eyes would turn toward her own father.

Because of this, more than anything, her heart was heavy as she sought out her grandmother's chamber.

At her granddaughter's entrance Doña Gitana turned slowly from the window before which she was seated, her old eyes filling with love at the sight of the young girl.

How beautiful Aurora was—and growing lovelier with each passing day. Even the pain that shadowed her wide blue eyes did not detract from her dark, wintry beauty, but rather made it more haunting.

Doña Gitana sighed. The girl's first season was nearly past, and as yet she had no husband—or even a *novio*.

It was not right, the elderly woman thought. Aurora should be out enjoying her youth, attending parties and balls, dancing the nights away with the handsome *caballeros* who would, Doña Gitana had no doubt, fly to the girl's side like bees to a fragrant flower. Instead she was content to pass her hours quietly, mostly in her grandmother's room; and whenever Doña Gitana suggested that Aurora ought to accept some of the many invitations that came her way, she only smiled wistfully and shook her head.

"I am not interested in parties and balls, Abuela," she would say. "There are always so many people present, crowding in upon me until it seems I can scarcely breathe; and I never know what to say to them all. Perhaps if I weren't so shy, it would be different. I don't know. I have tried, Abuela; truly I have! But it is difficult for me to laugh and flirt and chatter like a parrot with people who are strangers to me; and they don't understand my reticence. Instead they think I'm haughty and aloof. I've—I've even heard some of the *caballeros* call me the Ice Maiden because I seem so cold and distant. But, *Madre de Dios!* How can I respond to them when they stare at me so? It is most uncomfortable, as though they are undressing me with their eyes. . . ."

"Oh, come, Aurora, not all of them, surely," her grandmother would chide.

"No, perhaps not, but those men who do not strip me naked with a glance fawn about me like puppies waiting to be patted upon the head. And when I cannot return their affection they look so sad it makes me feel guilty. No, there is no man in Madrid for me. I am happy to go only to those functions it is absolutely necessary that I attend."

Aurora did have her own circle of intimate friends, of course; and with these she was quite gay and garrulous. But still she preferred her grandmother's company above all else; and it was, without fail, Doña Gitana whom the girl sought out when troubled, as she was now.

"No word today, then?" the old beldam asked quietly, correctly interpreting Aurora's downcast expression.

"No, Abuela, no word today."

Once more Doña Gitana sighed, blinking her eyes to keep at bay the tears that had started there. Her health was failing badly now; each day she grew more frail. Yet somehow she continued to cling to life, fighting to survive. She was a de Navarra. Her family needed her. She could not die now—not yet.

"*Venga*. Sit beside me, *niña*"—she patted the chair next to her own—"and tell me what else is wrong. It is more today than no news from Basilio. I can see in your eyes that something horrible has happened. No . . . do not try to spare me, *niña*. I am not as fragile as you think."

"Oh, Abuela, it's—it's Don Pedro. He—he shot himself this morning!" Aurora blurted out in a rush, beginning to weep.

The elderly dowager was silent for a moment, absorbing the shock of this information. At last, however, she spoke again.

"And now you fear for my son." It was a statement, not a question. "Hush, *niña*, hush," Doña Gitana ordered softly, putting her arms about the sobbing girl and hugging her close. "Felipe is not Pedro. He is strong . . . my son. Pedro, for all that he was a good and kind man—God rest his soul—was weak."

"But, even so, Abuela, how can Padre possibly hope to stand up to a man as powerful and mean as Don Juan? It is said the souls of half the men in Spain have been bought and paid for by that devil! And think of what they did to Don Pedro. Torched his vineyards. Terrorized his tenants. Raped his wife—"

"Aurora! Where did you hear that?" Doña Gitana queried sharply about this last. "You must not speak of such things! You, a young girl—"

"But it's true, isn't it? Everyone whispered about it; and Doña Dorotea had to retire to a convent, didn't she?" Aurora cried as she recalled the kindly woman who had tried to shield her from being interrogated by Don Juan's henchmen the night of Basilio's marriage.

"Even so, you must never mention it again," the beldam stated firmly, horrified that the tale of Doña Dorotea's brutal molestation had reached Aurora's ears. "For all we know it was but *bandoleros* or *guerrilleros* who did these awful deeds. Times are hard, and there are many rebels in the hills—"

"Oh, Abuela, I wish I could believe you. But you know in your heart, as I do, that it was Don Juan and his hirelings who brought about Don Pedro's downfall. The swine sits like a king in his townhouse and swats us as though we are flies—" Aurora's voice broke, and she bit her lip.

"No, *niña*, never that. He may take from us all we own, but he will never rob us of our pride. We are *la casa de Montalbán*," Doña Gitana said proudly. "Not insects to be crushed by beasts such as Don Juan. Now . . . dry your tears. There is much to be done if we are not to fall into that madman's clutches: for, much as I hate to admit it, I believe you are right; and it was indeed Don Juan behind all of Pedro's troubles."

With difficulty Aurora ceased her sobs and gazed hopefully at her grandmother. If there were aught that might be done to spare her family from Don Juan's vengeance, Doña Gitana would know of it.

"What must we do, Abuela?" Aurora questioned, afraid. "What must we do?"

"We must go to court," the dowager replied.

Aurora inhaled sharply, surprised by the answer, for she had not expected it.

"But—but Padre doesn't like court life," she protested lamely, overwhelmed by the thought of being thrust directly into the hub of Spanish society. "He's always said the best way to survive Spanish politics is to stay at home, where you don't attract attention to yourself."

"Nevertheless, he must go," Doña Gitana uttered resolutely. "We all must. We must gain the queen's favor, and there is no other way to do that than by going to court."

"You and Padre and Madre, *sí*, I can understand that. But—but why me?" Aurora questioned, confused now and strangely dreading her grandmother's response.

"Think, *niña*! The queen is a young girl, scarcely

older than you and, also like you, very shy and unsure of herself. That is why she is so easily manipulated by her mother and cruel, ambitious men like Don Juan. If you were to find favor in her eyes—become her friend— Don Juan would be forced to think twice about harming *la casa de Montalbán*. After all, no matter how powerful he is, he is no more than one of Isabella's close courtiers and counselors, while you, Aurora, can become her intimate confidante and companion, privy to her innermost thoughts and desires. Do you follow what I am saying, Aurora?"

"*Sí*, Abuela," she answered thoughtfully, comprehending very well indeed but still petrified by the idea of entering into life at court.

Her grandmother, however, grasped the meaning of the unease in her eyes.

"I know it will be hard for you, *niña*. As you noted earlier, you are a demure girl; and, of your own choosing, you have led a somewhat sheltered, solitary life. Though your parents and I have encouraged you otherwise, we have not pressed the issue because it was our feeling that you would eventually overcome your timid nature. Modesty is a perfectly natural trait, and we believed that pushing you into leaving the nest before you were ready would do more harm than good. But now—now it is time, Aurora. For all that you are shy, you are strong too, and there is fire in your spirit when you allow it freedom from its restraints. You must fight, *niña*—for all of us. You must learn to overcome your fears and self-doubt, and put yourself forward in the company of others. You must win Isabella's confidence and affection. Can you do it, Aurora? Can you?"

"I—I will try, Abuela. Truly I will, but I do not know

if I can succeed in what you wish. The queen may not like me at all."

"I believe she will, *niña*. Though there are many who would be her allies, she is still alone, for most of those who surround her do so out of ambition and greed. You will want nothing from Isabella but her friendship. Thus you will be different from the others, and she will be drawn to you above the rest."

"Oh, Abuela, I hope you are right."

"I have read the cards, Aurora, and they do not lie. Go now. Your destiny awaits you."

PERHAPS it was her grandmother's mention of the cards that triggered it. Aurora didn't know for sure. But that night she dreamed again of the overgrown maze and the man.

When she awoke, her body was still aching with loneliness; and she once more wondered who the man was and if she would ever find him.

"Who are you?" Aurora asked aloud softly in her dark chamber, as she had so often before. "And where are you, *mi amigo?*"

But in answer there was only the chiming of her small, ornate bedside clock as it struck midnight.

Chapter Seven

Laredo, Texas, 1848

THE sad little melody of his watch stopped abruptly as Salvador snapped the lid shut and turned back to reflecting upon the coast in the distance, which was drawing ever nearer. His long journey was almost over, and he was glad. Except for a brief interlude in Cuba, where he had changed ships, his feet had not been firmly planted upon land for several weeks now; and he had grown very tired of the ceaseless roll of the ocean. Moreover, in switching vessels he had lost the company of Don Basilio and Doña Francisca; and after parting from them he'd missed the newlyweds, his only friends in the New World, more than he'd thought possible.

Because of the cramped quarters aboard the *Santa Cruz*, the three of them had grown close in the passing weeks of the long voyage, exchanging many confidences during conversations that had lasted late into the evenings. The visconde had not learned the couple's true surname—Montalbán—but he *had* discovered they had fled from their mutual homeland under circumstances somewhat similar to his own. Though the newlyweds had not known him well enough to entrust him with the name of the vindictive man who had necessitated their flight from Spain—any more than Salvador had dared to allow his half brother's name to pass his lips, fearing, as they had, reprisals even this far from home—he had gathered that someone at court and high in the queen's favor had been behind their furtive escape. The visconde had thought it was rather ironic that Isabella, who was basically a kind person, should through the viciousness of those who surrounded her be the cause of so much grief.

On a more pleasant note, Salvador had also been enlightened as to the identity of the girl in the portrait in the timepiece he had bought from Basilio. She was, much to the visconde's relief, the young hidalgo's sister.

"I find Aurora a strange name for one who resembles the night," Salvador had remarked upon learning the girl's identity.

Basilio had smiled fondly, recalling his beloved sister and wondering what she was doing now.

"Everyone does," he'd claimed, "unless they know the rest of her name. It's Leila. Aurora Leila."

Salvador had smiled then too.

"Understanding dawns," he'd declared, then laughed along with the others at the unintentional pun. "Aurora Leila. Dark dawn. Sí, it suits her cool beauty, for she is indeed like a wintry sunrise, soft and dark and lovely. Your sister is obviously very dear to you, Basilio, and the watch is all you have left of her now. Much as I regret parting with it, I must return it to you."

"Oh, no, señor," Basilio had protested. "You bought it in good faith and paid far more for it than it is worth—if one discounts the sentimental value it holds for me. You saved my life—and Francisca's—by purchasing it, Aguila. I know that Aurora would want you to have it."

"Very well, then," the visconde had acceded. "Since you insist, I shall keep it until such time as you are able to buy it back. That way you will be forced to keep in touch with me, and perhaps someday I will be able to meet your lovely sister."

Basilio's eyes had clouded a little at this, but still he had nodded in agreement.

"I hope so, señor," he'd uttered earnestly. "But I'm afraid, with the way matters stand now, that I will never see her again. Peru is a long way from Spain, Aguila, and I have no way of knowing when it will be safe to contact my family. And until I am cleared of this false charge of treason—and Francisca as well, for I've no doubt that Don . . . the man responsible for this wrongful accusation has named her as my accomplice—we can never return to our homeland."

"But . . . Peru? Why have you decided to settle there, Basilio?" Salvador had asked interestedly.

The young hidalgo had shrugged.

"I don't know. I've heard the legend of El Dorado, of course, and it fascinates me, though I'm certain the city doesn't really exist. You'd think someone would have found it by now if there truly were such a place. Still, *quién sabe?* I might get lucky.

"Besides," Basilio had continued, "I have heard there is much money to be made in Peru, in sugarcane, coffee, and *guano*. Perhaps Francisca and I will be able to afford a small plantation. I had vineyards, of course, at—at my estate back home." He'd paused as painfully he'd remembered Jerez. Then he'd gone on. "In addition to this, Peru was colonized by Spain. The people will speak Spanish; the culture will be similar to our own. . . .

"How about you, señor? Why have you chosen *los Estados Unidos*—and *Tejas* at that? I've heard it is a wild place, inhabited by red savages who scalp their enemies."

"*Sí*, I too have heard such tales," the visconde had confessed. "But I've relatives there, and I hope to find them."

"Well, I wish you the best of luck, Aguila. Once we reach Cuba, we'll be parting company, the captain says. "I don't know how we'll keep in touch, but—"

"Write to me in care of the Hotel Placido in Laredo. The captain has informed me that, although the inn is not as calm as its name would imply, it is a decent place to stay. I'll be staying there for a while until I can make some inquiries about my relatives and Santa Rosa, the town from which they wrote to my mother upon their arrival in the New World twenty years ago. I imagine they've probably moved on by now, but I intend to locate them if I can."

"Oh, I do hope you find them, señor," Francisca had said. "It is terrible to be so far from home, without family or friends. . . ." Her voice had trailed off wistfully.

"Please do not hesitate to send word to me if you're ever in need of aid," Salvador had insisted, worried about the newlyweds' welfare. "I did not leave Spain destitute, and I am more than willing to help you both, should you ever desire my assistance. We victims of Spanish politics must stick together," he'd remarked lightly but sincerely.

"*Muchas gracias*, Aguila," Basilio had rejoined. "You have been more than kind. *Vaya con Dios*."

"Y ustedes también, mis amigos. Hasta luego, y buena suerte."

Now, recalling the conversation, the visconde was more concerned than ever about the couple's well-being. Though they had tried to make light of their difficulties, Salvador had known that, despite his purchase of Basilio's watch, they were nearly penniless; and they'd been too proud to accept any more money from him. He hoped they would indeed write to him, as they'd promised. Besides the fact that he'd genuinely liked them both, Basilio was Salvador's only slender link with Aurora, the girl in the portrait, who continued to haunt him. It was ridiculous, the visconde knew; and he was now more certain than ever that some odd madness had come upon him: for, despite all his wishes to the contrary, he believed he had fallen desperately in love with the face in that picture.

It wouldn't do, of course, even if by some chance he finally met Aurora. Salvador was definite about that. He had gradually come to the conclusion that he was accursed. All he'd ever loved had been torn from him—violently, painfully. The visconde could not endure that again. He must stifle his inexplicable feelings for the girl in the portrait. He had to—or something terrible would happen to her, as it had all the others.

No, much as he wished it were otherwise, Salvador could not allow himself to love anyone ever again.

It was the noise of Texas that struck Salvador first. As though they must be the biggest and best at everything, its rough-and-ready inhabitants were loud of voice and swaggering of behavior, quite unlike the soft-spoken, genteel nobility of Spain.

Laredo too was unlike any city the visconde had ever

known. It bustled with a hubbub of activity that made the quietly conducted business of his homeland seem tame and insipid; and the riverfront crawled with riffraff whose insolent and blatant animosity was far different from the obsequious attitude of the poverty-stricken in Spain.

He had no sooner disembarked from *La Bruja del Mar,* the riverboat that had brought him up the Rio Grande from Fort Brown, than he was witness to a heated argument that broke out on the docks and ended in a fatal shooting. As worldly as he'd believed himself to be, Salvador was nevertheless shocked at such open murder, for the man killed had been armed only with a knife.

The visconde wondered if perhaps he oughtn't to have landed in Galveston or Corpus Christi or stayed in Fort Brown, where he had disembarked briefly. Then he dismissed the matter with a shrug. Going by riverboat to Laredo had saved him many miles of overland travel to Santa Rosa, and Salvador had no intention of losing his hair to the red savages who were said to populate Texas. Besides, no doubt the other towns he'd previously considered as his initial destination were just as bad as Laredo appeared to be.

"Oh, señor!" Pancho exclaimed, horrified by the killing they had just witnessed. "We shall be murdered in our beds here. *Heridas de Cristo!* Let us return to Fort Brown at once. At least there they have soldiers to maintain order."

With a single sharp glance the visconde silenced his quivering valet.

"We were more likely to have been murdered in our beds in Spain, Pancho," he pointed out coolly. "Now go, and see to our trunks while I take care of Nieblo."

Once the valet had departed (superstitiously crossing

his breast and grumbling loudly to himself about his master's lack of good sense in bringing them to the uncivilized New World), Salvador turned back to the riverboat, where the men who worked the wharves were even now attempting to unload his prized Arabian stallion, Nieblo. The terrified horse was screaming, rearing, lashing out wildly with his hooves, and straining furiously against the ropes that secured him. The visconde hurried forward, knowing the men would be unable to control the beast much longer.

"Nieblo, *mi beldad*," Salvador crooned softly to the frightened animal as he approached it. "It is all right. No one is going to hurt you," he went on as he caught the ropes willingly relinquished to his grasp.

At the sound of his master's voice the stallion quieted somewhat, though he still snorted and rolled his eyes with fear. Nevertheless, he allowed the visconde to lead him down the gangplank on to the pier. There Salvador tied the horse to the back of a wagon that Pancho had found and hired to take them to the Hotel Placido. The visconde would have saddled and ridden the beast, but he realized that Nieblo had been too long without exercise to be trusted to the crowded streets of Laredo; and besides, Salvador wanted to bathe the animal first, to rid the stallion of the camouflaging stain that encrusted his once-satiny white coat.

At last they were under way to the inn, and the visconde was able to take a better look at his surroundings. Laredo was, to his eyes, a new city, for it was less than a hundred years old, having been founded in 1755, by Don Tomás Sanchez de la Barrera y Gallardo and a handful of settlers. The marks of its Spanish antecedents were curiously interwoven with those of what Salvador guessed must be American influences; and he studied with interest the main center of activity, the San Agustin Plaza. It too buzzed like a beehive.

It was here, among the many persons who flocked about the square, that the visconde caught his first sight of what he knew must be an Indian, for the man's skin bore a copper sheen that Salvador had never before beheld; and though he wore a fringed buckskin jacket similar to others the visconde had noted, his long, coarse black hair was adorned with feathers and beads. Salvador did not think the Indian looked particularly savage—there were, at any rate, no scalps hanging from his belt—and in his ignorance the visconde decided the tales he'd heard of such men must have been grossly exaggerated. Without further thought he dismissed the Indian, his attention caught by a couple on horseback.

It was the girl he noticed immediately, for her ebony tresses reminded him of the portrait of Aurora; and, before the impossibility of this struck him, Salvador thought it was she. However, he soon recognized that the girl upon the dappled-grey mare had nothing in common with Aurora other than the color and length of her hair. This girl's skin was not paler than cream, but tanned as gold as honey by the sun. Her face too, though captivatingly beautiful, was stamped with a hard knowledge of life that Aurora's innocent countenance lacked. The girl was, besides—Salvador's senses suffered another shock—garbed in pants and riding astride, which would have been unthinkable for a well-bred lady of Spain. The visconde wondered if this were, however, the acceptable custom for Texas women; then, seeing that others too were staring at the couple, he guessed it was not so.

He shook his head, pondering the girl's background. Perhaps she had never seen a dress. Indeed, that might be true, for she was gazing so raptly at a red one in a store window that her mare nearly collided with the pinto stallion her tall dark companion was riding. The man, who was clothed completely in black and silver, said something to the girl, then dismounted, leading her into the shop. Salvador smiled with amusement as a few minutes later he watched the store's proprietress remove the red gown from the window.

He would have liked to see the girl in the dress, for he had no doubt her escort was buying it for her; but the wagon had moved on down the street, and the visconde had lost sight of the shop. A pity, Salvador thought, for, despite her improper attire, the girl had been most attractive. He wondered if the man accompanying her had been her husband. Probably. He had certainly taken the girl's arm possessively enough. The visconde sighed, then smiled once more to himself. It was just as well, perhaps. He was here to find his relatives, not dally with pretty *tejanas;* and the deadly looking pistols in the gunbelt slung low on the hips of the girl's protector had appeared well used. He was one man, Salvador decided, whom he would not have liked to have for an enemy. Even his half brother Juan's wicked demeanor seemed to pale when compared with the steely grit that had chiseled the dark face of the girl's companion.

On impulse the visconde asked the driver of the wagon if he knew the man's identity.

The driver spat a wad of tobacco in the dust, then nodded curtly.

"If it be the breed 'pon that pinto you's meanin', then I reckon I does. But you don't wanna be messin' with the likes of him, mister. He goes by the name of El

Lobo, 'n' he kin draw a gun 'n' kill you quicker 'n a rattler kin strike."

The driver paused, chewing his tobacco as he considered the matter. After squirting another stream of brown liquid onto the road, he continued.

"I heerd tell that El Lobo took a wife a ways back, so I reckon that was her with him. Purty, ain't she? Wonder what it was 'bout that breed what done took her fancy? You wouldn't of thought she was the kind of trash what'd mix with him, wouldya? Jest goes to show you cain't never tell 'bout women, kin you? Nawsir," he answered himself, "you jest cain't never tell.

"Here," the driver grumbled, suddenly recalling himself to the present. "Giddyup there, Nellie. We won't never git to the durned hotel at this rate."

"What do you mean by 'breed'?" Salvador inquired curiously. "Except for his hair, the man looked pure Spanish to me—and of good blood."

"Well, durn if you ain't a green 'un," the driver drawled with disgust. "I swan. Even if yore man here wasn't to of hired me to take you to the hotel, I'd of still knowed you jest got off the boat, mister!

"That there El Lobo ain't got no blood but bad blood. He's half-Comanche 'n' half-Mexican; 'n' ain't nobody got no use for Injuns, dead or alive, 'n' even less for breeds. The way I got it figgered, they's the scum of the earth. Ain't no respectable white woman what'd spread her legs fer one of them red devils. Heck. Even them what's whores charge 'em double. Yep, they shore do.

"Goshdurn it, Nellie!" the driver shouted, vigorously flapping his reins. "Giddyup there, 'fer I take my whip to you!"

Salvador digested this information in silence, more

than ever uncomfortably aware that he had a lot to learn about the New World. Although he could manage to converse in his schoolboy English, he had not realized the country itself would be so alien. It was thus with a faint sense of relief that he saw they had reached the inn.

The Hotel Placido was indeed noisy, as the captain of the *Santa Cruz* had warned him; but after his initial glimpse of Laredo the visconde was not surprised. The inn, despite being loud, appeared decent, however: and Salvador was glad he had taken the captain's advice to put up there. Lord only knew where he might have found himself otherwise.

He strode inside to make arrangements for a room, feeling a disquieting sense of loss he had not known for many years.

Chapter Eight

ALTHOUGH Aurora had known her grandmother possessed a certain amount of power and influence, she had never realized how much until one evening Doña Gitana announced that, by unspecified means, she had made arrangements for her granddaughter to join the ranks of the queen's ladies-in-waiting.

Aurora was stricken by the news, for in her mind she had planned vaguely to befriend Isabella without becoming too involved in court life. The girl's images of living quietly at the queen's residence, chancing to meet and grow acquainted with Isabella in one of the long corridors or the gardens of the palace, now faded abruptly. Whether she wished it or not, Aurora was to be thrust directly into the hub of Spanish society.

New gowns, more expensive and ornate than any she had ever owned, were created for her by the most renowned seamstress available. Boxes and boxes of gorgeous hats, lacy chemises, morocco slippers, and hand-painted fans arrived by the cartload. Her father sent to Quimera for her costliest jewels, and flacons of fragrant perfume were carefully packed away in her trunk. A dancing master was hired to brush up her knowledge of intricate court dances, and a voice teacher was acquired to make certain she spoke with a perfect Castilian lisp. Aurora lived in fear that she would somehow blunder socially and not only disgrace her family, but provide Don Juan with the means to drive a stake through the heart of the house of Montalbán.

Thus it was with a great deal of trepidation that she took her place beside her grandmother in Don Felipe's well-sprung coach, which would take them to Aranjuez, the queen's country palace, to which Isabella had retired for the summer.

The short journey passed pleasantly enough, for the sun was bright and golden in its warmth, and the brown-and-ocher countryside of Spain was in full bloom. Fields of ripening wheat and barley stirred gently in the slight, arid breeze that whispered to the olive trees and rustled the verdant branches of the evergreen oaks and pines.

Here and there small herds of sheep—the long-wooled churro, the short-wooled merino, and the manchegan— and goats and cattle grazed contentedly upon the plains carpeted with tall prairie grass and threaded by a few straggling wildflowers. Now and then came the soft peal of a bellwether, answered by a low baa or moo; and sometimes a donkey brayed in response to its master's voice and whip as the beast pulled a heavily laden cart to market.

From the wagons loaded high with fruits and vegetables wafted the pungent aromas of olives, grapes, figs, and oranges; potatoes, beans, onions, and sugar beets. The sharp, tangy scents mingled tartly with the odor of fresh manure that dotted the dry, dusty road.

The hooves of the horses thudded dully against the earth, the steady rhythm occasionally accented by the jingling of the harnesses worn by sturdy mules drawing gaily painted caravans filled with gypsies dark of eye and skin.

These Aurora studied curiously as they passed, wondering if when they looked at her, they knew her ancestor had been one of their own. She thought that, had it not been for a twist of fate, she might have been one of the women dressed in bright, sometimes garish peasant skirts and blouses, their earlobes, throats, and wrists adorned by gold and silver bangles and multicolored glass beads. She too might have begged a few coins for her hungry child or read the palm of a *gorgio* for a piece of silver.

But though a faint trace of gypsy blood coursed through Aurora's veins, she was basically pure *castellana*.

She drew back from the window of the carriage. They were stopping at an inn for the night, since Doña Gitana tired easily and already looked ill and fatigued by the trip. Although worried about her grandmother's health, Aurora was secretly glad they were halting. If they never arrived at Aranjuez, it would be fine with her.

THE morning dawned bright and clear; and as nothing untoward prevented Don Felipe's coach from continuing on its way (much to Aurora's dismay) the Royal Palace of Aranjuez was in sight by midafternoon.

Located about fifty kilometers south of Madrid, near the place where the Rio Tajo joined the River Jarama, the palace had been built on a site once occupied by a castle that had belonged to the Caballeros de Santiago, an order of note during the Spanish Crusades against the Infidels. In the sixteenth century King Charles V, having no use for the castle, had converted it into a hunting lodge; and some years later his son, King Philip II, had ordered the country palace built. Unfortunately fire had destroyed the residence on at least two occasions. Thus the structure that Aurora saw, as they slowly approached the palace, dated from the eighteenth century, when it had been rebuilt by Santiago Bonavia, an Italian, for King Ferdinand VI.

The main courtyard of Aranjuez was a huge square dominated primarily by paving blocks and surrounded on three sides by the residence itself. The palace was a long low building only two stories high except for the central edifice, which contained a third floor. At the corners where the two wings, with their terraced roofs and galleries, joined the main structure, were small, lantern-topped domes capping squat turrets with round windows. An arcade adorned by statues of Spanish kings ran along the front of the main block; and stretching from one wing to the other, subdividing the central courtyard, was a barricade composed of square white stone pillars between which were sections of black spiked-iron fencing. The edifice itself was built primarily of the same white rock as the pillars but was accented by red stone set above the many windows, which gave the palace a pleasing, rococo architectural style.

Aurora, who had an eye for beauty, thought the residence, for all that it was small, was far grander and more impressive than the ugly grey Royal Palace of Madrid, which was said to resemble the Palais du Louvre in Paris. In fact, the girl was glad that Aranjuez was not overly large; perhaps it would not be as crowded.

The Montalbáns were admitted without difficulty to the palace and shown to their lodgings. Her grandmother and her parents had chambers of their own, but Aurora was to share a room with three other ladies-in-waiting to the queen. At present, however, the chamber was empty; and the girl was glad to be able to get settled in before meeting her fellow occupants.

She and her maid, Lupe, had just finished unpacking the contents of Aurora's large trunk and hanging up her gowns in her half of one of the two large armoires that stood in the room, when the other ladies-in-waiting arrived. To her surprise, for she had not really known what to expect, Aurora discovered all three were only slightly older than she was.

Blanca, the youngest, was from Barcelona. Small and fine-boned, she reminded Aurora of a china doll, with her porcelain skin, silky blond hair, and cornflower-blue eyes. In sharp contrast to Blanca was Fátima, who hailed from Granada and was as tall and dark and tawny as her Moorish ancestors had been, with brownish-black tresses and eyes so brown they seemed almost black. The last girl, Concepción, who came from Bilbao, was a redhead with green-gold eyes and warm golden skin.

With a great deal of talk and laughter they made Aurora welcome, exclaiming over her appearance and wardrobe, this last of which they showed no hesitation in dragging out and examining scrupulously. Upon perceiving that her clothes were the latest fashion; her jewels were real, not paste copies; and her perfume was the costliest of jasmine, they pronounced themselves delighted with her and rang for Madeira to celebrate her coming.

Aurora wondered briefly what her welcome would have been like had she been poor and plain, then pushed the thought from her mind. From now on these three women would play a major part in her life, and there was no point in antagonizing them, even had she been able to conquer her shyness long enough to speak up. If they seemed much too interested in worldly possessions for her liking, it was doubtless due far more to the influence of the court than to any flaw in their own personalities. María Cristina of Naples, the queen's arrogant and domineering mother, was fond of luxury; and those who wished to retain Isabella's favor found it prudent to share her mother's opinions.

Aurora realized she would already have one enemy at Aranjuez—Don Juan—and she was wise enough to recognize that outwardly she too must adopt the attitudes of María Cristina or garner a far more dangerous foe at court. To oppose Don Juan was perilous. To oppose María Cristina was fatal.

Not for naught had Isabella's mother succeeded in persuading her late husband, King Ferdinand VII, to deny his brother, Don Carlos, his rightful place as heir to the throne of Spain and to name young Isabella, a female, instead. Spain had revolted immediately upon Ferdinand's death, crying out for Don Carlos and rejecting young Isabella. But María Cristina, as regent for her daughter, had kept her iron grip on the queen's crown. Even now, five years after Isabella had been judged old enough to rule alone, her mother was the real power behind the throne.

So Aurora let her new friends' covetous posture pass without comment, taking comfort in the fact that they had been so animated about her belongings she'd scarcely had to talk at all and had managed to fend off adroitly the few truly personal questions they'd asked.

The Madeira was brought; and, Aurora apparently

having received a close enough inspection for the time being, the conversation turned to other matters.

Of primary importance appeared to be the subject of the queen's upcoming masquerade ball. Aurora grew faintly excited at the prospect of this. She had never attended such an affair before and wondered if, hidden behind her mask, her identity unknown, she might find the courage to take the initial steps toward becoming an integral part of Isabella's court and saving her family from Don Juan. Yes, she must do it, no matter her qualms. The fate of the house of Montalbán rested solely in her hands; she could not let her family down. She must put aside her fears, as Abuela had said, and learn to fight. Already she had made a beginning. She had gained three friends she had not had yesterday.

Curiously, from beneath half-closed lids, Aurora studied them, noting for the first time the lack of innocence in their eyes, the hard knowledge of life stamped upon their young faces. It occurred to her that once they had been like her, and, like her, they had been forced to learn to survive—a prerequisite at court, a necessity in life.

. . . you are strong . . . and there is fire in your spirit when you allow it freedom from its restraints.

I shall do it, Aurora vowed suddenly with unaccustomed fierceness as she recalled her grandmother's words to her. I shall not shrink from the challenge flung at my feet but fight as no woman before me has ever done. I shall not let *la casa de Montalbán* be beaten to its knees by Don Juan!

Without warning an unfamiliar sense of confidence was born within her at the thought; and to Aurora's surprise she found she felt almost invincible with the unexpected rush of determination now flowing through her veins. Her eyes flashing suddenly with the conquering light of one who has joined a battle, she tossed her head back proudly and, smiling, raised her glass in a silent toast to destiny.

Chapter Nine

THE Royal Palace of Aranjuez was an odd jumble of rooms, but because the residence was small, Aurora had soon learned her way about easily enough. This morning, dressed in a most becoming damask gown of light summer silk, she made her way down the long corridors to *el Salón de los Espejos*—the Hall of Mirrors—where she was to await her first audience with Queen Isabella.

Since it was still early, the salon was yet empty; and Aurora was glad to have a few moments of privacy, as such instances at the palace were rare. Lost in thought, she reveled in the time alone: for although, since her arrival at the residence nearly a month ago, she had grown to enjoy the company of Blanca, Fátima, and Concepción, she was still a solitary girl; and sharing her chamber with three other women had proven a difficult adjustment. Especially hard was the fact that Aurora must share her bed with Blanca, who was a restless sleeper and sometimes came and went at odd hours of the night. Aurora had no doubt the porcelain blond had a lover whom she was meeting. At the thought Aurora

felt an acute pang of loneliness and, for the first time,
wished that she too had a handsome *caballero* to chase
away the twinges of homesickness and emptiness that
sometimes assailed her.

Life at Aranjuez was so different from that of Madrid.
Here Aurora must rise early to begin her careful and
lengthy toilet. There was no lying about in bed or
donning the first dress she happened to pull from her
armoire. No, each day she must sparkle as freshly as a
dew-kissed flower—whether she wished to or not—for
wilted blooms were noticed and remarked on at court
and soon became easy prey for the powerful and the
ambitious. A word whispered here, and an ailing minister might be removed from his post. A hint dropped
there, and a weary courtier might be permanently
dispatched to foreign parts. A slyly solicitous suggestion
made to the queen, and a fading lady-in-waiting might
be married off to an unattractive old man or forced to
retire to a convent. There was no room at court for
those who did not join in the frivolity so beloved by
Isabella.

Aurora strode across the inlaid tile floor to examine
herself in one of the salon's large, ornate wall mirrors.
The girl thought she looked a trifle tired—there were
mauve shadows beneath her eyes—but other than this
she could find no fault with her appearance. Her gown
of summer silk was all that could be wished, with its
tight, three-quarter-length sleeves, scooped neckline,
sashed waist, and graceful folds. The damask color
brought out the blush in her cheeks, and the black lace
trim emphasized the creamy whiteness of her skin.

Her long ebony tresses had been drawn back, neatly
plaited, and intricately coiled at the back of her head,
showing off the swanlike elegance of her facial bones

and throat and making her sapphire-blue eyes seem to dominate her pale countenance.

Nervously but unnecessarily Aurora smoothed her hair and gown, as though to make certain the mirror did not deceive her, that all was indeed in place. Then she turned from her self-scrutiny to walk to the French doors of the salon, which opened out onto a small balcony. As the hot rays of the stifling midday heat would not invade the hall for some time, the doors, as well as the louvered shutters that prevented the sun's entrance during the day, stood open, enabling her to step out upon the balcony.

There she breathed deeply of the slight morning breeze, which yet bore a trace of coolness from the mountains. Soon the gentle whisper would be gone, leaving the plains still and arid; but now the air stirred ever so softly, and Aurora welcomed it with open arms. She broke a rose from the blossom-laden trellis that clambered up the palace wall to the balcony. The flower's scent was sweet, heady, mingling aromatically with the many blooms that grew in the carefully cultivated and irrigated gardens below. The bright splashes of the multicolored petals that interwove themselves among the verdant leaves and trees of the gardens seemed incongruous against the dull lifelessness of the brown-and-ocher countryside beyond; and strangely enough it was the pleasant, peaceful gardens that did not appear to belong.

As the sun rose higher in the startlingly azure sky that stretched above the Spanish plains, the golden rays of growing warmth permeated Aurora's senses, making her feel sleepy, and drowsily she leaned against the balustrade, soaking up the beams that caressed her.

Soon the heat would be rising in shimmering waves

off the land, distorting the distant terrain and making it seem like a mirage. Even now the scene before Aurora's eyes was wavering, becoming hazy, as though she viewed a vignette. She blinked once, twice, to clear her vision, but it worsened instead, everything blurring without warning, beginning to fade from sight. The girl staggered dizzily, disoriented, and clutched the railing for support. Yet irrationally she still retained her hold on the rose she had picked earlier.

The man was coming to her as he always did, upon the wings of mist swirling up to engulf her. But this time, fearing she might topple over the balustrade, Aurora fought to remain conscious. Presently, after she took several deep breaths, her eyes once more focused upon her surroundings.

She saw that, despite her efforts to prevent it from happening, all about her was changed. Aranjuez was gone, and in its place was an ancient hunting lodge.

Somewhere in the distance a bell tolled softly—an angelus bell.

"Querida, querida."

Aurora turned toward the voice that had called out to her. There he was. The man of her dreams. He was mounted on his white Arabian stallion and laughing as he cantered toward the balcony where she stood watching. As she spied him her heart swelled to bursting with an unfamiliar and unfathomable emotion she had never felt before.

Inexplicably she thought: I have looked for love in all the wrong places. It has been here with me all the time.

She marveled at the revelation. Why, oh, why had she never realized it until now?

The man came closer. Just beneath the balcony he

reined his horse to a halt and paused for a moment, gazing up at her. A sudden, overwhelming longing— and something more—pervaded Aurora's being at the look upon his dark visage. She had seen such a glance before—on Basilio's and Francisca's faces the night they had gotten married.

Aurora's heart began to pound erratically in her breast. Was it—was it possible that the man loved her, as she did him? Was that why he had come to her all these years?

He dismounted and, as though he had done it a hundred times before, swiftly climbed a nearby tree and dropped from its branches to the balcony.

"*Muñeca mía*," he murmured huskily. "It seems as though I have been waiting for you forever."

And then he kissed her.

Aurora felt no fear at the intimate caress, no desire to withdraw from him, as she had recoiled from the *caballeros* who had danced with her during the parties and balls of her debut into Spanish society. Instead she felt as though his mouth, fringed with the black mustache he had grown, belonged upon hers, that his lips were familiar—and dearly beloved.

Yes, oh, yes! She loved him.

He was what she had been seeking, what she had yearned for all her life. How could she not have known? Before, she had been but half a being, solitary, incomplete. Now—now she was made whole—more than whole, for together they had created something grander than either of them alone would ever have known.

Her mouth parted willingly for his, pressed eagerly against his lips, gave way gladly to the onslaught of his probing tongue as it explored her mouth gently, tenderly searching out the sensitive, secret places within, encouraging the petals of her passion to slowly awaken and unfurl.

Aurora was a child no longer, but a woman who loved deeply and was loved just as truly in return. She wanted this moment to last forever. If she must give up her present life to remain lost in the past with this man, then she would do it, somehow, some way. No sacrifice was too great if it meant having him beside her always. Aurora must speak and tell him what was in her heart, quickly, before he faded away.

But even as the thought occurred to her the man began to slip from her grasp, though she held on to him tightly, willing him to stay.

"No! Don't go!" Aurora begged, tears filling her eyes at losing so soon that which she had only just found.

"I must, *querida*," he told her quietly. "But this I promise you: Our time will come. Soon—soon we shall be together. This I vow. Swear that you will wait for me, *muñeca*, that you will be mine, only mine, always mine—now and forever. Swear it!"

"I do so swear, *mi amor, mi alma*, for there can never be another who holds my heart. If it takes a hundred lifetimes for us to be together, I shall wait for you—now and forever."

The man kissed her fiercely, possessively, once more. Then he departed the same way he had come. With a forlorn cry of bittersweet pain Aurora flung her rose to him so he might have some remembrance of her when he was no longer with her. Then after watching him ride away she laid her head upon the balustrade and wept for what she had known so briefly—and now lost.

When Aurora lifted her eyes the hunting lodge had

disappeared, and Aranjuez was again as it had been. Her beloved was gone. No part of him remained.

Yes, yes, it did, she saw as she glanced down at her hand. There a tiny bead of blood from where a thorn had pricked her still lay, like a tear, in her palm. Tenderly she pressed her lips to the spot, her throat choked with emotion.

I stood here, she thought, in another time. Here I swore to my beloved that I would wait for him—if it took a hundred lifetimes. . . . Oh, my love, my love, I am still waiting. . . . Where are you, *mi corazón?* Will I ever find you in this life?

The clatter of horses' hooves in the courtyard interrupted the girl's reverie, reminding her that the palace was beginning to come alive with the morning. With a sigh Aurora drew away from the balcony and returned to the salon. She wanted to sit quietly for a minute and think about what had occurred.

Still bemused, she sat down upon one of the ornate, gilded, velvet sofas that lined the walls of the salon. Something inexplicable yet highly momentous had just happened to her. She was either mad, or she had for a moment relived a fleeting interlude from another life. Aurora shuddered. She was not crazed; of that she was certain. The blood on her hand was real enough. But to be forced to accept the other alternative was just as frightening.

She must never tell anyone about the experience. She would surely, as Abuela had once warned her, be condemned as a heretic, for such beliefs were sacrilegious. Though finally abolished in 1820, the horrible Spanish Inquisition had not yet been forgotten, for how did one wipe away centuries of horror in a few decades? Aurora wondered if even now she might be thrown into prison and subjected to the rack, be branded with hot irons or have her thumbs pierced by screws. No, she could share the knowledge of her experience with no one, not even her grandmother, for Doña Gitana was already ill and would only be upset by the information.

There was no time for further thought. Already Aurora could hear laughter in the hallway, and soon the salon was filled with people. She hoped to pass unnoticed in one corner, but this was not possible. One of the queen's ministers beckoned to her and reminded her that today, after nearly a month of waiting, she was to have an audience with Isabella. The minister made certain that Aurora understood when and how low she was to curtsy before the queen, then left her, saying he would summon her when Isabella was ready to receive her.

There was nothing for the girl to do then but wait, her heart pounding jerkily in her breast as she thought of how the very lives of her family depended on the outcome of her meeting with the queen. What would occur, Aurora wondered, shivering, should any discover what had happened to her this morning?

QUEEN Isabella II of Spain was just seventeen years old that summer of 1848. Like her mother, she was tall and gracefully built, with fair skin, chestnut hair, and large dark eyes. Perhaps because her father, King Ferdinand VII, had been one of Spain's worst and most malicious monarchs, Isabella was kind to a fault and frivolous to the point of absurdity. Although she had been tutored by the learned Argüelles, it was generally agreed that her education had been so poor that even had she been intelligent—which she was not—she would not have proven a competent ruler. To make matters even worse, not only was the queen uneducated and less than bright, but she had on several occasions appeared to be lacking even the slightest degree of plain common sense. Whether or not she was actually as stupid as she seemed no one knew. She had, perhaps understandably, been given few chances to prove her leadership ability.

At the beginning of her reign she had been too young to rule, and her mother, María Cristina, had governed in Isabella's stead. María Cristina had few admirable qualities, however; and though she had managed (with the aid of her sister, Luisa-Carlota), during the first years of the first Carlist war, to retain her daughter's crown, María Cristina had vacillated constantly between the opposing factions involved in the fighting, needlessly making numerous enemies on all sides.

The crowning blow had fallen when María Cristina had made a morganatic marriage to a member of the Corps of Guards, named Muñoz, thereby losing what little of the people's respect she had held.

On April 31, 1839, with the signing of the Vergara Agreement, the first Carlist war had officially ended, and its hero, General Baldomero Espartero, had appointed himself head of the government. Shortly thereafter María Cristina, sensing the danger to herself if she remained and caring less for her daughter than she did for herself, had cleverly resigned her regency and left Spain. Espartero had then ruled as regent until 1843, when he had been succeeded by a coalition that had declared the thirteen-year-old Isabella of age to reign alone.

In 1844, a triumphant María Cristina had returned from exile to Spain, once more to act, albeit unofficially, as the real power behind the throne. The intrigues of her government had been numerous, and popular opinion had held that only a strong husband at Isabella's side would check her iron-willed mother's meddling in affairs of state.

At last, on October 10, 1846, in a double wedding, the queen had married her cousin Don Francisco de Asís, Duke of Cádiz; and her sister and heir, Luisa-Fernanda, had wed King Louis-Philippe of France's fifth son, the Duke of Montpensier.

The marriages had not answered. It was rumored that Don Francisco was not only weak, but impotent; and the queen, generous with her favors, had begun to take lovers and to appoint them to high government posts. General Serrano y Dominguez, it was said, was an especial favorite; and it was for this reason that General Narváez, now the official head of the government, had packed him off posthaste to Granada. King Louis-Philippe, who had hoped for a French succession through his son's alliance with Luisa-Fernanda, had, this year of 1848, indirectly lost his own throne due to the Spanish connection. Even more disastrous, infuriated that Isabella had not wed her cousin, Don Carlos's son, the Count of Montemolín, whom many still believed was the rightful king of Spain, the *Carlistas* had begun restating their claims to the throne; and the second Carlist war had broken out.

The country was rife with unrest, particularly in the Basque and Catalonian provinces, where the hills were alive with rebellion.

Worst of all was the fact that the thoughtless, impulsive queen, who had always been overly zealous in her religion, had fallen under the spell of a fanatical, power-grasping nun by the name of Sor Patrocinio. During the first Carlist war the allegedly miracle-working nun had been accused as an imposter and branded with a hot iron as such. She had never forgotten or forgiven the insult and now, restored to favor, was a dangerous adversary at court.

Aurora, whose grandmother had imparted all this information to her, was naturally skeptical about being able to win Isabella's friendship. Nevertheless, the girl knew she must try. As much as she was able she pushed the morning's highly emotional events from her mind and, calling up every ounce of her strength and determination, held her head high as she was ushered into the audience chamber to kneel before the queen.

"Oh, do rise, Doña Aurora," Isabella tittered absently, making eyes from behind her fan at one of her generals and scarcely paying any heed to the girl, who had been curtsying before her for several long minutes. Only the general's discreet cough recalled the queen to the present. With a little moue of disappointment she finally turned her attention fully to Aurora. "So . . . you are my new lady-in-waiting, are you not?" Isabella asked, then went on without waiting for a reply. "Well, let us hope you prove less of a trial than the last. Though I did my best for her, Doña Pilar would pine after Don Sebastian all the same—and of course, to no avail, as he was promised to Doña Natalia, whose dowry was a fortune. Poor Pilar. She killed herself in the end, you know." The queen sighed with sorrow at the thought.

"Doña Pilar was a temptress and a heretic, señora la Reina"—someone standing just behind Isabella spoke up—"and thus unworthy of your tears."

Trembling with apprehension, fearing that somehow the secret of her sacrilegious brush with the past this morning had already been ferreted out, Aurora glanced surreptitiously at the woman who had dared to rebuke the queen. It was not María Cristina, for the woman was clothed in a nun's habit. This, then, was Sor Patrocinio. Aurora suppressed a shudder, for it seemed as though the nun's eyes burned right through her, prising open her innermost soul, laying it bare for meticulous examination. There was, moreover, something in Sor Patrocinio's gaze that sent a chill of terror and repugnance down Aurora's spine. If she were not mistaken, the nun's eyes were filled with an unnatural lust when they raked her. *Madre de Dios!* No wonder so many at court whispered that Isabella's relationship with Sor Patrocinio was a scandalous affront to the Church and human nature!

Quickly, stricken, Aurora lowered her eyelashes against the nun's piercing stare, half afraid that Sor Patrocinio intended to denounce her as a heretic at any moment.

"You are right, of course, dear Sor Patrocinio," the queen said, confirming the nun's identity. Then, perhaps prompted by a desire to save Aurora from Doña Pilar's sad fate, Isabella inquired, "Have you a *novio*, Doña Aurora?"

"N-no, señora la Reina." She stumbled over the half-truth, for how could she speak of her beloved from the past?

Like a child, the queen smiled, delighted, and clapped her hands together.

"Then we must find one for you at once. Don Juan" —she beckoned one of the courtiers forward—"you will be pleased to show Doña Aurora the gardens."

"But of course, señora la Reina," the *caballero* uttered smoothly as the court smothered its sniggers.

As though Isabella's affairs weren't bad enough, now she must be matchmaking between her subjects.

Embarrassed at being made a spectacle, overcome by shyness, and still overwhelmed by her instinctive fear of Sor Patrocinio, Aurora's mind scarcely registered the name of the courtier commanded to escort her to the gardens. She knew only that the man was now approaching her, and she could not bring herself to look into his face, not wishing to see the amusement she was certain filled his eyes. Thus she blushed and glanced away as, murmuring his pleasure, Don Juan bowed low and kissed her hand.

It was only later, after conquering her emotions at last, that Aurora realized with horror that the man leading her from the queen's presence was none other than the hated Don Juan Rodolfo de Zaragoza y Aguilar!

Chapter Ten

Aurora knew with certainty that she was doomed. Not only had she been so bemused by the morning's events that she had failed to make an impression on the queen, but she had inadvertently aroused the unwelcome interest of Sor Patrocinio and had been delivered into the hands of the man she despised above all else. Nothing could have been worse!

She had failed. All of her grandmother's fine plans had been in vain, for doubtless Don Juan had already poisoned Isabella's mind against the house of Montalbán. Why else would the queen have chosen him—of all the *caballeros* who'd lingered in the salon—to escort Aurora to the gardens? She quivered with fear, and her heart thudded sickeningly in her breast. She found she could not bring herself to look up at the marqués again, to face the smirk of wolfish triumph she was sure was twisted upon his visage.

Was it only her imagination, or had his hold upon her arm tightened ever so slightly, mocking her? How she longed to snatch herself from his grasp and run away as fast as she could. Still she dared not. No doubt Don

Juan would catch her easily enough; and besides, where would she go?

Lost in uneasy thought, it was therefore several moments before Aurora, relieved beyond measure, at last recognized that the marqués had no notion of her identity.

"You must forgive the queen, Doña Aurora," he was saying politely as the girl brought herself back abruptly to the present. "Isabella is very young and often very thoughtless. Her command that I show you the gardens was meant kindly. She did not realize how it would appear to the court. You should have known as much and laughed along with the rest; but then you are new here, for I'm certain I've not seen you before." His eyebrows lifted in faint inquiry.

"N-no, señor," Aurora stuttered nervously. "My coming-out ball was but a few months ago, and I'm afraid I've spent relatively little time in society since. My—my grandmother has been ill, you see, and I did not want to leave her. I arrived at court only two weeks ago. Abuela said I . . . was wasting my youth on an old woman—as though I cared for that—and so she . . . made arrangements for me to become a lady-in-waiting to the queen."

Aurora faltered over the lie her grandmother had concocted earlier for just such an occasion as this.

"I see," Juan said, bored by the entire conversation. The girl beside him was too small, too fine-boned, too blue-eyed for his taste; she reminded him of his mother, whom he hated. How he longed for Francisca, who had been tall, flame-haired, and dark-eyed. But Francisca was gone and, like Basilio and Salvador, was not to be found. Though the marqués had, after weeks of diligent inquisition, traced all three of the refugees as far as Cádiz, there the search had abruptly turned up short. Juan had no way of knowing that Salvador had bribed the captain of the *Santa Cruz* to obliterate Basilio's and Francisca's names, as well as the visconde's own, from the ship's passenger list. The marqués knew only that he was intensely angered and highly frustrated by his inability to discover the whereabouts of the three. Well, never mind; he would find them all eventually—if it took him a lifetime to do so—and they would pay for their crimes, as Don Pedro and Doña Dorotea had paid.

Juan took immense satisfaction in the fact that he had destroyed Francisca's parents—though he had thought them poor substitutes for Francisca herself. Still he had enjoyed Doña Dorotea's screams as he and his men had raped her repeatedly, and the news of Don Pedro's suicide had brought the marqués further pleasure. He hoped that Francisca, wherever she was, had learned of her mother's brutal molestation and her father's death and was suffering agonizingly, as Juan had suffered over her rejection of him.

He glanced down at the girl beside him. She was pretty enough, but he found her dull, insipid, and as stupid as the queen. How dare Isabella foist off this miss just out of the schoolroom on him? Why, he could hardly even recall her name. Doña Aurora. That was it. He pointed out one or two of the more exotic flowers that bloomed in the gardens and tried to make conversation with her; but as she had scarcely two words to say for herself, the dialogue soon fell flat. As quickly as possible the marqués made his excuses and left.

Aurora heaved a great sigh of relief after he had

gone. The fiend! She didn't know how she'd managed even a semblance of courtesy toward him when all the time she'd been longing to slap his cruel, impudent face, to choke the life from his wicked body.

Thank God, he had not known who she was, had not recognized her as the scullery maid his henchmen had interrogated that night at the de Ubrique townhouse! She could be grateful for that at least. She had no doubt their stroll in the gardens would have been quite different, had Don Juan been apprised of her identity. As it was, she was certain she would have very little time in which to win Isabella's friendship before the marqués discovered that the young lady-in-waiting whom he had escorted through the gardens was none other than the sister of Don Basilio Enrique Montalbán y Torregato!

Aurora was sure that after learning that, Don Juan would find her much more interesting than he had today. She shivered at the thought. She must gain the queen's affection—and soon.

It was but a few weeks later when Aurora's opportunity to accomplish her goal arose. One fine summer day the queen, wishing amusement, decided to take her ladies-in-waiting to the local *plaza de toros,* where the much-admired matador Raimundo de Oliva, who had recently joined the court, was going to perform. Only Aurora, who had become sick at the one and only bullfight she had ever witnessed as a child, had no wish to go. However, Isabella, pouting, insisted on her presence, saying the girl's absence would spoil the day for the others; so Aurora had no choice but to attend. She was surprised and faintly apprehensive that the queen had singled her out for attention, and she wondered if Don

Juan had discovered her identity at last and set Isabella
against her. Finally, however, Aurora determined this
could not be the case. The marqués would scarcely
have ignored her under such circumstances, and the
queen, while somewhat distant, had been pleasant enough
to her. No, it was simply that Isabella, like a child,
could not bear to be thwarted.

Swallowing her nausea at the spectacle the bullfighting
would present and recalling that she wanted the queen's
goodwill, Aurora reluctantly climbed into the carriage
with the others.

She wished her grandmother and her parents were
still with her. But Doña Gitana, after seeing her granddaughter settled at court, had returned to the townhouse
in Madrid; and a few days ago, after receiving word that
some of his vineyards had been torched, Don Felipe
and Doña Ynez had journeyed to Quimera. Aurora had
been worried sick at the news, knowing that Don Juan
had begun his vindictive assault upon the house of
Montalbán.

The queen's entourage arrived at the *plaza de toros*
at last, and Aurora had no time to dwell further on her
uneasy thoughts. Along with the others, who were
laughing and chatting gaily about the forthcoming event,
the girl took her place upon the tiered benches that
surrounded the *corrida*. She was glad of the shade
provided by the brightly colored canopy that had been
erected especially for Isabella and her ladies-in-waiting,
for it was already hot, the sun beating down relentlessly
upon the Spanish plains. Aurora waved her fan steadily
to stir a slight breeze and wished the queen had not
brought along her favorite spaniel, which was yapping
shrilly with excitement.

Presently the spectacle began. Led by two bailiffs

mounted on dappled-grey Arabian geldings, the grand procession slowly crossed the arena amid the cheers of the audience gathered there. The cries of delight were as much for the brilliant costumes of the troupes that would be performing as for the beginning of the entertainment, for the bullfighters were beautifully garbed, their ornate garments making bright splashes of color against the brown earth of the bullring.

After the parade the *presidente municipal* of Aranjuez, who was seated in a place of honor next to Isabella, rose and handed down to one of the bailiffs the keys to the bull pens. Then all except the first troupe retired from the field.

With a flourish the performers removed their heavily embroidered satin dress capes, bowed low to the queen and the rest of the spectators, then took their respective positions in the *corrida*. The senior matador signaled for the start of the bullfight, and one of the bailiffs opened the bull-pen door. As the bull rushed through it an attendant perched above deftly attached a colorful silk rosette to the beast's massive shoulders. Aurora knew this indicated from which special breeding ranch the animal came, but, having seen only one bullfight previously, she could not recognize the colors belonging to each ranch. It was Fátima who enlightened her.

"Ahhhhh," the older girl sighed with pleasure. "The bull will be fierce indeed, for it comes from the Ganadería de Goya."

With interest Aurora studied the beast closely, aware that it had been specifically bred and tested for strength and savagery. Today would be its one and only appearance in an arena. If it were an especially clever and vicious animal, it perhaps would kill one or more of its opponents before the bout had ended. Several performers had lost their lives in a bullring. Aurora, who did not like bullfighting, secretly hoped the bull would do as much damage as possible before its death, though she knew that, even so, it would not survive the day. Already she could hear the sounds of the vendors outside the *corrida,* setting up their displays, where the meat of the freshly slaughtered beasts would be sold to the spectators.

The bull hunched its enormous shoulders and charged into the arena. One of the *banderilleros* stepped forward and, with one hand, gracefully caped the animal with his *muleta* so the matadors could determine whether or not the beast showed a marked preference for attacking with one horn or the other. Bulls who demonstrated no such favoritism were more dangerous, as they were less predictable.

After that the matadors, in order of seniority, began their work. The initial passes—in this case, the basic *verónica*—were beautifully done; and the spectators applauded enthusiastically with appreciation. Aurora's breath caught in her throat as she watched the elegant swirling of the capes. She knew the red side was believed to enrage the bull, but it was not so. The beasts were color-blind and attacked, with equal fervor, the yellow side. The real reason for the *muletas'* red color was so they would not show the blood with which they would soon be stained.

Once the initial passes had been completed, a bugle sounded, signaling the entrance of the mounted assistants and the start of the first of the three acts that would constitute the bout.

The bull snorted and pawed the ground, shaking its large head at the horses before it charged. With great skill one of the *picadors* stabbed his pike pole into the junction of the bull's neck and shoulder blades—the only acceptable point of entry—then swiftly yanked it free. Aurora gasped and turned away, ill, as the first of the horses went down, its blood and intestines spilling out over the earth in a crimson gush as its rider deftly leaped clear.

Shouts of *"Olé! Olé!"* filled the air for a deed well done.

With difficulty Aurora choked down the vomit that rose in her throat. It would be disastrous for her to be sick, especially as she appeared to be the only one horrified by the horse's agony. She could only be glad when its screams of pain finally ceased, and with one last convulsive shudder it lay still. Unfortunately she was forced to witness two more such inhumane deaths before the mounted assistants retired from the field.

Again the bugle shrilled, and the *banderilleros* went to work. With cries and gestures they provoked the bull into charging them, stepping aside at the last moment and skillfully implanting their *banderillas* into the beast's flesh. Soon the animal looked as though it were wearing some strange, ornamental headdress, for the short, barbed staves were decorated with brightly colored paper. Aurora thought the gay, carnival-like streamers ironic in light of the bull's suffering.

By now the beast's powerful neck and shoulder muscles had been severely weakened, and its head hung low, giving evidence of the damage done to it.

Once more the bugle was blown; and the third act, known as the Hour of Truth, ensued. Alone, the senior matador approached the queen's box. With his *montera* held aloft in his right hand and his cape and sword in his left hand, he formally requested the *presidente municipal*'s permission to dedicate the bull to Isabella. Then, with a graceful flourish, he tossed his hat to the queen and returned to the field.

After several more passes to prove his complete mastery over the animal, he prepared for the kill. This he did by the more common method of *al volapié*, in which man and bull attacked each other from a stand-still position. The alternate method, *recibiendo*, in which the matador stood still and received the beast, was rarely performed, as it required great skill and courage.

The man and animal charged. The matador, who was not allowed to touch the bull except with his *estoque*, attracted the beast's attention with his *muleta*. The animal lowered its head, and the man thrust his sword into the junction of the bull's neck and shoulder blades, severing its aorta. The beast died almost instantly.

All the *toreros* circled the bullring, smiling and bowing at the cheers and applause of the crowd, who waved their handkerchiefs to signal their approval of the bout. In response to the spectators' demand the *presidente municipal* awarded the matador one of the bull's ears as a trophy, the traditional honor for excellence. If the matador had been unusually outstanding, he would have received both ears; if he had been phenomenal, he would have gotten both the ears and the tail of the bull. After claiming his prize the matador then retrieved his *montera* from the queen, who returned the hat along with a purseful of gold coins.

A *puntillero* entered the *corrida* to cut the bull's spinal cord from the base of its skull in a final coup de grace; and the carcass was dragged, by mules, from the arena to be butchered and dressed for sale outside the bullring. Other attendants hurried forth to rake the *corrida* in preparation for the second bout.

It was not until the sixth and final performance of the day that Raimundo de Oliva, the highly acclaimed matador, appeared. By then Aurora wished for nothing more than to return to the Royal Palace of Aranjuez. Not only had several more horses been killed, but three men had been seriously gored, and one of them had already died from his injuries. Despite the fact that the girl was glad a few of the bulls had given as good as they had gotten, the gorings had still been horrible to watch; and of course, Aurora was sorry for the men unfortunate enough to have fallen prey to the beasts' vicious horns.

Raimundo de Oliva's skill was so great that, during the second act, he did the placing of the *banderillas* himself, much to the audience's delight: for the previous gorings had only whetted the crowd's appetite for blood, and the risks taken by the renowned matador now honed its excitement to a feverish pitch.

Even Isabella's favorite spaniel was yapping loudly, struggling so frantically in her arms that she was having difficulty controlling it. Dismayed, she attempted to hand the dog over to one of the courtiers who sat in the box; but somehow during the exchange the spaniel escaped and tumbled into the arena. The queen rose to her feet, screaming. The sudden confusion distracted both Raimundo de Oliva and the bull and frightened the dog into running wildly toward the center of the bullring. Raimundo de Oliva narrowly missed being gored as the bull turned without warning and charged straight toward the terrified spaniel. The dog, suddenly sensing its danger, searched desperately for a means of

escaping from the *corrida;* but there was none. It ran
back toward Isabella's box while the spectators, frozen
with shock, looked on in horror as they finally realized
what was happening.

Why she acted as she did then Aurora never knew.
Had she thought about it first, she would have recognized how foolhardy she was. But she did not think; she
acted blindly and solely on impulse, her mind filled
only with the thought that the small spaniel was about
to be impaled on the bull's deadly horns, trampled
beneath the bull's deadly hooves. Skirts flying, she
flung herself over the side of the arena, scooped up the
dog, and tossed it into the queen's box. Then, hearing
behind her the thundering of the bull's hooves upon
the hard ground, Aurora tried to climb back into the
box herself. To her horror she discovered she lacked the
strength to do so. Her heart pounded horribly in her
breast. Her mouth was dry with sudden, mind-numbing
fear. In moments she would be killed, gored to shreds
by the bull's horns, crushed to pieces by its hooves.
Oh, *Santa María,* have mercy!

Miraculously the girl's prayers were answered when
several *caballeros*, with their strong arms, rapidly hauled
her up the side of the bullring, preventing her from
certain death as the bull struck the wall savagely again
and again.

Aurora gasped with relief at her narrow escape as her
knees suddenly collapsed beneath her, and she fainted.

Isabella herself was waving a vial of smelling salts
beneath Aurora's nostrils as at last she began to stir.
Her dark blue eyes fluttered open to see the queen
bending over her. A look of concern and profound
gratitude was upon Isabella's face; and when the queen

spoke Aurora knew she had accomplished her goal of winning Isabella's affection.

"My dear Doña Aurora," the queen said, her eyes filling with tears, "how can I ever repay you? When I think of what you did to save poor Trapos's life . . . *Dios mío!* It's a wonder you are alive. Tell me—how can I ever repay you for such a courageous gesture?"

"It—it was nothing, señora la Reina," Aurora uttered weakly, still devastated by her near brush with death. "I acted solely on impulse, I assure you, and not from bravery at all."

"Nevertheless, it was a deed well done and must be rewarded. What would you have, my dear Doña Aurora? Gold? Land? There must be something," Isabella insisted.

Aurora saw her chance, and she took it.

"I—I would ask nothing more of you save your friendship, señora la Reina," she declared, "for I wish only to serve you to the best of my ability."

"Then know that you are indeed my true friend," the queen announced, touched by the unusual request. "Come. You shall have a place of honor at my side."

Raimundo de Oliva was no fool. Seeing what had happened in Isabella's box, he rose heroically to the occasion. Like the master he was, he dedicated to Aurora the bull that had nearly killed her. Though she knew it was a signal honor, still she could not be pleased by the gesture; for it somehow made her feel responsible for the beast's death, something she could take no delight in, though the animal had almost caused her own.

She was immensely relieved when the bullfight was over and she could return to the palace to rest. Her only joy of the entire day was that she had

managed to secure a place in the queen's heart. Had
Aurora realized how news of her escapade would
travel through Aranjuez, however, she would not
even have been able to find happiness in this, for it
brought her to the attention of the two people she
had hoped most to avoid: Sor Patrocinio and Don
Juan.

Chapter Eleven

THE summer heat of Laredo was almost unbearable, Salvador thought as he gazed at his hand. Even the cards he held were damp with sweat and stuck to his fingers when he attempted to discard a deuce and a seven, which were of no use to him. The first new card he drew was the nine of clubs, also of no help; but the second one was the queen of hearts. Inwardly the visconde smiled, though outwardly his face showed no emotion as he studied the four ladies he now held in his hand.

As though bored by the whole affair he drummed his fingers lightly upon the table and glanced about the *cantina,* searching for the ripe, blowsy girl who had waited upon him earlier. Catching her eye, Salvador signaled for her to bring him another glass of whiskey, the only halfway decent liquor he had managed to discover since his arrival in Texas. He shuddered as he sipped the rotgut drink slowly. Accustomed to fine wines and brandies, he was still unable to bring himself to bolt down the awful shot as did the hard-drinking men who frequented the western frontier.

He was just getting ready to make his bet when a

gunslinger pushed open the shuttered doors of the saloon. For a moment the visconde could not place the man who walked with a soft jingle of silver spurs across the floor to the bar. Still Salvador was certain he had seen the gunslinger before. But where? It had had something to do with red... a red dress... and a girl.... Yes, he had it now. This was the notorious man they called El Lobo.

The visconde stared with interest at the gunslinger, who appeared to be unaware of how silent the *cantina* had fallen at his entrance. The man drank the glass of mescal, which he'd ordered, with a single practiced action, then turned to survey the saloon. Upon spying the card game, he swaggered toward the poker table.

"Damned half-breed," one of the players, named Hayes, muttered under his breath. "I suppose we'll hafta deal the bastard in."

"I reckon so," said another man, called Jenkins. "I cain't rightly say as how I'd like to offend the murderin' son of a bitch. I got a wife 'n' kids to think of. They wouldn't have no means of payin' the rent without me; 'n' I ain't about to leave 'em homeless on account of some two-bit, half-breed Injun what jest happens to have a draw like greased lightnin'. Ain't decent, a piece of scum like that bein' able to yank them pistols outta them holsters that fast."

"Ain't it the truth," Hayes replied, spitting a stream of tobacco on the floor in disgust. "I wonder if he scalps the bodies afterwards, like they say? I wouldn't be a'tall surprised, him bein' sech a heathen 'n' all."

"Mind if I join you... gentlemen?" El Lobo asked.

Startled, the two men who'd been discussing him blanched with fright, wondering if he'd overheard their remarks. How had he sneaked up on them so silently?

Damned Injun blood! That's what it was, made him able to creep up, without a sound, on decent white men.

"No, no, not a'tall," they hastened guiltily to reassure the gunslinger, giving his pistols a surreptitious, apprehensive glance as he pulled out a chair and sat down.

"We'll jest finish this here round, if you don't mind, then we'll deal you in," Jenkins told him.

"Right."

El Lobo lit a thin black cigar and dragged on it, then leaned back in his chair to blow a puff of smoke into the air. The cloud wafted up in a blue haze of rings.

The tension at the poker table crackled like a whip. Only Salvador was unmoved by the strain. Calmly he leaned forward and tossed his money on the pile in the center of the table, calling the last bettor. Those who'd remained in the game showed their cards, and the visconde raked in his winnings, ignoring the grumbling of one of the men across the table.

"'Pears to me like yore doing right well, mister," the disgruntled player, named Will, sneered. "You got some furrin way we dunno about of charmin' that there deck?"

Salvador smiled, unruffled by the man's animosity.

"When you yourself dealt, señor?" the visconde pointed out. "No, I think not. It is simply that Lady Luck has chosen to be kind to me this afternoon," he went on. "Perhaps another day she will not be so generous, no?" Receiving no answer, Salvador shrugged. "*Quién sabe?* As the gypsies in my country say: 'It is all in the cards.'"

The visconde noticed that El Lobo looked at him interestedly at that, but the gunslinger said nothing. The antagonistic Will made a few more hostile remarks, then, seeing that nobody was paying any attention, he motioned for the men to get on with the game.

Time passed. Salvador's winnings grew. Will became more and more vocal in his complaints until finally he jumped to his feet and accused the visconde outright of cheating.

Once more the saloon fell deathly still. Again the tension in the air was so thick it could have been cut with a knife.

"I dunno where yore from, mister," Will growled, his eyes narrowed and threatening, "but here in Texas, we shoot card cheats."

Salvador quirked one eyebrow upward dangerously, his whole body tense and ready to spring.

"Does anybody else at this table have cause to doubt my honesty?" he inquired in a deceptively calm voice.

"No," El Lobo uttered flatly, tipping back his black, flat-brimmed hat to get a better look at what was happening.

"Now, Will," another man, called Matthew, whined placatingly, standing up as though to restrain his friend, "there ain't no call fer you to git so riled up. 'Member what Hayes 'n' Jenkins said earlier." He cast a quick sly glance at El Lobo, fearing the gunslinger might have ideas about butting in. "You got a wife 'n' kids too, 'n' you don't want no trouble. That there furrin feller's done played his cards fair 'n' square, near as I kin reckon. Yore jest likkered up; that's all. Why don'tcha go on home to Sally. Mebbe she'll fix you sumpin' to eat; 'n' then you kin sleep it off."

"I ain't goin' nowheres, Matthew, till I teach this here card cheat a lesson he won't soon fergit; 'n' if yore my friend, you'll stand by me in this, 'cause I ain't figgerin' on bein' shot in the back by no interferin' son of a bitch." He glared angrily at El Lobo before turning his attention once more to Salvador.

"Hell, we're all yore friends, Will; you know that. But, Jesus Christ, man!" Jenkins rose to his feet as well. "That there furrin feller ain't even wearin' a gun, jest a little ole dinky sword what don't look like it would skewer a gnat's ass."

"Then you or Hayes give him yore pistol, Jenkins, 'cause I'm aimin' to show him he cain't come in here— wearin' them fancy duds 'n' lookin' like a stuck-up ole spinster of a schoolmarm—'n' think he kin bamboozle us with his lowdown tricks. Damned furriner! If he wasn't so damned dark, I'd swear he weren't nothin' but a slick mick on the make! What's he doin' here anyhows?"

"That, señor, is none of your business," Salvador replied coolly. "However, I shall be happy to give you satisfaction, as I comprehend that you are challenging me to a duel. If you will be so good as to name your seconds, señor, and the time and place. I shall meet you there—with the weapon of my choice, of course, as it is you who have provoked this quarrel."

To the visconde's surprise and irritation only loud guffaws greeted this statement.

Matthew howled like a hyena, dancing about and slapping his knee; and Hayes laughed so hard he doubled over the table, choking on his drink, and had to be thumped on the back—by an equally hooting Jenkins—several times before he could catch his breath. Only Will didn't think the matter was funny.

"You tryin' to make a fool outta me, mister?" he snapped.

"Not at all, señor," Salvador responded, slowly getting up and warily laying one hand upon his rapier. "It seems to me that you're quite capable of doing that all by yourself."

At that Will lost his temper completely and, like an enraged bull, went for his gun. With years born of long practice the visconde just as rapidly yanked his sword free of its scabbard. Like a silver streak of lightning, the blade flashed through the air, knocking the revolver from Will's grasp just as the pistol went off. Then with a quick lunge forward Salvador kicked over the poker table and, his rapier at his opponent's throat, forced Will up against one wall of the *cantina*.

It was not until he heard the sound of a gun being cocked behind him that the visconde realized his danger and cursed his foolishness at having turned his back on the other men.

"I wouldn't do that if I were you," El Lobo quietly warned a much-startled Matthew, who had pulled his revolver, intending to shoot Salvador in the back with it.

Matthew pivoted around to see two cold steel gun barrels trained straight at his heart.

"I don't hold with card cheats," El Lobo continued in that same silky voice, "and I don't have any respect at all for backshooters. That gentleman there"—he indicated Salvador—"played an honest game and won fair and square, despite the fact that your friend Will was dealing from the bottom of the deck—and quite poorly too, I might add—and had a card or two up his sleeve to boot. So I would suggest that you four . . . *cabrónes*" —he snarled the derogatory Spanish word employed for Salvador's benefit—"clear out of here before my trigger finger starts getting real itchy, and I decide to scratch it."

The men needed no further urging. Sullenly grabbing their hats and cursing to themselves under their breath, they left the saloon. With a flourish of his hand the guitarist, who had abruptly ceased playing when the fight had broken out, strummed his strings loudly; and a lively flamenco dancer began to sway to the click of her castanets. Bottles clinked against glasses, and the *cantina* returned to normal.

"*Muchas gracias, mi amigo, para todo el mundo,*" Salvador thanked the gunslinger. Then the visconde sheathed his sword, righted the poker table, and sat down. "Allow me to buy you a drink, señor. A small gesture of appreciation for saving my life, no? But, nevertheless, the only one I can think of at this moment. Permit me to introduce myself. I am known as La Aguila, late of Spain and quite obviously, I'm afraid, only recently arrived in the New World."

Salvador extended his hand, felt it shaken by a firm, steely clasp.

"They call me El Lobo," the gunslinger announced tersely.

"So I have heard. So, señor. What will you have? Beer? Whiskey?"

"Mescal."

"Conchita"—the visconde motioned to the waitress— "a bottle of... mescal for me and my friend here."

When Conchita had thumped the bottle down on the table, then departed, with a wink and a smile, hips swaying, Salvador poured the drinks and raised his glass in a toast to the gunslinger.

"To you, señor," he announced.

"*Salud!*" El Lobo rejoined.

"You speak Spanish, señor," the visconde noted after sipping the unfamiliar mescal and finding it not unpleasant. "And not just Spanish, but the Spanish of Spain. I take it that you are originally from the Old World, then."

"Once, a long time ago," the gunslinger replied in a voice that encouraged no such further observations.

Tactfully, sensing that this was a subject to be avoided, Salvador changed the direction of the conversation.

"*Sí*, it seems years since I have seen my homeland too. And as you can doubtless apprehend, I have much to learn about the New World."

"Well, I'd say you got a real important lesson today . . . Aguila, wasn't it? A gunfight—or duel, as you called it—can happen in the blink of an eye out here, and it's very seldom polite. Take my word for it: You won't last long in the West if you persist with those fancy, drawing-room manners of yours; and if you've got any brains at all, you'll get rid of that pig-sticker, and buy yourself a pair of Dragoon Colt revolvers."

"*Sí*, I can certainly see the wisdom of that."

"Just what in the hell *are* you doing here—if you don't mind my asking?"

"Not at all, señor. I am making arrangements for a guide, transportation, and provisions in order to journey to a small town called Santa Rosa."

Salvador thought he had never seen such an abrupt change in a man as that which suddenly came over El Lobo. All traces of previous friendliness gone, it was as though the gunslinger had, without warning, donned a cold hard mask, so chillingly forbidding was the expression now upon his face.

"Did I—did I say something wrong, señor?" the visconde queried, puzzled.

"No," the gunslinger grunted curtly. "It's just that

I—I used to live thereabouts, and I don't have much liking for the place."

"I'm sorry to hear that, señor. But perhaps you know the man for whom I am searching then. An older gentleman, he would be now, by the name of Don Diego Ramón Delgados."

At that El Lobo suddenly clenched his shot of mescal so tightly the glass shattered, cutting open his palm.

"Clumsy of me," the gunslinger stated coolly as he ripped his bandanna from his throat and began to wind it about his bleeding hand. "If you'll excuse me, señor . . ."

"But of course." Salvador spoke courteously, rising, more confused than ever.

What could he possibly have said to cause such consternation in the man? It was obvious to the visconde that El Lobo, for all his outward calm, was inwardly a mass of tension.

"I'm sorry if I have inadvertently caused you some distress, señor," Salvador apologized.

"No, no trouble at all. *Buenos días*, señor. Thanks for the drink."

With that the gunslinger was gone.

Salvador sat thoughtfully for some minutes in the saloon after El Lobo's departure, going over and over in his mind the conversation just past. Just what had brought about the gunslinger's sudden, strange behavior? For the life of him the visconde could not think what it might have been. Finally, shrugging, he dismissed the matter. Whatever it had been was unimportant. Doubtless he would never see El Lobo again.

THE man they called El Lobo leaned against the wall of the alley behind the *cantina* and took several deep breaths to steady his nerves. It had been a long time since he had felt so shaken.

The past, which he had thought long forgotten, had suddenly risen up in the shape of La Aguila to haunt him. Who was he—this man, La Aguila, who had spoken so casually of Santa Rosa and Don Diego Ramón Delgados? El Lobo had to know, for he had not always been the gunslinger known as the Wolf. His real name was Rafael Bautista Delgados y Aguilar; and the man for whom La Aguila searched was El Lobo's father, dead for fifteen years, murdered for a piece of land, Tierra Rosa, where his family had lived just outside of Santa Rosa. El Lobo had been only twelve years old at the time; but to this day he could still see his father crumpling to the ground, blood spurting from the mortal bullet hole between his eyes. The gunslinger could still hear the terrified screams of his mother, Doña Anna María, as the murderer Gabriel North and his men had raped her until she had died of internal injuries. El Lobo could still taste the vomit he had retched up that horrible day as he'd stood weeping helplessly.

Half-breed, the murderer Gabriel North had called the twelve-year-old boy, thinking him the product of a lowly Mexican and a white whore. Half-breed. He, who in Spain, before the treachery of Don Manuel de Zaragoza had caused the gunslinger's family to be exiled from their homeland, had been the Visconde Torreón. Don Rafael, they had called him then. Don Rafael Bautista Delgados y Aguilar.

But Don Rafael, Visconde Torreón, was no more. In his place stood El Lobo, gunslinger, bounty hunter, savage, a man who walked both sides of the law when it pleased him. El Lobo's jaw set with determination. He

would discover who this La Aguila was, and if the
gunslinger did not like what he found out, he would kill
the man whose life he had just saved.

THE valet Pancho slept with the sounds of a man who
has drunk to his heart's content. His loud snores rose
up from his pallet on the floor, where he slumbered at
the foot of his master's bed, and filled the air with a
rhythmic noise that most would have found irritating.
Salvador, however, was exhausted and slept on, oblivi-
ous of the valet's familiar, stertorous breathing. Neither
man heard the slither of a body shimmying up a post to
the overhanging roof of the first story of the Hotel
Placido, nor did they discern the soft thud of boots
across the red tiles to their second-story bedroom window. Neither was wakened by the stealthy scraping of
the knife that eased its way beneath the sash, prying it
open, nor were they alarmed by the creaking of the
window itself as it was slowly raised.

With the barest whisper of movement the shadowed
figure outside reached in, pushed the ruffled cotton
curtains aside, and climbed into the chamber, fully
aware that his entrance was unobserved, unheard, by
the two men who slumbered within. It was not for
naught that, after the deaths of his parents, El Lobo
had lived with the fiercest band of Comanche Indians
on the Great Plains and learned their ways of life. He
could sneak up, without a sound, on a man who was
wide-awake and fully alert. Two who were sleeping
therefore posed no difficulty at all for him.

Cautiously, after his eyes had grown accustomed to
the change from moonlit night to almost total darkness,
the gunslinger glanced about the room. It was stifling,
and he wondered that his prey slept at all, so hot and

humid was the chamber. El Lobo had been surprised to find the window closed; but no doubt these two, only recently arrived in the New World, had felt safer with it shut. Now a slight breeze soughed beneath the sash, rippling the curtains and allowing a scattering of moonbeams to filter inside. The hazy stream struck the weapon the gunslinger still held in one hand; the silver blade glittered, cold and deadly.

With skill born of long and torturous practice the gunslinger caught the sleeping visconde in a murderous grip and pressed the knife's point to Salvador's throat.

"Don't struggle, and don't make a sound," El Lobo hissed as the visconde started wide-awake at the sudden assault. "I'm just as good with this blade as I am with my revolvers."

"El Lobo," Salvador breathed in recognition, his tense body relaxing a little, although he was careful not to move, not wanting to have his throat slit.

"Yeah," the gunslinger said. "I've got a couple of questions for you; and your answers better be damned good, Aguila, or you're not going to be talking to anybody except your Maker."

"You've made your message clear, señor," the visconde replied. "Surely we can discuss, like two civilized gentlemen, whatever you wish to know. I am aware, from watching you today, that you are not really the savage you pretend."

"No?"

"No, Lobo. You too inhabited a drawing room once, or you would not have recognized the manners that belong to such a world."

"I'll say this for you"—the gunslinger's eyes glinted with a flicker of approval—"you're a cool one, greenhorn or no. All right. We'll do it your way, provided you give me your word—as a gentleman—that you won't try anything funny."

"My word, then—as a gentleman."

Slowly El Lobo released his bone-crushing hold and drew back, sitting down warily upon a chair next to the night table. Just as carefully Salvador tossed back his single sheet and sat up on the edge of the bed. With steady hands he lit an oil lamp, trimming the wick so the light was low.

"Would you like a drink?" he asked. "I'm afraid I don't have any mescal, but there's some whiskey here someplace."

El Lobo nodded.

The visconde stood and, moving cautiously so as not to waken Pancho, found the bottle and two glasses. He poured out the liquor, then toasted his night visitor, reflecting on the odd trust and admiration that had so strangely developed between them. The gunslinger had come to the Hotel Placido to kill Salvador; of that the visconde had no doubt. But Salvador's composure had won El Lobo's respect. As for the visconde—he did not fear the gunslinger; he was merely curious about him. After they had drunk and refilled the glasses, Salvador spoke again.

"I was right. I *did* say something this afternoon that disturbed you, Lobo, disturbed you so greatly, in fact, that you followed me here from the *cantina* and waited until dark before creeping up here to interrogate me. What was it, señor? What chord from your past did I inadvertently strike to bring you here like this tonight?"

Once more El Lobo's eyes gleamed unfathomably.

"Not only cool, but clever too," he observed. "I'm beginning to think you really are a specter."

"Come to haunt you, señor?" the visconde queried.

"Quick on the uptake as well. My estimation of you is getting higher by the minute, Aguila. Yeah, you're a ghost all right, a ghost from my past; and I want to know what you're doing here. This afternoon you mentioned a name—two names, actually. Santa Rosa . . . and Don Diego Ramón Delgados. I want to know what your interest in them is."

Salvador shrugged.

"There's no secret about it, Lobo, I assure you. Don Diego is my uncle—"

"No!" The gunslinger inhaled sharply, his whole body suddenly once more tense and wary. "No, it can't be!"

"What can't be, señor?"

"Cousin? Salvador?"

The chamber was silent for a moment, each man gazing at the other with astonishment and disbelief. Then the visconde whispered:

"Rafael? *Mi primero?* Rafael?" His voice rose. "*Dios mío!* Rafael!"

In an instant the two men were in each other's arms, hugging each other tightly, unable to believe that, after all the long years that had separated them, they had found each other again. After a time they drew apart and sat down, still staring, taking in the changes the years had wrought.

"Jesus Christ! Salvador," El Lobo murmured, shaking his head. His voice choked with unaccustomed emotion. "I never would have believed it. After all this time. Salvador. My God. Do you know how long it's been since someone called me Rafael?"

"Too long, *mi amigo querido*, too long. Oh, *mi primero*, I can see by your eyes that it is a very long and sad story. Tell me. Tell me what has happened to Tío Diego and Tía Anna María. Tell me what has filled your soul with such wariness and your heart with such pain and hate."

And so until dawn the two men talked while Pancho slept on, unaware of the joyful yet sorrowful reunion that was taking place. At long last the visconde sighed.

"Your parents dead. Murdered. Oh, Rafael, I am so sorry, so very sorry," Salvador said, the knowledge of the loss of his relatives as hurtful to him as it had been to his cousin. He buried his face in his hands for a moment, trying to regain his composure. At last he went on. "I can offer you no consolation for their deaths, Rafael, only the small and bittersweet satisfaction that Don Manuel lies too in his grave. I killed him. *Sí*, I drove my rapier through his black heart in repayment for your exile, my father's murder, and my mother's abuse at his cruel hands. Afterward I was forced to flee from Spain. My half brother has managed to ingratiate himself with the queen. Need I say more?"

"No, Salvador, *mi amigo querido*. From the time we were small I knew that Juan hated you. He would have stopped at nothing to see you dead."

"He hunts me still, as though I am an animal; I am certain of it," Salvador declared. "That is why I came here to the New World. That—and my longing to find you. *Mierda*. How my poor mother will suffer to learn her sister has been dead for fifteen years."

"Tell her—tell Tía Catalina that my mother's murderer will pay," El Lobo stated flatly. "Tell her that someday Gabriel North will pay—as you forced Don Manuel to pay for his crimes against us."

"I shall, Rafael. I promise. So, *mi primero*. Where do we go from here?"

"To my hotel room, Salvador." El Lobo suddenly

smiled tenderly, as only a man deeply in love can do. "I want you to meet my wife."

HER name was Storm Aimée Lesconflair, and she was even more beautiful up close than when Salvador had seen her from a distance, buying the red dress that had been in the shop window. His breath caught in his throat when he saw her: for her cloud of long blue-black hair and her fine bones reminded him so much of Aurora's miniature portrait in his watch that it actually hurt the visconde to look at his cousin's wife. Only Storm's eyes were different, a keen clear shade of grey and filled with a painful knowledge of life that did not belong in the eyes of a sixteen-year-old girl. Salvador's heart went out to her. It was plain that her past was haunted by as much suffering as his own and El Lobo's were.

With a courtly flourish the visconde bowed low and kissed Storm's hand.

"It is a pleasure to meet you, Aguila," the girl said, her soft, cultured voice tinged with a slight French accent. "I did not know my husband had any living relatives, particularly here in Texas."

"I . . . have only recently arrived, señora," the visconde explained without further elaboration.

Both he and El Lobo had previously decided the past was not to be discussed. The gunslinger, like Salvador, had his own reasons for not wanting his true identity known—not even by his wife. The conversation was therefore of inconsequential matters, and the visconde was somewhat relieved when he was able to take his departure.

Storm was not Aurora: but somehow, nevertheless, she continued to recall the girl's picture to Salvador's mind, and his heart was pervaded by a strange ache that would not be banished. It was not his cousin's wife whom he bid good night, but Aurora—she whose eyes were bluer than the Spanish sky and filled with the innocence of youth.

Chapter Twelve

Aurora's sapphire-blue eyes, which so often of late had been haunted by shadows, now sparkled with happiness. She was so excited she could hardly contain herself. At last, after months of waiting, a letter from Basilio had come! She glanced down at it again, scarcely daring to believe she held the precious paper in her hands. Beside the girl, Doña Ynez, who, not daring to trust a messenger, had come personally to Aranjuez to deliver the good news to her daughter, smiled tenderly, blinking back the tears that the letter had brought to her eyes.

"He and Francisca are well, he says," she told Aurora, repeating from memory the words written on the paper, as though to reassure herself of her son's well-being. "They have managed to buy a small plantation, but it is in such disrepair that it will require a great deal of money and hard work to make it even slightly profitable. . . . *Santa María!* I can only imagine what a ruin it must be, for they had only what little Don Pedro's purse contained when they left here and are desperately in need of funds. Of course, your father and

I are making what arrangements we can, but... Peru is such a long way from Spain. Yet even there they do not feel safe. I do not blame them. They go by the name of Montoya.... Oh, poor Francisca! How can I tell her what has become of Don Pedro and Doña Dorotea? Has not the poor girl suffered grief enough? Have not we all?"

"Shhhhh, Madre," Aurora murmured comfortingly, patting Doña Ynez's hand. "The attacks on Quimera—and Jerez too—have ceased, have they not?"

"Sí, but at what price, *mi hija?* Don Juan—the fiend!—is far too clever to offer us insult or injury now that Isabella has so pointedly befriended you, and he has learned your identity. No, now the monster seeks to court you, as though your father would ever be fool enough to give your hand to such a demon! *Ay, caramba!* I would fling Don Juan's flowers in his face and spit upon the ground he treads if I were you! I do not know how you can bear his attentions. You know he hopes to wed you only so you will be rendered totally powerless against him, and he can punish you in place of Basilio. There is no love in the marqués's heart for you, Aurora."

"I know, Madre, I know," she whispered, a lump of hatred and shame rising in her throat. "Do you not believe I despise the way his cold eyes appraise me, as though I am nothing but a slave upon a block? Do you not think I am filled with loathing each time he seeks to take my hand in his? If I were a man, do you not realize I would cut out his wicked heart and feed it to the rats that lurk in the dark corners of Aranjuez?

"Oh, Madre. I am sick unto death whenever the beast approaches me! But what can I do? The queen—God bless her kind nature, for it is her only saving grace—has no sense or insight whatsoever. Don Juan has convinced her he is mad for me, and I am but playing coy. Dear Isabella, to whom love comes as easily as a breath of air and who has, of course, been so cleverly guided by the marqués in her thinking, has decided it was her matchmaking that day at court that has led to this pass. Naturally she is delighted that one of her favorite *caballeros* wishes to marry me, her good friend.

"I have made every conceivable excuse to avoid the entanglement, Madre, but the queen persists in leaving me alone with Don Juan at every turn. I cannot risk offending Isabella, for she is as fickle as a bee that flits from bloom to bloom. The marqués knows this only too well and has taken full advantage of it. Oh, Madre" —Aurora's voice was a sharp cry of despair—"I do not know how much longer I can hold out against the two of them."

"Aurora, *mi hija*, I am so sorry," Ynez apologized, tears of self-reproach trickling down her cheeks. "Forgive me. I have been selfish and unthinking, wrapped up in my own fears. I should have realized I was not the only one who was suffering and afraid. How hard indeed this must have been for you. You were always such a shy and solitary child. I can't imagine how being thrust into the center of attention at court has affected you. Of course, I know you haven't encouraged Don Juan, that it is only the queen who forces the issue. Oh, if only Isabella weren't so very foolish and frivolous!"

"She cannot help it, Madre, and she does try; truly she does. It is not her fault she was born with beauty instead of brains."

"I know." Ynez sighed. "I must go, Aurora. I promised your father I would not travel at night, and already the sun sinks in the sky. Take heart, *mi hija*. At least we

know now that Basilio and Francisca are safe. There is
comfort in that."

"Sí. Take care, Madre," Aurora said wistfully, sorry
to lose her mother's company so soon. The girl hugged
Ynez close and kissed her. "Vaya con Dios."

After her mother's departure Aurora sat quietly in
the gardens for some time. Today, fortunately, she did
not have to worry about being accosted by the marqués
and compelled to listen to his false flattering of her.
Don Juan had gone hunting and would not return to
the palace until late. Aurora's mind was indeed troubled, as she had informed her mother. The pressure
being brought upon her by Isabella to marry the marqués
was almost more than the girl could bear.

She shuddered involuntarily at the thought of being
helpless in Don Juan's grasp. Should she be forced to
wed him, Aurora had no doubt that in the end he
would kill her. She remembered the unnatural expression of joy upon his face, the other day when he had
crushed a bug in the gardens. The pleasure he had
derived from stomping his boot down upon the insect
and, with his sole, grinding the pitiful creature into the
ground had appalled Aurora. She knew the marqués
would take the same delight in tormenting and abusing
her, should she ever fall into his power.

But far more frightening than this was a matter that
Aurora had not been able to bring herself to discuss
with her mother, for the gentle Ynez would have been
shocked and horrified by it.

It was Sor Patrocinio. Though she hid it well, the
fanatical nun deeply resented the queen's affection for
Aurora and was doing everything possible to undermine
it. Still more terrifying was the fact that Sor Patrocinio's
hot, covetous eyes, filled with unnatural lust, followed

Aurora's every move. The girl was afraid that Sor Patrocinio's vulturous designs on her were behind the nun's sly, subtle attempts to discredit her with Isabella.

Just last week Blanca, who had confided to Aurora her own overwhelming fear of Sor Patrocinio's intentions toward her, had been found dead in the nearby woods, where many of the courtiers and ladies-in-waiting often went riding. Aurora had not seen her friend's small, mutilated body, but the rumors about what had been done to her were bad enough. Not only had Blanca been severely beaten and burned by her torturers, but she had been savagely raped as well, in some manner so hideous even the most hardened of those at court still refused to speak of it.

Aurora shivered at the thought. She was not ignorant of the physical relationship between a man and a woman, but she had little knowledge whatsoever of the sadistic perversions that were practiced by some. Fátima, who had been unfortunate enough to discover Blanca's corpse, had described to Aurora and Concepción—in terse, quietly outraged detail—just what had been done to the girl's body. Aurora and Concepción had been so stunned, so stricken, that they had not believed their friend.

"What innocents you both are," the older Fátima had sneered at their incredulous protests. "If you had been born in Granada and reared on the tales of the Infidels' atrocities, you would know I speak the truth. I saw Blanca's corpse, I tell you! I know what was done to her; and I also know, without a doubt, that it was Sor Patrocinio who did it. The evil *puta!* She hides her sickness behind her robes and Bible: but God and I, Fátima, see her for what she really is. Are you blind that you have not observed how the altar boys and young novitiates shrink from her very presence? She's a witch, I say, who works not miracles, but spells!"

Once more Aurora trembled as she recalled the whispered conversation. Despite Fátima's pronouncement, Aurora still would not have believed her friend, had the girl not seen with her own eyes Sor Patrocinio's peculiar, triumphant smile as Blanca's body had been lowered into its grave. Aurora had glanced away quickly at the sight, horrified, lest the nun realize that her gloating expression had been noticed.

Now, like the rest of the ladies-in-waiting, Aurora no longer rode in the woods.

She could fight Don Juan's wickedness, though cruel and vicious, because she understood it. She did not know how to combat Sor Patrocinio's evil, however, for it was a thing that Aurora could not comprehend. Her very mind and soul reeled at the shock of such sacrilegious behavior. How could God allow such a nun to exist? The girl had no answer. Her own crime of believing in a past life seemed very small in comparison to Sor Patrocinio's trespasses. Aurora wished she could talk to her grandmother, for Doña Gitana was old and wise and had seen many things in her lifetime; but she was ill, and Aurora did not want to trouble her.

The girl sighed and closed her eyes, feeling, as she did so, time slip from the present into the past. She was not surprised, then, when she looked up, to see the man—now her dearly beloved—standing over her. For an eternity, it seemed, he stared down at her, his eyes searching her face. Then he asked:

"Why so still and quiet, *querida?*"

"Oh, *mi corazón*," she whispered with anguish, for she knew he had come to plead for her hand—and she could not give it to him. Her father had refused his consent to their marriage, though she had begged him to relent. "There is no hope for us. I know it. Though I would wed you tomorrow and be glad of it, my father will not permit it. Of this I am certain. For all that your blood is as blue as my own, *mi alma*, you have no fortune; and Padre, who is proud, will not see me wed a poor man. He is going to give my hand to another, a despicable creature but one who is a marqués and whose pockets are lined with gold."

How could that be? Aurora wondered even as she spoke the words. Had Don Juan too been present in her life long past? Had her father indeed promised her to him rather than to her beloved? Was that why now she instinctively shrank from the marqués?

"No!" her beloved cried, then swore. "*Sangre de Cristo!* He cannot do this to us! He cannot! I will not allow it!" He flung himself to his knees before her and took her hands in his. "You must resist your father's plans for you, *muñeca*," he directed earnestly, "for as long as you can. I will find a way for us. This I promise you."

With a start Aurora came back to reality, shaking her head to clear it. Sweet *Jesús*. The man's hold on her was growing stronger and stronger; and, because she loved him so, she was helpless to deny it. Still never before had he appeared to her in so public a place. It was dangerous. Anyone might have passed by and heard her speaking to him, and since no one could see the man except Aurora, it would have appeared as though she were talking to herself.

She glanced up warily at the sound of approaching footsteps. Had someone indeed spied her odd behavior?

Coming along the path that wound its way through the gardens was a striking older woman whom Aurora had never seen. Yet for some reason the stranger seemed almost familiar to the girl.

"*Buenos días*," the woman greeted her. "Forgive me for disturbing your reverie, Doña Aurora, but I was told I could find you here. You don't know me, but I would like to speak with you for a moment—if I may." The woman paused, then hurried on as though fearing that Aurora would otherwise deny her a few minutes' time. "Allow me to introduce myself. I am Doña Catalina Aguilar de Rodriquez de Zaragoza de Yerbabuena, Condesa de Fuente. A long name for one woman, isn't it?" she asked, smiling a trifle sadly.

"*Sí*." Aurora nodded, slightly perplexed by the condesa's sorrow and so curious about what it was that she wanted that her name scarcely registered.

"May I sit down?"

"But of course," Aurora agreed, rising with embarrassment as she suddenly remembered her manners. "Indeed, how rude of me to have kept you standing. I must apologize, señora. I'm afraid my thoughts were elsewhere."

"*Sí*, I would have to have been blind not to have seen that," Catalina commented as she settled herself upon the stone bench.

The condesa's hands plucked uncomposedly at the folds of her gown, and briefly, now that she sat beside the girl, Catalina could not bring herself to speak. Aurora waited awkwardly in silence until at last the woman found her voice.

"You are . . . very beautiful," she observed, "and very young. That is why I—I must warn you—"

"Warn me!" Aurora exclaimed, startled.

"*Sí*. Please hear me out, señorita. I am the mother of

señor el Marqués de Llavero, Don Juan Rodolfo de Zaragoza y Aguilar."

Aurora gasped, then froze with shock, her face blanching. She should have realized— But no. This quiet, lovely lady couldn't possibly have given birth to such a swine! The condesa, already apprehensive, misinterpreted the expression upon the girl's still countenance.

"I see I am too late," Catalina declared softly. "He has already poisoned you against me."

"What—what do you mean?" Aurora queried, more confused than ever.

"Doña Aurora, please forgive me, but I must speak plainly, and I'm afraid what I have to tell you is very painful to me. No, please"—she stayed the girl's interruption—"let me continue. I know now that you don't want to listen, but you must!

"It is no wonder that Juan has already succeeded in turning you against me. His lies are believed even by the queen, who is kindness herself. My son—my son despises me, because I have never been able to bring myself to love him. But I could not! Doubtless you think me an unnatural mother, and perhaps I was—at least to Juan. I hated his father, Don Manuel, my second husband, who was a most cruel and vindictive man. Manuel was powerful, greedy, and ambitious; and he would stop at nothing to obtain what he desired."

The condesa's voice was bitter with remembered agony. She inhaled raggedly, then went on.

"I—I was very young, as you are now, when he murdered my deeply beloved first husband, Don Esteban. Young and alone, with no one but our newborn son, Salvador, to protect me. I had one sister, Anna María, but her husband, Don Diego, was as much a victim of

Manuel's treachery as my own was. Diego tried, but he did not have enough power to prevent me from being compelled to marry Manuel. Diego was a *Carlista*, you see; and even in those days there was danger in such a political stance.

"The first thing that Manuel did on our wedding night was to send my son away. Then, while Salvador's pitiful cries of fright were still ringing in my ears, Manuel came to my chamber. He—he claimed his rights, and Juan was the result. God forgive me, but from the first I could not bear the sight of the child. His—his eyebrows swooped upward, just like Manuel's, and I knew he was the devil's spawn."

She was still for an instant, recalling, then continued.

"So it has proven. Some months ago Salvador, in a rage, killed Manuel in a savage duel at our townhouse in Madrid. And I was glad. God forgive me, but I was *glad!*" Catalina's voice rose fiercely. "But I have paid dearly for my joy at Manuel's death. Juan went to the queen and accused Salvador as a murderer and a traitor to the Crown. Salvador was forced to flee from Spain, to the New World; and now I shall never see him again."

Again she paused, weeping, then recovered her composure.

"I have told you this story because—because I have heard rumors. . . . Oh, señorita, I pray you: Do not marry my son Juan. He will hurt you, as Manuel hurt me, as Juan goes on hurting me in Manuel's place—" She broke off abruptly, biting her lip.

Aurora was stunned by the tale and at a loss for words as she tried to absorb the impact of the condesa's confession.

"Doña Catalina, I thank you for warning me against the marqués," the girl said soberly, "but I believe you are laboring under a terrible misapprehension. If I too may speak plainly?" At the older woman's nod Aurora went on, her tone as bitter as Catalina's had been. "Frankly, I hate your son Juan. He accused my brother Basilio of being a *Carlista,* and, like your son Salvador, my brother was forced to flee from Spain. The only reason the marqués wishes to wed me is so he can punish me, because Basilio has escaped his vengeance!"

"But—but this is horrible!" the condesa cried. "I knew nothing of this. I thought—I thought that Juan wanted you, had—had somehow managed to hide his true nature from you. . . ."

"No, señora. No. I know him for what he is."

"You must get away, Doña Aurora," Catalina stated firmly. "If you do not escape, Juan will find some means of compelling you to marry him, just as Manuel did me. I cannot allow that to happen. I will not allow it!"

"Doña Catalina, I deeply appreciate your concern for me—more than I can say. But I cannot run away, not now. My grandmother is ill, and she needs me. Besides, if I do not stay at court to retain the queen's goodwill, the marqués will resume his attacks on my family. No, it is impossible, señora. I cannot leave Spain."

"But you must!" the condesa protested, highly agitated. "Do you not understand what I have told you?"

"*Sí,* Doña Catalina. I understand everything you have said. I know it is the truth. But I must think of my family."

There was silence for a minute as the older woman pondered this. Then, exhaling sadly, she replied, "Of course. You are right; I see that now. I apologize, señorita. I'm afraid I was carried away by my fear for you. But please, if you ever change your mind, if you ever need assistance, do not hesitate to call on me." She pressed her card into Aurora's palm. "My husband— my third husband—Don Timoteo Yerbabuena, owns several ships. It was he who arranged to have Salvador smuggled safely out of Spain. Timoteo and I will help you. Please do not forget."

"No, señora, I will not," Aurora replied gravely. "Thank you for coming here today. I hope your son Salvador is well."

"As do I, Doña Aurora. I have had no word from him, but perhaps tomorrow . . ."

"Sí, of course. I am certain you will hear from him." The condesa rose and took Aurora's hand.

"It is a great pity that Salvador is not here, señorita," Catalina remarked wistfully. "It might have been he who courted you—instead of Juan. I—I believe I should have liked very much having you for a daughter."

"Gracias, señora. You are most kind."

"Adiós, Doña Aurora. God keep you."

MANY nights later Aurora's beloved came to her again. He was, she thought, as she had so many times before, the most handsome man she had ever seen. He reminded her of an eagle, proud and arrogant, with his lean, hungry face and sharply defined features. There was something primitive and animalistic about him too. He exuded power, and for the first time he gave her pause.

There was something about him tonight that was different, something that had been coiled within him all the while but that only now had been unleashed. As his dark eyes raked her she stepped back slightly, a little frightened.

What did she really know about him, other than that she loved him? She had grown up with him, and yet it seemed she knew him not at all. The easy camaraderie they had shared as friends was gone, had been replaced by something more intimate and intense.

He was no youth now, but a man. A man whose eyes appraised her body deliberately as he walked toward her, sending a strange thrill of excitement mingled with fear down her spine.

"What—what is it, *mi vida?*" Aurora questioned hesitantly, one hand going to her throat. "What is wrong?"

"I am going away," he said slowly, still studying her intently.

"Away!" she cried, stricken. "But . . . to where?"

"To South America, to make my fortune. Your father has at last relented and has given his consent to our marriage, provided that in three years' time I can restore my family's riches."

"Dear God," Aurora uttered softly. "Dear God."

"*Sí,*" her beloved said bitterly. "He drives a hard bargain—your father—does he not?"

"Oh, *mi alma!* Take me with you! Take me with you!" Aurora whimpered. "I do not think I can bear to be parted from you—ever!"

"You must," he declared firmly, though his face was filled with pain and fury at his helplessness. "You could not survive in the Amazon jungle, where I am going. You are so frail, so fragile. Sometimes I fear for you."

He turned away, his mouth tightening with worry. Of late she had seemed so pale and ill—and there was too that small, nagging cough that disturbed him, frightened him.

"Then you have come to—to say . . . goodbye," she whispered.

"*Sí*, for that . . . and other things." His gaze lingered on her mouth, then moved to her eyes. "I will be gone a long time, *querida*," he murmured gently, "and who knows what may happen in the coming years? I may never see you again." Indeed, in his heart he had a terrible foreboding that it would be so, that she would be dead long before he ever managed to return to Spain. "*Te quiero, muñeca mía*. Now. Tonight. *Comprendes?* Do not deny me that," he pleaded passionately.

Young and afraid, Aurora stared at him, conflicting emotions warring in her breast. All her life she had been taught to save herself for her husband, that to do otherwise was a mortal sin. But three years was indeed a long time, a time in which anything might happen to separate them forever. She too was filled with ominous premonition. Though she had made light of it to spare him, she knew her cough was worsening; her health was failing with every passing day. Had her father not been so stern, she might have spent her last years with her beloved. Now there would be nothing for them; Aurora knew it. Tonight was all they would ever have, her one chance to share with him the joyous fulfillment that their intimacy would bring. She would not die without that knowledge, would not allow this one moment of happiness to be lost because she hesitated. It would be her secret, and by the time it was discovered it would not matter. She would be dead, and the memory of her beloved would be safe within her— forever. No, they would not snatch that from her grasp.

"No, *mi amor*," Aurora answered softly, fiercely, "I will not deny you."

Then awkwardly she turned away, not knowing what was expected of her. Slowly her fingers began to untie the lacings of her filmy wrapper. Minutes later the wisp of material slipped from her body and slid to the floor. From behind, the man placed his hands on her, pushing the sleeves of her negligee down until her shoulders were bare. Then tenderly he pressed his lips to the nape of her neck. A shudder of delight tingled up her spine, and Aurora did not resist when he suddenly whirled her about and took her in his arms.

It seemed as though he kissed her forever, savagely, his mouth moving on hers until she was weak and breathless with desire and laughing too, for his mustache tickled her. He kissed her cheeks, her eyelids, her temples, the strands of her ebony hair. Then his mouth claimed hers once more. But this time his lips were gentle, tantalizing. Expertly they played upon Aurora's senses, setting her blood ablaze, inflaming her until she was a fire burning wildly, longing to be quenched by the man who held her in his strong embrace.

His tongue traced the outline of her mouth, parted it as he forced his way inside to savor the nectar within. Aurora quivered at the intimate contact, for his tongue was rough and yet somehow as smooth as silk as it teased her, taunted her, demanded that she yield to him. It explored every crevice within her lips, entwined about her own tongue, imprisoning it, as the man had imprisoned her, with love. Her breath mingled with his, coming in quick little gasps, as though she could not get enough air—and yet she did not care. Nothing mattered except the man and the things he was doing to her.

Her head was spinning, and she was sure she would have fallen, had he not held her so tightly. Moments later he lifted her, so she was cradled in his arms, and carried her to the bed. He laid her down, then drew back to gaze at her as though scarcely daring to believe that she was there, was real. His eyes dwelled upon her face, small and white against the disheveled tresses billowing out like a black cloud upon the pillow. He stared lingeringly into the fathomless depths of her sapphire-blue eyes, noting the dark, half-moon shadows her thick, sooty lashes made against her pink cheeks when she closed her lids. He followed with pleasure the outline of her finely chiseled nose, its nostrils flared with arousal. He longed once more to taste her sweetly vulnerable mouth, now bruised and swollen from his kisses.

A small pulse beat rapidly at the hollow of Aurora's throat. The man felt his loins quicken with desire at the sight. He wanted her—and he would have her. Now. Tonight. He would wait no longer.

He lay down beside her, covering her body with his own. She could feel his white linen shirt and, where the lacings were open, the mat of dark hair across his chest, both damp upon her skin where he pressed against her, molding himself to her, compelling her to give way to him.

He nipped her earlobe and whispered in her ear, words of love and passion she heard only dimly as tingles from his warm breath chased down her spine, making her shudder with excitement. Her arms wrapped around his broad back. Her fingers dug into his flesh, kneading the sinuous muscles that bunched and rippled beneath her palms, reminding her of a cat as it crouches, ready to spring upon its prey.

With a low cry of surrender Aurora flung back her head, exposing the length of her bare throat to her beloved's lips. They traveled down the slender column, and his teeth grazed her skin lightly before sinking gently into that soft place upon her shoulder where it joined her nape. Flashes of electric anticipation shot through her body as she moaned and instinctively arched against him, writhed beneath him, her loins taut and aching.

The man laughed huskily, wrapping her cascading mane about his hands, his fingers tightening in the locks as he muttered something against her throat.

What had he said? She didn't know. The words escaped her, were swept away by the sheer, overpowering tide of desire he was wakening in her. Her earlier timidity vanished. She wanted him, whatever the price.

His hands tore at her negligee, ripping it from her body to expose her naked flesh to his gaze. Aurora trembled a little, for no man had ever looked at her so. She tried to cross her arms to hide her bare breasts— but to no avail. Her beloved pushed away her defense and cupped the melonlike globes, ripe and full, that thrust eagerly against his fingers. Sharp circles of delight radiated from her nipples as his palms slid caressingly over the pink buds that soon grew hard and stiff with excitement. Yet he did not cease the sensuous movement. On and on he fondled the rigid little peaks, teasing them to even greater heights. With exquisite finesse his thumbs flicked the tiny buttons that strained against his hands, begging, aching, to be touched. The man's lips closed over one flushed tip, sucking, tongue swirling about it deliciously in a manner that made Aurora feel faint.

A surge of primitive, instinctive emotion whirled up to engulf her as, without her even realizing they did so, her fingers crept up to entwine themselves in the thick rich strands of his glossy jet-black hair, to draw him even nearer.

Lightly his teeth caught her nipple, held it fast for the quick, darting movements of his tongue as it fluttered like a butterfly's wings over the crest he had claimed as his. Over and over the man tormented her until Aurora thought she could stand no more, would go crazy with wanting. And just when she believed her sweet torture was at an end, his mouth scorched its way across her chest, seeking her other breast and taking possession of it as hungrily as he had its twin.

Then suddenly, without warning, the man released her. Aurora's eyes flew open; her lips parted with a small sharp cry of surprise and disappointment. Oh, cruel, cruel the man was to have aroused her so when he'd had no intention of sating the terrible craving that had seized her in its grasp. Didn't he know that she had become a wild thing with the passion clawing its way through her veins? Didn't he know that deep within the secret place of her womanhood, desire was coiled like a tight spring, just waiting to be unwound?

"No, don't leave me, please," she pleaded, her arms outstretched to him with yearning.

He lifted one dark brow and smiled.

"Do you truly think I would deny myself now that which I have so long coveted, *querida?*" he queried. "I am but taking off my shirt."

Naked now to the waist, he again lowered himself over her, pressing his chest against her own so she could feel his heart pounding rapidly, even as her own was.

The man's loins tightened, racing with an excitement that he feared, for an instant, he would not be able to control. He took several slow deep breaths to still the furious thudding of his heart, the trembling anticipation of his limbs. He must take her gently, gently, at first: for this giving of herself to him was a precious thing, a treasure to be cherished always and remembered. No matter what happened in the future the love they

shared between them tonight would never die but
would endure to span the eons of time. The man would
see to that, somehow, some way.

"I love you," he said. "You are my destiny, *muñeca*,
now and forever, as I am yours."

He cast away his remaining garments. Aurora shivered
as she saw his obsidian eyes grow even blacker with
passion and desire as he again caressed her. Once more
his mouth closed over hers, hard, demanding, yet filled
with a fierce tenderness that wiped away the last vestiges of her virgin fears.

Her hips arched against him provocatively as his
hand trailed down to part her thighs, to stroke rhythmically the secret, swollen folds of her womanhood, the
tiny bud of pleasure that throbbed achingly for his
touch. His fingers slipped inside the warm wet core of
her, fluttering lightly along the length of her. Then,
almost before she realized what was happening, Aurora
felt his hard shaft probing her, finding the dark chasm
of her inviting cleft, and piercing it swiftly.

She cried out at the stabbing pain of his invasion
until he muffled her sobs with his lips, kissing her softly
and murmuring words that soothed the hurt, assured
her it would not last.

Presently, as he began to move within her, Aurora
found this was indeed the case. The ache was gone, had
been replaced by deliciously growing waves that swelled
within her before they crested and broke joyously across
the sands of rapture.

Again and again the man drove into her, spiraled
down into the beckoning cavern of her womanhood,
taking her to the heights of ecstasy—and beyond.

Finally, with one last, convulsive shudder of delight,
he collapsed upon her and was still. After a while he

withdrew. Aurora lay quietly beside him, afraid to move, lest she cause the hands of time to shift and find herself alone in her chamber.

"*Mi corazón,*" she breathed sweetly in the darkness. "I cannot go on if you leave me."

"I must, *querida*. It is our only chance at happiness."

Aurora reached out to grasp her dearest treasure, an intricate little carillon clock that sat upon her night table. She wanted the man to have it, so he would be reminded of her always.

"Then take this with you when you go," she told him, "and know that I am with you every hour of every day. *Vaya con Dios, mi amor.*"

AURORA started wide-awake, agony tearing at her breast. Her beloved was gone! He was gone, and he was never coming back! Frantically she reached out for him and only succeeded in disturbing Úrsola, the young lady-in-waiting who had taken the dead Blanca's place. Úrsola stirred, then rolled to a new position and resumed her gentle snoring as Aurora sank back upon her pillow, realizing at last that she was in her bed at Aranjuez.

How vivid that interlude from the past had been! Even now she could still feel herself throbbing with passion, could still feel the sheen of dewy moisture that beaded her flesh. She trembled as she moved her hands marvelingly over her body, as though she somehow expected to find it changed. But it was not.

I am still a virgin, she realized, and yet I have experienced love.

She hugged herself tightly at the thought. How beautiful it had been! She knew now that she could never give herself to any man but her beloved. Some way she

must find him, now, in the present, and pray that he
knew her—as Aurora was certain she would know him.

She glanced at the clock on the night table; it was
still there, as she had guessed it would be. Quietly,
under her breath, she hummed the sad little melody
that the small, ornate carillon clock from the past had
played. She had heard its song before—but where? And
then Aurora remembered. The jeweler's shop where
she had once bought a gold watch. The tune it had
chimed had struck some strange chord within her, and,
intrigued, she had purchased the timepiece, not even
quibbling with the jeweler over the price. Now she
knew why she had wanted it so. It was a link with the
past and dear to her heart and soul. She had given the
watch to Basilio because she'd had no husband, and it
had been too masculine for her. But Aurora knew the
timepiece truly belonged to her beloved.

"I will count the hours until I find you again," she
whispered fervently; and as though in answer, an angelus bell rang out softly in the distance.

Chapter Thirteen

AURORA was trapped, cornered like an animal in a seldom-used salon of the palace; and there was no escape for her—not now, not ever. Her eyes, wide and wild with panic, stared at Don Juan's vile, victorious face as slowly he again stalked toward her.

"It is hopeless, you stupid little pig!" he sneered. "You cannot get away from me. There is no one to hear your squeals and come to your aid, so you might as well stop fighting me. I shall have you in the end, and you know it."

"No! Never!" Aurora panted, her breasts heaving with rage and fright.

Oh, how could she have been so foolish as to allow herself to be caught alone with the marqués? If only she had examined more closely the note that had been delivered to her earlier! If only she had paused to think first before impulsively dashing to Concepción's aid! Aurora would have recognized that the handwriting was not her friend's; she would have realized that Concepción had no need to meet her secretly when they already shared a chamber.

But Aurora had not thought. Instead she had rushed down the long corridors of the palace to this small, out-of-the-way hall; and when she had hurried inside, searching for her friend, it had been Juan who'd slammed the door behind her and locked it, placing the key in his pocket for safekeeping.

Smiling mockingly at her fear and confusion, he had walked toward her purposefully.

"You bitch!" he had spat when she'd indignantly demanded to know the meaning of his ruse. "You have scorned my proposal of marriage and succeeded in deterring the queen from my suggestions. You have made me look a fool at court. Well, you shall not escape after all. I have friends too, my dear, very powerful friends. And once we have done with you today, you will beg me to wed you before any learn of your disgrace at our hands! Then you will be mine, all mine, to do with whatever I please. Oh, how your brother Basilio will cringe when he discovers that his little sister shares my bed! He shall be sorry, then, that he took Francisca from me."

Then Juan had lunged at her so quickly that Aurora had not had time even to think, much less run. In moments his jeering, carnal mouth had cruelly claimed her lips, grinding down upon them with such brutality that she had nearly swooned from pain. No one had ever abused her so; and at first she'd been too frozen with shock to defend herself. It was only when the marqués had begun to tear at her garments, and Aurora had realized he fully intended to rape her, that she'd started to struggle in earnest.

Savagely she had lashed out at him—clawing at his face with her nails, beating his chest with her fists, kicking his shins with her feet. Juan, believing her physically helpless against him, had been unprepared for her sudden, whirlwind assault and had fallen back to catch his breath and inspect the injuries she'd inflicted upon him.

Upon discovering these last were but minor, he now sought to regain his control over her.

Aurora was terrified. She had screamed and screamed, but no one had come to her aid. This part of the palace was little used; and doubtless none could hear her beyond the tapestry-covered walls and sturdy door anyway. If she did not find some means of escaping from him soon, the marqués would rape her, and she would indeed be forced to marry him before anyone learned of how he had defiled her, for he would be quick to boast of his conquest of her; and who would have her then? Public disgrace would be unbearable. God forbid that she should fall into Juan's merciless clutches in such a manner! Why, he might even get her with child! The thought of the marqués's seed growing inside of her made Aurora want to vomit.

"Keep away from me, you *bastardo!*" she warned as he stealthily approached. "Else I shall kill you!"

But even to her ears she sounded more pleading than threatening.

Juan only laughed, a horrible, mirthless chuckle.

"As you can see I am quaking in my boots, my dear. You foolish child! You are merely postponing the inevitable. It will go much easier for you if you simply submit."

"Never!" Aurora reiterated feverishly.

Once more the marqués lunged at her, this time pinning her up against the wall. The pounding of her heart sounded so loud in her ears that Aurora thought it would deafen her as again she struggled furiously to defend herself. Only dimly did she hear the further rending of her gown, comprehend that her bodice had now been ripped to her waist, exposing her breasts completely. Frantically, piercingly, she screamed over and over before Juan roughly clamped one hand over her mouth, his voice low and evil as he cautioned her to be still. Then he crushed his lips down hard on hers once more, his disgusting, encroaching tongue compelling her tender, already-bruised mouth to open for his rapacious assault. His palms slid down to grasp her breasts, squeezing them painfully and pinching her nipples savagely when the tiny buds refused to grow excited by his advances. The girl's lack of response angered him. The marqués considered himself an expertly tormenting lover, able to elicit an unwilling, anticipatory reply from even the most frightened and frigid of women. It was this that gave him the greatest satisfaction of all, knowing that despite their hatred of him, they wanted him still. It was obvious that Aurora did not.

How could she, when only last night her beloved from the past had shown her the joy and beauty of sharing such intimacy? She would not allow Juan to destroy that image. She would not! She would kill him first!

Again Aurora tried to cry out, but the marqués's lips still stifled her own. She felt as though she were suffocating and attempted desperately to gasp for air. The length of Juan's body pressed against her, smothering her; she could feel his hard fat manhood jammed up against the secret place between her thighs. Maliciously, feeling her writhe in helpless protest against him, he rubbed himself against her, cursing her skirts, which hampered his assault. Viciously, without warning, he swung her around to fling her down upon one of the many small velvet sofas that sat about the salon.

Aurora exhaled sharply as the wind was knocked out of her by the blow. Dazed, she lay powerless for a moment, her strength seeming to drain from her limbs as the marqués began to push her gown up about her thighs. One hand yanked at her undergarments while the fingers of his other fumbled with his pants. The girl tried to bring her knees up, but Juan had them pinioned beneath his own; and she knew there was no hope for her. In minutes he would have his way with her.

She gave a low moan of horror, her head lolling from side to side like a broken doll's. Again her arms flailed out wildly, striking a china figurine, which sat upon a nearby table, and tipping it over. Blindly Aurora's hand searched for, found, and seized the porcelain statuette. The marqués, his eyes fastened upon her now-exposed womanhood, did not observe his danger. He was too busy savagely probing the soft, downy curls; the dry, narrow passage that denied entry to his ravaging fingers.

Discovering sudden strength in her fury, Aurora brought the china figurine up, smashing it as hard as she could against Juan's triumphant, smirking visage. The porcelain statuette shattered against his cheekbone, snapping his head sharply to one side. With the jagged shard that Aurora still held she gouged an agonizing wound down his cheek while several smaller, uncontrolled splinters pierced his flesh like arrows, deeply embedding themselves into his skin. He squealed, horrified, as a chip flew into his eye; and blood began to spurt from the terrible gash upon his face. The unexpected blow had knocked him off-balance, and he fell back, rolling upon the floor, his hands clawing at his red, watering, squinted eye and the pieces of glass that pitted his countenance.

Not certain she had truly conquered him Aurora struck out at him again for good measure. The heavy base of the china figurine hit his temple, and the marqués crumpled into a heap and was still.

For an instant, as she knelt over him, Aurora thought that Juan was dead and that she was guilty of murder; but then she saw his chest move slightly, and she realized he was still breathing. Her head spinning, she sat back on her haunches, frozen once more with shock. Presently, great, strangled sobs began to rack her trembling body, and she wept with relief. Choking down the vomit that rose sickeningly in her throat, she ran her tongue over her bruised lips. Her breasts and nipples ached, and the tender folds of her woman's place were raw with pain where the marqués had tried to force his fingers inside of her. Most of all. Aurora knew an overwhelming sense of dirtiness and shame. She longed to strip off her tattered clothes and wash every inch of herself. But there was no time now for self-pity. Somehow she must manage to pull herself together. Sooner or later someone was bound to investigate the locked door and discover her and the marqués.

Shuddering with distaste, Aurora searched Juan's pockets until she found the key to the salon. Then she stood. She gasped as she caught sight of herself in a mirror that hung upon one wall.

She looked sick and disheveled. Her mouth was swollen; there were purplish-blue blotches on her arms and breasts; and her garments were torn beyond repair. She daren't traverse the long corridors of the palace in such a state! As best she could Aurora drew the ragged edges of her bodice together and, with her fingers, combed her tangled tresses. Then she replaited the disordered mane and pinned it back up with a few of her hairpins that lay scattered here and there upon the floor. What had befallen her would be obvious to any who happened to see her. No one would believe her honor was still intact. The marqués might as well have accomplished his evil purpose.

Well, there was no help for it. She would hardly be less remarked on if she were spied wearing Juan's bloodstained jacket.

Squaring her small shoulders determinedly, Aurora unlocked the door to the salon—and inhaled sharply. She could not believe her ill fortune! Surely God could not be so cruel! But He was: for there, just outside in the corridor, stood Sor Patrocinio. The nun's face was sly as her narrowed, gloating eyes took in the girl's obvious fright and disarray.

"No," Aurora whimpered helplessly. "No."

She backed away, startled and more apprehensive than ever. The wheels of her mind churned furiously. Sor Patrocinio's appearance was just too convenient to be believed. Why, it was as though the nun had been listening at the keyhole! To her horror Aurora suddenly realized that Juan must have arranged for Sor Patrocinio to discover them in the act of coupling. Doubtless once he had raped and subdued Aurora, he had meant to admit the nun to the salon. Perhaps Sor Patrocinio too had planned to have a taste of her before claiming she had willingly, sinfully, fornicated with the marqués.

Yes, that was how it must have been. That was what Juan had meant earlier when he had said he had very powerful friends.

And once we have done with you today, you will beg me to wed you before any learn of your disgrace at our hands!

Of course, Sor Patrocinio would have insisted that

Aurora had tried to seduce her—a nun!—as well. Between them they would have blackened the girl's name and reputation so badly even the queen could not have saved her, and Aurora would have been utterly at her enemies' mercy. Oh, yes, she would have begged Juan to marry her, would have suffered his and Sor Patrocinio's advances—the price of their silence, of course. Anything to spare her from being tortured as a heretic and doubtless hanged or burned at the stake. Did they still do that to people? Burn them to death? Aurora wondered. Even if they didn't, she was certain that somehow the nun would have managed to arrange it.

Without a sound Sor Patrocinio closed the door to the hall, her eyes taking in the salon at a glance, flickering briefly, scornfully, over the marqués.

"I warned him you were clever," the nun said as she advanced slowly, intently, toward Aurora. "I see I was right, and you have managed to save yourself after all. Or have you?" She laughed shortly. "No matter. I am not such a fool as Don Juan. If he has left you a virgin, so much the better."

Like a snake, the nun's tongue darted out to lick her lips; her clawlike fingers caressed suggestively, almost lewdly, the unusually large wooden crucifix that hung about her neck. Aurora watched, mesmerized, swallowing hard as she recalled what Fátima had said had been done to Blanca's body. Was it possible that the crucifix was the instrument that had been used? Sacrilege! Aurora fully expected to be stricken down by God for even suspecting such a thing. It was not possible— surely it was not possible that even Sor Patrocinio had stooped to such sacrilege.

The nun held out her hand.

"Give me the key to the door, Doña Aurora," she

whispered, her rasping voice tinged with lust and excitement.

"No," the girl breathed, shaking her head with shock and revulsion. "No."

"You cannot escape," Sor Patrocinio told her. "Already Don Juan is regaining consciousness. You cannot fight us both."

To her horror Aurora realized this was the truth. Frantically her eyes searched the salon for some sort of weapon. Cautiously, surreptitiously, she edged nearer to the fireplace, where a heavy brass poker reposed in an ornate stand.

"Give me the key, slut!" the nun hissed, suddenly lunging at the girl.

Almost simultaneously, fueled by the power of sheer terror, Aurora grabbed up the poker and struck Sor Patrocinio a vicious blow. The nun staggered and went down, moaning, as the marqués, groaning, raised his head at the commotion.

Quickly, knowing she had no time to lose, Aurora wrenched Sor Patrocinio's hood and robes from her fallen, faintly struggling body. They would serve to disguise the state of the girl's hair and clothes until she could reach her chamber.

"Witch!" the nun uttered weakly, still dazed. "Demon's bride! You bear Satan's mark upon your body!"

She pointed to Aurora's bosom, where the ragged edges of the girl's bodice had fallen open to reveal a small mole upon one breast. Aurora gasped. Surely no one nowadays believed such superstitious nonsense!

"You'll pay," Sor Patrocinio intoned, raising herself feebly from the floor. "You'll . . . pay . . . for this. . . ."

Then she collapsed. Aurora didn't wait to see if the

nun were still alive, for Juan was now stirring, trying to rise. Instead the girl pulled on Sor Patrocinio's hood and robes and ran from the hall as though the devil himself pursued her.

Chapter Fourteen

THERE was no time to lose, Aurora thought as she made her way to the stables and asked for a horse to be brought around. Soon Don Juan and Sor Patrocinio would be pouring out to the queen their highly distorted version of what had occurred today; and Isabella would be forced to believe them, whether she wished to or not. The kindly queen was too religious not to be horrified by an attack on a nun, especially when Isabella was doubtless unaware of Sor Patrocinio's true, wicked nature. Somehow, despite the rumors at court, Aurora could not believe the nun had exposed her real self to the queen. The girl must escape immediately—if she were to get away at all.

She had hurried furtively to her room and, relieved to discover it was empty, had rapidly changed into her riding habit and packed up her purse and jewel chest. The rest of her belongings would have to be left behind. If they were not confiscated, Lupe, Aurora's maid, could bring them later to the townhouse in Madrid. Then, after leaving a short, warning note for

Lupe, instructing her to depart from the palace as quickly as possible, Aurora had hastened to the stables.

Now, as a mount was brought around for her, she hoped she had not made a rash decision. The hills were roiling with rebellion, and she did not even know if she could, unescorted, manage to reach Madrid. Any number of evils might befall her. She might be waylaid, assaulted, robbed, raped, or even murdered by *bandoleros* or *guerrilleros*. Nevertheless, she must try. It was certain that her fate was sealed at Aranjuez.

Aurora had ridden all her life, and she was a superb horsewoman. Expertly she whipped up her mount and galloped from the palace courtyard.

Doña Gitana's proud old face was grave as she listened to her granddaughter's tale. Despite the elderly dowager's best-laid plans and an initial modicum of success, Aurora had failed. The combined wickedness of Don Juan and Sor Patrocinio had proven too much for her. It was a marvel that she had managed to outwit and escape from them. It was a miracle that she had somehow reached Madrid unharmed.

Though dying, Doña Gitana was not yet finished. If it were the last thing she ever did, she would save her granddaughter's life.

"Felipe"—the beldam spoke to her son—"send for Don Timoteo Yerbabuena and his wife. We are going to need their assistance."

"But—but Doña Gitana!" Doña Ynez, who was sitting by her husband, protested vigorously. "We don't even know if we can trust them! Just because the woman approached Aurora, told her a sad story, and gave her a card in case she should ever need help doesn't mean the condesa will be sympathetic to our plight. For all we know, the woman is hand in glove with her son—the monster!"

"Don't be a fool, Ynez!" Doña Gitana snorted. "Don Timoteo is the son of one of my late husband's oldest and dearest friends." The dowager always referred to her husband as though he had only recently passed away, when in reality he had been dead for over twenty years. "You remember Raúl Yerbabuena, surely; and a fine man he was too. I hear the son followed in his father's footsteps. Besides, I recollect when young Don Esteban Rodriquez was murdered, and a ghastly thing it was. And the way his poor widow, Doña Catalina, immediately married Don Manuel de Zaragoza afterward. It wasn't decent, you know; why, Don Esteban was scarcely cold in his grave at the time! I always did think there was something peculiar about that. Now I know what it was. It's my belief the woman is to be taken at her word. She said she and Don Timoteo would aid Aurora if ever the need arose. I think they will. Felipe, do as I told you."

So it was that sometime later Aurora found herself on her way to Cádiz, to board one of Don Timoteo's ships bound for the New World, for Peru, and Basilio's ruined plantation. Beside her, in her father's well-sprung carriage, sat her younger brother, Nicolas. The boy was only eleven; and his eyes were red-rimmed from crying, for understandably he had not wished to be wrenched from his home to accompany her. But their parents had insisted. Aurora could not travel alone, with no man to protect her; and Nicolas had been the only male relative available. Felipe must remain behind in Spain to defend his wife and his mother, who was too ill to be moved.

The parting from their family had been tearful and

heartbreaking. Especially hard for Aurora had been bidding her grandmother *adiós*, for the girl had known she would never see Abuela again. Doña Gitana too had realized this.

"Do not weep for me, *niña*," the beldam had said as she'd lovingly stroked Aurora's head, laid in her lap. "I am old, and I have lived a long and happy life. I am ready to meet my Maker."

"Oh, no, Abuela, no!"

"*Sí*, Aurora. It is so. When you have lived as long as I have, you no longer fear death, *niña*. It is instead a welcome release. I yearn for my late husband—and for my friends too who have passed on to their rewards; and I know they will be waiting for me in heaven. My only regret is leaving you, Aurora, for you have been my pride and joy in the winter of my years. I love you, child of my heart. Be strong, *niña*. For both of us, for I will be with you in spirit—if not body. *Vaya con Dios*, Aurora. May your destiny be grander than gold and glory too."

Now, as she recalled sorrowfully her grandmother's words, Aurora was puzzled, for what could be grander than gold and glory? Money and position were all. At sixteen, she had already learned that bitter fact. Had she been rich and powerful, she would not have fallen prey to Don Juan and Sor Patrocinio. She and Nicolas would not have been forced to leave their home and family. A terrible, empty sadness overwhelmed her at the thought. She hoped her parents and Abuela would be safe. Don Timoteo and Doña Catalina had declared that they would stand by the house of Montalbán. Already, quietly, since his marriage to Catalina, Timoteo had been searching for others who had been harmed by Juan's perfidy. By now the Conde de Fuente had

discovered enough injured families to form a small band
of resistance against his evil stepson. En masse they
would try to defeat the marqués. Their first action
would be to see that Lupe, Aurora's maid, got safely
away from Aranjuez.

"I felt so guilty about leaving her behind," Aurora
had explained to the kindly, lame hidalgo. "But there
was no time to try to locate her. She might have been
anywhere, for she was very loyal to me and acted as my
eyes and ears at court."

"Do not worry, señorita," Timoteo had stated comfortingly. "I will take care of the matter. Despite Juan's
machinations, I am still a man of some consequence in
Madrid. If the maid is found unharmed, do you wish for
her to join you in Cádiz?"

"Sí, that would be nice, but only if Lupe agrees to come,
señor el Conde. After all, Peru is a long way from Spain."

A long way from Spain. The words seemed to echo in
Aurora's mind as the ship that she, Nicolas, and Lupe
had boarded in Cádiz pulled slowly away from the
wharf. The girl was glad that her faithful maid stood
beside her on the deck, for Lupe, who was clever, had
proven herself an invaluable friend and ally. After reading Aurora's note the maid had managed, with the aid
of Fátima and Concepción, to escape from Aranjuez,
bringing away what she knew were the dearest of
Aurora's possessions: the girl's Bible and rosary that her
grandmother had presented to her the day of her
confirmation, the carillon that her parents had given
her on her sixteenth birthday, a silk *rebozo* from Basilio,
and a hand-painted fan from Nicolas. Further, before
leaving, Lupe had endeavored to give the impression
that she was heading toward Quimera, thus throwing
Aurora's pursuers off the track and buying the girl

precious time. The maid had actually been en route to Madrid when Don Timoteo's men had found her and had escorted her to Cádiz.

It had been Lupe who, when the captain of the *San Pablo* had asked them to sign the vessel's passenger list, had deliberately upset the inkwell, obliterating their names from the page; and it had also been Lupe who, upon inspecting their accommodations on board the ship, had loftily informed the captain that a mistake had been made, that Señorita "Montoya" and her brother had bought first-class tickets, not steerage, and that they intended to complain to Don Timoteo Yerbabuena himself if they did not receive what they had paid for. They had immediately been placed in private cabins when the somewhat unscrupulous captain had been made aware that, this time, he was not dealing with a couple of ignorant peasants.

How was he to have known, the captain asked himself later, that Señorita Montoya was not as helpless as she had at first appeared? Don Timoteo, who had a kind heart, was always assisting some poor, stupid wretch in need—most of them political refugees, his captains had no doubt. Why else did so many of them board secretly at night and keep glancing about as though they feared to be arrested at any moment? Sometimes, out of pity, Don Timoteo even gave them free passage on one of his vessels if they could not afford the fare. It was small wonder that his line did not prosper as so many others did, that his profits were less than they might have been otherwise. What did it matter if his captains, who considered themselves underpaid and overregulated, occasionally helped themselves to a bit of extra coin if they thought they could get away with it, charging first-class prices for steerage and then pocketing the difference? The travelers so cheated were usually in no position to complain; and after all, a captain's life was not an easy lot. Still it was a risky business, and Don Timoteo ruled his line with an iron fist. If he discovered the stringent maxims had been broken, he did not hesitate to fire the man who had disobeyed them. The captain of the *San Pablo*, all smiles and falsely apologetic, had therefore deemed it wise not to swindle Señorita Montoya, lest he earn Don Timoteo's wrath in the process.

Aurora, for her part, could only be glad that she had had Don Timoteo's name and word to protect her. She shuddered to think how she, doubtless an obvious refugee, would have been cheated otherwise; and she wondered if Basilio and Francisca had been forced to journey to the New World, packed in the dark, dank, cramped quarters of steerage belowdeck. Surely not. Surely Basilio would have found some means of obtaining a first-class cabin for his bride, no matter how limited his funds.

Basilio. The prospect of seeing him once more was Aurora's only small comfort as the coast of Spain grew distant and at last disappeared. For somehow, as she stood at the ship's rail, watching her homeland fade from sight, the girl knew in her heart that she would never see Spain again.

BOOK TWO

Dawn of Desire

Chapter Fifteen

The Amazon River, Peru, 1848

IT would have been late autumn in Spain, nearly winter, so Aurora, who knew little about the seasons in relation to geography, was surprised to discover that it was late spring on the Amazon River, almost summer. The captain of the *San Pablo* had told her it was because they had passed the Equator and were now in the Southern Hemisphere, that the seasons were reversed. She was puzzled by the information, for she did not understand how it could be true. How could it be autumn in one place and spring in another? It was as though the planet Earth had been turned upside down; and she wondered what other surprises were in store for her in the New World.

Already the weather was hot and humid; and Aurora, who was used to the dry, acrid climate of Spain's Meseta, thought she would die from the combination of heat and moisture. Her hair was lank and damp with sweat; little tendrils had escaped from her neatly coiled braids and curled most annoyingly about her face. The material of her gown, unsuitable for the unfamiliar climate, was stuck unpleasantly to her back and clung heavily to her petticoats as well, making her even hotter. She waved her fan vigorously to stir the stifling air, but the slight breeze she evoked did little to alleviate her distress. Once more, with her handkerchief, she wiped the perspiration from her forehead and thought longingly of a tall cool drink.

"It's terrible—the heat," complained Nicolas, who stood by her side at the ship's rail, watching as the coastline of Brazil drew near.

He too looked most uncomfortable, with his broadcloth jacket plastered to his shoulder blades and the lace on his linen shirt hanging limply over his striped waistcoat.

"It will be worse where you are going," said the captain of the *San Pablo,* who'd overheard the boy's remark. Then he explained, "You can't get away from the humidity in the Tropics, for the rain falls almost continually. It causes mildew to grow on nearly everything—letters, books, clothing, boots, saddles—and soon practically all that you own is rotten."

Naturally neither Aurora nor Nicolas was cheered by this information. The girl bit her lip, thinking that surely Basilio could have found a more hospitable place to settle. No doubt whoever had owned the ramshackle plantation her brother had bought had been glad to be rid of it! She was not looking forward to the long, dangerous part of their journey down the Amazon River, which still remained. She would have been more than content to stay in the city of Belém, where they were now slowly pulling into port.

Located on the Bay of Guajará, part of the vast Amazon Delta, Belém was very old, having been established, as Fort Feliz Lusitânia, in 1616, and having attained city status in 1655. In later years it had been known as *Nossa Senhora de Belém do Grão Pará*—Our Lady of Bethlehem of the Great Pará River—and as *Santa María de Belém*—Saint Mary of Bethlehem. In 1772, it had become the capital of the Brazilian state of Pará. Though the town was sometimes still called Pará, a reminder of its antecedents, it was the simple name *Belém*—Bethlehem—that finally had been formally adopted.

Through the centuries the city had been noted for its raising of sugarcane, rice, cotton, and coffee, and its cattle ranching. Over the years, due to its convenient location, it had grown to be the main export center for the Amazon Delta. Thus it was a lively, productive town, as busily bustling as a beehive and filled with people of every race, creed, and color.

Yes, Aurora would have been happy to remain here, for Belém's beautiful plazas, gardens, and tree-lined streets reminded her of Spain. Santo Alexandre, the oldest of the city's churches, brought back memories of her own cathedral in Madrid, where she had always heard Mass, and her heart ached with homesickness.

She, Nicolas, and Lupe disembarked to oversee the unloading of their baggage and to make arrangements for accommodations until such time as they would continue on to Peru; and after finding a pleasant hotel Aurora was finally able to quench her overwhelming thirst. Seated on the wide, shady veranda of the hotel, she slowly sipped the strange drink that had been served to her, discovering it to be quite refreshing, though unlike anything she had ever tasted. It was made, the waiter had informed her, from the berries of the assai palm.

Still she would be glad when Lupe had finished unpacking their trunks and had ordered Aurora's bath. Then she could go upstairs, bathe decently for the first time in many long weeks, and change her garments for something more suited to the steaming climate. At least she was safe on dry land again! Aurora had not enjoyed the lengthy ocean voyage, for their first-class cabins had been small and stuffy. She couldn't imagine how they would ever have endured traveling in steerage, for those belowdeck had been packed together like sardines and had smelled just as rank. All manner of sicknesses had swept the ship, due, Aurora was certain, to the terrible conditions in steerage. She thought it was a miracle the vessel hadn't been quarantined by the Brazilian immigration officials, who kept a sharp eye on Belém's port.

Aurora sighed. She was tired, so very tired. She knew it was due more to her depressed feeling of being utterly bereft than to any physical exertion on her part. Still she could not help feeling old and worn out. She was only sixteen, but already she felt as though she had lived a lifetime; and to think that scarcely half of her exhausting journey had been completed!

She shuddered as she contemplated the remainder of their trip. At least Basilio had chosen to settle in eastern Peru, near a small Iquito Indian village at the mouth of the Nanay River. She had wondered why he'd selected the remote site—until the captain of the *San Pablo* had told her it was a good area for raising both sugarcane and coffee, the earth being richly alluvial soil, in which such crops flourished. In addition, land there was much cheaper because it was so isolated. Not many people wanted to venture so far inland. But apparently Basilio had; no doubt he had been worried that Don Juan would seek him even in the coastal cities of the New World. It was just as well, Aurora thought. Otherwise she would have faced another long, grueling ocean voyage around Cape Horn, for passage across the Andes to western Peru was nearly impossible, the hard and torturous way through the mountains being known to only a few native Indians.

As it was, Aurora and the others must journey up the seemingly endless Amazon River, a prospect no more enchanting. There was, the captain of the *San Pablo* had informed the girl, no civilized means of transportation up the river: for though there were isolated towns here and there, the Amazon Basin was largely uninhabited, as few cared to brave the hazardous jungle that covered most of the area. They would have to travel upriver as others centuries before them had done—in what were literally crude, dugout canoes manned by Indian guides.

Aurora had seen several of the small boats, heavily laden with wares, being silently paddled from port by the stoic-faced Indians; and she did not relish the thought of entrusting her person to either them or their unsafe-looking crafts. Nevertheless, she could not stay in Belém, as she wished, with no one but her eleven-year-old brother and Lupe for protection. Basilio and Francisca were family; and Aurora must join them—if only because she carried, carefully hidden in her trunk, the money her older brother and his wife so desperately needed.

Yes, she would go to Peru, to the remote plantation Esplendor that Basilio had purchased. She must. She had no other choice. Don Juan and Sor Patrocinio had seen to that.

* * *

IT was known by many names—Amazonas, Solimões, Marañón, Maranhão—but whatever one called it, it was, in volume, the largest river in the world. Its earliest explorer was Vicente Yáñez Pinzón, who had investigated the lower section in 1500. He had been followed by the more well-known Francisco de Orellana, in 1541, who had traveled from one of its Andean headwaters to the Atlantic. Orellana had claimed to have been attacked, during his long journey, by a tribe of tall, powerful, female warriors such as those of the Greek legend, and thus had given the river its fanciful name, Amazon. Other brave, daring men had come after these: Pedro de Ursúa, in 1559; Pedro Teixeira, in 1637, who had gone from Belém all the way to Quito, in Ecuador; and Charles de la Condamine, in 1751, who had brought back to Europe the deadly Indian arrow poison, curare.

It seemed quite impossible to believe that, centuries before Aurora's time, such men had battled through the dense, steaming jungle of South America, under the most primitive of conditions. And for what? Gold, most of them had sought—or so the stories told by the Indians claimed. Most especially searched for had been *El Dorado*—the Gilded One—a lost city, where it was said even the streets were paved with the yellow ore so hungered for by men. El Dorado had been found only once, or so the Indians whispered, by a young Spaniard, Don Santiago Roque y Avilés, who had been cursed by the gods for plundering the Gilded One and had gone mad and died, the secret of the way to the city going with him to the grave.

These tales and others the Indians imparted to Aurora as they journeyed down the Amazon in the crude, dugout canoes that carried them ever forward toward

Peru, to the place where the Nanay River flowed into the Amazon. To her surprise Aurora had discovered that the small boats, which she had originally deemed highly unsound, were, in fact, very finely and painstakingly crafted and were quite light besides, almost skimming over the waves. This was important, as, for all its vastness, there were parts of the river where a vessel could draw no more than eighteen to twenty feet of water.

Aurora had learned, as well, to like and trust the Indians who served as guides and manned the strange crafts they had fashioned. Most had been a part of the Amazonian trade system for years, so almost all of them spoke both Spanish and Portuguese, as well as their own native languages and dialects. As the days passed she grew especially fond of Mario, a half-breed with a Portuguese father and an Indian mother. *Mestizos*, such persons were called.

The first day of their trip, Mario, upon spying Aurora's pale skin, had clucked his tongue and shaken his head, smiling.

"You will be roasted alive, señorita," he'd announced. "Even with your hat, you will be roasted alive. A tasty treat for the Jívaros, should you happen to fall prey to them!"

"The Jívaros?" Aurora had questioned hesitantly, suspecting she did not want to know what he was talking about.

She had guessed correctly.

"Headhunters, who are doubtless cannibals as well, señorita." Mario had grinned.

Aurora had shivered, unamused.

"I shall keep well inside my hut, Mario," she had stated firmly, for the center of each canoe was covered by a peaked, thatched roof, protection against the pouring rains. "And if we are indeed attacked by such fiends, I shall lose no time in pointing out how much fatter you are than I am!"

"I don't know about the wisdom of that, señorita," Mario had slyly rejoined. "After all, it'd be just that much more work for them to shrink my big head!"

Everyone had laughed, Nicolas hardest of all; and Aurora had flashed Mario a grateful look for making her brother smile. Nicolas had been so downcast since leaving Spain that she had begun to worry that he would never regain his previous mischievous disposition.

Despite her earlier declaration, once the excursion got under way, Aurora found it was almost impossible to remain inside the hut. There was too much to see, all of it strange, exotic, and fascinating.

The tidal forests of the delta were soon left behind as the Indians, with their long poles, paddled the canoes through the Straits of Breves. Ranges of hills that were several feet high began to appear, vaguely reminding Aurora of the mountains of Spain, though the knolls here were smaller and not capped by snow. Farther on, the rolling crests sloped down to border almost on the river's bank; beyond in the distance were wide, open grasslands, called *campos*. Then after many days they reached the heart of the rain forest that covered the major portion of the Amazon Basin.

Never before had Aurora seen such plants and animals. So thick and luxuriant was the vegetation, so tightly woven was the canopy of the vast rain forest through which they traveled, that life in the Amazon Basin was literally an intense, continuous battle to garner a place in the sun. Mario told Aurora that portions of the forest were so dark that not even the

Indians penetrated the deepest portions of the jungle's interior, for fear of becoming lost in the blackness within.

Great silk-cotton trees, Para nuts, fruit-laden sapucaia, and blue-blossomed sucupira rose up like obelisks against the azure sky, where the sun blazed so brightly, so closely, because of the nearness of the Equator, that it seemed as though Aurora could actually reach out and touch the flaming ball.

Beneath the forest giants were myriad smaller trees. Thorny acacias mingled with climbing bignonias, whose branches were laden with trumpet-shaped flowers. Bombacaceae, Brazil nuts, and pink-blossomed cacao trees sprouted alongside cecropias, cedrelas, and figs dripping with pear-shaped fruit. Evergreen laurels, mauritia, and myrtles with white or rose blooms and black berries grew among leaf-crowned palms; hard, dark-colored, fragrant rosewoods; and rubber trees. All were covered by a veritable profusion of cacti, ferns, liana vines, peperomia, pineapples, pipers, Spanish moss, and an endless, riotous display of yellow daffodils, multicolored orchids, water lilies, and other brilliant tropical flowers.

There were aerial plants whose roots never touched the ground, content to embed themselves in their larger, stronger brothers for support. There were trees and bushes whose roots crept out in tangled tendrils to form a massive maze of undergrowth. And then there were the killers, the huge, cablelike stranglers that encased their hosts, gradually squeezing them to death to gain a precious bit of earth, a vital ray of sun. Aurora saw more than one giant tree that, now rotting, had fallen prey to the stranglers.

At night when they made camp along the shore, she

found that the forest itself teemed with animals of every imaginable kind. Hordes of small black flies, called *piums*, and mosquitoes buzzed and swarmed, as did fireflies and stinging bees, hornets, and wasps. Masses of droning locusts filled the air; thousands of gossamer-winged butterflies fluttered along the riverbanks. The earth crawled with armies of ants, beetles, centipedes, cockroaches, scorpions, spiders, termites, and ticks.

Aurora and the rest were cautioned early on to keep their limbs well inside the canoes, no matter how tempting it might be to wet one's lace handkerchief to cleanse oneself or to trail one's bare feet idly in the water: for many of the river's inhabitants were vicious and known to attack man. Barklike caimans, relatives of the crocodile, lurked like rotting logs upon the surface of the river. Giant catfish, electric eels, and stingrays moved with lightning speed to prey upon the unsuspecting and the unwary. It was said that aggressive, blood-thirsty piranhas could kill a man in moments, virtually stripping the flesh from his bones. Huge anacondas, some nearly forty feet in length, could slither up stealthily to coil themselves about their victims, crushing them to death in a matter of minutes, then swallowing them whole.

The Indians frightened Aurora with their stories of how the deadly snakes could devour a man as large as six feet and weighing more than a hundred and fifty pounds.

Less dangerous were the huge turtles, which, along with their eggs, were a primary food supply. There were gentle manatees, sometimes called sea cows; and often during the day playful freshwater dolphins came alongside the canoes and, with aquatic antics, entertained the travelers. Aurora never tired of watching these and applauded enthusiastically for tricks well done, laughing as the mammals bobbed a kind of bow in return. The unusual pink dolphins were especially revered by the Indians, who told tales of how the mammals sometimes changed their forms so they resembled human men and went ashore to take native females as their lovers. The children of such women were said to look like their dolphin fathers.

Sleep was made difficult in the evenings by the croaking of the abundant frogs and toads; and the slithering through the tall grass of lizards and iguanas, some of which grew to be more than six feet in length and resembled prehistoric monsters. They gave Aurora the shivers, and she screamed when she spied one perched upon her pallet, its tongue darting out rapidly as it stared at her with its beady eyes.

Tough-shelled armadillos, silky anteaters, and prehensile-tailed porcupines waddled about cautiously. Brocket deer, easily alarmed, crashed through the forest, startling raccoonlike coatimundi, agouti, and capybaras, which looked like giant guinea pigs and were the largest rodents in the world. Furry, white-spotted pacas searched the ground for morsels dropped from trees and, like the sleek otters, took with a splash to the water when pursued. From deep within the thick undergrowth came the grunts and squeals of peccaries and massive tapirs, their cries mingling with the eerie, womanlike screams of the occasional puma, jaguar, and ocelot, none of which Aurora was anxious to view.

High in the trees hung two- and three-toed sloths, some of whose fur, she noticed, was actually tinged green by the algae that had accumulated in it. She couldn't imagine hanging upside down without moving for so long that plants might grow in her hair.

Swinging from branch to branch were capuchin monkeys, howler monkeys, owl-faced monkeys, spider monkeys, and woolly monkeys, all of which chattered angrily when disturbed, stirring up the hundreds of thousands of bats and birds that shared their limbs.

At the edges of still, forest ponds that Aurora sometimes glimpsed in the distance stood elegant herons, sun bitterns, marabou storks, and cormorants, which looked down their long beaks at the lesser ducks and geese. Here and there perched untidy hoatzins, brilliant-plumed tanagers, funny-faced cotingas, gaudy macaws, big-billed toucans, and fat curassows. Tiny hummingbirds in search of nectar flitted from flower to flower while, overhead, gulls called, and sharp-eyed harpy eagles and king vultures hovered threateningly, waiting for the old, the sick, and the weak to die.

It was splendid, fascinating, savage, frightening, and glorious; but most of all, the jungle was awesome. Man had encroached upon it, but still it remained unconquered.

Aurora and the others were overwhelmed by it, for they had never dreamed that such as this existed. At night they lay by their campfire, listening to the sounds of the darkness that was alive with a million creatures.

The girl didn't know what they would have done without the Indians. They paddled tirelessly, singing and telling anecdotes to pass away the time.

Expert hunters and fishers, they had keen eyesight, and their marksmanship was beyond compare. More than once Aurora saw an animal yards away dropped by a bow and arrow, or a darting, quicksilver fish skewered by a spear.

The Indians showed Aurora and the others how to crush certain leaves and berries to make a thick paste to smear upon their skin to prevent their flesh from being ravaged unmercifully by mosquitoes and *piums*, whose bites caused red welts that itched for days. It was also the Indians who scraped the bark of cinchona trees for the bitter, white crystal salts that kept malaria at bay.

For a time Aurora could have sworn that she had been afflicted by the disease, for several weeks after their long journey began she was stricken by a fever that alternately burned and chilled. Progress downriver was halted as the Indians stopped to care for her, mixing various potions whose contents were known only to them.

Flushed and delirious, Aurora lay upon her pallet, certain that she was dying. Her hallucinations were made worse by the fact that she continued to experience the time travel that carried her back into the past; but now she no longer saw her beloved. Instead she found herself lying all alone in the bed where they had made love so passionately. Her body was wasting away from the lung phthisis; and though she tried desperately to retain her fragile hold on life, still it slipped from her fingers. Presently, after crying out her beloved's name, all was blackness.

When Aurora finally regained consciousness she was startled to find herself alive and well. She was even more bewildered to feel the man's presence watching over her, though he no longer appeared to her on the wings of time. She thought she understood the reason for this—in her past life she was dead now. But she could not comprehend why she should believe he was somehow still with her, guarding her—or why the closer they got to Esplendor, the stronger the feeling became.

*   *   *

AFTER many long weeks of travel they arrived at the
boat dock of Basilio's plantation. Strangely silent now,
the Indians deftly unloaded their passengers' trunks
and supplies, then moved to depart, their dark eyes
filled with fear as well as sadness as they bid Aurora and
the rest farewell.

"Mario," the girl ventured, "why are the Indians
behaving so oddly? Surely they are glad to be going
home."

"Sí, sí, señorita, it is so," the *mestizo* replied. "Nevertheless, they are afraid to leave you here."

"But—but why?"

"Your brother's plantation, señorita . . . it—it is be-
lieved to be both accursed and haunted." Mario shrugged.
"For myself, I have always thought it was only a story.
But the others . . . well, they believe. *Adiós*, señorita.
God keep you."

After the Indians had gone Aurora glanced about
warily, trying not to let her vivid imagination, which
had been piqued by Mario's words, run away with her.
She told herself that it was 1848, not the Middle Ages,
and that curses and ghosts simply didn't exist. But it
didn't help much. The plantation was eerily, deathly
still; and as, after ordering Nicolas and Lupe to stay with
the trunks and supplies, Aurora started up the winding
dirt road that led to the house, she felt a sudden chill of
foreboding tingle down her spine. It seemed as though
eyes peered out at her from behind every tree and
bush, and try as she might Aurora could not shake the
feeling that she was being watched.

"Nonsense," she muttered under her breath, squaring her small shoulders determinedly.

But, casually, all the same, with a coolness she did

not feel, she bent to pick up a stout branch that lay upon the road. It was at least some sort of a weapon, she thought. She had felled Sor Patrocinio with a fireplace poker. With a stick, Aurora could surely handle anyone else, for no one else could possibly be as evil as the fanatical, perverted nun had been.

Like a ribbon, the road to Basilio's plantation wound its way through the vegetation that over the years had stealthily encroached upon it. So thick was the growth in places that Aurora was unprepared when at last she pushed aside a branch hanging heavy with Spanish moss, and the house itself burst upon her.

For an eternity, it seemed, she stood frozen with shock, gasping—not because the manor was such a ruin, but because she realized instantly that it was the strange white manor house that Abuela had seen so long ago in the cards when she had read Aurora's fortune. As Abuela had first said before correcting the interpretation, it resembled a tomb. Nevertheless, for all its peculiarity and unfamiliarity Aurora felt somehow as though she had come home, as though the house had been built especially for her. . . .

I am going away . . . to South America. . . .

"No, it can't be," she whispered, stunned as she recalled her beloved's words. "It can't be."

Then she flung away the limb she had thought to use as a weapon, if need be, and began to run toward her brother's plantation.

"Basilio! Basilio!" she shouted as she reached the steps leading up to the porch.

But there was no answer. All was strangely hushed; and Aurora's voice echoed oddly in the silence.

There's something wrong, she thought. There's something terribly wrong.

Inhaling sharply, her hands trembling, she pushed open the heavy wooden doors of the house, not bothering to knock.

"Basilio?" she called more quietly. "Basilio?"

Still there was no answer. Aurora stood hesitantly, gazing about the decayed hall. She could tell that it had been magnificent once. But now it too was in sad disrepair. She did not know how to proceed. The manor appeared to be empty, bereft of life. Was it possible that a mistake had been made, that this was not Basilio's plantation after all? From the pocket of her gown she withdrew her brother's precious letter, now creased and dirtied, one corner torn from having been read so many times. Basilio's bold handwriting leaped out at her.

We have purchased a small plantation called Esplendor.

No, there could be no mistake. This *was* Esplendor. The faded, weather-beaten wooden sign at the boat dock had proclaimed as much.

"Can I help you?"

Aurora glanced up, startled by the unexpected sound of the voice that had spoken to her, for she had not heard the approaching footsteps, so softly had they fallen.

A tall, dark-skinned woman stood before her. A *mestiza*, Aurora guessed, for fine Spanish and native Indian features intermingled upon the woman's face, giving her a proud, mysteriously attractive appearance. Her dark sloe eyes, half-veiled, were cold and suspicious; her eyebrows were lifted in haughty inquiry. Aurora flushed guiltily beneath the woman's unrelenting stare, for it made the girl feel as though she had been caught trespassing. Then she remembered who she was and where she was and that she had a right to be here; and she drew herself up proudly.

"I'm looking for Don Basilio Mon . . . toya," Aurora announced, "and his wife, Doña Francisca. I am Don Basilio's sister, Doña Aurora. Would you please be so kind as to take me to him at once."

Briefly the woman's slanted black eyes flickered, with both fear and malice, Aurora would have said, puzzled, had someone asked her. Then once more the woman's face was like a mask—impenetrable.

"I am Ijada," she uttered regally. "I did not know that Don Basilio had any relatives. However, that is unimportant now. I am afraid, señorita, that you have chosen a poor time to visit." She seemed to stress the last word. "Had I known you existed and planned on coming here, I would have persuaded you against the idea. Don Basilio is ill. He has contracted a tropical fever and can see no one. The disease is contagious. It will be better if you return home before he learns of your presence and unduly excites himself."

"I shall do no such thing, of course!" Aurora declared, more confused and concerned than ever. She was right. There was something terribly wrong here. She was certain of it. In his letter Basilio had written that both he and Francisca were well. How could things have so drastically changed? "Where is Doña Francisca? I wish to speak to her immediately."

"I regret that that too will be impossible, señorita," Ijada informed her coolly. "Doña Francisca is dead. She died three days ago—from the same fever with which your brother has been afflicted."

Aurora blanched, shocked and stricken by the news. Francisca dead? How could that be? It simply wasn't possible. Three days ago. Oh, if only Aurora had arrived three days sooner!

"Then I must insist, madam, that you escort me to my brother. I am not afraid of contracting the disease."

Not for naught had Aurora been reared in the house of Montalbán. She met Ijada's gaze unflinchingly, refusing to back down. At last the woman nodded.

"Very well, señorita, since you insist. But do not say I didn't warn you."

THE man who lay in the dirty, unkempt bed was not Aurora's brother. Surely this pathetic, emaciated, yellow-skinned man was not her healthy, handsome brother. Slowly, as her eyes grew accustomed to the darkness that pervaded the room, which was shuttered against the stifling midday heat, Aurora approached the shrunken, skeletal figure who moaned and tossed upon the bed. Anxiously she pushed aside the insect dung-clotted mosquito net and bent to examine him.

"Basilio?" she breathed, her heart aching. "Basilio?"

At the sound of her voice the man started and stirred. His heavy-lidded eyes flickered open to reveal dull, glazed irises, as though he were drugged rather than ill. He stared at her uncomprehendingly for a minute, then finally recognition dawned.

"*Niña*," Basilio rasped weakly, his voice cracked and dry, the barest of whispers. He tried to hold out one wasted hand to her, but the effort proved too much for him. "*Niña*."

"*Sí*, Basilio, it is I," Aurora replied, appalled. "No. Don't try to speak now. Just rest. We can talk later, when you are better. In the meantime I have come to take care of you, to see that you get well. Go back to sleep now, *mi hermano querido.* I shall take care of everything."

Basilio nodded, his eyes closing. The girl couldn't even be sure he'd understood her. Quietly she left the room, softly pulling the door shut behind her. She shook with anger as she faced the outwardly serene and composed Ijada. To think that Don Basilio Enrique Montalbán y Torregato, Visconde Jerez, had been reduced to this! To think he, who was descended from some of Spain's finest nobles, lay amid filth such as Aurora had never seen in her life!

"Madam"—the girl spoke curtly to Ijada—"since I do not know your position in my brother's household, I have no idea what you hoped to accomplish by allowing him to lie—ill and helpless!—in such a state. However, that is neither here nor there. You are dismissed from your post and will leave these premises at once!"

"No, I will not, señorita," the older woman rejoined, unruffled. "It was Don Basilio who hired me. It is for him to send me away—not you."

"Why, you insolent, insufferable . . . Get out! Get out immediately, I say."

"And who is to force me to leave if I do not choose to go?" Ijada asked, then laughed throatily. "You, señorita?" She raised one eyebrow frostily. "I think not."

Then she turned and walked away.

"Come back here!" Aurora called fiercely. "Come back here, you impudent wench! How dare you defy me in such a manner?"

But her words echoed in the barren rooms of the deserted manor, for Ijada had disappeared.

Furious, Aurora stalked down the hallway, seeking the way she had come earlier. It was no use. She was lost. The knowledge only further enraged her. She wasted several long minutes, stumbling along the maze of corridors, before finding her way back to the grand, horseshoe-shaped staircase leading down to the main entry. There was no sign of Ijada. With a sigh, Aurora straightened her shoulders and went outside to fetch Nicolas and Lupe and inform them of the dreadful, depressing state of affairs at Esplendor.

Chapter Sixteen

IJADA had not departed. Like a sly cat, stealthily, sound-lessly, she reappeared when Aurora returned with Nicolas, having wisely, after her earlier confrontation with the *mestiza*, told Lupe that she would have to continue to guard the trunks. This time Ijada's face was twisted into a scowl of displeasure.

"Señorita," she inquired icily, "what is the meaning of this? You have seen for yourself that Don Basilio is in no position to be entertaining guests."

"Pay no attention to this woman," Aurora instructed Nicolas, who was glaring darkly at Ijada. "She is not to be spoken to, to be paid any wages, or to be given room and board. She has been dismissed from her post, whatever that may have been. If, under the circum-stances, she chooses to remain until such time as she is forcibly removed from the premises, that is her foolish affair. Do you understand, Nicolito?"

"*Sí, mi hermana.*" The boy nodded vigorously.

"Just who do you think you are?" the woman hissed venomously to Aurora. "It is *I* who have run Esplendor since your brother's arrival. I warn you: You are meddling in something that does not concern you, señorita. You have been well advised to return home. I must insist that you do so immediately."

"It is clear to me that you are an inordinately dense woman, madam," Aurora rejoined coolly, although inwardly she was shaking. "You are in no position to insist on anything. Nicolas and I have not come to *visit* our brother; we are not *guests* in this house. We have come here to live. Why do you seek to drive us away?"

Ijada was momentarily nonplussed. She had not realized, until this instant that Nicolas was also related to Don Basilio. The situation was now made more complicated than she had previously imagined. She licked her lips.

"I—I . . . Don Basilio is very ill with the fever, señorita," she said more respectfully, determining to switch her tactics. "And there are only a few poor servants here to help me, as Don Basilio could—could not afford a complete staff. I—I did not feel that I could properly care for *el patrón* and entertain his family as well; besides, I feared you would contract the disease too. It is hard enough work looking after Don Basilio without having more sick people on my hands. That is all. I did not realize that you had—had come to stay."

Aurora stared suspiciously at the woman but could find no trace of Ijada's previous insolence. The girl bit her lip, now assailed by indecision. She still did not like or trust the woman, but if indeed Ijada were willing now to acknowledge their right to be here, perhaps she could be useful.

"Very well, then," Aurora said at last. "We will forget this morning's unfortunate misunderstanding. My maid, Lupe, is still at the dock, overseeing our trunks. You will make arrangements for someone to transport her and our baggage to the manor. I will take Don Nicolas upstairs to see his brother. Since I have already exposed him, as well as myself, to the fever, there is no point in worrying about whether or not we will contract the disease. Besides, it does not seem to have affected you, Ijada."

"No, señorita, but then I have lived in Peru all my life and have developed a resistance that most foreigners lack to many of our tropical illnesses."

"Doubtless that is so," Aurora conceded the point. "However, we will just have to hope for the best. This afternoon we will convene in the small salon—I assume this house does have one—to discuss what must be done."

"Sí, señorita," Ijada responded, her glance downcast as she gave a slight curtsy: but beneath her half-closed lids her dark eyes glowed with triumph.

She had managed to retain her position at Esplendor. Her employer—her *true* employer—would be most pleased.

THAT night, just as the moon slipped up over the trees, Ijada made her way furtively from the house to a tiny glade that lay some distance from the manor. Earlier she had gone up to the cupola, where she had lit a candle that had blazed like a beacon in the darkness. She had waited until far away an answering light had flickered in the jungle. Then she had extinguished her own flame.

Now she smiled with satisfaction as she traversed the narrow path that wound its way through the tangled brush. He had replied. He would be waiting for her at the meeting place.

Despite her thick leather boots, protection against

poisonous snakes, she moved soundlessly along the road. It was a talent she had carefully cultivated over the years, one that had often proven of benefit and, because of constant use, was second nature to her now. As she walked she glanced about cautiously. The jungle was alive with stirring creatures at night, and she had no wish to become a tasty meal for some hungry beast.

For a moment, to reassure herself, her fingers caressed the short, hollow tube at her sashed waist. Ijada had made the weapon herself. It was not as long as the ones men carried, so its tiny arrows did not achieve any great distance or speed; but it was good enough for her own purposes. She was not a hunter, like many of the men who belonged to her tribe. She wanted only to be able to protect herself. She had used the blowgun twice in the past—once against a massive tapir that had charged at her from the undergrowth, and once against a gleaming-eyed ocelot. In minutes both had died, poisoned by the curare in which she dipped her darts, which also hung at her waist. She had informed her tribe of the killing of the tapir, and several of the men had butchered the animal before it could be devoured by other predators. She had skinned the ocelot herself, retaining the pelt and claws before sharing the meat with her tribe.

Though born of a Spanish father and an Indian mother, Ijada had always considered herself an Iquito, like her mother. She did not like the Spanish, those murdering conquerors who had brought disease and death to the South American Indians. Had Ijada had her way, she would have had nothing whatsoever to do with the Spanish. But those Indians who were fortunate enough not to be unlawfully enslaved by them were paid with silver coins to work for them, coins that bought food and other essentials when the Indians fell upon hard times.

It was difficult always to be moving from one place to another when the soil wore out and no longer produced the crops that were necessary to the Indians' survival. It was especially hard in the Amazon basin, where the jungle had to be slashed and burned to clear even a small piece of land. Spanish coins bought an end to the constant, grueling struggle to survive, so Ijada took them, though she despised those who paid her.

The man who waited for her at the meeting place was not a Spaniard, however; he was a Dutchman, which made him seem even lower in Ijada's eyes, for he did not possess even the rudimentary understanding the Spanish had acquired of the South American Indians. Still, because the Dutchman paid her well, Ijada suffered his attentions. One day she would kill him, but in the meantime she needed him.

"*Hola*, señor," she greeted his shadowed figure as he stepped from the trees at her arrival.

Then, knowing he expected it—indeed, would demand it if she refused—she allowed the Dutchman to take her in his arms. Crushed against him, her lips opening beneath his passionate kisses, Ijada felt the familiar, uncontrollable surge of desire that always erupted between her thighs when he touched her. How she hated him for that! But she was powerless to resist him; she always had been.

The Dutchman laughed huskily, triumphantly, as she molded her body against his. He could feel her heart beating rapidly, her breasts heaving; and for a moment he pondered taunting her until she begged him to take her. But his need for her was too urgent, and he pushed the thought aside.

With a low growl he forced her down upon the

ground, yanking impatiently at her garments until her skirts were bunched up about her flanks and her womanhood lay exposed and inviting. With his hand he cupped the dark, silky triangle that twined between her thighs, probing the soft folds of the furry mound that quivered eagerly with anticipation beneath his intruding fingers.

The Dutchman gave a short grunt of satisfaction. She was already wet and hot for him, as always. Deftly opening his breeches, he plunged his hard shaft into her. Savagely, again and again, he drove between her flanks, faster and faster, until she cried aloud, a primitive moan of surrender. She arched her hips against his own, her nails raking his broad back, her fingers kneading his muscular buttocks. A long, sighing shudder ripped through her body, and then his; and then they lay still.

After a time the Dutchman rolled off her and stood, fastening his pants.

"So, my little tulip, apart from what we just did, why did you want to see me? Have you located either of the documents I told you to look for?"

"No, señor," Ijada said, rising also and straightening her clothes. "I have searched everywhere. The papers are not to be found. It is my belief that thief Gilberto Huelva took the deed. As for the map..." Ijada shrugged. "I do not think it exists."

"It must!" The Dutchman swore, slapping his fist into his other hand. "The story rings too true to be merely an old Indian tale."

Once more Ijada shrugged.

"The legend does not lie, señor: but much time has passed since its beginning, and who can say what has been lost or forgotten over the centuries? I will keep on searching for what you seek, of course. But that is not why I summoned you here tonight. Another problem has arisen."

"Oh?"

"Sí, señor. Don Basilio's sister and brother have come to Esplendor."

"Well, get rid of them."

"I tried, señor, but they are not to be budged. They plan on taking up residence at the manor."

"Really, Ijada! Must I instruct you about every little thing? You know what to do."

"Forgive me, señor, but . . . will it not seem strange? Four deaths—five, counting the sister's maid, a clever girl, who would have to be disposed of as well—so suddenly, and from a 'fever' that no one else in the household has contracted? No, señor. I do not think this will be believed. Don Basilio and his wife were not all alone in the world, as we thought. His sister and brother have already come. Perhaps more relatives will follow, and who can say how rich or powerful they may be? The sister has money. I saw her take it from one of the trunks. I tell you no, señor. We must think of another plan."

The Dutchman frowned, then nodded.

"Yes, I see your point. Very well. Do whatever you believe is best. Perhaps you can frighten them away, although that didn't succeed with Don Basilio and Doña Francisca."

"That was because they had no funds with which to leave Esplendor, had they wished to go. It is different with the sister. Sí. I will try to scare her off. For herself I do not think she has much fear; but the boy may prove useful. If she grows afraid for him . . . Sí. It might work." She abruptly changed the subject. "It's getting late, señor. I must go."

"So soon, my little tulip?"

The Dutchman smiled, slipping his hand beneath her blouse to fondle her breasts.

"Well, perhaps I can stay a little longer," Ijada conceded, her nipples hardening with excitement at his touch.

Chapter Seventeen

The Staked Plain, Texas, 1848

HIGH in the Palo Duro and Tules, on the *Llano Estaca-do*—the Staked Plain—the Comanche band known as the *Kwerharehnuh*—Antelope-People—had made their winter camp. Here too had come El Lobo and his cousin, Salvador, to bring goods and guns to the Indians.

No wonder everyone thinks he's a half-breed, the visconde marveled as he gazed at his cousin. For El Lobo, upon reaching the winter camp of his adopted Comanche family, had changed from his black-and-silver western garments to the beaded-and-fringed leather accoutrements worn by the braves who had gathered around the campfire to smoke their pipes and to dicker with the men who had come to trade with them. Combined with his long black hair and dark skin, the hand-crafted buckskin clothes did indeed make El Lobo appear to be more Indian than white. Only his midnight-blue eyes belied the image.

I will never get used to it. Salvador sighed. This savage land filled with savage people. Who, I wonder, is

more civilized here—the white men or their red enemies? God forbid that someone should ask me. I would
have to say the Indians, and then I would be an outcast
like Rafael. Worse, because at least Rafael belongs
here. He is as much a part of this land as the mesquite
trees and sagebrush, while I—I have no place here at
all. Had Don Manuel allowed me to come to the New
World with Tío Diego and Tía Anna María, I would have
been like Rafael. But now—now I am too old to learn.
Spain is too much a part of me. I should have gone to
Peru, as Basilio and Francisca did, or to some other
place where the language and culture are of Spanish
origins. This *Tejas* . . . it is too American for me. Even
with Rafael to teach me . . . No, he has his own life to
live and a wife to look after besides. He cannot be
traipsing about with me just because I'm ignorant of
this country's ways and don't belong here. *Sí*, I must
leave *Tejas* and find someplace more like home in
which to settle. Tomorrow, I will tell Rafael. He will
understand, for though our worlds are now different,
nothing will ever break the bond of blood and affection
between us. *Sí*, tomorrow I will tell him that I must
go.

GILBERTO Huelva was not the thief that Ijada had
scornfully called him. A poor, simple peasant, he was an
honest and loyal man. He had indeed taken the deed
that Ijada had accused him of stealing, but he had done
so only because Don Basilio had instructed him to.

Gilberto would have done anything for *el patrón*, for
it had been Don Basilio who, in the city of Manaus, on
the banks of the Amazon River, had saved his life.

He was a tailor by trade, a profession in which it was
necessary to work many long hard hours to eke out

even the most meager of livings. The day that *el patrón*
had come into Gilberto's life had been an especially
difficult one.

One of his assistants had fallen ill, and the other had
had the misfortune to be killed by a pair of runaway
horses hauling a heavily laden freight wagon. Gilberto
had wept with despair when he had learned the news.
José had been his best assistant, far more skillful with a
needle than the sick Luis; and Gilberto had counted on
José to help him complete a very important order that
had to be finished by the following morning.

There had been nothing for Gilberto to do but work
late into the night all by himself. Though exhausted, he
had pushed himself relentlessly, egged on by the thought
of the many pesetas that would be paid for the beautifully tailored suit the next day. Gilberto had deemed it
one of his most excellent creations. It must be perfect.
So he had ignored his heavy-lidded, blurring eyes, his
aching head, and had worked on.

At what time he had finally fallen asleep he did not
know. He did not remember nodding off or laying his
head down on his worktable; and he certainly could not
recall knocking off the oil lamp that had sat to one side.
So tired had he been that even the crashing of the glass
upon the floor had not wakened him.

In moments his entire shop had been in flames. Had
it not been for Basilio, who had been passing by on his
way back to the poor lodgings he and Francisca had
found for the night, Gilberto would surely have died.
Through the window of the blazing store, Basilio had
spied the tailor's inert figure slumped over the worktable and had rushed inside to save him from the burning
building.

Gilberto, his lungs afire with hot, acrid smoke, his

mind reeling with shock over the destruction of his shop and the near loss of his life as well, had flung himself to his knees to kiss his savior's feet.

"Oh, thank you! Thank you, señor!" he had cried, sobbing with emotion. "To brave the fire to rescue a total stranger . . . Oh, how can I ever repay you, señor?"

"Truly there is no need, sir," Basilio had murmured, embarrassed by the tailor's gratitude. "Anyone would have done as much for you as I did."

"No, oh, no, señor. An act such as yours required a great deal of courage. Why, you might not have escaped yourself; the flames might have consumed us both. See how the roof has caved in!"

In the end the now-destitute Gilberto, learning of Basilio's straitened circumstances, had determined to serve as his valet and would not be dissuaded from this decision.

"But I have no funds with which to pay you, sir," the young hidalgo had protested vigorously.

Still the tailor had not been deterred. His store was gone, destroyed by the fire; and there had been nothing else to keep him in Manaus.

"Do you think I care for that, señor?" Gilberto had asked indignantly, his pride injured. "Gladly shall I devote myself to you—and for no money at all. I owe you my life, señor. It is a debt of honor that must be paid!"

And so the tailor had become Basilio's faithful and trusted servant. No one had grieved more than Gilberto when *el patrón* and his lovely wife had fallen so ill. The tailor had done all he could for them—and more—but still it had not been enough. Doña Francisca had died, and Don Basilio, fearing for his own life, had insisted that Gilberto fetch the small, locked chest carefully secreted under the bed, wherein a few coins, painstakingly hoarded for emergencies, and the deed to Esplendor had been kept.

Taking the key from his neck, *el patrón* had opened the casket and removed the leather pouch and the paper. He had asked Gilberto to bring him a quill and ink, and then he had shakily scrawled some words upon the deed and signed his name. After he had sealed the document, he had fallen back among the pillows, exhausted. He had closed his eyes tiredly and licked his dry, cracked lips.

"My . . . friend"—Basilio had spoken slowly—"my beautiful bride is . . . dead, and I am . . . dying. What little money there is left . . . is yours. Use it to—to go to Laredo, to the . . . Hotel Placido." He had paused, then, with effort, continued. "Give the deed to—to a man who calls himself . . . La Aguila. Tell him—tell him that Esplendor . . . and the watch . . . are his. I—I owe him a debt of honor, and it . . . must be . . . paid. . . ."

Though confused about the timepiece, for there was no watch in the chest, Gilberto had understood the rest at once. Still he had protested.

"I do not wish to leave you, *el patrón*," he had declared. "You are very sick and need me now more than ever. Ijada is sly, and I do not trust her to care for you properly, señor."

"Do not . . . worry, my friend. I am as good . . . as dead anyway."

In sorrow Gilberto, knowing this was the truth, had gone.

Now he stood uncertainly in the lobby of the Hotel Placido, wondering if he had done the right thing in leaving Don Basilio and Esplendor. *El patrón* had been so ill. Doubtless he was dead by now.

Oh, if only Don Basilio had accepted the offer that had been made to him some months previously! A Dutchman, Paul Van Klaas, newly arrived in Peru, had wanted to buy Esplendor and had named a handsome purchase price. But *el patrón* had refused to sell, even though he and Doña Francisca had desperately needed the money.

"No," he had told Gilberto, "I will not part with Esplendor, for where would we go? We cannot find another plantation as cheap as this one was; and in the meanwhile we would have to live. By the time we found another place we would have spent a great deal of Señor Van Klaas's money, and doubtless then we would not be able to afford to buy another manor. No, my friend, we will stay here. Though the house is a ruin, the land itself is good. Soon it will produce many vegetables; the forest is plentiful with game, and the river is filled with fish besides. If we are careful, we can survive and, in time, rebuild Esplendor. Then it will be worth much more than Señor Van Klaas has offered. No, I will not sell."

So the Dutchman had been forced to settle for another estate upriver. Capricho was in much better shape than Esplendor, and Gilberto had wondered why the Dutchman had wished to purchase *el patrón's* plantation in the first place. It was said to be both accursed and haunted, a claim the manor's previous inhabitant had stoutly asserted was true.

"It has been nothing but a constant headache to me since I bought it, señor," Señor Gomez had told Basilio when he'd asked why the hidalgo wanted to sell the house. "There is an old Indian tale that says that Don Santiago Roque y Avilés, the man who originally built Esplendor, did so with gold he had stolen from El

Dorado, the lost city. The Indians claim the Inca gods were so angered by Don Santiago's pilfering of the Gilded One that they cursed both him and the manor. Don Santiago died a madman, or so I have been told, murdered by a band of mercenary knights who thought he'd buried a fortune on the grounds. Subsequent owners met with equally brutal fates. One was drowned in the Amazon River. Another was bitten by a lancehead viper. Yet another hanged himself for reasons that were never discovered. Because of this—though there is still talk of a buried treasure there that has yet to be discovered—over the years the place gradually fell into the ruin you see before you now.

"Once I too thought, as you, that something could be made of the estate. I tried; God knows, I tried. But the Indians, a superstitious lot, fear to set foot on the place, so finding laborers was difficult. Oh, some will work, provided you pay them enough, but even they won't remain on the plantation after dark. They claim that ghosts haunt the house. I don't know. I always thought it was all a great deal of nonsense myself; that is, until I lost my leg. An accident, of course, but all the same . . . I'm dying, you know. Gangrene. Nothing to be done."

"I'm sorry to hear that, señor," Basilio had sympathized.

"At any rate, that's why I'm selling the manor—and so cheaply too. I'll be glad to be rid of it!"

"And the treasure, señor—do you suppose it really exists?" Basilio had asked curiously, faintly excited by the prospect.

"Oh, that. Now don't go letting that idea get hold of you, señor. Men have dug up the grounds for centuries and never found it. If you waste your time searching for it, you're liable to become obsessed by it, as so many others before you have; and then you're certain to meet a bad end. There was one man who looked for years. The villagers found him one morning, dead. He'd slipped somehow, fallen into one of the holes he'd made, and broken his neck. Dug his own grave, you might say. At any rate, the peasants buried him right there, just covered him up and left him.

"No, if there ever really were a treasure—or even a map showing its location or the way to El Dorado, as some say—it's long gone by now. Well, I wish you the best, señor. *Buena suerte*. You're going to need all the help you can get!"

Doubtless the Dutchman, Paul Van Klaas, had heard the story of the buried fortune, and that was why he'd wanted to buy Esplendor, had kept on pressing his offer until it had been firmly refused. Now Gilberto wished fervently that *el patrón* had sold the estate, for by keeping it, Don Basilio, as so many others before him, had met his fate there.

His master must surely be dead. Gilberto felt certain of it. Now the accursed plantation belonged to this man La Aguila, whom *el patrón* had sent Gilberto to Laredo to find. He shivered a little and crossed his breast. He did not envy Esplendor's inheritor.

Slowly Gilberto walked up to the desk in the lobby of the Hotel Placido.

"*Buenos días*," he said to the innkeeper. "I wonder if you could help me, sir. I'm looking for a man who calls himself La Aguila."

"*Sí*, he is here," the innkeeper replied. "Room number five. But you'd best hurry if you wish to catch him. He is leaving for Mexico today and will be down shortly to check out."

"*Gracias*." Gilberto nodded his thanks, then started up the stairs to room number five.

*   *   *

SALVADOR sighed as he glanced about the chamber to
be sure that Pancho had not forgotten anything. The
visconde's parting from his cousin and Rafael's wife had
been sad and difficult, but they had understood why he
must leave them. He was not a part of Texas, as they
were; he must find his own niche in the world.

Bound for Mexico, he had stopped off at the Hotel
Placido in Laredo to see if by some chance a letter from
Basilio and Francisca Montoya had come for him; but
there had been no word. Salvador had been disappointed, for he'd hoped the couple would write to him. He
wondered if they'd been able to purchase a small
estate, as they'd hoped, and if they were doing well.

Well, he shook his head, tossing off the last of the
whiskey in his glass, it would do no good to brood about
them. Doubtless he would never see them again. The
idea filled him with a strange sense of loss, and he
thought again of Aurora, the girl in the portrait. Now
Salvador would probably never get a chance to meet
her, to discover if the real woman were as lovely as the
face in the picture.

Once more, at the thought, the visconde gave himself a mental shake. What good would it do to meet the
girl? He couldn't allow himself to love anyone ever
again. He was accursed. Bad things happened to those
he cared for; it would be far better for Aurora if the two
of them never came together.

A knock upon the door interrupted Salvador's silent
musings.

"*Venga*," he called, glancing up without interest,
expecting the maid had come to make up his room.

The visconde was therefore surprised when a strange,

uneasy-looking man cautiously stuck his head inside, then hesitantly entered the chamber.

"Your pardon, señor," the man said, "but I was told I could—could find a man called La Aguila here."

"You're looking at him," Salvador drawled, tensing slightly, not realizing how much of his cousin's wary, fear-instilling demeanor he'd picked up during the few months he'd spent with Rafael. Unconsciously he laid one hand upon his new Dragoon Colt revolver. "What do you want?"

"I—I am Gilberto Huelva, señor. I have a—a message for you, from Don Basilio Montoya."

"Montoya!" the visconde exclaimed, rising. "Come in, sir. Sit down. How is Don Basilio? Well, I trust."

Gilberto, some of his fright at Salvador's appearance fading, shook his head.

"No, no, señor, he is not. In fact, when I left *el patrón* he was very ill indeed. No doubt he is dead by now."

"Dead?" the visconde uttered, stunned. "But—but how?"

"He was afflicted with some sort of tropical fever, señor. Each day, he grew a little weaker until . . . I'm sorry, señor. There was nothing to be done."

"And his wife, Doña Francisca?" Salvador asked, trying to absorb the impact of the awful news just delivered to him.

"She—she is dead too, señor. She had contracted the disease as well and died a few days before I left Esplendor."

"Esplendor?"

"Don Basilio's plantation, señor."

The visconde sank to his chair in dismay. The Montoyas dead? No, it just couldn't be. It just couldn't be. They had been so alive, so young, so much in love. As he thought about them he recalled his earlier notion that he was accursed, and he became more certain than ever that it was so. He had befriended the couple, and now they were dead.

"*Mierda*," Salvador swore bitterly. "What a shame. What a goddamned shame!"

"*Sí*, señor." Gilberto paused, then cleared his throat respectfully, not wishing to intrude upon the visconde's grief. "Señor, if I may . . . *el patrón*, he charged me, with his dying breath, to bring this to you." He removed the deed to the manor from his pocket. "There— there was no time for Don Basilio to make a will, you understand. But *el patrón* managed to sign this paper over to you before he—before he . . . It is the deed to Esplendor, señor. Don Basilio wanted you to have it . . . and his watch, señor. This last, however, I did not comprehend. I'm sorry, señor. There was no timepiece among *el patrón*'s possessions. I can only assume he was delirious with fever and rambling."

"No." Salvador spoke softly. "No, sir, he was not. I have the watch to which Don Basilio referred. I purchased it from him some months ago and was keeping it until he could buy it back."

"Well, then, it is yours, señor, for *el patrón* clearly said you were to have it," Gilberto stated firmly, relieved the matter had been explained. He was silent for a moment, then, his conscience bothering him, Gilberto rushed on. "Oh, señor, do not go to Esplendor!" he cried as the visconde perused the deed. "It is an evil, accursed place, haunted by ghosts. All who have owned it in the past have died violently, as Don Basilio died. I beg you, señor: Do not go to Esplendor!"

Salvador looked askance at the man, wondering if he too had caught his master's disease and was raving.

"Tell me, sir," he directed, puzzled and concerned, "tell me about the plantation and why you have warned me against it."

And so Gilberto, inhaling raggedly, began the ancient story of Don Santiago Roque y Avilés and Esplendor.

Chapter Eighteen

"The bitch!" Basilio spat, suddenly trying to sit bolt upright in bed and pointing a trembling finger at Ijada. "She poisoned me!" he accused, then fell back among the pillows, dead.

Aurora stared, stunned, at her brother, then turned her eyes, wide with horror, toward Ijada.

"It was the fever, señorita!" Ijada declared frantically. "*El patrón* was out of his mind with delirium! He did not know what he was saying! Why should I wish to poison Don Basilio when it was I who cared for him all this time? It was the fever, I tell you!"

Aurora's brain, numbed by the shock of her brother's death, scarcely registered the *mestiza's* words.

"Of course, Ijada," she murmured mechanically.

She knew how hard the woman had worked, caring for Basilio, bringing him soothing drinks and soups, trying to get some nourishment in him to combat the disease. But it had been hopeless. Each day Basilio had grown worse until today he had died.

He had been like a madman at the last, wild-eyed and shouting, flailing about uncontrollably upon the bed until Aurora had been forced to restrain him by binding him to the four posts of the canopy. His body had been racked with such agonizing pain that now the girl could only be relieved that his terrible suffering had ceased.

She held his wasted hand in hers and wept until she had no more tears. Then, resolutely putting aside her grief, she drew the sheet up over Basilio's body, squared her small shoulders determinedly, and went to make arrangements for his funeral. It would have to be held immediately because of the tropical heat. There could be no lengthy vigil by the coffin in the salon, no casket lying in church while Mass was said. Already flies buzzed sickeningly about the corpse; and Aurora knew she must hurry before the body began to decompose.

A simple wooden coffin was rapidly constructed; a grave beside Francisca's was quickly dug. The priest, who had been summoned from the nearby mission, administered the last rites to the corpse and said the proper words as Basilio was lowered into the ground. To Aurora—who was used to the days of vigil, the long funeral Mass—the ceremony seemed over before it had even begun.

She tossed a handful of earth upon the casket. Then, weary at heart, she walked back to Esplendor, feeling as though she bore the weight of the entire world upon her shoulders.

THEY would not return to Belém. About this Aurora was determined. With his dying breath, Basilio had accused Ijada of poisoning him; and though earlier Aurora had discounted his words as the ravings of a feverish mind, now, some hours later, a small, niggling doubt assailed her. She could think of no reason why her brother should have been murdered by the *mestiza*, for it appeared that Ijada had nothing whatsoever to gain and everything to lose by such an act. But suppose that Basilio *had* spoken truly! Aurora remembered her initial dislike of the sly, imperious Ijada and how the woman had at first attempted to drive them away from the manor. Her explanation had been believable enough, but still . . . Was it possible that Ijada had killed Basilio? The more the sorrow-filled Aurora dwelled on the thought, the more suspicious she became. She decided they could not leave Esplendor until she had discovered the truth of the matter one way or another. She owed her brother that.

If Basilio's accusation had been the ramblings of a delirious brain, then she and the others would go in peace. But if her brother had spoken the truth, then Aurora must stay and see his murderess punished.

THE next morning Aurora decided the first thing she must do was go over the estate to determine what needed to be done to make it hospitable. If they were going to stay here, they must be able to live; and from what little she had seen of the ruined plantation, she wondered that anyone survived here at all. She didn't know how Basilio and Francisca had managed to exist at Esplendor as long as they had. The house itself was going to require extensive work to make it even halfway habitable. As for the land . . . if the few meals, consisting of some scanty vegetables, that Aurora and the rest had eaten were any indication of what was produced here, the vast acres surrounding the manor were in equally bad shape.

Until now, however, the girl had not been able to do

anything about this, since from the moment of her arrival, the nursing of Basilio had taken all her time.

She explored the house first. It was huge, consisting of some thirty rooms; but, of course, none except the few opened up for use were livable. The whole of the west wing was closed off completely, it being considered unsafe because its supports were so weakened. The rest of the chambers were devoid of furniture and swathed in dust and spiderwebs. Ceilings leaked; walls were cracked; windowpanes were broken or missing entirely; and floorboards were so rotten it was actually dangerous to walk across many of them. Paint and plaster both were peeling in numerous places. Evidently, although attempts at repair had been made, they had been given up in despair.

Most depressing of all was the fact that creatures of all kinds had invaded the house. There were hordes of bats in the cupola and attic; rats scurried in every nook and cranny; and, worst of all, snakes had slithered in to hide in dark corners. The most vicious and poisonous of these was the barba amarilla, a lancehead viper often called, although wrongfully, a fer-de-lance. Aurora shuddered as one uncoiled itself to glide away at her approaching footsteps. She was glad of the stout boots she wore with her riding habit.

No wonder Basilio's limited funds had been enough to buy the place. No one else must have wanted it.

Upon reaching what was left of the tumbling-down stables, Aurora discovered there was no horse, or even a mule, to be had. She was dismayed but not surprised. Her next act then must be to acquire a mount.

There was no city near Esplendor; the closest, Manaus, was almost fifteen hundred kilometers away. The nearest thing to a settlement was a small military outpost, which could scarcely qualify as a fort. Beyond its walls was a scattering of peasants' huts and a mission. The town, if it could even be called that, did not even boast a name. Some distance from this was an Iquito Indian village. That was all.

Well, there was no help for it. Aurora must walk to the outpost. Setting her chin, she started down the dusty, overgrown road.

She had not gone very far when she was startled to see a team of horses and a carriage coming toward her. To her surprise the driver reined the showy chestnuts to a stop beside her.

"Good day, señorita," the man greeted her in Spanish heavily overlaid with some accent that the girl didn't recognize. "Allow me to introduce myself. I am Paul Van Klaas, from the neighboring estate of Capricho. You must be Doña Aurora, Don Basilio's sister."

"*Sí*," she replied, more perplexed than ever.

The man laughed.

"Forgive me, señorita. You are puzzled that I know who you are, I can tell. The explanation is simple. Both the Peruvian peasants and the Indians have a love of gossip, and word around here travels fast. When I learned of your arrival I thought to pay my respects and check on your brother's progress as well. He has been very ill, has he not?"

"*Sí*, señor," Aurora responded soberly. "He died yesterday."

"Oh, please forgive me, señorita," the man apologized, his voice filled with sympathy. "I am most sorry to hear of your bereavement. Naturally, had I known . . . How unfortunate to have traveled so far only to meet with such a tragedy."

"*Sí*, señor. It has been . . . a difficult time for us all.

My brother Nicolas and I loved Basilio dearly. His . . . death has been a—a terrible blow, as was his wife Francisca's, though we did not know her well."

"Please, señorita, if there's anything I can do to be of assistance to you, just let me know. I imagine you will be wanting to return home now. . . ."

"No, señor. We have decided, for the time being, to stay at Esplendor. The journey here was very long and hard, and I do not feel up to another trip down the Amazon just yet."

"Of course. I understand. Please forgive me. I've intruded on your grief long enough. You were on your way to the cemetery, I take it?"

"No, señor, to the military outpost. We are so very isolated here, without means of transportation. It is necessary that I acquire at least a horse. I do not know how—how Basilio managed without one," Aurora ended, near tears as her sadness at her brother's death threatened to overwhelm her.

"Well, in that case you must allow me to take you to your destination." Paul Van Klaas spoke politely, pretending not to see the moisture that welled up in her eyes.

"Oh, *gracias*, señor. You are most kind, but I do not wish to impose. . . ."

"It's no imposition at all, señorita, I assure you. This region of Peru is so remote that we have to stick together out here. Besides, it won't do at all for you to walk so far alone. Not all of the Indians are as friendly as the Iquitos."

"Then I will be happy to accept your offer, señor."

At the girl's words Paul jumped down from his sturdy carriage to assist Aurora inside. Once she was settled, he clucked to the team, turned the vehicle around, and started down the road. Aurora wiped her tear-filled eyes with her handkerchief, then studied her benefactor curiously.

He was a big man, with blond hair and blue eyes, which stood out startlingly in his tanned face. She supposed he was handsome, and he certainly was well dressed; but he did not appeal to her for some reason. She imagined fancifully that his capable hands, holding the reins so confidently, looked brutal, as though they could easily have crushed the life from someone. As the morbid idea crossed her mind she thought once more of her brother's accusation against Ijada.

Was it true? she wondered. Had the *mestiza* really poisoned Basilio? No, surely the notion was ridiculous! What could the woman possibly have hoped to gain by such an act? By this time, of course, Aurora had heard the legend of Esplendor; but she had dismissed the story as being little more than an Indian fable. Though the tale bore a grain of truth, she thought it was much exaggerated; and the idea that there was a treasure buried somewhere on the plantation grounds only amused her. The history of Peru was colored by numerous such legends, stories of lost cities where the streets were paved with gold. Like *El Dorado*—the Gilded One—Esplendor's fabled fortune must be just a myth. Besides, the Indians, including Ijada, thought the estate was both accursed and haunted. Only Ijada was brave enough to remain at the manor after dark, and this was, or so she claimed, only because she was a powerful *bruja* and had much magic to protect her.

No, even if Ijada believed the legend of Esplendor, she would hardly have murdered Basilio over a treasure that, even if it existed, had yet to be found. Had her brother actually possessed such a fortune, Aurora could have understood the matter. But Basilio had been virtually penniless, having no more than a few pesetas at most. All he had owned of any value was the watch that Aurora had given him last year on his birthday. It was true the timepiece had not been among his things, which she'd gone through after his death, but the girl simply could not believe her brother had been killed merely for a watch. It was far more likely that what Ijada had claimed was true, that Basilio's former valet, Gilberto Huelva, who had departed from Esplendor the day before Aurora's arrival, had stolen it.

Abruptly Aurora recalled herself to the present. She had been silent for so long that Paul Van Klaas probably thought her the rudest person imaginable.

Clearing her throat, she apologized and began again to make conversation.

"How did you come to end up in Peru, Señor Van Klaas?" she asked.

"Oh, it's a long story, señorita," he declared, "but, basically, I quarreled with my father, back home in Holland; and he disowned me. Before I married I'd done the Grand Tour, of course; and so I spoke a little Spanish, among other languages. I heard there was money to be made here, in sugarcane, coffee, and *guano*, so I packed up my wife, Heidi—no children, unfortunately—and came to Peru.

"I didn't have a lot of funds, you understand, so I tried to find something cheap. I made your brother an offer for Esplendor, you know, but he wouldn't sell. I'm afraid I had to settle for Capricho, which cost a good deal more than what I'd wanted to spend." He shrugged. "But it's working out all right, I guess. At least the crops seem to be doing well, and it looks like the place might show a small profit after the harvest, so I can't complain.

"What about you, señorita? Why did you come here to live with your brother?"

"Oh, times were hard at home, in Spain," Aurora said vaguely. "We thought we'd do better here, with— with Basilio." She paused, grief-stricken once more, then pulled herself together again and continued more brightly. "So . . . you're from Holland. That accounts for your accent, then."

"Yes. Well, here we are. Let me help you down."

The military outpost was small and, as Aurora had assumed, could not really be called a fort at all. It did, however, possess some good stock; and Coronel Xavier de la Palma, the man in charge of the outpost, was happy to sell the girl two well-bred horses and several mules—which she planned to use for plowing—as well.

After her business there had been concluded she visited the village just beyond the outpost's walls and succeeded in hiring several Peruvian peasants.

The Dutchman shook his head at this, explaining that most all the plantations in the area used Indian slave labor, which, although illegal, was the standard practice in South America.

"Perhaps it is," Aurora agreed, "but not only is it against the law, but I have discovered that it is virtually impossible to get Indians to work at Esplendor. They all believe that awful legend, which says the manor is both accursed and haunted, and they fear to set foot on the place. With the exception of Ijada the few who do come each day won't stay after dark. Eventually—provided, of course, that Nicolas and I decide to remain permanently—I've got to have laborers who will live on the land."

"I see," Paul remarked noncommittally.

"You think I'm making a mistake, don't you, señor?" Aurora questioned. "That I'll never be able to make a go of the estate all by myself."

"Forgive me, señorita, but many *men* have tried and failed. What can you, a mere woman, hope to accomplish?"

Aurora was rankled by the Dutchman's attitude. She tossed her head.

"I am of the house of Mon...toya, señor," she uttered haughtily. "And we are a family of fighters."

"Well, we shall see, señorita," Paul Van Klaas commented strangely. "We shall see."

Then he smiled smugly to himself. There was really no need to scare the lady off. She could not possibly succeed at what she planned. The Dutchman was certain she would presently grow discouraged and leave Esplendor of her own accord. If Ijada helped her along, so much the better! One way or another Paul was sure he would soon be rid of Basilio's sister.

In the days that followed, Aurora worked herself unsparingly, alternately cursing and weeping when she discovered how much there was to be done. Oh, how could Basilio have accomplished so little in the many long months he had lived at the manor?

The land was so overgrown with vegetation it had to be slashed and burned to clear it, an arduous, lengthy process that was not only difficult, but downright dangerous. One wrong swing of a machete and a man could accidentally but severely injure himself or a fellow worker. One miscalculation when setting fire to the brush and the blaze could burn out of control, raging through the forest, causing destruction that would take centuries to repair. Poisonous snakes lurked too in the undergrowth, coral serpents and lancehead vipers that struck viciously when disturbed.

And it seemed that nothing went right from the beginning as each day brought a fresh disaster.

One man was crushed to death beneath a huge tree that crashed to the ground before expected. Another was maimed by a friend's hacking blade as they tried to clear the verdant tangle. Still another was bitten by a barba amarilla, and yet another fell prey, in an especially swampy area, to a sharp-toothed caiman that had crawled out of the water to bask in the sun.

Here and there, there were deep, crumbling pits into which the men often stumbled. When Aurora inquired as to what had caused the holes, Ijada informed her that Basilio had believed the story of the buried treasure and had spent most of his time digging up the grounds in search of it. The girl swore at the knowledge. No wonder her brother had achieved almost nothing toward rebuilding the estate!

Aurora was soon beside herself with despair as the difficulties continued; and she did not blame the peasants when many of them, crossing their breasts superstitiously, informed her that they could no longer work for her. Even she had begun to believe the Indians were right, that Esplendor was accursed. Desperate, she doubled the wages of those men and women who remained.

Work on the house itself was equally problem-filled. A pillar on the porch collapsed, causing the roof to sag perilously. On one outside wall a slab of marble was shaken loose by the pounding of the hammers inside and fell, narrowly missing Nicolas, who was passing by at the time. The men making the repairs crashed through the rotten floors, and, although none was killed, one peasant broke his arm. The hordes of bats that were stirred up screeched and attacked everyone, their skeletal wings and vampiric mouths inflicting bruises and wounds that festered and sometimes led to disease. A fire was somehow started in the kitchen, where the women were cooking for their hungry men, and a child was badly burned. Lupe found a scorpion lurking in Aurora's bed.

The list of disasters was as endless as the list of supplies that Aurora needed when Mario returned downriver to trade with the plantation owners of the Amazon Basin.

Had she had time to think, the girl would have grieved for Basilio, for Francisca, and for herself. But there was not a day's moment to be lost in reflection, and at night she fell into bed so exhausted that she didn't even dream. The recurring vignette, which had so haunted her in Spain, troubled her sleep no more. For her, reality was a nightmare that filled her every waking hour.

Sometimes she gazed at the strange white manor house and wondered if she were mad to stay, if she would, like Basilio, meet her end there, if that were the destiny that Abuela had seen in the cards for her. She thought if she had any sense at all, she would forget her brother's dying words and return to Belém. She was no closer now to discovering whether or not Basilio had been murdered by Ijada than she had been the day of his death. The regal *mestiza* came and went as stoically as ever, not even deigning to comment when Aurora informed Nicholas that he was not to eat or drink anything that had not been prepared by Lupe's faithful hands.

Aurora watched her younger brother like a hawk,

fearing some ill would befall him too, and she chastised herself ceaselessly for endangering his life by remaining at Esplendor. Besides almost being hit by the falling marble, the boy had narrowly missed being the victim of several other accidents. Aurora knew she should take him away from the plantation, but still she did not feel she could leave without knowing the truth about Basilio's death. Had Ijada truly poisoned him, as he'd claimed— or had it really been Esplendor that had killed him?

Esplendor. Beautiful, savage Esplendor. Alive with a million sounds of the jungle, it was as though the ruined manor lived and breathed, waiting, always waiting; and eerily, on a moonless night, Aurora could have sworn she heard an angelus ringing. Twice she went up to the cupola to stare down through the hole in the floor to the attic below, where a huge solid-gold bell, dulled by time, lay covered with dust and cobwebs. She had thought to reinstate it to its proper place in the cupola, but the superstitious peasants would not touch it. Twice she went to the attic to examine the angelus, to be certain it had not been moved, that it was not possible it had been ringing.

I am going mad, she thought. Mad...

But Aurora refused to give up. Despite all her difficulties, she had an uncanny feeling of being protected at Esplendor, as though, although he no longer appeared to her, her beloved were watching over her here.

Even now she could see him, as though he really stood there before her. . . .

Aurora blinked, then rubbed her eyes. He truly *was* there, standing upon the steps leading up to the porch of the manor.

The earth reeled beneath her feet. No. It could not be. The wings of mist that always signaled his coming

had not swirled up to engulf her, to transport her back
through time. The plantation had not suddenly changed
in appearance, as each place had always done before.

Heridas de Cristo!

The man was alive. He was real.

Slowly, her heart pounding erratically in her breast,
Aurora walked toward him, her fate, her destiny, for all
time.

Chapter Nineteen

THE man was tall and strongly muscled, his tough, sinuous body as lithe as a whipcord. His skin was dark, swarthy; and his hair was as black as a moonless night. Beneath his jet-black brows, dark eyes, as black and gleaming as obsidian, appraised her; and his full, sensuous mouth, set below a fine, aquiline nose and a clipped black mustache, smiled boldly, white teeth flashing. His cheekbones were high, elegantly chiseled; the planes of the cheeks themselves were spare, giving him a lean, hungry look. The set of his jaw was arrogant, determined, as though in all his twenty-seven years he had expected and received what he'd demanded.

His powerful shoulders and broad chest tapered down to a narrow waist and a firm flat belly; and the thrust of his pelvis was casually provocative, emphasizing his loins and thick, corded thighs.

Except for his shirt, which was of fine white lacy linen, he was clothed completely in expensive black broadcloth garments. A black, flat-brimmed *sombrero* sat upon his head. About his neck was a black silk cravat pierced by a pearl stickpin. A black waistcoat with pearl buttons, and a short, well-tailored black jacket trimmed with a stripe of white brocade on each sleeve, hugged his body. At his waist a black leather belt was fastened with an ornate silver buckle. Across his belly, within a specially made holster, lay a black-barreled revolver with a walnut stock. A narrow scabbard bearing a deadly looking silver rapier hung at his side. Tight black breeches, also adorned with stripes of white brocade on either side, encased his legs; and black leather boots with gleaming silver spurs were upon his feet. In one hand he held a pair of black leather riding gloves and a whip, which he tapped idly against the side of one high boot.

Yet for all his refined appearance there was something savage about the man that frightened Aurora even while it attracted her. He was not evil, as Don Juan had been, but the girl suspected he could be just as cruel and ruthless if the need arose. She did not think if he wanted something that he would allow anything—or anyone—to stand in his way. She quivered a little at the thought. Except for Nicolas and a few peasants there was no one at Esplendor to defend her.

The man continued to stare at her as though he could not tear his eyes away from her.

She was here. She was real. No longer just a face in the portrait in his watch, but a woman alive and standing before him, gazing at him as though she saw a ghost. She was more beautiful than he had ever imagined. How could he have forgotten? The odd thought was gone as quickly as it had come. Except for her picture he had never seen the woman before. And yet . . . it was as though he knew every strand of her blue-black hair that had loosened itself from its neatly coiled braids and now wafted tangled, untamed, about her piquant face; as though he knew every plane of her lovely countenance, every glance of her dark, sapphire-blue eyes, every curve of her lips, every beat of the pulse fluttering wildly at the base of her throat.

Salvador's heart thudded in his breast; his chest was filled to bursting with unaccustomed emotion; his loins raced with excitement. He wanted to run to her, sweep her up into his arms, and kiss her passionately until she cried out her surrender and gave herself up to his all-enveloping embrace; and in that moment he swore she would be his.

"*Querida*," he breathed. "*Muñeca mía.*"

Aurora did not hear the words. She was caught, held as he was, by something so strong it overwhelmed them both. It was as though they had known each other a hundred lifetimes in the past, as though some unknown force had drawn them to this place, to each other. A soft wind soughed plaintively through the jungle, rustling the deciduous trees, as though to nudge them into alertness with its eerie whisper; and a still, breathless hush fell upon Esplendor, which had been waiting, waiting for three hundred years to be wakened in just this manner.

Aurora thought, strangely, inexplicably: He has come. At long last my beloved has come.

She knew no more. A haze of blackness whirled up to envelop her, and she fainted.

Salvador leaped down the steps to rush to her side, to bend with concern over her inert form. Tenderly, trembling, scarcely daring to believe he held her at last in his embrace, he gathered her slender figure in his strong arms and carried her into the house. Unhesitantly, unerringly, he moved through the rooms until he found the small salon. He did not question how he knew his way, for from the instant he had first seen the manor, he had felt that he had come home.

Gently he laid Aurora upon the sofa. Then, spying a nearby vase filled with flowers, he wet his handkerchief in the water and began to caress her face and wrists with the white square. As he did so, he could have wept with sadness and vexation. He had been so swept away by the girl's beauty that he had for a brief moment opened his heart to love. But he must not let that happen again. He had spent just a few minutes with her, and already she had fainted. What bad things would befall her in an hour, a day, if he allowed himself to love her? His love was a curse; everyone he had cherished had suffered because of it.

Presently her eyelids fluttered open.

"Doña Aurora," he said politely, stifling his impulse to take her once more in his arms, "are you all right?"

"You—you know my name. How?" she asked marvelingly, wondering if she did, after all, but dream.

"Sí, señorita. I was a friend of—of Don Basilio and Doña Francisca. Your brother spoke often of you to me. I am called La Aguila. Did he . . . never mention me?"

"No, señor. But by the time I arrived at Esplendor, he was . . . very sick. Sometimes he did not even recognize me. He's—he's dead, you know."

This last was but a broken sob.

"Sí. That is why I have come," Salvador explained, his voice kind but carefully reserved as he fought his longing to pull her to him, hold her close, and protect her. She was too delicate, too fragile, too vulnerable, to be so alone, so grieving. "Doña Aurora, forgive me, but . . . you do not seem well. Where are the servants? Can I ring for someone?"

"No. No, señor. I'm fine," she answered, trying to

get hold of herself. "It was just the heat. *Sí*. It must have been the heat that caused me to swoon. As for the servants, what few there are, are working in the fields and the kitchen. As you may imagine, with my brother's death, these are not... the best of times. I'm afraid we are ill equipped to entertain guests, señor. Have you—have you come a long way to Esplendor?"

"*Sí*, from *Tejas*, in *los Estados Unidos*. But I am not a guest, señorita. I am—I am very much afraid that what I have to tell you will come as a shock to you. Before he died your brother signed the deed to this place over to me, and his former valet, Gilberto Huelva, delivered it to me in Laredo. I am the new owner of the manor."

"No!" Aurora gasped, stunned. "That cannot be!"

"I assure you that it is, señorita. I have the deed right here." The visconde removed the paper from his pocket. "You may, of course, wish to have a lawyer examine it, but I am certain it is in order."

The girl stared at the deed, stricken. She knew nothing of such matters, but the paper did indeed appear to be legitimate. Though she could barely recognize the scrawled words and signature as Basilio's own, she knew, nevertheless, that the handwriting was her brother's. Doubtless he had been in the last stages of the fever when he had signed Esplendor over to the man who now sat beside her.

Slowly, still dazed, she handed the deed back to Salvador. All the money she had spent, all her hard work, all the recent disasters that had befallen the plantation were all for naught. Esplendor did not belong to her, had never been hers.

"Señor, I—I don't know what to say," she whispered in despair, her wide blue eyes haunted by shadows. Now she would never be able to discover whether or not Basilio had been murdered. "I will need a few days to pack—"

"Doña Aurora!" Salvador interjected, eager to explain that this was not at all what he had intended. He had no wish at all to lose this exquisite creature when he had only just found her. He might not be able to love her, but at least he could offer her his protection. "You surely cannot think I mean to put you out of your home! Oh, no, señorita, you have misunderstood me. Of course, you must stay. Don Basilio was my friend. How could you believe I would turn away his sister?

"Please, señorita." He took her hand in his. "Your brother's death, the plantation, the heat, my arrival—all have been too much for you. It is no wonder that you fainted. It is obvious even to me, a stranger, that you are filled with grief and overcome by exhaustion. Do not allow my presence to force you to make a hasty decision that you may later regret. In a few days, when you are rested and feeling better, there will be time enough to decide what must be done.

"Until then Esplendor is your home. Indeed, I am certain that Basilio, had he known of your coming, would not have signed the manor over to me at all. I informed you that he had done so only because I wished to spare you from the terrible burden of rebuilding the plantation, which I see you have taken upon yourself. I promise you, I did not mean to drive you away."

Aurora gazed at him, still quite unable to believe he was actually here. What would he say if he knew what she thought? That he was her beloved from a past life, the man of her dreams; that the mere glance of his eyes, the touch of his hand, set her heart to beating in the strangest manner; that she longed to lay her head upon his shoulder and feel his strong arms about her, protecting her from the rest of the world; that she yearned to shift the burden of her problems from her small shoulders to his broad ones.

No, she could not tell him, a stranger to her, these things. He would think her mad—and perhaps she was. Why else did she want nothing more than to remain at Esplendor, by his side? She had known him but a few minutes, yet it seemed as though she had known him a lifetime, a hundred lifetimes.

Mi corazón, mi alma. . . .

"You are very kind, señor," she said at last. "And, *sí,* it would indeed be wonderful to rest for a while before making any more decisions. It seems I have made so many lately." Aurora rubbed her eyes tiredly. Her head ached, and she did indeed want to lie down and rest for a time. "But perhaps your wife will not like having so many strangers living in her new home."

Salvador smiled.

"I have no wife, Doña Aurora," he said. "Except for my mother, in Spain, and my cousin, in *Tejas*, I am quite alone in the world. So, you see, if you leave Esplendor, I shall have no one at all to keep me company."

Aurora could not refuse him. She knew then that she could not refuse him. She too knew what it was like to be alone.

"Very well, señor," she murmured. "I will stay at Esplendor for a little while until I can determine what is best to do."

"I tell you, señor, I have tried everything!" Ijada cried frantically to the Dutchman, knowing he was angry with her tonight and fearing he meant to cast her aside. "I loosed a slab of marble from the side of the house and pushed it off when the boy passed by, but it missed him. I started a fire in the kitchen, but it burned a child of my own tribe! *Sangre de Cristo!* What do you think the Iquitos would do to me if they discovered that? I put a scorpion in the sister's bed; but that clever maid, Lupe, found the creature when she turned down the sheets, and she crushed it with a shoe. I tell you, señor, I have tried everything to drive them away, and nothing has worked."

"No matter." Paul Van Klaas shrugged. "I have seen the sister, a fragile, hothouse blossom not fit for the savage jungle of Peru! She will soon grow discouraged and leave of her own accord."

"That may be," Ijada agreed. "But she is no longer important, for now—now!—yet another difficulty has arisen! A stranger has come to Esplendor. He has the paper that you wanted, señor, the deed to the manor. Don Basilio, before he died, signed the plantation over to this man, this La Aguila, and sent that thief Gilberto Huelva to deliver the paper to him. That is why I could not find it when I looked for it, though I searched everywhere."

The Dutchman's eyes narrowed dangerously, but Ijada went on.

"The house is in an uproar," she said. "This La Aguila has turned everything upside down, and the sister has permitted it! She is overcome by grief and exhaustion and has taken to her bed, leaving everything in La Aguila's hands. The first thing he did was say he had no use for superstitious peasants and Indians who would not do a full day's work, and then he fired them all. He has hired terrible, rough men to take their places, mercenaries from *Tejas*, who have no fear of the jungle, much less an old Indian legend.

"Already they have cleared more land in a day than the others did in a month. Señor, I do not know what to do. It seems your plan has failed."

Paul's jaw tightened with anger at the *mestiza*'s words. He had been so close to obtaining possession of Esplendor—and now this! He was beside himself with rage. There was a treasure buried somewhere on the manor grounds—or at least a map hidden in the house itself, which showed the location of the fortune or the way to the lost city of El Dorado—and the Dutchman meant to find it.

If only Don Basilio had sold the plantation to Paul to begin with! But no, the foolish Spaniard had been determined to discover the treasure himself, and he had started digging up the land in search of it. Paul couldn't permit that. He'd ordered Ijada, his eyes and ears at the estate, to poison Basilio slowly, so it would appear the Spaniard had acquired some fatal tropical fever. Basilio's widow, Doña Francisca, would sell Esplendor; the Dutchman had been certain of that.

Unfortunately Francisca had inadvertently drunk some of the potion intended for her husband. The dose had been too strong for her, and she had died. Even then Paul had not despaired. The couple had no family, or so he had thought. He could buy the plantation once it came on the market again. But then the sister and another brother had come; and though Ijada had done her best to frighten them away, they had refused to go. And now—now, this man, La Aguila, had turned up!

Paul ground his teeth with impatience. He would never get his hands on the treasure at this rate!

"This man Aguila, is he the type to be scared off?" the Dutchman asked Ijada.

"No, señor. In fact, I should not wish him for my

enemy. He has much gold, far more than the sister, and is very powerful besides. I think he is a *brujo*, señor, who possesses much magic, for the house has changed somehow since his arrival. I—I can't explain it, señor. It is not just the men he has hired to work there. It is as though Esplendor itself has come alive, as though it were only sleeping before and has now awakened. The manor has accepted him. I don't know why, but for some reason Esplendor wants him to stay."

"Oh, Ijada, that's just superstitious Indian nonsense!" Paul declared, frowning. "You talk as though the house is human, for Christ's sake! Well, you'll just have to get rid of him—and the others as well. You know what to do."

Ijada blanched, and she bit her lip.

"I—I am sorry, señor, but I cannot," she stated nervously.

"And why not?"

"Don Basilio—Don Basilio, before he—he died, he—he accused me of—of poisoning him, señor. The sister heard him; and though she said little afterward, perhaps believing, as I claimed, that he was but delirious and raving, now neither she nor the others will eat or drink anything that I have prepared."

"Goddamn it!" the Dutchman swore, more infuriated than ever. "Well, I'll just have to think of something else. Go on back now, and keep me posted, as usual."

"Do you—do you not want me tonight, señor?" Ijada questioned, ashamed and humiliated that she was so hungry for him, she would stoop to begging him to take her.

"No, you stupid bitch!" Paul spat. "You've bungled everything, and I'm in no mood even to look at you." With swift, impatient movements he mounted his horse and in a voice heavy with sarcasm reminded the woman, "If you wish me to love you, my little tulip, then you must not fail me."

Alone, untouched and unsatisfied, Ijada watched him ride away, then slowly turned and walked into the blackness of the jungle.

Chapter Twenty

IT was now impossible for Aurora to leave Esplendor, even had she wished to. Today Nicolas, attempting to build a tree house, had fallen and broken his leg and would not be able to travel for some weeks. Although she was relieved that her younger brother's injury was not serious, Aurora did not know how she could bear to remain so close to Aguila, feeling about him as she did. She did not love him; she was certain of that. After all, she had known him but a few days. Still he haunted her, disturbed her in some manner she could not explain. Had he been her beloved in a past life, as her instinct told her? Or was he a stranger that she, in the grip of some odd madness, had mistaken for a long-lost love? Perhaps she was coming down with the tropical disease that had allegedly taken Basilio's and Francisca's lives. Yet Aurora did not feel as she had when she'd been stricken with fever on the Amazon. In fact, since Aguila's coming, she had been relieved of many of her burdens and was now well rested and in better health than ever. Still she had never felt so strange.

She respected Aguila, admired the way he'd taken

over. He had been well informed about the conditions at Esplendor, and he had come well prepared to deal with them. The men he had brought with him— *bandoleros* and *comancheros* mostly, he'd told Aurora— while rough, worked hard and tirelessly and were not afraid to remain on the estate after dark. Already in just a short time things at the plantation were starting to take shape.

Courteously, never mentioning the fact that in actuality it was he who owned the plantation, and not once criticizing Aurora's management, Aguila had suggested that it would be best if the men devoted most of their time to the land, as it was of primary importance for survival. The house could wait. Repairs that were absolutely necessary to the manor would be made, but that was all.

"Things will be accomplished much faster and more smoothly, señorita, if the work force is not divided," Aguila had explained.

Aurora had not argued, though, deep down inside, her pride had caused her to be resentful of his easy command of the situation, so different from her own struggle. Aguila knew what he was doing, and she obviously did not. She had never run a large estate before. Through sheer determination she had made some slight headway, but it had not been enough. Now she would watch and learn; and someday when she owned her own plantation she would know how to manage it properly.

"*Buenas noches*, señor," she greeted Aguila politely as she entered the dining room for supper.

"Doña Aurora," Salvador said, rising and pulling out a chair for her. "And how are you feeling this evening? Better, I think. You look rested at least. The shadows are gone from your eyes. I trust, then, that Nicolito's mishap was not serious."

"No, señor. His leg is broken, as I feared, but it will soon mend. In the meantime he cannot travel, of course. I am sorry, señor, but I'm afraid that we will have to impose on your hospitality a little while longer than I had thought."

"Aurora," the visconde murmured, pushing away his plate. "May I call you that, without the doña? For I hope we are going to be friends." At her nod he went on. "*Bueno*. I think it is time now that you and I talked. I have been giving the matter of the disposition of Esplendor considerable thought; and I have a proposal to make that I hope you will agree is in everyone's best interests."

Salvador paused, to be certain he had piqued her curiosity, then he continued.

"Señorita, your brother Basilio was a political refugee from Spain. No, do not deny it, for I know it is the truth. Montoya, I presume, was not his real surname, nor is it yours. You would not therefore be using it unless you too fled from our homeland under conditions similar to your brother's.

"Oh, do not look so alarmed, Aurora. I do not care what you did or whom you offended at court; and I certainly don't intend to report you to the Peruvian authorities for deportation, if that is what you are thinking. I too did not leave Spain under the best of circumstances politically; and in Spain there is doubtless a price on my head far larger than the one on yours. Ah, that relieves your mind, does it not?"

He grinned, his black eyes dancing; and Aurora thought how good it would be to laugh with him. Doubtless he would smile even in the face of death.

She felt a little better, a little braver, and smiled back at him.

"Please go on, señor."

"Very well. Am I correct then in assuming also that outside of Spain, to which you cannot return, you have no relatives or friends—no one to turn to for assistance?"

"Sí, señor. It is so. That is why we came here to Peru, to Basilio."

"And now he and Francisca are dead. He did not know you were coming to Esplendor, I am sure, else he would have made some provision for you. Instead he left his plantation, and his watch, the only things of value he owned, to me.

"Aurora, I cannot in good conscience take what is rightfully yours. However, it is also clear to me that you cannot manage this estate alone. I am not criticizing you, you understand. You made a tolerable start in the face of overwhelming adversity. But Esplendor requires massive reconstruction and a great deal more money than I believe you have. So what I propose is this: Let us become business partners, with equal shares in the plantation, and rebuild Esplendor together."

Aurora was stunned, for she had not expected this. Her first instinct was to refuse the offer at once, but her wiser second thoughts prevailed.

Of course, once Nicolas was well, he, she, and Lupe could return to Belém, as they'd planned, or go to some other place. But even so, how long would it be before Aurora was forced to apply to her parents for further aid? After all, she had never held a job in her life, and the past few months at Esplendor had shown her just how unsuited she was for manual labor. Besides, workers were paid cheaply in South America, or not at all; and why would those who owned Indian slaves want to hire her? Perhaps she could become a governess, but even so, she had no past experience as such and no references either. Who would entrust the care of their children to her under such circumstances? And what if her parents could not help her? Perhaps after her departure from Spain, Don Juan had succeeded in bankrupting her father. If that were so, to whom could she turn?

It was not as though Aguila had made her an indecent proposition. Indeed, since his arrival he had treated her with the utmost courtesy and respect. Now he was offering her a chance to secure her future and asking for nothing in return except her friendship. Aurora would be a fool to turn him down.

She took a deep breath, aware that she was about to change the course of her life forever.

"Señor," she announced, "I would be happy to accept your kind offer."

Slowly Salvador's tense body relaxed, and he exhaled with relief. She was going to stay. He had not lost her.

"Muchas gracias, señor el Cristo," he said softly under his breath. *"Muchas gracias para todo el mundo."*

IN the days that followed, Aurora was to question many times her decision to stay at Esplendor, for on more than one occasion, Aguila infuriated her. He did not mean to do it; of this she was certain. But, nevertheless, scarcely a day passed that he did not in some way unintentionally insult her.

Determined not to be a burden to him, Aurora tried hard to pull her own weight at the plantation—but to no avail. Every time she gave an order, Aguila countermanded her authority, politely but firmly. The girl thought she would scream if she heard him say—just one more time—"Aurora, things will be accomplished much faster if . . ."

On several occasions she tried to explain to him how inadequate and useless he made her feel, but Aguila refused to take the hint.

"You are not to worry yourself, Aurora," he told her. "Running an estate is a man's business after all. You have enough to do as it is, overseeing the house and caring for Nicolas."

"But I don't want to be dependent upon you!" she cried. "You said we would be equal partners."

"And so we are. Come, come. Is there aught of importance about which I have not consulted you?"

"No," she was forced—reluctantly—to admit (for he *had* consulted her; he simply had ignored her advice).

"Well, then, if you have nothing more to discuss with me, the men are waiting. . . ."

And so it went.

Oh! Just once, Aurora fumed silently, I'd like to break through that icy reserve of his! This isn't how it was supposed to be. I just know it! Aguila is my beloved from the past. I'm sure of it. So why isn't he interested in me? Why doesn't he make some loverlike gesture toward me, a glance, a smile, anything to let me know that he remembers too? Is it—is it possible he isn't aware of the bond between us? Is that why he maintains such a distance between us? Can it—can it be that I am mistaken about him?

The more Aurora dwelled on this notion, the more it began to obsess her.

Salvador did nothing to answer the questions that disturbed her mind. More than anything he yearned to have her working at his side, as she so obviously wished to do, but he did not think he could bear to have her so

close. As it was, he could scarcely restrain himself from
snatching her up and claiming her for his own. If he
were to be near her constantly, looking at her, talking to
her, smelling the fragrance of her perfume, innocently
touching her, he did not think he could control himself.
And he must. For her sake. Perhaps it was only super-
stition, but he did not dare to challenge the fate that
had brought them together. To love Aurora would be to
bring disaster to her, for the misery that plagued his
dear ones proved he was accursed.

The visconde worried about her every time she left
the manor, fearing that some ill would befall her, and so
when she wasn't with him he tried to keep her inside
the house as much as possible. He knew she was
puzzled and angered by his actions, but he could not
bring himself to enlighten her about the reasons for his
overly protective behavior. Doubtless she would think
him mad.

He knew that Aurora watched him too, when she
thought he was not looking, even as he studied her, his
expression controlled, lest she see his hunger and anguish. He wanted her. But each time that Salvador
thought to throw caution to the wind and ask her to be
his, his conscience prevailed over his desire. Who was
he to risk hurting Aurora in order to satisfy his turbu-
lent emotions? But it was agony to do so, a torture the
visconde didn't know if he could continue to endure.

Once, after helping Aurora dismount from her mare,
he yanked his hands away so quickly from her waist that
she nearly fell. And though, instinctively, he reached
out to steady her, Salvador could not bring himself to
touch her again. His palms felt as though they were on
fire, burning up with aching for her. At Aurora's searching, bewildered gaze he turned away, mortified by his

behavior. He had hurt her feelings; he could tell. But he could not explain that to him her wounded pride was a small price to pay for her safety. Instead he kept silent and bitterly cursed the capricious destiny that had brought him to Esplendor—and to Aurora, whom he could not have.

Each day that passed was a constant struggle for him as he warred against himself, not knowing that Aurora too fought the same kind of battle within her own being. She told herself that she had no interest in Aguila—but it was not true. Even had he not been her beloved from the past come alive in the present, his cool, distant attitude toward her would have rankled, pierced her pride even more sharply than had his overriding her management of the estate. Though they had thought her cold, many of the Spanish *caballeros* still had sought, with pretty speeches and gallant attentions, to win her hand and heart. To be ignored as a woman was not within the realm of Aurora's experience. She did not know how to cope with it. She alternately raged between wanting Aguila desperately and resenting him with a fury. She searched determinedly for a means to break through his hard shell, to become more to him than just someone he had befriended out of pity—but she found none.

With despair she thought: I am justly punished. The Ice Maiden is enamored of a man even colder than she.

Aurora noticed that Aguila often stared at her like the eagle whose name he bore, and she wondered at the painful longing on his dark visage when he thought she did not see. What did it mean? She pondered the question endlessly but could discover no answer. Once, she touched his cheek lightly in a gesture of concern. To her mortification, Aguila shuddered and withdrew from her. Aurora did not realize he had shivered with desire. She believed she had repelled him; he had responded to her gentle caress as he would have to a snake slithering across his skin. She turned away, her eyes filled with tears at his rejection.

She could not bear it. She knew what it was to love and be loved deeply; and though she had never truly experienced passion, the interlude from the past that she had shared with her beloved had shown her the beautiful joy that such intimacy could bring. Especially after Don Juan's horrifying attempt to rape her, Aurora had had no wish to experience again the passion her beloved had shared with her on the wings of time. Now she recalled the episode in detail and found herself stirred by Aguila as she had been stirred by her beloved.

Sometimes just the sight of Aguila's bare chest when he worked in the fields was enough to bring a blush to her cheeks and a fire to her blood. On several occasions she fled into the house to hide from him her confusing emotions toward him. How terrible it would be if he should discover her yearning for him when he so obviously did not want her. Aurora would not only be highly embarrassed but humiliated as well. So she steeled herself against the tide of feelings that overwhelmed her and, shrugging, insisted to herself that she cared nothing for the block of ice she called Aguila.

Yet the more distant he was to her, the more intrigued by him she became. More fervently than ever she tried to strip away his polite, frozen veneer to find out what lay beneath—but still Aguila forestalled her at every turn.

The most bitter blow of all had come today. A large black jaguar, evidently in hot pursuit of some small, fast-fleeing quarry, had lunged unexpectedly from the

outskirts of jungle, causing Aurora's mare first to shy
and then to bolt wildly. Her mount's sharp, sudden
movement had been so rapid that even Aurora, as
brilliant a horsewoman as she was, could not control the
beast. Before she'd even realized what was happening,
she'd been thrown violently from the saddle. With a
blow so forceful it had left her momentarily stunned,
she'd hit the ground. Only instinct had caused her to
fling herself from beneath the mare's flailing hooves
before they could strike her.

The men working in the fields had hurried to her aid;
but it was Aguila's hand she'd reached for, Aguila's arms
she'd wanted to feel about her, Aguila's chest she'd laid
her head upon as the tears had come.

Was it her nearness that had caused his heart to pound
so? Had he longed to enfold her in his warm embrace?
she'd wondered. But he had not. Instead he'd inquired
calmly if she were injured. Then, upon discovering that
she was not, he had courteously but firmly set her from
him and, after ordering one of the laborers to escort her
back to the manor, turned his back on her.

Hurt and hatred had welled up in Aurora's breast as
she'd watched him walk away. Silently she'd cursed
Aguila and the day he had come to Esplendor. Surely
he was not her beloved from the past! If he were, he
could not have been so cruel, so callous. What a
horrible jest fate had played upon her. It had given her
hope when there was none to be had. The flame that
had been kindled in Aurora's heart at Aguila's coming
had flickered and then died. He was a stranger to
her—nothing more.

AURORA could not sleep. Her bed, a relic left, like the
rest of the furniture, by a previous owner of Esplendor,

seemed more than unusually uncomfortable this night. It was hot too, its one thin sheet damp with her sweat and clinging to her flesh like a lover. She tossed restlessly, trying to find a more acceptable position; but it was useless, and at last she gave up the attempt.

Pushing aside her mosquito net, she rose, drew on her wrapper and slippers, then moved to the shuttered French doors that led to the gallery just beyond and kept the darkness at bay. Though she feared the jungle at night and normally, despite the stifling heat, kept the shuttered doors closed, now she flung them wide, glad of the cool air that filtered inside.

Sighing, she stepped outside onto the veranda, drinking in the breeze that stirred ever so softly. She glanced up at the sky, for she never tired of looking at the stars of the Southern Hemisphere, so different from those that had sparkled over Spain. But this eve the firmament was black, without a trace of starlight. Even the moon was subdued, ringed with a misty halo that diffused its edges into a silvery vignette.

As the wind soughed again plaintively, rustling the leaves of the trees that grew thick and lush in the jungle, Aurora realized suddenly that it was about to storm. She shuddered, for Esplendor, always so especially eerie at night, grew terrifying when a storm raged.

Nevertheless, she did not go inside, not yet. The moment of solitude was precious. She would not throw it away.

Though some months had passed since Aguila had come to the plantation, it seemed that Aurora was no closer now to knowing him than she had been in the beginning. He was a strange man, she thought. He behaved just as a gentleman should toward her, never seeking to take advantage of her relative aloneness with him. Still sometimes when he believed she was not looking, she caught him watching her with a peculiar expression upon his face.

It's as though he really is an eagle, she mused, for his eyes fix upon me exactly as that bird does its prey.

The notion made her shiver slightly, reminding her of just how isolated they really were at Esplendor. On occasion, now that things were somewhat settled at the plantation, they had guests. Coronel Xavier de la Palma and some of his officers came to dine now and then; and once, Paul Van Klaas and his pretty wife, Heidi, had paid them a visit. But usually Aguila was Aurora's only company.

If he were amenable, they rode together in the mornings, surveying the progress of the estate, then returned to the manor to discuss further plans or changes, all of which were always Aguila's ideas. Sometimes Aurora was so frustrated by this she wondered why he bothered to ask her opinion at all. They took their meals together in the dining room. They played both chess and cards together in the small salon, in the evenings. This was the time that Aurora loved best, for she took no small delight in beating Aguila at every opportunity. It was a petty revenge, to be sure, for his attitude toward her—but nevertheless, it was one she could not help taking, even though sometimes she was certain, from the strange smile upon his face, that Aguila had deliberately let her win.

Still he remained an enigma to her, thus piquing her interest in him.

At first Aurora had thought he would eventually ask her to marry him. After all, it seemed the ideal thing to do, especially as she knew the neighbors gossiped scandalously about their living together, though the presence of Nicolas and Lupe made it perfectly respectable. But no hint of any such proposal had crossed Aguila's lips; and if it had, Aurora could not honestly have said what her answer would have been.

The Indians, she knew, feared Aguila, believing him a powerful *brujo* with much magic. They claimed that Esplendor had somehow come to life since his arrival. Aurora would have laughed at this, had it not seemed to her so eerily true. Even she felt more vibrantly alive when he was with her, and she longed passionately for him to kiss her just once, so she might quench the strange yearning for him that she had in her heart.

She pulled her wrapper more closely about her. It was growing cooler; the dark thunderheads now racing across the sky heralded the coming storm. Soon the fury would begin. Aurora turned, about to go back inside when her attention was caught by a flicker of flame in the distance. It burned steadily for some time, then abruptly vanished. She waited for a while, but the light did not reappear. She shrugged. It was nothing more than a lamp lit at one of the neighboring plantations, she supposed. Someone else, it seemed, could not sleep this evening.

The wind moaned once more, its breath soaring, then falling to a low whine. The jungle murmured in response, then all was again still, the silence broken only by the soft whisper of footsteps across the carpet of rich green grass.

Footsteps?

Curiously Aurora leaned furtively over the balustrade, wondering who was up and about at Esplendor at this time of night. Presently she spied Ijada, making her way down one of the narrow dirt roads that led from the manor into the jungle. The *mestiza* glanced back at the house, and instinctively Aurora secreted herself behind one of the pillars that lined the gallery. Then, waiting until the woman had vanished into the brush, Aurora hurried impulsively to the steps, which wound down to the ground below, and followed.

Her heart beat with excitement. Where was Ijada headed? Was the light that Aurora had seen a signal?

As she pushed her way through the undergrowth, her determination to discover Ijada's secret mission faltered. It was dark; the night was alive with a million creatures; and Aurora did not know where she was going. Now she recognized how foolish she had been. Her slippers were thin; she might easily tread on a snake or some other dangerous small animal. She might lose her way along the twisting, overgrown path.

She turned back, only to find that the brush had swallowed up the road in the blackness. Every tale ever told to her by the Indians returned to haunt her. Even they did not penetrate the darkest reaches of the jungle, for fear of becoming lost. Her heart lurched with panic. Her arms flailed wildly at the overhanging branches that barred her way. She must get back to Esplendor. She must!

By now frantic, she did not realize she was making enough noise to attract the attention of any large predator, to say nothing of the monkeys, birds, and bats she disturbed. The wind was stronger now, rising, the spine-chilling whistle mingling with the cries of the animals in the jungle. The trees seemed to come alive as monkeys stirred, screaming warnings to each other, swinging to branches that offered greater protection from the coming storm. Birds called shrilly, winging into the night sky to settle on more-sheltered perches. Bats rose in hordes that blacked out the hazy moon, leaving the jungle in total darkness.

Aurora tripped over a root, stumbled, and fell, cringing as her hands clutched the grass. She imagined that armies of ants and spiders crawled over her fingers. Was that some awful creature she heard skittering through the brush?

She staggered to her feet, pushing on desperately through the undergrowth. Thunder clapped loudly and jagged lightning flashed. Moments later the thick, dark, massive clouds hanging heavily in the sky opened up to disgorge their contents. Sheets of blinding rain pelted down, drenching her to the skin in minutes. Her filmy nightgown and wrapper clung to her legs, making it almost impossible for her to move. She lifted the sodden skirts and forced herself to go on.

Suddenly a shadowed figure loomed before her, approaching menacingly from the trees.

Aurora screamed and screamed again, terrified. Not knowing if the form were man or beast, she tried to run, but the pouring rain and her soaked negligee hampered her efforts to flee. The figure crashed after her, knocking her to the ground. Gasping for breath, she lay dazed for a moment from the force of the blow. Then she began to struggle wildly against her attacker.

SALVADOR could not sleep, and aware from past experience that he would find no rest no matter how long he lay in bed, he rose and dressed, sighing. It was going to be another endless night, as so many since his coming to Esplendor had been. If only he could get Aurora out of his mind! But he could not. He kept his distance when they were together, but when he went about his daily duties thoughts of her tormented him. His longing to caress her overpowered him, and he pictured her in his arms, her red lips pressed against his own, her heart beating in rhythm with his.

Today had been even more trying than usual, for the visconde had given way to her request to accompany him to the fields. And what had happened? A jaguar had burst from the outskirts of the jungle, frightening Aurora's mare and causing the girl to be thrown. She might have been killed! Salvador's heart had leaped to his throat when he'd spied her lying so still upon the ground. The big cat, startled by the sight of so many humans, had bounded back quickly into the brush, relinquishing the prey it had been chasing; so the visconde had not feared the jaguar would attack the girl. It was instead the horse that had worried him. Until Salvador had reached Aurora and discovered she was unharmed, he'd feared the mare's wildly flailing hooves had struck her.

When she'd stumbled to her feet and flung herself into his arms, he could have wept with relief. He had yearned to hold her there against his breast, to explore her body and assure himself that she was truly uninjured. But he had not. Instead, summoning up every ounce of his strong will, the visconde had set her from him and turned his back on her so she would not see how affected he was by her nearness and the very thought of losing her. It was growing more difficult each day to fight against loving her. The fact that she deeply resented him, viewed him as an interloper who had usurped her ownership and management of the estate, helped his cause, however. When he ignored her suggestions as to how the plantation ought to be run and saw anger rise in her deep blue eyes, he was grateful. Rage was better than love; it would keep her safe from him.

Still the visconde also realized that in this he had been unfair to her. Much of her advice was sound. Often she pointed out things he ought to have seen for himself. It diminished his stature. He was the man. It was his responsibility to prove a competent manager, especially when in his mind Esplendor truly belonged to Aurora. He wanted to do his best for her, and he was trying; but her constant comments to him about his deficiencies only highlighted his failure.

He could not love her. He could not even adequately protect her. The thought galled him bitterly.

His mouth tightening with wrath at himself and his helplessness, Salvador went down to the small salon and poured himself a glass of whiskey. With unaccustomed lack of appreciation for good liquor he bolted down the shot and refilled it. After several stiff drinks he began to feel somewhat better. After several more he had reached the conclusion that he was not at fault at all. It was Aurora and her ceaseless meddling that were to blame for the state of affairs at Esplendor. A woman ought to keep her mouth shut, even if she *were* intelligent, damn it!

A noise outside caught the visconde's attention. He lurched toward the shuttered French doors that opened out onto the veranda.

Over the past few weeks Salvador had become aware that there was something wrong at Esplendor. More pits had been found. Since he had ordered the ones that Basilio had dug to be filled in, it was obvious that the holes recently discovered were new. Someone else was digging up the grounds. It was not one of his men; the visconde felt certain of this. Most of them had lived too long with harsh reality to be taken in by the legend of the buried treasure; and, besides, they worked too hard during the day to be digging at night as well. No, someone who did not belong at Esplendor was sneaking onto the estate after dark and searching for the fortune. Salvador had posted guards about the plantation, but so far nothing had turned up.

Now he swore silently to himself. *Por Dios!* If the idiot digging up the grounds were back, the visconde would catch him and put a stop to his treasure hunting at once! Unsteadily Salvador made his way outside and peered through blurred eyes into the darkness. *Sangre de Cristo!* It was Aurora stealing about in the blackness. What in the hell was the witch up to now?

"I'll teach her," he mumbled drunkenly to himself. "I'll teach her who wears the pants around here!"

Then he threw away his empty glass and loped after her.

AURORA sobbed, terrified, as the figure that had loomed toward her out of the shadows now pushed her down upon the earth. Oh, why had she ever left the safety of the house, especially with a storm coming on? She was going to be killed. She just knew it!

"Aurora!" the visconde shouted over the roar of the wind and rain as he pinioned the frightened, struggling girl to the ground. "Aurora, it's I, Aguila!"

Dimly, through the stinging downpour, she recognized him. How he had come to be there, she did not know or care. It was enough that he had come. She gave a little whimper of relief; she was not about to be mauled to death by some savage animal! Her body crumpled as her terror drained away, and she stopped fighting and clutched him instead.

Silently Salvador helped Aurora to her feet. Too drunk and angry to be kind, he pulled her roughly along the overgrown path as he looked for some sort of shelter. The path back to the house seemed to have disappeared, but Aurora knew that Aguila must have eyes like his namesake—the eagle—for somehow he spied a large, rotting, fallen tree that was partially hollow on one side. He dragged her toward it and kicked at it several times with one foot. A snake, unhappy at being disturbed, slithered out and vanished into the brush. Despite her protests, the visconde propelled Aurora inside. Within the huge trunk there was room enough for them to lie pressed close to each other, safe from the rain drumming down on the bark overhead.

Aurora shivered, certain that grubby insects were creeping up her legs. Thinking she was cold, Salvador hugged her nearer, cradling her head against his chest. She could feel his heart beating within his breast, a sound as primitive, in that instant, as the tattoo of the rain above.

Slowly Aurora became aware of other things: the clean, fresh, spicy scent of soap and cologne that clung to Aguila's flesh; the carnal curve of his mouth so close to her own; his warm breath tinged with the aromas of whiskey and the thin black cigars he smoked; his fine linen shirt, open to reveal his chest; the dark mat of hair that curled crisply upon his breast; the hard length of his body next to hers, one leg thrown carelessly over her own.

She inhaled raggedly and looked away, glancing out beyond the close confines of the fallen log. Thunder boomed; lightning crackled. The rain pounded down relentlessly, forming swirling puddles on the ground, flooding the jungle grass, which gave way helplessly beneath the water's onslaught. The gale whipped the trees about mercilessly, making the verdant branches shudder and groan.

Once more Aurora trembled, her body pervaded by an odd, inexplicable thrill. Now that she was safe, there was something peculiarly alive and exhilarating about the storm.

She turned back to Aguila. His black eyes glowed like twin coals in the darkness, reminding her of the jaguar that had so frightened her mare this morning. When the visconde shifted his weight to find a more comfortable position, the muscles in his lithe lean body rippled against her, tense and powerful, as though he were an animal about to spring upon its quarry.

Aurora wondered what he was thinking, if his nerves were as raw and taut as her own, if his blood raced as hers did. She did not care to dwell on the notion, not wishing to know the answer. For all his consideration of her, Aguila was, after all, a man—and an extremely handsome and virile one at that. The intimate press of their bodies was bad enough. If it should become something more . . .

Without warning a flash of lightning suddenly illuminated Salvador's hawklike face and confirmed Aurora's worst fears. She gasped, startled, for the brief electric bolt had revealed to her a man she had never seen, an Aguila as wild and primitive as the tempest. His obsidian eyes, suddenly even more dark and gleaming than before, gazed at her hungrily, openly naked with desire. She shook with a new kind of apprehension and excitement, her heart thudding erratically in her breast, a small pulse fluttering at the hollow of her throat. Her nipples, already cold and rigid, strained even harder against the sheer material of her nightgown, standing out like twin peaks beneath the wet, diaphanous fabric.

The visconde would have had to be blind not to have seen. He swore, the sound emanating like a low snarl from his throat. Then, suddenly, remembering his intention to teach her a lesson, he roughly caught the strands of her dripping blue-black hair and lifted her face to his. His other hand tightened on her waist.

Time stood still as he stared down at her, devouring her fine-boned countenance: the dark, fiery gems that were her sapphire-blue eyes; the sooty, half-moon shadows her long black lashes made against her damask cheeks; her delicately chiseled nose, its nostrils flaring slightly with fright—and something more; her lush scarlet mouth, so vulnerably parted and tremulous.

He inhaled deeply her jasmine perfume, which wafted toward him enticingly on a breath of wind.

Her silky wrapper had fallen open to reveal the creamy swell of her ripe, heaving breasts outlined beneath the translucent material of her negligee. He could plainly see the tips of the rosy crests, stiff little buttons just aching to be touched and tasted.

Yes, he would show her who the man at Esplendor was.

His fingers crept up to lightly brush one of the beckoning globes.

"*Bruja*," he breathed, his voice thick and husky. "*Te quiero. Te quiero!*"

Aurora quivered involuntarily. The violent storm outside seemed minor in the face of this new danger. This was not the polite, icy *caballero* who had always treated her with such courtesy and respect. No, this man was a stranger to her, a savage beast who would take what he wanted. And he wanted her. . . .

Her blue eyes wide with apprehension, she began to struggle against him, trying to free herself from his grasp so she might run back out into the storm and the jungle. They were elements she could fight, and she did not know if she could resist Aguila.

A surge of sudden desire now rushed hotly through her blood; the secret place between her thighs had begun to pulse with an aching throb; and she knew that she wanted him as much as he wanted her. It was true. She could not deny it.

Yet she whispered, "No." And again hoarsely, "No."

It was unthinkable. She felt as though he had held her like this a hundred times before; still somehow this time it was different. This was no memory of a life long past, no dream. This was real and vibrantly alive, frightening her with its fierceness. What she had longed for was happening. Their veneers had been stripped from them, exposing their innermost selves to each other.

Salvador paid no heed to her pleas for release. Instead he pressed his mouth hotly to her throat, his hands cupping the full mounds that thrust eagerly against his palms, filling them to overflowing.

"I have wanted you from the first moment I ever saw you," he muttered. "Do not deny me, *muñeca mía*. I know you felt it too."

Muñeca mía. He had called her *muñeca mía*. Oh, what cruel twist of fate had made him choose that name for her, that name only her beloved from the past had ever called her?

"No," she moaned. "No, I don't want you."

But it was not true, and he knew it.

With a low growl he claimed her lips, and a shocking tide of desire swept through her at his kiss. Her head spun dizzily, and her belly shuddered, as though the earth had suddenly reeled beneath her. His tongue darted forth, tracing lingeringly the soft sweet shape of her mouth before nudging her lips apart to taste the nectar within. Her mouth grew heated, sizzling like smoldering embers as his searing tongue continued its slow onslaught, branding every curve, every crevice, of her lips. Soon her mouth opened to him of its own accord; then at last Aurora was kissing him back, her own tongue entwining feverishly with his, her hands wrapped in his mane of rich black hair.

This was what she had waited for, yearned for, all her life. Yet now that it had come, she was terrified by its intimacy, its intensity. Never before had she felt so utterly lost, as though she were drowning in the wave of emotion that rushed up to engulf her.

Even now, despite her willing it otherwise, her young, treacherous body was wantonly molding itself to his; her very bones were melting inside of her. Her wayward heart beat fast within her breast, pounding louder than the rain that thrummed against the hollow log.

Outside, the storm howled, but Aurora did not hear it above the roar of passion that filled her ears. She was deaf and blind to everything but Aguila and the desire he was wakening in her being. On and on he kissed her, his tongue plunging between her trembling lips, plundering her mouth until it seemed she was nothing more than sensation, as electric as the lightning that streaked crookedly across the firmament.

His lips slashed like a whip across her face to her cheeks, her temples, her hair, her ears, her throat, then back to her mouth, until it was bruised and swollen from his kisses.

Aurora gasped for air. Her upper lip was beaded with sweat, as was the valley between her breasts. Slowly, tantalizingly, the visconde licked away the rivulet that trickled its way down the hollow. Then he groaned and buried his face between the soft mounds.

The sudden motion jolted Aurora, recalling her to her senses. What was she thinking of to allow herself to be ravished, to permit herself, a Montalbán, to be taken upon the ground as though she were no better than a common harlot?

"No, no," she whimpered.

Then, the element of surprise on her side, she wrenched herself free, rolled from his grasp through the opening of the fallen tree, sprang to her feet, and began to run.

"Aurora!" Salvador called, starting after her. "Aurora, come back!"

But still she raced on blindly, knowing all the while that she was fleeing not from him, but from herself and her own passionate desire.

Somehow she found her way through the jungle back to Esplendor. Somehow she managed to climb the winding steps leading to the gallery, stagger inside, and bar the French doors to her room.

There, shaking all over, she sank down upon her bed, mortified by the emotions that had been unleashed within her this night. She had thought that Aguila, though reserved, was at least her friend. She had been mistaken. Why, he was no better than Don Juan! But the marqués had not made her feel like this with his kisses, his caresses. No, Juan had repulsed her, revolted her. But Aguila . . . ah, how she had wanted him, still wanted him. She buried her face in her hands, ashamed. What was wrong with her? She felt so strange and confused. Perhaps she really was going mad. Perhaps the images she had believed were of a past life truly *were* the delusions of an imbalanced mind. Maybe she had experienced the visions so often she could no longer distinguish fantasy from reality. If she woke up presently, she would be safe at her father's townhouse in Madrid, and everything would have been but a horrible nightmare: Don Juan, Sor Patrocinio, the flight to South America, the journey down the Amazon,

Esplendor, Basilio's death, and Aguila. Ah, Aguila. She had made him up and wished him to appear; and now that he had come, she did not know what to do.

In her fantasy he had loved her; in reality he only wanted her. That was the worst of all. She had wished for love and had received desire.

Aurora flung herself down upon the bed and wept, her heart shattering into a million pieces. She had waited a hundred lifetimes for him, and her beloved did not recognize her.

Chapter Twenty-one

SALVADOR awakened slowly, disoriented for a moment. He blinked his eyes, trying to figure out where he was—and then he remembered. He was on the sofa in the small salon at Esplendor. He groaned, attempting to uncoil himself from his cramped position. His body felt as though someone had beaten it with a stout stick. His head throbbed with a dull ache, and his mouth tasted like cotton. As he moved to sit up, his belly lurched and roiled, its contents sour and nauseating. He had gotten drunk last night, very drunk indeed. That was the only explanation for his behavior, and even that was no excuse. He had ruined everything! *Heridas de Cristo!* How could he have been so stupid?

The combination of the whiskey he'd drunk, brooding over Aurora; the wild, savage intensity of the storm; and the girl's dishabille, when he'd found her in the jungle, had proven too much for him. Instead of taking her back to Esplendor, as he should have done, he had propelled her into the hollow log and had attempted to force himself upon her.

God. What must she be thinking? Aurora was a lady,

and he had treated her like a whore—worse, for the fallen tree had been rotten and filthy, unfit for a slut, much less the woman he cherished. Doubtless she hated him now, and he could not blame her. He had fought loving her, and now he had made it next to impossible to keep her near him.

AURORA scrutinized her appearance carefully in the crazed mirror that hung above her washstand. She wanted to look her best. This morning she must face Aguila, and to do that after last night, she needed all the courage she could muster. Being well groomed would help give her the confidence she so desperately required.

She wore a becoming gown of sprigged, icy-green muslin. It had bell-shaped sleeves that gathered at her elbows, and a heart-shaped bodice that exposed just a hint of her full ripe breasts. The narrow waist was banded by a sash that tied in a bow at the back, and the folds of the dress swayed enchantingly over her many petticoats. From beneath her skirts peeped dark green morocco slippers, and in her hands she carried a delicately painted fan.

There were mauve shadows under her eyes, but that couldn't be helped. Other than that, she thought she looked well. Her long, glossy hair was plaited and coiled neatly about her head, unlike the wild blue-black mane that had tangled down about her so wantonly yesterday evening.

She shivered at the thought, remembering.

Aurora had given the matter considerable thought, and she knew she must leave Esplendor. There was no way she could possibly remain after what had happened last night. Except for Nicolas and Lupe, who really were scant protection, she was all alone with Aguila at the manor. Before, it had not mattered; he had been a gentleman in every respect. But now she could no longer trust him. She must get away before he succeeded in having his way with her.

Oh, if only he had come to love her, had wished to marry her! But he had not. He only wanted her. He had made that quite plain.

Well, today she would make it equally clear that she was not to be had in such a manner.

Brushing the tears from her eyes, Aurora went downstairs to inform Aguila that she was leaving Esplendor.

HE was already waiting for her in the dining room, looking so handsome that Aurora's heart gave an odd little lurch upon seeing him.

"Buenos días," he said, and then, as though delivering a speech he had rehearsed several times, he went on in a rush before she could speak. "Aurora, forgive me. My conduct last night was unspeakable and inexcusable, and I do not blame you if you hate me for it. I apologize deeply. I can only say that I had been drinking and that I am terribly sorry. I know that isn't much, but I do not know what else I can do to make amends. Of this I assure you: You can be certain that such a thing will not happen again."

Aurora was surprised and thrown off-balance by his statement, for she had not expected it. The man she had glimpsed last night was not the one who stood before her this morning. She had come downstairs fully prepared to deal with a ruthless cad. Instead she found herself facing an extremely contrite gentleman. She did not know what to say. The haughty, stinging words she had been prepared to deliver to him died on her lips, for they seemed hateful and churlish now and totally unnecessary in light of his obvious embarrassment and self-reproach.

She knew if she had any sense whatsoever, she would leave Esplendor as she had planned. But now all her old anxieties about how she would support herself, Nicolas, and Lupe rose up again, and she was torn by indecision. If they left the plantation, there was no telling what evil might befall them; if they remained, they would at least have some measure of security. A great deal of the land had been cleared and was ready to be plowed and planted come next spring; and the house itself was beginning to take shape.

Of course, Aurora thought, now that she was an equal partner in the estate—and had the necessary legal papers to prove it—she could direct that her share of the profits be sent to her in Belém or some other place. But even so, suppose she left and Aguila decided not to stay at Esplendor either. Who would run the manor? No one, of course; and where would she be then? Right back where she had started from. She could not manage the plantation by herself, and now she could not sell it without Aguila's consent. No, it was hopeless. If he really wished to force himself upon her, he had numerous means at his disposal to compel her compliance.

It was better to stay, she determined, and hope his remorse was sincere. She took a deep breath.

"Very well," she said, her eyes veiled, her cheeks flushed. "I accept your apology, señor. We will forget that last night ever happened, and we will go on as before."

But this was not possible, of course. All had changed

between them. The facade of friendship that had concealed their desire for each other had been stripped away. It would not easily be replaced.

As the days passed, Aurora grew more and more aware of the spark of passion that had been ignited between them that night of the storm. Aguila, more courteous than ever, if that were possible, watched her hungrily when he thought she was not looking; and she knew he too had not forgotten. And though she yet feared him, it was as though some strange force too strong for her to deny drew her to him anyway.

When he rode out over the estate she was often at his side, studying him covertly from beneath her half-closed lashes. Her blood raced to see him sitting tall and proud upon his ghostly white stallion, Nieblo, his muscular legs gripping the horse casually, confidently. Her heart beat too fast when, after returning home, he helped her dismount, his powerful hands clasped tightly about her waist.

Once, up earlier than usual, she chanced to pass by his room while he was at his morning toilet. His door was open, and Aurora could not prevent herself from staring as she glimpsed him, shaving before his washstand. He was naked to the waist. His dark skin, tanned even browner by the tropical sun, glowed with a rich bronze sheen. The sight of the crisp black curls that furred his broad chest reminded her sharply of the close press of their bodies that night in the hollow log. She saw that the dark mat trailed down his belly to disappear in his tight breeches, and she shivered, remembering the feel of his racing loins against her own. The muscles in his back rippled sinuously as he moved, and she thought of how they had felt beneath her palms as she'd clung to him so wantonly before finally wrenching herself free.

His gaze locked on hers in the mirror, and for a breathless moment she could not look away.

The obsidian eyes that challenged hers were naked with wanting and slightly mocking too, as though they had looked into her soul and ferreted out her desire for him. Aurora gasped, turned aside, and ran down the long corridor to the sanctuary of her room.

Trembling, she sank down upon her bed, wondering if he were indeed the demon the Indians claimed, to haunt her so tormentingly. She did not know. Aurora knew only that she wanted him, and she did not know how much longer she could deny what was in her heart.

Chapter Twenty-two

Esplendor, Peru, 1849

THOUGH the Indians had fallen silent with apprehension, as they usually did upon reaching this particular place, Mario looked eagerly downriver toward Esplendor. It had been over a year since he had left the lovely Spanish señorita at the plantation, and during that time he had worried about her welfare. Through the grapevine he had heard that she was managing well—other traders had occasionally delivered supplies to the manor—but still he was concerned about her well-being. His conscience had troubled him, and he wished to be assured that he had not made the wrong decision in leaving her at the ruined estate. Besides, he had what he hoped would be good news for the girl—a letter from Spain.

As they drew near Esplendor, Mario's eyes widened with disbelief, and the Indians began chattering rapidly among themselves, awed. Surely this could not be the same plantation they had seen a little over a year ago!

Acres and acres of land had been cleared and neatly

subdivided into fields that were even now being plowed by strong, determined men guiding teams of mules across the terrain. Work had been started on the house as well. The roof had been fixed; the pillars across the front had been repaired; and all the broken or missing windows had been replaced. The west wing was in the process of being restructured so it could be once more opened up and put to use. There was still a great deal to be done, but it was evident that excellent progress was being made.

Mario was stunned. He had not thought the fragile-looking Doña Aurora capable of accomplishing such deeds. He would never underestimate a woman again!

"Mario! Mario!"

He glanced down the road to see the girl running toward the new boat dock, smiling and waving and eagerly catching the ropes the Indians tossed to her to secure the dugout canoes. Close on her heels were a tall dark man, whom the *mestizo* did not recognize, and Nicolas. Mario chuckled as he spied the monkey that was perched on the boy's shoulder.

"*Buenos días*, señorita," the *mestizo* called, still grinning as he climbed ashore. "I have worried for many months about your being left all alone at this accursed place, but now I see my fears were unnecessary. If there were ghosts at Esplendor, you have driven them away. You have prospered, señorita," he observed, his eyes burning with curiosity.

"*Sí*," Aurora agreed. "But come. You are no doubt tired and hungry. Come inside, and we can talk. You remember Nicolas?"

"Of course. How could I forget? You are well, Nicolito?"

"*Sí*, sir. I broke my leg a while back, trying to build a tree house, but the limb has mended."

"*Bueno*. And who is your small furry friend there?"

"I call him Bribón."

The boy had recently found the monkey in the jungle, bending forlornly over its mother's dead body. Moved to pity, Nicolas had brought the sad, abandoned animal home and tamed it.

The monkey eyed Mario suspiciously, then suddenly shrieked and buried his face against Nicolas's shoulder. Everyone laughed. Then the *mestizo* turned questioningly to Salvador, and Aurora presented her business partner to Mario.

As they all walked to the house the *mestizo* expressed his surprise and pleasure at the changes that had been wrought at Esplendor.

Mario was so excited about the story he would have to tell his friends when he returned to Belém, and there were so many arrangements to be made to acquire the things written on Aurora's long list, that it was not until he was ready to leave the plantation that the *mestizo* remembered the letter he had brought with him.

"Oh, *señorita!*" he exclaimed, stricken. "I almost forgot. I have a letter for you, from Spain. The captain of the *San Pablo* brought it. I hope it is good news."

"*Sí*, so do I," Aurora uttered as she recognized her mother's handwriting.

Though she was aware that the others were waiting expectantly, she could not bring herself to open the letter before them. She tucked it into her bodice to read later, in the privacy of her chamber.

*   *   *

At last Aurora was alone in her room. She lit the oil lamp that sat next to her bed and adjusted the wick so the light shone brightly. Then she broke the wax that sealed the envelope containing her mother's letter, removed the folded sheets of paper, and began to read.

November 14, 1848

My dearest daughter,

I hope this letter reaches you and finds you, Nicolas, Basilio, and Francisca well. Your father and I are doing fine, so please do not worry about us. The time here has been hard, but, thanks to Don Timoteo, Doña Catalina, and others who have become our allies, we have managed to survive and to retain the family titles and estates.

The Queen was most upset by your disappearance, but she must have suspected the veracity of whatever story Don Juan and Sor Patrocinio told her, for she has issued no warrant for your arrest, as they wished her to do. Despite this, your father and I do not think it is wise for you to come home. Isabella is beset by problems at Court, and we do not feel, under the circumstances, that she has either the time or the inclination to resume your friendship. Her affection for you has caused her much distress, as, naturally, Don Juan and Sor Patrocinio have done their best to blacken both your name and reputation, all of which gossip has reflected badly on the Queen.

Don Juan is still obsessed by his desire for revenge upon la Casa de Montalbán. I don't wish to upset you, but I feel I must warn you that we have reason to believe the Marqués has somehow discovered you are in South America. Even as I write, he is making

*plans to set sail for Brazil, from where he doubtless
intends to continue his search for you. I am frightened for you, niña, as I do not think he will rest until
he has achieved his vengeance.*

*The china figurine with which you struck him
during your struggle has left a terrible scar on his
face, and he can barely see out of his eye.*

*Because of this, he is more determined than ever
to wed you, to have you utterly at his mercy. I
believe he is quite mad.*

*I am afraid I have even more bad news for you,
niña. A few days ago your grandmother—God bless
her soul—died. She passed away quietly in her sleep,
so she did not suffer. Her last words were of you. She
said you should look for the eagle. I have no idea
what she meant by this; I can only assume her mind
was wandering.*

*Well, I must close for now. Take care, niña. Your
father and I send our love to you, Nicolas, Basilio,
and Francisca.*

Madre

Aurora's first thought upon reading the letter was
that it had crossed with her own to her parents. By now
they must know that Basilio and Francisca were dead.
Then the girl wept for a very long time over her
grandmother. Thus it was only later, much later, that
she recalled Doña Gitana's dying words.

Look for the eagle.

At first Aurora was puzzled by the cryptic message.
Then, suddenly, she understood. *The eagle.* Aguila.
Somehow her grandmother had known about Aguila.
Unfortunately Aurora couldn't decide if Doña Gitana
had meant the words as a warning or a recommendation.

Aurora shivered as she thought of Don Juan, perhaps even now on his way to Peru, to Esplendor, to take his revenge upon her. Would Aguila protect her from the marqués? Perhaps. But, then again, perhaps he would not. After all, by Aguila's own admission there was a price on his head in Spain for dueling, which was against the law. Even if he were willing to help her, it would mean exposing himself to Don Juan. The marqués was very powerful at the Spanish court. He had spies everywhere and knew everything and everyone. Suppose he recognized Aguila and turned him over to the Peruvian authorities for deportation! Was it possible that could happen? Aurora didn't know. She knew nothing about the government of Peru. What law there was, was on the west coast, in the capital of Lima. Only a handful of soldiers kept order in the Amazon Basin.

As for marrying Don Juan—why, the idea was ridiculous! How could he possibly believe he could force her to wed him, even if he found her? He must indeed be mad, as her mother had claimed. Nothing could induce her to marry the marqués. Aurora shuddered at the awful notion, remembering how Don Juan had attempted to "persuade" her once before. There was no way she could allow herself to become his victim.

One way or another, Aguila must be brought to defend her, despite the risk to himself. Aurora bit her lip at the thought. She knew without a doubt what he would want of her in return.

THE short distance down the corridor to Aguila's chamber seemed the longest walk that Aurora had ever made in her life. Halfway there she was tempted to turn back, but she forced herself to go on, her mind made up. Hesitantly, assailed by last-minute doubts, she raised her hand to knock upon his bedroom door.

What would he think of her after tonight? No well-bred lady would do what she was about to do. What if he mocked her, laughed at her, humiliated her, and then refused her? She would never be able to face him again! Nevertheless, Aurora decided that was the chance she must take. She had no choice. It was Aguila or Don Juan; and Aguila, for all that he frightened her and aroused her in that strange, disturbing manner, was infinitely preferable.

She rapped timidly upon his door.

"*Venga*," Salvador called, glancing up with interest to see who sought his chamber at such a late hour. "Aurora!" he exclaimed, surprised, then closed the book he was reading, laid it aside, and rose from his bed. "What are you doing here?"

"I—I need to talk to you," she said. "Please. It's—it's very important. Do you have a minute?"

His dark eyes flickered briefly, unfathomably.

"But of course," he replied. "Won't you sit down?"

He indicated a nearby chair, but Aurora shook her head, rejecting the offer.

"No, *gracias*," she answered. "I—I prefer to stand."

The visconde raised one eyebrow, slightly mocking.

"Oh? Then perhaps you would care for a brandy before you begin?"

"*Sí, gracias*." She nodded.

Anything to postpone the moment when she must tell him what she had come to ask of him.

Looking at Aguila furtively, Aurora noticed that his shirt was open, revealing the crisp black curls that covered his chest. Her eyes strayed lower, to his tight-fitting breeches, and involuntarily she shivered, wondering again if she were making the right decision.

As though unaware of her scrutiny, Salvador strode over to the dresser, where a fine crystal decanter and four fragile glasses sat upon an ornate silver tray. After unstoppering the bottle he poured the amber liquid into two of the snifters, one for Aurora and one for himself. He handed the girl hers, then raised his own glass in the familiar Spanish toast.

"*Salud*," he said.

"*Salud*."

Aurora tossed off the brandy in one quick gulp, thinking it would steady her nerves. Instead the fiery liquid burned down her throat, causing her to choke. She gasped. Tears stung her eyes. She coughed several times, trying to catch her breath. And all the while the visconde watched her, saying nothing, although he knew the matter she had come to discuss with him must be serious. Why else would she be seeking courage from a bottle?

At last the brandy mellowed in her belly like a low flame, sending its warmth through her body.

Aurora set her snifter aside, inhaled deeply, then started to speak.

"Before I begin," she explained anxiously, "I—I need to know something." She paused and bit her lip, still uncertain, then went on in a rush. "Do you—do you still—still want me as much as you did that night of the storm?"

Salvador, who had been in the act of sipping the amber liquid in his own glass, stopped, his hand in midair. Startled, he gazed searchingly at the trembling, white-faced girl before him, wondering where this was leading. Was she about to offer herself to him? Why?

His eyelids swept down to veil his thoughts. Aurora swallowed hard, thinking he wasn't going to answer her.

"If—if you don't," she stammered, flushing, "then there's no reason for me to continue. Please. I already feel humiliated enough as it is."

His eyes appraised her deliberately, challengingly.

"And if I say *sí*," he asked, "that I do want you, what then?"

"Then—then you can have me."

There, she had said it, the shameful thing she had come to tell him.

"I see," he remarked slowly, then paused, considering. "And what are the terms of this interesting proposition? I assume you do not plan to give yourself to me simply out of the kindness of your heart."

"Well, no," Aurora replied, then picked up her snifter and held it out to him. "Please, I believe I would like some more brandy, and I—I think I *will* sit down now too, if—if you don't mind."

"Not at all, señorita," the visconde responded politely as he refilled her glass, then moved to take a chair as well.

This time Aurora sipped the fiery liquid slowly, as it was meant to be drunk. Then, her hands cradled about the snifter to keep the brandy warm, she went on.

"There is a man searching for me, a very evil man," she elucidated. "His name is not important, but his rank and riches are, for he is a marqués, and he stands very high at the Spanish court. Thus he wields much power. It was he who denounced Basilio as a *Carlista* and succeeded in persuading the queen to issue a warrant for my brother's arrest. As you know, Basilio managed to escape, however, fleeing from our homeland. Because my brother eluded the marqués's clutches, taking with him Francisca, whom the marqués had wished to marry, the marqués sought revenge against my family, wanting to punish us in Basilio's place.

"He had already destroyed Francisca's parents, and to save ourselves we determined to go to court, where it was hoped I would be able to gain Isabella's friendship. This I did. When the marqués saw this, not wishing to lose the queen's favor, he ceased his attacks upon my family, deciding that I alone would be the recipient of his vengeance. Cleverly playing upon Isabella's love of romance, he began to court me, seeking to wed me, knowing that then I would be helpless against him; and as I suffered at his cruel hands, so would my family suffer.

"My father, of course, refused his permission for any such betrothal; but the marqués was not deterred. He started to work on the queen, attempting to persuade her to order our marriage. She began to waver in his direction but apparently not fast enough for the marqués. He determined to take matters into his hands. Through a ruse he managed to get me alone, and he tried to—to rape me."

Aurora paused, shuddering, as she recalled how Don Juan had attempted so brutally to force himself upon her. Salvador inhaled sharply, silently cursing his own attack upon her. Small wonder she had been so upset that night; what amazed him was that she had been able to bring herself to remain in the same house with him afterward! Regaining her composure, Aurora continued.

"I managed to save myself, however, with a porcelain statuette. I struck the marqués with it. When it shattered it gouged a terrible wound upon his face. A chip of glass flew into his eye too, momentarily blinding him and giving me time to make my escape. I had by then learned that the marqués was in league with a fanatical nun, Sor Patrocinio, who also wields much power at court. I could not fight them both. Spain was no longer safe for me, so I fled here to Peru, to Basilio.

"Now somehow the marqués has discovered my whereabouts and is perhaps even now on his way here to find me. Because I succeeded in besting him, and left him with a horribly disfiguring scar upon his face as well, he has become obsessed with gaining his revenge against me. He is, I believe, quite mad."

"And you want me to defend you from him," the visconde stated, his cool tone revealing nothing of his thoughts. "And in return for my protection you offer yourself to me."

"S-sí," Aurora answered softly, ashamed. "I thought—I thought it was a—a fair bargain. After all, you yourself said there is a price on your head in Spain. Doubtless the marqués will recognize you, and you will therefore be risking your own life to save mine."

"Sí," Salvador agreed. He was silent for a moment, then went on. "You realize, of course, that you can't keep an arrangement like this a secret. People are bound to find out about it sooner or later, and you will be branded a social outcast for becoming my mistress."

The girl glanced up sharply at this, stricken, dismayed. Her face blanched.

"Oh, no, señor! You—you have misunderstood me!" she cried. "I did not mean . . . that is, I—I thought . . . I hoped you would—would marry me," she concluded lamely, mortified.

"I see," the visconde said.

Then he rose and came to stand before her, not daring to show the sudden excitement that raced within him as at last he threw caution to the wind. The black cloud that hung over those he loved was an intangible thing, something he might, in fact, only have imagined. But the threat to Aurora from this marqués was real. Salvador knew he must protect her. He could not forsake her. To do so would almost certainly consign her to doom. He had looked out for her this long. Surely he could continue to do so. And finally she would be his, truly his, irrevocably his! It was even better than he had hoped. As his mistress she would have been free to leave him at any time, but as his wife... Salvador would never let her go. Never!

"I warn you, Aurora," he declared, "to consider this matter carefully before you decide for sure upon this course of action. If you wed me, our marriage will indeed last 'until death do us part,' for I shall not release you from such a vow, once made. Moreover, I have been... without a woman for many long months now. Do not think, once we are wed, that you can draw back from our bargain, pleading maidenly fears or any other such nonsense. I will not permit it. I am a man, a very virile man," he asserted, his voice low, "and I will take what is mine. Do I make myself clear?"

"*Sí,*" she whispered, her blue eyes wide and haunted by apprehension as she stared up into his black ones, which were glittering with triumph.

The way he was towering over her filled her with fright, and she shivered a little at the thought of placing herself so irretrievably in his hands. Against her will her eyes strayed to his bed, and her cheeks flushed painfully as she recalled how the length of his hard lean body had pressed against hers when they'd lain together in the hollow shelter of the fallen tree.

"Well?" the visconde queried sharply, jolting her back to reality. "Is it a bargain or not?"

Once more Aurora looked up at him, wishing he were not so tall and dark, so—so satanic in appearance. This was not the gentleman she knew but the ruthless devil she had glimpsed that night of the tempest. How could she do it? How could she marry this man who, for all their time together, remained such a stranger to her? How could she not? she asked herself as she remembered Don Juan. At least if she were wed to Aguila, the marqués could not somehow force her to marry *him!* Yes, better to face the unbridled lust of Aguila than the mad cruelty of Don Juan. Nervously she licked her lips.

"*Sí*," Aurora replied. "It is a bargain."

Salvador exhaled slowly with relief. It was done. She was his. He would find a priest as soon as possible to make sure of it.

"Come here, Aurora," he ordered softly, his obsidian eyes dark and unfathomable.

"Why?" she inquired timidly, her body still pervaded by fear.

What did he mean to do to her, this demon into whose keeping she had just given herself so completely?

"Know this from the beginning, señorita: If you are to be my wife, you must learn to obey me—and without question," the visconde informed her.

Slowly Aurora placed her glass of brandy on a nearby table and stood, walking toward him hesitantly, as though dazed.

He reached out his hands, removing the pins from her hair and loosening the cascading mass. For a timeless moment he stared down at her, dwelling on her tremulously parted lips; the pulse beating jerkily at the hollow of her throat; and the swell of her breasts as they rose and fell with her rapid breathing at his nearness. His fingers tightened in her silky blue-black strands, pulling her to him. Frightened, Aurora began to struggle against him.

"No, *querida*," he muttered warningly, "do not fight me. I do but want a taste of what I have been promised."

Then his mouth came down on hers—hard and possessive as he claimed her for his own.

Chapter Twenty-three

THEY were married in the chapel of the mission, Nuestra Señora de Ayuda Perpetua, which lay just beyond the walls of the small military outpost governed by Coronel Xavier de la Palma. The coronel himself and one of his officers, Teniente Miguel Sanchez, were the only witnesses.

Aurora wore a dark blue silk gown, as there had been no time to have a proper wedding dress made. The frock had no sleeves, so her shoulders were bare except for the white ruffle trimmed with satin ribbon that formed straps on either side and continued on down to edge the heart-shaped bodice, which was cut low to reveal the swell of her breasts; at their hollow nestled a small bow. The layered folds of her full skirt fell from a tight waist to sweep out over her many petticoats, from beneath which her matching morocco slippers peeked. In her hands she carried her Bible and her rosary.

Her long blue-black hair was unbound—Salvador had insisted on this—and the glossy mane cascaded down her back in a riot of curls as she knelt white-faced with apprehension before the priest.

The visconde was garbed in a fine white linen shirt with a lacy ruffle down the front, complemented by a narrow black silk string tie. His short jacket, waistcoat, and tight breeches were of black velvet adorned with ornate gold braid. High, shiny black leather boots were upon his feet. A black flat-brimmed *sombrero* with a gold band hung down his back.

Aurora thought he had never looked so handsome. Still her soft voice trembled as she repeated the vows that would bind her forever to the man kneeling by her side, and her hand shook as he placed his plain gold ring about her finger.

The priest wrapped his stole about their entwined hands and blessed them; then suddenly Aguila was kissing her, and the ceremony was over. The rite had taken half an hour, but to Aurora it seemed as though it had scarcely begun before it had ended. All too soon she had become Aguila's wife.

Salvador signed his name with a flourish upon the wedding license, then handed the quill to Aurora.

"You understand"—he spoke quietly in her ear, so the others could not hear—"that you must sign your real name—none of this Montoya business."

She nodded, swallowing hard. Of course, she could not sign a false name; their marriage wouldn't be legal. She glanced at the paper before her. For the first time it occurred to her that she didn't know her husband's true name either, any more than he knew hers. She looked down at his bold black signature: *Don Salvador Domingo Marcos Eduardo Valentín Rodriquez y Aguilar, Visconde Poniente, de España*.

All of a sudden the license seemed to blur before her eyes, only two words standing out clearly: *y Aguilar*.

Don Juan Rodolfo de Zaragoza y Aguilar.

Juan went to the queen and accused Salvador as a murderer and a traitor to the Crown. Salvador was forced to flee from Spain, to the New World. . . .

Aurora gazed with horror at her husband. What had she done? Dear God, what had she done?

"*Dios mío,*" she breathed. "You are the marqués's half brother!"

And then she fainted.

NONE of the men present had any smelling salts, of course, so Salvador solved the problem of his wife's swoon by setting fire to the quill and waving the burning feather beneath her nostrils. Soon the acrid smoke brought her to her senses. Dazed, she looked about confusedly for a moment. What had happened? Where was she? Then she saw Padre Guillermo, the priest, eying her worriedly, and she remembered. Slowly she sat up on the pew upon which the visconde had laid her earlier.

"Gentlemen"—Salvador turned to the three men who hovered about anxiously, puzzled and concerned—"if my wife and I might have a few minutes alone?"

"But of course," Coronel de la Palma said, pretending as though nothing were the matter. "Come, Teniente, Padre. We will wait outside for the newlyweds."

The three men left the chapel, and the visconde refocused his attention on Aurora.

"What is it?" he asked quietly. "What is wrong?"

"Why didn't you tell me?" she uttered accusingly, angry and afraid. "Why didn't you tell me who you were? Or are you a part of Don Juan's plot against me as well?"

"Don Juan?" Salvador questioned, puzzled, for he had not heard what she'd whispered before she'd fainted.

"Don't pretend you don't know whom I'm talking about!" Aurora spat. "Señor el Marqués de Llavero, Don Juan Rodolfo de Zaragoza y Aguilar, your *half brother!*"

"Ahhhhh," the visconde sighed. "Now I begin to understand. It is against *him* that you wish my protection. He is the man who is searching for you; and, not knowing my real name, you did not realize until today that he was my half brother. And now—now you are frightened, for you fear I will not keep my bargain with you. You little fool!" Salvador snapped impatiently. "Do you really believe I have any love for Juan? It was he who forced my exile from Spain! *Ay, caramba*, Aurora! If only you had told me his name in the beginning, willingly would I have protected you—and without the bargain you so temptingly offered me—for gladly would I drive my rapier through that evil serpent's black heart!"

"You mean—you mean I married you for nothing!" Aurora cried, indignant.

The visconde smiled slowly, his eyes raking her intimately.

"Oh, not for nothing, *querida*. Never for nothing, I assure you," he said softly.

How Aurora longed to slap that knowing smirk from his face! Oh, how could she ever have thought he was a gentleman, much less her beloved from the past, the man of her dreams? She really must have been mad; and now—now!—she was married to the devil, and there was nothing she could do about it.

She shivered, thinking of the night to come, and thought she must die: for how could she live through it? How could she bear to have him touch her?

"Aguila..." she began hesitantly.

"Salvador," he corrected gently. "You know my true name now. As my wife you must learn to use it."

"Oh, very well; Salvador, then. Our marriage . . . is a . . . terrible mistake. I—I cannot go through with it."

He ceased grinning abruptly enough at that, his jaw tightening stonily.

"Then that is your misfortune," he stated icily. "I warned you how it would be. It is too late now for you to change your mind. The wedding has taken place. You are my wife—the Viscondesa Poniente, if that means anything to you—now and for always. Now, come. The others are waiting for us."

Miserable, feeling as though she were being marched out to face the executioners of the Spanish Inquisition, Aurora allowed him to lead her from the chapel. His hand, imprisoning her arm, felt like an iron band; and she walked so slowly the visconde asked sarcastically if she had shackles on her ankles.

"Smile!" he hissed. "You look as though you are on your way to a funeral rather than coming from a wedding. Where is your pride, Aurora? Do you wish for the entire Amazon Basin to know you are unhappy?"

"No, of course not."

"Then smile."

So Aurora laughed and flirted with Coronel de la Palma and his handsome young lieutenant and chatted with Padre Guillermo, excusing her swoon by saying she had been overcome with emotion. After all, it was the truth, she thought bitterly. The three men, however, interpreted her explanation as she had intended and smiled.

"So young, so much in love." The older Coronel sighed while the kindly priest, who had performed the ceremony, beamed in jovial agreement, his earlier worry vanishing.

Coronel de la Palma, upon learning they did not as yet possess any such vehicle of their own, graciously insisted the newlyweds ride back in his own carriage to Esplendor.

"You can tie your horses behind," he said, eying Salvador's white Arabian stallion skeptically, "for I do not think that any of my men will be able to return that spirited beast to you, eh?"

"No," the visconde conceded. "No one but me has ever ridden Nieblo."

"I thought as much. Well, no matter. I'll send some of my men over in a day or so to collect the vehicle. *Hasta luego, y buena suerte.*"

After thanking the three men for their participation in the wedding, Salvador assisted Aurora into the carriage, then sprang in beside her, gathered up the reins, and clucked to the dashing bay team. The vehicle started off down the winding dirt road that led to Esplendor—and the visconde's chamber.

"I think, *sí*, I really think, Aurora, that you have had more than enough wine," Salvador informed her, taking away her glass and setting it aside. "I have waited long enough, *muñeca mía*. Now it is late, and I grow impatient. It is time that we retire for the evening."

Aurora glanced up at her husband, frightened. The others of the household, not knowing the true circumstances behind the wedding, had earlier celebrated the newlyweds' marriage and had long since gone to bed, leaving the couple alone. But still Aurora had been unable to bring herself to climb the stairs leading to the visconde's room. So she had sat in the small salon, pretending she was not yet tired, though she had known, from the pointed looks he'd given her, that she was not fooling her husband.

She did not know how much of the rich red wine she had consumed to bolster her courage for the coming night—nor did she care. She knew only that it wasn't nearly enough. She was still afraid.

Aurora had thought to find Salvador's eyes mocking her triumphantly when she gazed up at him; but to her surprise she saw no trace of any such emotion there. Instead they were dark, unfathomable, and somehow curiously gentle.

He held out one hand to her.

"*Venga,*" he said.

She had hoped that Lupe would be there to help her, but obviously the visconde had instructed the maid otherwise. The chamber was empty except for the hundreds of multi-colored flowers that filled it to overflowing. Aurora stared, stricken, at the vibrant bouquets, for it was as though her dream of being lost in the overgrown maze had come true, and she felt momentarily trapped in a nightmare. A bath too had been prepared and was waiting, the water still steaming; and her wrapper, negligee, and slippers lay upon the bed. None of these things escaped Salvador's notice.

"I will wait outside, on the gallery," he remarked, "until you are ready. Do not dawdle, *querida.*"

Then he opened the shuttered French doors and stepped out onto the veranda. Aurora briefly studied his silhouetted figure, as though to be certain he did not intend to return until she called. Then she slowly undressed and slipped into the hammered-brass bathtub, where fragile-blossomed water lilies floated.

Aurora would have cursed her maid's romantically inclined thoughtfulness, but she realized that Lupe was unaware of the real reason behind her mistress's marriage and could not be blamed for trying to make the wedding night a special one.

The water was warm, soothing. The essence of jasmine that Aurora always used wafted sweetly to her nostrils. The maid must have poured some of the heady scent into the bathwater. Aurora leaned back, her lashes closing. Oh, if only she might linger here a while! But there was no time for that. Her husband was waiting. Sighing, she opened her eyes and reached for a nearby cake of soft soap and a sponge, then began to lather herself vigorously.

After she had rinsed herself off she cast a quick glance toward the gallery. The visconde was still outside, his back to her; he raised his arm, and she watched the ember of his thin black cigar glow against the night. Hastily she toweled herself dry, then pulled on her negligee, wrapper, and slippers. As she began to remove the pins from her hair, Salvador came in.

He gazed at her quietly for a time, finding pleasure in her presence; and when she picked up the silver-handled brush the efficient Lupe had placed upon the dresser, he moved to stand behind her.

"Let me," he said.

Wordlessly Aurora handed her husband the brush. As he started to work the stiff bristles through the long, silky mane, Aurora, despite herself, reveled in the soothing, intimate contact, feeling a pleasurable tranquility wash over her. A man who would offer to brush her hair and perform the task so tenderly, so caressingly, surely could not be all bad. Perhaps he would use her body gently as well.

She bit her lip and prayed it would be so, as the

visconde laid aside the silver-handled brush and led her
to the bed. Hesitantly, aware of his eyes on her, Aurora
shrugged off her wrapper and slippers, then slid beneath the single light sheet. Salvador blew out the oil
lamp, stripped off his clothes, slipped in beside her,
and drew the mosquito net around them.

For a moment there was a tense, awkward silence
between them. Then her husband touched her, and
Aurora knew her time of waiting was at an end. Her
heart pounded wildly when his thumb stroked her
cheek, as though he wished to reassure himself that she
really did lie there beside him, that she truly was real.

For an eternity, it seemed, the visconde stared down
at her, his eyes black and fathomless in the darkness,
which was lit only by the moonbeams that streamed in
through the open French doors. To Aurora he appeared
like some ancient pagan god touched by the moonlight,
with his jet-black hair and dark gaze; his hawklike face,
with its proud, aquiline nose; and his bronze skin
beneath which his muscles rippled.

She shivered a little as he continued to study her, his
eyes caressing, compelling. Her mass of ebony hair was
spread like a Spanish fan across the pillows, and her
sapphire-blue eyes met his briefly, then closed against
his scrutiny, her long black lashes making crescent
smudges against her flushed cheeks. Her nostrils flared
a little with fear—and something more; and her lips
parted.

His glance swept lower, to the sheer bodice of her
translucent nightgown, which revealed the swell of her
breasts, rapidly rising and falling at his nearness. Like a
man starving, Salvador feasted on the sight, devouring
her already-hardened rosy nipples that strained against
the light material of her negligee.

He inhaled sharply, his hand suddenly catching the shimmering waterfall of her blue-black tresses. His fingers tightened in the locks, twisting her face up to his.

"*Querida*," he muttered savagely. "*Muñeca mía.*"

Then his mouth came down on hers hard.

Aurora, unprepared for his sudden assault, began to struggle against him, pushing at his broad chest, trying to free herself from his grasp. But he was too strong for her and subdued her easily, pinioning her wrists above her head, his hard lean body covering her own. She caught her breath at the sudden, intimate contact of their flesh, the feel of his weight upon her, of his thighs pressed against her own.

"I am your husband," the visconde growled fiercely, "and you will not deny me."

"I must. I will!" she protested desperately, feeling strangely, inexplicably, as though she were about to be swept by some unknown force that had destined her forever for this moment. "Please, don't."

But Salvador paid no heed to her pleas. She was his, and he wanted her. . . .

She started once more to fight him, but it was futile. She was no match for his strength and desire. He would have his way with her in the end; she knew that. All that Aurora had done with her frantic writhing was to exhaust herself and excite him. She gasped for breath, her limbs ceasing their movement, weak and drained of energy. She was helpless against him; and suddenly she hated him for that, despised his dark, handsome visage that again bent near to hers.

She would have told him of her animosity, spat her enmity in his face; but he gave her no chance for that. As though he guessed her thoughts, once more, rough-

ly, demandingly, his lips imprisoned hers, shutting
off the hostile words she would have uttered. Savagely his tongue encroached upon her mouth, compelling her soft, vulnerable lips to open so he could
ravage the sweetness within.

Aurora choked with outrage against his onslaught
upon her senses, but there was nothing she could
do to prevent it. He was determined to possess her.

Oh, if only he loved her, she reflected wistfully in
some dark corner of her mind. Gladly would she
have given herself to him. But he did not. He only
wanted her, as he had doubtless wanted—and taken—
a hundred other women. It was this thought that
tormented her more than anything as his carnal
mouth continued to move sensuously on her own,
bruising her tender lips. He did not love her.

But it did not matter. In the end it did not matter:
for it was as though her body had a mind and will of
its own, responding to her husband's kisses, his
caresses, as though he alone knew how to melt her
frosty exterior, turning her to flame.

Again and again the visconde's tongue darted
forth to outline lingeringly the full lush shape of her
scarlet mouth before parting her lips to taste the
honey of her upon his tongue, sweet, sweet. Aurora's mouth grew hot, tingling with sparks of electricity as his tongue sought out every soft, hidden place
within until at last, against her will, she was kissing
him back, her own tongue entwining with his, her
teeth nipping at his lips, even as his bit urgently at
hers.

Her head reeled, as though she had drunk too
much wine; but she knew it was not so. It was
Salvador and the things he was doing to her that

caused her to feel faint. Her belly shuddered; her blood boiled within her veins. Her traitorous body molded itself to his until she was like the doll he called her, limp, yielding, without bones.

This was no dream. This was real, vibrantly alive, as Aurora herself was. She moaned low in her throat, consumed by sensation, her flesh prickling with excitement wherever her husband touched her.

How had he aroused her so quickly? He knew, without being told, just where her body most craved his touch. It was eerie, peculiar. Was his a knowledge gleaned in some embrace long ago? Even now, did it not feel as though he had held her like this a hundred times before, kissed her, caressed her, made love to her?

Sí, sí, her heart cried to her, to him. Oh, *mi amor, mi alma*. . . .

Madre de Dios! What was he doing to her?

His mouth burned like a brand across her cheeks to her eyelids, her temples, her hair. He whispered in her ear, his voice thick and husky with passion. What had he said? Aurora did not know; she did not care. She was lost, adrift upon the waves of overwhelming emotion that swirled up to engulf her.

His breath was warm upon her face. She could smell the spicy aroma of the soap and cologne he used, mingling heatedly, intoxicatingly, with her own jasmine scent and the floral fragrance that suffused the chamber.

She shivered as his tongue gently traced the shell-like contours of her ear, then licked its way down her throat. His teeth grazed softly the slender column, so bare, so vulnerable, so trustingly offered up to him in surrender, before his mouth kissed the pulse fluttering rapidly there, then found that sensitive place upon her shoulder where it joined her nape. His tongue teased it lightly, ceaselessly, so that Aurora writhed against him, shuddered beneath him. Her nipples puckered with anticipation, grew even harder as ripples of shock and delight coursed through her treacherous body.

Salvador loosened his restraining grip about her wrists. One hand caressed her face, trailed down languidly to close about her throat, tightening there briefly.

"You are mine," he breathed. "Mine! Always mine. Say it! Say it is true!"

Aurora stared up into his black eyes boring down into her own blue ones. He might have been a demon, so satanic did he look, dark and fierce with desire. She inhaled sharply, for it seemed to her as though he were demanding not only her body, but her soul as well. Still she could not deny him. Now she could not deny him.

"Sí, *mi corazón*, I am yours, now and forever," she whispered.

Was that really her voice that had answered, so soft, so filled with yearning?

The visconde laughed throatily, triumphantly. Then with a low snarl he caught the bodice of her filmy nightgown. In a single, sharp movement he ripped the constraining garment down to free her breasts. Like ripe melons, the full mounds burst forth eagerly.

Aurora gasped, young and afraid, and started once more to struggle to cover herself. But she could not. Her husband pushed her arms away easily, once more exposing the pale globes to his gaze. He laughed again, the sound victorious and mocking.

"You are my wife, *querida*," he said. "What you would hide is mine for the taking."

Then his palms closed about her breasts, squeezing

them tenderly. How invitingly they thrust against his fingers, filling his cupped hands to overflowing.

As though they had a will of their own, Aurora's fingers crept up to entwine themselves in his rich black hair; her arms fastened around his neck to draw him even nearer as he pressed his scorching lips to the hollow between her breasts.

Hungrily Salvador fondled those alabaster globes of perfection. Like marble they were, so translucent he could trace the blue veins within through which her life's blood flowed. Their stiff pink crests blushed even more rosily as his palms glided across the tiny buttons in a slow, circular motion that sent tingles of pleasure radiating through Aurora's body in all directions.

For an instant the girl felt a strange warm fluttering in her belly, a primitive, unexpected longing to be filled by her husband's child. Then the feeling passed to be replaced by something even more instinctive as the visconde's thumbs flicked the rigid peaks gently, teasing them to even greater heights. His mouth closed over one flushed bud, enveloping it, sucking it. Tenderly, his teeth caught the tip, held it prisoner while his tongue whirled about it deliciously, fluttering about it like a butterfly's wings, licking it, savoring it.

Involuntarily Aurora cradled him even closer, her fingers digging into his broad back, feeling his strong, powerful muscles ripple beneath her palms. She arched her body against his lips, his hands, hungry for more. Her captive nipple felt as though it were on fire, a flame that burned inside his mouth.

Aurora could bear no more; she knew she could not. Already she was like a wild thing with the passion clawing its way through her quicksilver veins. She strained feverishly against him, a throbbing ache building between her thighs where a void yearned to be filled by Salvador—and him alone.

She whimpered a little. To her shame, dimly, she heard herself begging him to take her. But her husband only laughed again softly and went on tormenting her.

"Patience, *muñeca,* patience," he told her. "It is better that way—the first time. We will have many days and nights such as this, I promise you."

Aurora bit her lip, humiliated. Oh, how could she have behaved so disgracefully, so wantonly? How could she have pleaded with him so desperately to make her his? She tried to pull away from him, but he only held her closer.

His taut loins raced with excitement, and with difficulty he forced himself to breathe deeply, to relax, to go slowly with her. This giving of herself to him was a precious thing, a treasure to be cherished—and loved.

Like wildfire, his mouth seared its way across her chest, seeking her other breast and setting it ablaze, as he had done its twin earlier, until it too was like a smoldering ember, burning with desire.

Deep within the secret place of Aurora's womanhood, the ache that had started to pulse earlier now beat like a drum, faster and faster, more demanding than ever. She yearned desperately for her husband to quiet the pounding tattoo of her body, but he did not. Instead he went on kissing her, his lips as soft as a sigh as they floated down her belly, his mustache brushing against her like a feather.

His tongue gently explored her navel, tickling her, then traced its way back up to her mouth before he half rose to kneel over her.

His hands tightened for a moment on her slender hips. Then languidly his fingers slid down her legs, following the shape of her calves, then moved back up, slipping around to tease the backs of her knees. Aurora quivered as he touched the sensitive spots, for she had not dreamed she could be so aroused. He found one daintily arched foot, picked it up, and kissed it. He sucked her toes one by one, taunting them with his tongue.

Then slowly—oh, so slowly—his fingers began to trail along the insides of her thighs, up and down, over and over, until Aurora was shaking with longing and anticipation.

With a little cry of agony she caught his hands, trying to make him cease the sensuous movement; but he did not. Instead he captured her wrists once more and went on stroking her.

Gradually his knees nudged her own apart, forcing her to open to him, like a budding flower unfolding its petals. Deliberately he sought the swollen pink crests of the valley that curved beneath the downy black curls, soft as velvet, that twined between her legs. Lingeringly, tantalizingly, he fondled the warm wet folds that trembled and throbbed beneath his searching hand. At long last he found the dark chasm that beckoned to him so enchantingly, so irresistibly. His panting mingled with Aurora's own as he slipped his fingers inside of her to probe her hot moist cavern.

She gasped at the thrill of fear and excitement that shot through her at the intimate contact, for no man had ever touched her so. The pulsing of her womanhood momentarily eased, then began anew, even stronger than before, as his thumb lightly flicked the tiny bud that hardened beneath it.

With each fluttering of Salvador's hand, Aurora's yearning deepened until she thought she would burst from the force of it. Tremors of delight surged within her, growing stronger and stronger.

Then suddenly, before she became aware of what he was doing, the visconde, certain now that she was ready for him, withdrew his fingers, replacing them with his manhood. The bold shaft pressed against her briefly, then entered her without warning, plunging down swiftly with tender fury into the warm, receiving core of her.

Aurora cried out sharply at the unexpected, stabbing pain, involuntarily jerking upward against her husband, thereby unwittingly aiding him in his assault.

Once he had fully settled into her, Salvador lay still for a moment, waiting for the ache to recede and accustoming her to the feel of him inside of her. He silenced her whimpers with his lips, murmuring gently that there was no need for her to be afraid, that it always hurt the first time.

"The pain will soon lessen, *querida*, I promise you," he said.

To her surprise, for she half feared he did but lie to her, Aurora discovered that he was right. Little by little the ache vanished, to be replaced by an even more powerful feeling of desire.

Her husband began to move within her, slow deep strokes at first, which heightened the throbbing of her body unbearably. Aurora was sure she was going to explode, and then incredibly she did. From her throat came a single, animalistic cry, a low moan of surrender; and she suddenly stiffened and clutched the visconde to her, her nails raking tiny furrows down his back. Gripped by uncontrollable passion, she arched her hips wildly against him, as a thousand shooting stars burst within her, blinding her to everything save him. Salvador spiraled down into her, faster and faster, like a comet, as his own release came almost simultaneously, whirling them through the galaxy—and far beyond.

For a fleeting eternity time stood still yet rushed by so quickly that Aurora felt as though she had not lived at all until this breathless moment. A strange sense of being made whole, complete, filled her being so strongly she knew her husband must feel it too. It was as though they had been but halves before and now were one.

Slowly, as though reluctant to withdraw, the visconde left her. But oddly enough Aurora felt no emptiness at his going. He was a part of her now, just as she was a part of him.

He pulled her close, cradling her head against his shoulder and kissing her sweetly, lingeringly, as they waited for the furious pounding of their hearts to return to normal.

"Sal—Salvador," Aurora questioned hesitantly at last, her voice a whisper of stunned awe, "is it—is it always like that?"

He did not need to ask what she meant. He glanced down at her, his eyes dark and filled with emotion.

"For us, *muñeca*, it will be so. I swear it."

And later, much later, when he once more took her in his arms, Aurora knew he had spoken truly.

BOOK THREE

Passion Flower

Chapter Twenty-four

Esplendor, Peru, 1849

A warm feeling pervaded Aurora's being as she glanced at her husband by her side. How handsome he looked this morning, with his jet-black hair, newly washed, still glistening with beads of water, and his skin darkly tanned. His obsidian eyes glowed with pride as he gazed out over the land, and his teeth flashed whitely beneath his mustache at some remark made to him by one of the men. He shook his head agreeably, then moved on, his tall figure striding imposingly across the terrain.

Always, as he passed, the men working in the fields stopped, doffed their hats, and called greetings to *el patrón*. And he smiled, nodded, and continued on his way, just as he did now. On the estate there was not a man, woman, or child whose name the visconde did not know. Aurora marveled at his ability to remember them all: for as word of Esplendor's miraculous rebuilding spread, people came from all over the area to the plantation, seeking work. Salvador studied each face for a long, silent minute before either offering or denying employment, hiring only those persons whom he believed would stay and make the manor their home. The workers loved him, for he was a fair, if stern, employer.

Aurora sighed. She could not deceive herself any longer, not after so many long weeks of being the visconde's wife. She loved him too.

If at first she had been bitter and angry, thinking herself humiliated and cheated by wedding a man who did not love her, who would have protected her regardless of the bargain they'd made, she no longer felt so. It did not matter that Salvador did not love her. He liked and respected her and wanted her physically. Aurora knew that many marriages had begun with less and flourished. She was determined that in time she would win her husband's heart, and he would grow to love her as she now loved him. Till then she would be content with whatever he offered. She was proud to have him by her side, proud of what they were accomplishing at Esplendor.

This last was a great deal indeed. The sugarcane cuttings they had planted earlier had grown tall, looking like a vast, verdant sea as they spread out, acre after acre, over the rich, fertile earth. The immature plants had been purchased from a neighboring estate, Musgo Morado. Now a shipment of *guano*, the fertilizer that Salvador had also arranged for, was being shoveled from carts onto the soil between the rows; and men armed with machetes were trashing the cane, removing any dead or dying leaves from the stalks.

In case the cane crop should fail there were coffee plants in other fields; the evergreen shrubs, covered

with berries, were lightly shaded by banana and pineapple trees.

Closer to the house were orchards and vegetable
gardens, where all manner of fruits and vegetables were
being grown. Aurora had not realized until now how
many of these, which she had always taken for granted
in her homeland, were actually native to Peru and had
been brought to the Old World, centuries past, by
Spanish explorers. Francisco Pizarro had discovered
tomatoes, calling them love apples. Other fruits origi-
nating in Peru were the avocado; the cherimoya, a
sweet fruit with white meat; the guava; the granadilla,
which came from the passion flower; and the papaya.
The lowly potato, so vital to the wild, gregarious race
that peopled Ireland, had its origins in Peru, as did
squash, pumpkins, chili peppers, and most beans, with
the exception of the broad bean and the soybean. Also
indigenous was the cacao tree, from which chocolate
was made. There were several of these in the orchards.
Indian corn, peanuts, and sweet potatoes, although not
native to the land, flourished in the gardens as well.

Soon Esplendor would have more than enough produce to sustain itself. The rest would be sold for a good
price.

In addition, the dark cool cellar wherein meat was
kept was no longer empty. Often Salvador and the men
he'd brought with him from Texas hunted, bringing
back plentiful game. This was immediately dried, salt-
ed, and preserved in barrels in the underground larder,
for meat could not otherwise be stored. If fresh and not
used promptly, it soon turned rancid in the jungle heat,
becoming infested with hordes of maggots.

On one of their outings the visconde and his men had
captured a young group of motherless peccaries as well.

The wild piglets were kept in a pen, where they were being fattened for butchering. At slaughter time Aurora planned on making hogshead cheese, a jellied meatloaf that Heidi Van Klaas had assured her they could prepare.

Aurora liked Heidi, Paul Van Klaas's wife. She was one of the few friends the girl had acquired in the remote Amazon Basin, where neighboring plantations numbered less than twenty and were scattered far and wide.

Sometimes the Van Klaases came for dinner, and Aurora and Heidi passed a pleasant evening together. But more often than not Paul rode over alone from Capricho. He seemed almost obsessed by the progress of Esplendor; but once when Aurora, puzzled by his interest, had questioned him about it, he had merely shrugged and informed her that he wished to implement some of Salvador's ideas at Capricho. Thereafter Aurora had ceased to wonder at his curiosity.

Still she could never rid herself of the fanciful notion she'd had the first time she'd ever met him: that his large, strong, spatulalike hands looked capable of murder. Whenever the idea occurred to her, she shivered, thinking of Ijada and wondering whether or not the *mestiza* had actually killed Basilio, as he'd claimed. To her sorrow and frustration Aurora had never discovered the truth of the matter, though she kept hoping she would. Ijada still went about her business as always, saying little.

IT was some months later that disaster struck.

The morning started out like so many others, with that odd, quiet hush that presages a summer storm, so Aurora thought nothing of the stillness when she awoke. In fact, she looked forward to what she believed was the coming rain, for the heat was stifling, and a shower would cool things down considerably.

She pressed her daintily tatted and scented handkerchief to her temples and wrists, then pushed a few stray tendrils of hair back into place before going downstairs to join the others at breakfast.

Nicolas, of course, was first with the news.

"There's something real peculiar going on in the jungle," he mumbled after stuffing himself with a hot, buttered roll.

"Don't talk with food in your mouth, Nicolito," Aurora chided gently, conscious that she must teach the boy manners in their mother's absence. Doña Ynez was counting on her to do that, Aurora knew. "And how many times have I told you to stay out of the jungle besides? You know it's dangerous, Nicolito. You could be attacked by a wild animal or become lost in the undergrowth." She shivered at the thought. "Even the Indians don't venture very far into the brush."

"I'm not afraid, Aurora," the boy countered cheerfully. "I've got my bow and arrows—and my blowgun—after all." He felt confident carrying the weapons that one of the Iquitos had made for him. "I'm real good with them now, and I can take care of myself. Do you want that?" He pointed to a banana on Salvador's plate.

"No, Nicolas," the visconde replied.

"Whether or not you can take care of yourself is not the point," Aurora stated firmly, exasperated, as she steered the conversation back to the subject at hand. "The jungle is a perilous place even for experienced men, much less an untried youth. Nicolito! Don't feed that monkey at the table!"

"It was only a banana, and Salvador didn't want it anyway. He said so."

"That was before I realized you meant to give it to that ill-mannered beast," the visconde declared.

"Well, how else is Bribón to learn what's expected of him, if he isn't allowed at the table?" the boy asked, with what he hoped was acceptable logic.

"Don't be impertinent, Nicolas," Salvador answered, with an ill-concealed flicker of a smile. "Monkeys don't dine with their betters. You know that as well as I, or you wouldn't have hidden that repugnant creature under the table. Now take him away at once, then come back to finish your meal."

"Sí, señor," the boy assented, not in the least rebuked, for he liked the visconde immensely.

Nicolas tugged on Bribón's leash, leading the offensive, chattering animal away. Aurora could have sworn they were both laughing. She was certain of it moments later when the boy returned, his eyes dancing with merriment.

"I left him in the kitchen, with Lupe," he explained.

He did not have to say more. The maid—now in actuality Esplendor's very capable housekeeper—had on more than one occasion taken a rolling pin to the mischievous monkey, who managed deftly to elude her at every turn. Lupe insisted that one day she would catch the irritating beast, and they would all have monkey stew. Nicolas was not alarmed by this announcement. He had on several instances observed the maid secretly indulging Bribón's craving for peanuts, which she shelled especially for him.

"Now"—Salvador spoke, once the matter of the monkey had been disposed of—"just what is it that's going on in the jungle?"

"Nothing," Nicolas answered.

"But you said something strange was occurring,"

Aurora pointed out, annoyed and thinking this was another one of her brother's pranks.

"That's just it," the boy insisted. "There's nothing happening. All the animals have gone, vanished, even the big cats. The place is as dead as a tomb."

"But . . . how can that be?" Aurora queried, puzzled. "I don't understand it. There are literally millions of beasts in the jungle. Where could they all have gone— and why?"

"I don't know." Nicolas shrugged. "A puma crashed through the cane this morning. It scared the men half to death, although it never even gave them a second glance."

The visconde listened intently to the boy's words, startled. Something peculiar indeed was occurring, for normally, with the exception of the jaguar that had caused Aurora's mare to bolt the day she had been thrown from the saddle, the big cats never came near the plantation.

In the brief, troubled silence that had fallen, far off in the distance could be heard a low rumbling, like thunder.

"Perhaps we're in for a really terrible storm," Aurora mused aloud, "and the animals are all searching for shelter."

"Maybe," Salvador agreed, concerned. "I think I'll ride out and take a look all the same."

In the end, however, this was not necessary. Just as the visconde was having Nieblo brought around, Teniente Miguel Sanchez, from the military outpost, came galloping up to them as though pursued by the devil. He reined his gelding in sharply, and not taking time to dismount, he shouted his warning.

"Army ants are coming. They're on the march and heading this way. You've got a few days, maybe, if you're lucky. Prepare yourselves for evacuation. I've got to go and warn the other planters."

Then he turned off toward the next plantation.

For a moment the lieutenant's words had little effect on Aurora. She did not realize that what sounded like distant thunder was the noise made by the millions of voracious insects traveling toward Esplendor. In her mind ants were tiny, pesky bugs that showed up at picnics.

What Indians there were on the estate had already disappeared; they had recognized the warning throb of the earth for what it really was and had fled in terror. The rest of the workers were gathering before the house, their eyes wide with confusion and apprehension as they waited for Salvador's instructions. Only the visconde's imposing, authoritative figure and his wise instinct in having chosen his men prevented panic, for already, horrifying word was being spread that the ants would eat everyone in their path alive.

"Why, that's ridiculous!" Aurora snapped when one woman suddenly cried out the news she had just been told, then, sobbing, fell to her knees and started to pray.

Salvador glanced sharply at his wife, for he had never known her to be so callous in the face of another's fright. Then he realized, with a start, that Aurora did not understand their peril.

Tactfully, so as not to scare the others even further, he drew her aside and spoke quietly in her ear.

"*Querida,*" he uttered, "I don't wish to alarm you, but what Natividad said is true. Oh, not in the sense that she meant. The ants move relatively slowly, and we are able-bodied and have plenty of time to escape. But if a man were injured, for example, and lay helpless upon the ground in the insects' path, they would indeed eat him alive in a matter of hours, literally stripping the flesh from his bones. This is why we must evacuate Esplendor—and in a quick, orderly fashion—as soon as possible. No one must be left behind, perhaps to panic, stumble, and fall, and be consumed by these ravaging bugs."

"Oh, Salvador!" Aurora gasped, stricken, as she tried to absorb the awful impact of this information. "I'm sorry. I did not realize. . . ."

"No, *muñeca*, I know you did not." His eyes were kind. "Now . . . let us hurry, for there is much to be done."

"Oh, Salvador!" Aurora exclaimed again as another thought occurred to her. "The cane!"

"It will be safe," he assured her. "The creatures are meat-eaters only."

She shuddered involuntarily at that. The ants must be monstrous in size to inflict such damage. Aurora fancifully imagined an insect as large as a cat or a dog, perhaps bigger, with terrible, crushing jaws and pincers. No, that simply could not be. No mere insect could be so huge, but whatever was coming, they must escape from it!

As though he guessed her thoughts Salvador squeezed her hand tightly, reassuringly, for an instant, then turned away to begin giving orders.

Even though the threatening rumble in the distance had ceased—the army ants rarely marched during the heat of the day, it seemed—the laborers worked rapidly to carry out the visconde's commands. Of primary importance were the peccaries and the chickens that Aurora had acquired from some passing traders. The animals could not be left penned up at the plantation. They would be devoured in minutes by the coming insects. Cages had to be constructed so the beasts could be transported to a place of safety. Aurora was glad that over the months the men had built sturdy wagons that would serve to carry the confined animals, as well as the many laborers who now worked at the estate.

Food also had to be prepared, for since no one knew how long the column of approaching ants was, there was no way of estimating the number of days all would have to be absent from the manor. The horde might pass in a single night or take as long as three days to march on.

Despite the amount of work to be done, fear proved a motivating taskmaster, and by the following morning everyone was ready to go. The wagons were loaded; and after making a final check to be certain no man or beast remained behind, the cavalcade from Esplendor set out for the higher hills that loomed in the distance. The crests were thought to be out of the insects' path; but if they were not, the knolls would at least provide a good vantage point from which to monitor the ants' progress so the party could move again if it must.

Because it was so large, the cavalcade traveled slowly. Earlier in the week heavy rains had soaked the ground, and it was now as sodden as the swamps near the rivers and the forest pools. As a result the winding dirt road they followed was like a steaming bog. The wheels of the vehicles sank into the mud. Several times women and children were forced to climb down from the wagons while their men tried to free the vehicles from the mire. The air was filled with shouts and grunts as the laborers hauled on mule harnesses, cursing the animals and pulling them forward, while their fellow workers, shoulders and backs pressed to the wagons, slipped and slid in the mud as they attempted to shove the vehicles along. Children yelled and laughed, scampering about as though it were all some grand adventure; and babies, unaccustomed to the noise, wailed ceaselessly.

It was small wonder then that neither Salvador nor Aurora heard Nicolas's frantic cry as his clever monkey, who months ago had figured out how to unfasten his leash and did so whenever he pleased, now freed himself, jumped down from the boy's shoulder, and scurried off into the brush.

"Bribón! Bribón!" Nicolas yelled, but it was no use.

The monkey was gone, swallowed up by the thick undergrowth. Without pausing to think of the danger to himself, the boy urged his horse from the road, compelling the mount into the jungle, chasing determinedly after the naughty monkey. Bribón spied Nicolas coming and, squealing with what sounded amazingly like laughter, began to swing from branch to branch as though playing a game.

Heedlessly the boy pressed on, following. It was some time before he recognized that he was lost.

"SALVADOR," Aurora sobbed over and over, distraught and scarcely able to speak as she buried her face against her husband's wide, comforting chest. "Salvador."

"What is it? What is it, *querida?*" he asked gently, holding her trembling body close to his to calm her. "What's wrong?"

"It's—it's Nicolas. He's gone!"

"Gone? Gone where?" the visconde questioned sharply, his hands tightening on his wife's shoulders.

"I don't know," she wailed. "I don't know. He—he

must have forgotten something at Esplendor and gone back to the manor. Nobody saw him leave. We don't even know how long he's been gone."

"Don't worry, *muñeca,*" Salvador said soothingly. "I'll go back and look for him. I'll find him. Don't worry."

"But the ants—"

"Are doubtless still a day's march away. I'll be all right. You stay here with the others, and supervise the camp until I return."

He kissed her swiftly before striding toward his horse, and the vital strength seemed to pour from his hard body into her own, giving her courage. After he'd gone Aurora touched her fingers to her mouth, as though to prevent the taste of his lips from fading. Her fears for Nicolas lessened a little now that she knew her husband had taken charge of the matter. If anyone could find her brother and bring him back safely, it was Salvador.

Taking a deep breath, she began to direct the making of the camp.

They had found a large, grassy glade where they could settle for the night. At the *comancheros'* suggestion Aurora ordered that the wagons be driven into a circle for better defense, and that the animals be unhitched and tethered within the formation so they would be safe from predators. Then she sent several of the men out to find wood to build fires and set the women to unpacking and preparing the foodstuffs. After that there were beds to be made. Those who could not fit into the vehicles would have to sleep upon the ground. Ferns and moss, gathered from the jungle, would serve as comfortable mattresses, and many were not used to more besides.

There was so much to do that it was some time before Aurora, glancing up at the sun, which was just starting to sink low in the sky, realized that almost three hours had passed; and Salvador had not yet returned.

Soon it would be dark, and the army ants would be on the move again. She bit her lip worriedly. The party from Esplendor had traveled slowly because it was large, and the mired road had caused difficulties for the wagons. A single man on horseback should have been able to traverse the distance to the manor and back in a little over an hour. All of a sudden Aurora was assailed by a dreadful premonition. Something was wrong! Something was terribly wrong! She could not huddle here like a coward when both her husband and her brother were in danger.

"Lupe," she called to her maid. "I want you to finish overseeing the camp. Get Jim Rawlings or one of the other *comancheros* to help you. Salvador says all those men from *Tejas* know how to live off the land. They'll know what to do. I've got to go and see what's become of my husband."

Before Lupe could protest, Aurora was gone, whipping her mare furiously toward Esplendor. After a moment the maid shrugged. In all the cacophony and confusion she had not noticed that Nicolas had disappeared; and she assumed that Salvador was somewhere nearby, perhaps scouting for supplies or searching for some sign of the army ants. Lupe did not know that *el patrón* had gone back to Esplendor to look for his wife's brother; and it certainly never occurred to her that Aurora would return, alone and unprotected, to the manor; so obediently she went to seek out Jim Rawlings in order to discover the best way to make coffee over a fire.

Since the rough but handsome American was sweet on the maid and had been making every effort to court her, he spent a considerable amount of time patiently teaching her how to perform the task. Happy that Jim Rawlings was interested in her, Lupe talked and laughed with him at some length, her duties temporarily forgotten. By the time she realized that her mistress, *el patrón*, and Nicolas were all missing it was too late to do anything about it.

It was dark, and in the distance could be heard the throbbing of the earth that signaled the march of the army ants.

Chapter Twenty-five

WHEN Aurora first spied Salvador, so unnaturally pale and stretched out motionless on the ground in front of Esplendor, she believed, for one heart-stopping eternity, that he was dead. Her breath caught in her throat; her heart lurched sickeningly; and her belly shuddered as though the earth had suddenly dropped from beneath her feet.

No! He just couldn't be dead! He was too vital and alive for that!

With a little sob of horror she hurriedly dismounted and raced to his side. To her relief she saw that, although unconscious, he was still breathing, albeit shallowly. Briefly she closed her eyes and said a silent prayer of thanks to God for that, then bent to examine her husband's inert figure, wondering what had befallen him.

There was a nasty gash on the back of his head, matted with dried blood and swollen the size of an egg. Aurora gasped as she touched the ugly wound, probing gingerly to see how bad it was. Salvador stirred and groaned, but he didn't awaken. Rapidly she went over the rest of his body. There didn't seem to be any other injury upon him, but his pallor and stillness frightened her. Doubtless he was suffering from shock.

Momentarily the sound of fading hoofbeats caught Aurora's attention. She looked up.

"Nicolas!" she cried. "Nicolas!"

Her voice echoed eerily in the hush that lay like a pall over the plantation. No answer came in response to her call. The estate was deserted. Whoever had been there was gone.

Quickly, her husband's comfort and well-being uppermost in her mind, Aurora ran into the house to fetch a basin of water and a blanket. Once outside, she covered the visconde and started gently to cleanse his wound, her fingers trembling as she realized the seriousness of the gash.

She studied him with concern, wondering if she should try to move him. At last Aurora decided against this. Salvador was heavy. She would have to drag him inside, possibly hurting him further; and perhaps even then she wouldn't be able to lift him onto one of the sofas. She knew there was absolutely no way she would ever get him upstairs to their room.

Tears filled her eyes as she bit her lip in self-reproach. Oh, if only she had brought Pancho, her husband's valet, or one of the other men with her! They would have been able to help. *Mierda!* Why was she always so damned impulsive? She decided it would be best to leave the visconde where he was until she could determine what must be done.

Oh, if only Nicolas were here. He would be able to assist her. But there was no sign of the missing boy. Was it possible her brother hadn't returned to Esplendor after all? Had she sent Salvador on a wild-goose chase with her hysterics?

Now that she had time to think, Aurora was puzzled as to what had happened to her husband. There was something about the awful gash on his head that disturbed her. It looked as though he had been hit a vicious blow rather than simply having tripped and fallen, as she had suspected previously.

Made suddenly uneasy by the notion, she glanced about warily, remembering the hoofbeats she'd heard earlier. When she spied the clublike branch lying a few yards from the visconde's side, she inhaled sharply, stricken. Salvador *had* been knocked unconscious! Near the top of the wood were dark bloodstains mingled with a few strands of her husband's jet-black hair. Yes, someone had definitely sneaked up behind him and brutally struck him down.

But . . . why? Why would anyone have wanted to do such a horrible thing? She did not know.

Suddenly very much afraid, Aurora dropped the branch and moved slowly back to Salvador's motionless form. She knelt down and, with shaking hands, pulled the heavy, black-barreled revolver from the special-made holster at his waist. She did not know how to use the pistol, but an intruder wouldn't know that; and the gun gave her a small measure of security. Then cautiously she forced herself to go back into the house.

Now she began to notice things that previously, in her haste, she had not observed. The few pictures that hung upon the walls were slightly askew, as though someone had tilted them, looking behind them. One had been removed from its nail completely; its back had been slashed open, and the canvas had been prised from the frame. Several of the furniture drawers were a little ajar, as though they had been hurriedly searched, then carelessly slammed shut. Some of the ornate cornice work and wainscoting on the walls had been pried loose, as though by a knife. A brick from the fireplace lay upon the floor of the main salon. Here and there were other signs of damage, though the upstairs appeared to be untouched.

Aurora forced herself to go through the entire house, top to bottom, except for the west wing, which was still under reconstruction and not yet considered safe. But there was no one to be found. The manor was empty.

Nevertheless, it was evident that during their absence from the plantation someone had come to Esplendor and had tried to search the manor . . . looking for what?

Aurora didn't know. All of their money, except for a few coins for emergencies, was kept in a sturdy iron strongbox carefully locked and hidden in the study. Perhaps that was what the intruder had wanted. But the vault's place of concealment had gone undiscovered, and the strongbox was undisturbed. Doubtless, had the intruder had time to make a more thorough search, he or she would have found the vault hidden under the rug and floorboards beneath the heavy desk that Salvador had had one of the men build.

Fortunately Aurora had arrived, scaring off whomever it had been.

Perplexed and concerned, she went back outside to her husband. He was still unconscious, but the beating of his heart was strong. She raised her head from his chest and suddenly was aware of another steady sound— the rumbling of the army ants. They were on the march again, and with each passing minute it sounded as though they were drawing closer.

Dear God. What should she do?

*But if a man were injured, for example, and lay
helpless upon the ground in the insects' path, they
would indeed eat him alive in a matter of hours,
literally stripping the flesh from his bones....*

Dear God.

After rapidly replacing Salvador's revolver Aurora
rushed back into the house to the kitchen, to the wood
box. Grabbing a nearby towel, she hastily loaded it with
as much kindling as she could carry. Panting, gasping
for breath, she made trip after trip after trip, until her
husband was completely surrounded by a large circle of
brush, and more logs were stacked within the formation, so there could be no chance of her running out of
wood. Then she ran down to the cellar, where the
whale oil for the lamps was kept. She lugged two small
barrels outside, her mouth dry, her heart racing frantically as the tattoo upon the earth became louder and
louder, and a hideous buzzing began to sound. Terrified, she went back as many times as she could, getting
food and water and brandy for Salvador, to keep him
warm and sedated, should he awaken.

Finally Aurora thought she had everything she needed.
Then suddenly she realized she had forgotten the tinderbox. Screaming as she saw by the last light of the
setting sun the appalling phalanx of dark red start to
gush like blood from the edge of the jungle, she fairly
flew into the manor, snatched up the metal tin, and
hastened back outside. With shaking hands she ripped
off the lid of one of the whale oil tuns and began to pour
its contents over the brush. Desperately she fumbled
with the tinderbox.

"Light, damn you! *Light!*" she shrieked as she scraped
the flint furiously, again and again.

At last the spark caught and held. She blew gently on

the tinder to fan the flame, then shoved it into the kindling. With the aid of the whale oil the brush blazed up immediately; and soon Aurora and Salvador were enclosed in a circle of fire.

To her utter horror the girl suddenly realized she had forgotten one last, very important thing: the grass.

Thank God, it was sodden with rain! Before the blaze could spread and burn them alive, Aurora grabbed up a cup she had taken from the kitchen, then crawled like a crazy woman over the ground, frenziedly gouging a small trench into the earth inside the circle. This she filled with the buckets of water she had managed to bring along, in case the fire got out of hand.

After that, physically and mentally exhausted, drained of every last ounce of her strength and courage, she collapsed, sobbing hysterically in the darkness.

The sound of her tears pierced the veil of Salvador's unconsciousness. His eyelids fluttered open; he moaned, dazed, his head pounding with pain. He tried to rise but could not and fell back once more, still groaning.

Immediately, her face brightening, Aurora ceased weeping and rushed to her husband's side.

"Salvador!" she cried. "Oh, Salvador!"

Dimly, confusedly, his eyes focused upon her.

"Aurora," he rasped. "Aurora."

"Hush. Don't try to talk. You've been hurt. Here. Let me get you some brandy."

She fetched the decanter, cradling his head and shoulders in her lap, and raised the rim of the bottle to his lips so he could drink. After several long swallows he managed to sit up on his own at last.

Still dizzy, he peered about uncomprehendingly at the circle of fire, then looked back at Aurora, taking in her utter exhaustion and disheveled appearance.

"*Heridas de Cristo, querida*, what is happening?"

As calmly as she could, not wanting to add to the burden of his aching head, she explained what had occurred.

"*Dios mío,* Aurora!" Salvador exclaimed, stunned, when she had finished, staring at her marvelingly as though he'd never really seen her before. "I don't believe it. You did all this—all by yourself?"

"*Sí.*" She nodded, some of her composure returning at the realization that she no longer had to face the army ants alone. "It was all I could think of to do. Even had I managed to drag you inside the house, I don't believe I could have lifted you to a place of safety. Besides, I couldn't build a fire in the manor, and I was certain that was our only hope."

"You were right, *muñeca.* You saved my life—at the risk of your own."

There was an emotion in his voice that had never been there before. Aurora looked away, her eyes filling with sudden tears. He was grateful to her, of course. Only she didn't want his gratitude. She wanted his love.

"I'll—I'll just put some more wood on the fire," she said. "We—we can't afford to let it die out."

"Our fire will never die out, Aurora," he replied softly, "for it is an eternal flame."

But she did not hear him. She had already turned away.

ALL through the long, torturous night the army ants, cannibals of the jungle, surrounded them. By the light of the blaze Aurora and Salvador watched the unending column, which was fully four yards wide and nearly half a mile long. As the stream of countless millions of shiny bodies passed, Aurora saw why they were called army ants. Like a military regiment, they marched in mass formation, busy workers making up the body of the battalion, tong-jawed soldiers guarding its flanks. All except for the winged males were blind. Even so, the horde flowed on unceasingly, killing and eating as it went.

Aurora saw a large iguana skittering over the grass, trying to escape. But it could not. In moments the dark river of ants swarmed over it, ripping it to shreds with their inward-curving jaws and vicious, hooked pincers. She shuddered, horrified. Such might have been her and Salvador's fate.

Those insects that had come away with bits of flesh scurried back to the phalanx, often colliding with their fellow creatures and fighting over who was to retain the meat. The victors disappeared into a tunnel created by the ants' own bodies.

Part of the column of bugs was carrying larvae, which had not yet become cocoons, and pupae, which had. There must have been hundreds of thousands of these, waiting to grow into more of the ghastly ants.

At last there came the queen herself, surrounded by faithful guards, their antennae wiggling excitedly as they conducted surveillance for possible danger to her, for the army ants could not survive without a queen. She was much bigger than the others of the colony, nearly two inches long, fat, and wingless. Her coat of armor glistened in the firelight, for when the insects rested, the workers cleaned and polished her body continually so she was always immaculately groomed. No royal highness on earth ever received better care or treatment. So distraught did the ants become if their queen died that they would actually cling, bereft, to her empty shell, as though trying to bring her back to life.

"*Santa María*, Salvador!" Aurora breathed. "They are going to go right through the house."

And so they were, for in her haste to prepare for the bugs' invasion of Esplendor, Aurora had left the front doors open—and doubtless the back doors as well—not that closing them would have done any good.

Straight through the manor the army ants marched, wiping it free of every snake hiding in the cool cellar, every rat lurking in a dark corner, every cockroach scuttling in a twisted cranny.

It was well after dawn before the last straggling insect disappeared, and Aurora and Salvador could breathe freely again. Their terrible, nerve-racking ordeal ended, they turned to each other's arms, embracing wordlessly in the peaceful stillness that had fallen over the jungle. Now they could put out the fire that had been their salvation and walk to the house. Salvador placed his arm about Aurora's shoulders to steady himself, for he still felt slightly sick and dazed from the painful blow he had received.

The visconde had not seen who'd struck him, but he had his suspicions as to whom it had been; and he knew for certain that he had been deliberately knocked unconscious and left upon the ground, in hopes that the army ants would make short work of his helpless body. Had it not been for Aurora, he would have breathed his last that night.

How he longed to tell his wife how much he loved her, now, more than ever, for she had risked her own life to save his. But Salvador said nothing of his overwhelming emotions toward her. He had seen the look upon her face when earlier, his voice choked with feeling, he'd thanked her for what she had done for him. Aurora had turned away, not wanting to encourage any intimate expressions from him. She had given herself to him; but she did not love him. She only needed him to protect her.

Sometime later, after he had rested and despite Aurora's protests that he was too ill to move, the visconde went back outside and whistled for his stallion, who'd sensibly run away last night. When Nieblo, still snorting with fear, finally appeared, Salvador mounted the beast slowly and went to alert the others that the army ants had come and gone. At the camp he formed a search party to look for Nicolas, who to the visconde's vast relief was discovered, scared but unharmed, along with Bribón, a few hours later.

After that Salvador instructed some of the men to clear away the circle of ashes in front of Esplendor and to plant a ring of flowers there in the grass to remind him always of Aurora's bravery.

Surely there was some spark of caring for him in her, else she would not have acted as she'd done last night, saving his life at the risk of her own. Salvador wanted very much to believe that. He *had* to believe that; otherwise he thought he would go mad.

Chapter Twenty-six

"SOMEONE struck you down viciously and attempted to search the house."

"*Sí*," Salvador replied calmly to Aurora's statement. "It is so."

"But—but why?" the girl stammered, confused. "What on earth was the person who did it looking for?"

"The treasure, *querida*. The fortune that Don Santiago Roque y Avilés supposedly buried at Esplendor centuries past."

"Oh, *that*," Aurora said flatly, disgusted. "I'm so sick of hearing about that. If there ever really were such a thing, somebody must have found it years ago and long since carted it away."

"No, they couldn't have, for the treasure never existed— at least not in the form of gold and jewels, such as everyone believes."

"How do you know that?"

"I don't know." The visconde shrugged, for indeed he really did not understand why he was so sure of this, any more than he'd been able to comprehend the strange feelings he'd had the first time he'd ever seen Esplendor.

When he'd first glimpsed the manor he'd been overwhelmed by emotion: for it had been as though he had been lost, wandering, for eons, and had at last come home. He'd even known his way unerringly about the house. How? He could not explain it.

"Simple logic dictates the answer," he continued to his wife. "If Don Santiago did indeed discover the lost city of El Dorado—and somehow I feel certain that he did—then he did, in fact, have a great deal of gold.

"But think, Aurora! Look about you at Esplendor, and imagine what it was like when it was first built, so grand and beautiful that it was breathtaking. Think what it must have cost to create this—this *splendor* in the midst of the jungle. The marble alone had to be imported all the way from Italy. I doubt when he was finished that Don Santiago had any fortune left; and for some reason I don't believe he ever returned to the Gilded One. El Dorado did not hold what he truly desired. His beloved Doña Arabela lay in a tomb in Spain."

"*Sí.* It's very sad, isn't it, his story?" Aurora uttered softly. "And this house . . . it's almost as though it were meant as a monument to her memory, like Shah Jahan's Taj Mahal in India. Don Santiago must have loved Doña Arabela deeply. How wonderful it must have been to be loved like that." Aurora spoke without thinking.

Then she glanced up quickly, mortified. Imagine what Salvador must be making of a statement like that! She blushed painfully under his odd, searching gaze and turned away.

"It is too bad that other men are so greedy," she

declared hastily, to cover her unintentional slip, "for in destroying Esplendor they have desecrated something far grander than gold and glory too."

Now why had she said *that*? She had but worsened the situation. *Madre de Dios!* Her husband would think she was little better than a lovesick schoolgirl, begging him for his heart!

"Even—even Basilio fell prey to the tale of the treasure," she continued hurriedly, knowing she was babbling but unable to prevent herself from doing so, "digging up the grounds when he ought to have been rebuilding the manor. It was that which took his life. *Sí*, in the end it was his greed that killed him, just like all the others. It was almost as though Esplendor knew somehow that he was a marauder like all the rest. I know it's only my imagination, but sometimes it seems as though this house is alive."

"I thought your brother died from a tropical fever," the visconde asserted, slightly puzzled, for surely it was the jungle that had taken Basilio's life.

"So everyone believed," Aurora said. "But with his dying breath my brother claimed that Ijada had poisoned him—and perhaps Francisca too, if Basilio spoke truthfully, and they really had not contracted some dread disease."

"Ijada!" Salvador exclaimed, startled. "But . . . why would she want to murder your brother and his wife?"

"I—I don't know," Aurora confessed. "It doesn't make any sense, unless she's also searching for that accursed treasure—which you say never existed anyway—and she thought that Basilio would find it before she did. But why did she not just wait for my brother to discover it and then kill him? That's what I would have done and saved myself the trouble of looking for it."

"*Sí*, but then it would have been obvious that Basilio had been murdered. If Ijada really did kill him, she certainly wouldn't have wanted your brother's death to look suspicious. A poison that caused the same symptoms as a fever would have been ideal."

Aurora shrugged.

"Maybe so. But on the other hand, maybe my imagination is just running away with me again. It might have been as Ijada said, that my brother was simply delirious and raving."

"Perhaps," the visconde agreed, but his eyes were troubled all the same and narrowed thoughtfully as he considered the information his wife had just imparted to him.

IT was time to harvest the sugarcane.

They chose a day when the wind was still to start, for they must take every precaution against the slightest risk of the necessary fires burning out of control. This also had been taken into consideration when the sugarcane cuttings had been planted; and between each of the fields, as well as between the fields and the jungle, there lay a wide strip of earth that was totally devoid of vegetation. This too would help guard against the flames spreading.

They would do each square of land separately so, once begun, the harvesting process could continue without interruption.

It was a fine morning, and as it was still very early, about an hour before dawn, the air was yet cool. Despite the fact that other landlords forced their workers—usually Indian slaves, who could not protest—to do it, Salvador had declared that no laborer of his would burn cane during the sweltering heat of the day.

This meant that there was much to be done before the sun rose high in the sky, but the men were able and willing to work hard for such a generous *el patrón*.

The first of the blazes was set, carefully calculated to do no more than lightly char the stalks in order to reduce the moisture they contained. This partial drying of the cane helped it to produce more sucrose.

Once the initial field had been burned, half the labor force moved on to the next. The other half began the cutting.

Salvador, naked to the waist, worked right alongside the rest, swinging his shining silver machete tirelessly. Row after row of the tall stalks fell, were topped, and laid aside to be gathered up by several other men, loaded onto the wagons, and transported to the shed where the cane would be milled. Aurora, mounted on her favorite mare, supervised most of this, gleeful that she had prevailed in the blistering argument she'd had with her husband when she'd insisted on helping. The visconde had been enraged, but she had stood her ground. She would no longer remain cooped up in the house—like a prisoner.

"If you don't let me out, *warden*," she had jeered, "I'm going to rebel, and then you'll be sorry. I'll make you sorry, some way, somehow! Why do you try to keep me locked up anyway? What's the matter? Are you afraid I might run off with somebody else?"

"If you dared, I would kill you," Salvador had replied.

"You'd have to find me first," she'd jibed, "and the world is a big place."

Her husband had at last relented; and Aurora had joined in the harvesting. Now, as she rode between the fields and the shed, she could not help but let her eyes stray toward her husband. His imposing figure stood out easily from the rest of the men; and she thought that even though he was working like a common laborer, no one could ever have mistaken him for such. His dark bronze skin glistened with sweat, inflaming her with its erotic sheen. The powerful muscles in his arms and back rippled sinuously with each strong slice of his machete. Aurora believed she had never desired him more than she did that day. There was something so absolutely godlike and yet beautifully, excitingly earthy about him, standing there among the tall green stalks, beneath the hot sun that was rising high in the endless azure sky. To her he looked as though he could defy the elements and conquer the world.

Irrationally—for she was a lady accustomed to fine, fragrant colognes; clean silk sheets; and soft, comfortable beds—Aurora wished her husband would take her savagely upon the hard ground amid the sugarcane, with the sweat of his labor still upon his lithe body. Her nipples flushed and stiffened at just the thought of his pressing her down upon the rough earth, his flesh driving passionately into her own. She shivered with desire as she caught his black eyes upon her, gleaming hungrily, as though he guessed her thoughts.

She blushed and turned away, and, as she did so, something new and exciting occurred to her, making her heart beat fast.

Why didn't she make love to her husband? She wanted his heart, desperately; and yet she had never given him even the slightest hint of encouragement when he had sought to take her, had never dared to tell him how much she loved him, fearing that he would merely laugh at her, mock her, humiliate her.

But what if he did not? Surely if she loved him, she

should be willing to take that chance. She had offered herself to him once in order to bargain with him. What if she gave herself to him freely, expecting nothing in return? Was that not the true measure of love? Perhaps he had even come to care for her a little and would not show it, believing that she wanted nothing more from him than his protection.

Oh, what a fool she had been! Aurora realized. Now that she thought about it, ever since the night of the army ants, he had made countless small attempts at intimacy, as though seeking to bring them closer; and she had rejected every one! Even the ring of flowers he had ordered planted she had dismissed as but a gallant gesture of appreciation for saving his life.

Aurora, you are indeed a fool, she told herself sternly. You have fought for everything you wanted at Esplendor— with the exception of your husband. And it is he whom you desire above all else. You hoped the seed of your friendship would grow to a blossom of love, yet you have done nothing to nurture the bud you would have bloom. A flower without sun and rain does not unfurl its petals. Why should Salvador give his heart to you when you have done nothing to show him that you wish to have it? Fool!

But he wants my body only—not my love. He has made that quite plain.

Has he, or is that only what you have told yourself so many times that you have come to believe it?

I don't know. I don't know!

Then try listening to your heart for a change, for it alone holds the answer.

Aurora bit her lip, the argument with herself over. She did not know if she could win Salvador's love, but she *did* know now that she must try.

The next time she visited the cane fields, she dismounted and, with her own hands, took her husband a cool drink, which she'd obtained from Lupe, who kept a sharp eye on the women who brought food and beverages as the day wore on. Salvador glanced at his wife, somewhat surprised by her action; and Aurora blushed.

"I—I think you should come to the mill now," she stammered, her heart hammering so loudly in her breast she was certain he must hear it. "They are getting ready to crush the first of the stalks."

"I'll come at once," the visconde replied. "It's nearly noon anyway and too hot to be burning the cane any longer. I'll tell the men it is time for a *siesta*, then join you at the shed."

"I'll see you there, then," Aurora promised and smiled, then took his empty glass back to one of the women.

Salvador stared after his wife for a long, thoughtful moment before turning away to shout instructions to the others.

THE mill was a long wooden building, set off some distance from the house. It was in this shed that the cane was processed.

The stalks were first chopped into shorter pieces, then fed several times through a roller-mill to be crushed. The precious juice that was extracted by this method was collected in barrels set beneath the grinding machine. The liquid was then poured into copper pans placed over furnaces that were fueled by the discarded trash or stalks. The first two pots burned at a higher temperature than the rest in order to concentrate the clear juice. After the liquid had been boiled, laced with lime, and skimmed, it was then transferred by stages to three subsequent pans, each smaller than the last, the process being repeated all along until the crude brown sugar, or magma, as it was called, was achieved. The two men who watched the final pot were the most important persons of the harvesting process, for it was they who determined just when to strike—to remove the contents of the last pan at the moment the sugar crystallized.

Aurora arrived at the mill first, and instead of waiting for Salvador to accompany her, she went on inside. It was even hotter in the shed than it was outside, but she was fascinated by the harvesting process and asked endless questions of the laborers.

"How do you know just when to strike?" she inquired of one man.

"Oh, sugar's just like a woman," he rejoined suggestively. "You just feel it, and you know it's ready."

Aurora gasped and blushed, embarrassed by the response. The workers just laughed, and finally, to save face, she joined in, unaware that Salvador was standing in the doorway, scowling ominously. Curtly, after checking to be certain that everything was going smoothly, he ordered everyone back to work, then yanked Aurora roughly from the mill.

Once outside, he shook her savagely.

"Now do you see why I don't want you around the men?" he growled. "They're crude and vulgar peasants— not Spanish *caballeros*."

"They were only teasing me, Salvador," Aurora protested. Though she *had* been shocked by the risqué witticism, it had been mild compared to some she'd heard at the Spanish court. "They didn't mean any harm."

"No? And just what do you think they're going to think about you now after you stood there and listened to that lewd remark—and actually laughed along with them? *Ay, caramba!* What kind of a lady are you?"

"A stupid one, obviously," Aurora retorted, angry now, "since I married a jealous idiot!"

"Don't push me, *querida*," the visconde warned through clenched teeth. "I'm only trying to protect you, yet you seek to thwart me at every turn. Why?"

"Because I don't like being treated as though I were a child! I'm a woman, damn it! Why can't you see that? Everyone else does!"

They glared furiously at each other for a moment, then Aurora pivoted on her heel and walked away. Briefly Salvador stared after her, then returned to the mill to deliver a few well-chosen words to the laborers. After that he left the shed. Though he knew relatively little himself about the harvesting process, he had chosen his men carefully and trusted them to do their jobs well. Aware of his pride and confidence in them, they put forth their very best efforts. Esplendor would have a small but profitable harvest.

Surprised that she had waited for him, the visconde rode back with a stony-faced wife to the house for lunch. Then after a few hours of rest he returned, with Aurora at his side, to the fields. Thus they established a pattern that continued throughout the harvesting process.

Each day, despite her wrath at him over the incident at the mill, Aurora's desire for her husband grew. Salvador, however, was so exhausted at night that he fell into bed and slept immediately, never once touching her, thereby unwittingly increasing her urgency to have him. By the time the harvest was nearly completed, Aurora thought her body would burst with the yearning for him that filled her. She had never in her wildest imaginings dreamed she could want a man so.

The evening before the last field was to be burned and cut, she could wait no longer. She determined that she would have her husband. As they were riding back to the manor, she suddenly reined in her mare.

"I—I've got to go back," she stuttered, flushing, as Salvador drew his stallion up beside her. "I—I dropped my riding crop."

It was the only excuse she could think of, and even to her ears it sounded like a poor reason for returning to the fields.

"Forget it, *querida*," the visconde said. "It's getting dark. We'll find it in the morning."

"No!" Aurora exclaimed, agitated; then at Salvador's startled glance she explained weakly, "I—I think Deleite is coming up lame. I'll have to ride Incendio tomorrow, and—and I'll need my whip to control him. You go on. I'll catch up in a minute."

Of course, she had no intention of doing so. Her plan hinged upon her husband's coming to look for her.

Aurora wheeled her mare around and galloped off before the visconde had a chance to stop her. Slightly perplexed, he gazed after her, pondering her odd behavior. Amazing . . . how she had cantered away so quickly on a mare that she had claimed was coming up lame. Aurora was a superb horsewoman. She knew better than to abuse a mount like that.

Her excuse for returning to the fields was feeble, and there was obviously nothing wrong with her mare. She had deliberately sought to deceive him. But why?

I'm a woman, damn it! Why can't you see that? Everyone else does!

Suddenly a terrible, terrible suspicion occurred to

Salvador as he recalled his wife's words to him the other day.

What's the matter? Are you afraid I might run off with somebody else?

Who was somebody else? Her lover? Was that why she had made the remark? Had she been worried that Salvador had discovered her infidelity? Had she thought subtly to test his reaction to the idea by teasing him? Had she looked relieved at his answer? The visconde couldn't remember. Damn her! Even today, after he'd specifically warned her against it, he had again caught her inside the mill, laughing with the men employed in the shed. Was it—was it possible that Aurora was actually interested in one of *them?* Salvador's hands clenched tightly on his reins at the notion. Impossible! He could not imagine her coupling with one of his own men, and his and Aurora's social acquaintances were few. Rapidly the visconde went over them in his mind.

He dismissed Padre Guillermo instantly. The man was middle-aged and a priest besides, for Christ's sake! Aurora was a devout Catholic. She would rather have died than borne such a sin upon her soul. Coronel Xavier de la Palma was sixty-five, if he were a day. Aurora couldn't possibly be interested in that doddering old man! Or could she? No, surely not. There was the Coronel's lieutenant, however, Miguel Sanchez, a foppish but handsome puppy. Salvador's lips tightened angrily. If Teniente Sanchez were the man, the visconde would kick him aside like a mongrel! Upon further reflection, however, Salvador decided the lieutenant had too great a sense of honor and duty to be trifling with another man's wife.

Well, who else was there?

Paul Van Klaas. Big, good-looking Paul Van Klaas,

with his lion's mane of blond hair and eyes bluer than the delft china of his homeland. Paul Van Klaas, who rode over to Esplendor a good deal more than was necessary for a friendly neighbor. Paul Van Klaas, whom the visconde suspected of being the person who had struck him down from behind that night of the army ants.

Through casual but careful questioning, Salvador had determined that the Dutchman was obsessed with the buried treasure he believed was hidden at Esplendor. It was he who had been digging up the grounds at night. The visconde had seen him late one evening. Upon discovering the identity of the intruder, Salvador had merely laughed to himself and dismissed the guards he'd posted earlier. If Paul Van Klaas wanted to spend his nights futilely shoveling dirt, then let him! Salvador had just been relieved to find it wasn't some vengeful worker he'd fired, out to destroy the crops, a possibility that had also crossed his mind.

But now another horrible thought seized him. What if the Dutchman were *not* obsessed with the buried treasure but had cleverly given that impression in order to hide his true interest at Esplendor? What if Paul Van Klaas's digging were simply a ruse in case he were to be discovered on the grounds at night? Oh, he'd look like a fool, another idiot bitten by the gold bug, out there with a shovel—but nothing more. At least no one would suspect him of having a secret assignation with Salvador's wife. Had Aurora been slipping out to meet the Dutchman? The visconde thought of the night of the storm, when he'd followed her and attempted to force himself on her. *Sangre de Cristo!* Had she even then been running to her lover's arms?

Salvador's stomach churned sickeningly at the idea.

It was he whom the girl had asked to marry her, to protect her from his half brother; but perhaps that had been only because Paul Van Klaas was already wed. Perhaps it was the Dutchman she truly wanted. Maybe *that* was why Paul Van Klaas had tried to kill him! Not because of the buried treasure, but because the Dutchman could no longer bear the thought of Aurora in the visconde's arms.

But she had been a virgin when he'd taken her! Or had she? Such things could be feigned, Salvador knew.

He gnashed his teeth with wrath and frustration at the thought. Well, he was not just going to sit here like an idiot. He was going after his wife and find out the truth—if he had to beat it out of her!

By now it was dark. Aurora had long since found her riding crop, which she had purposely dropped earlier to lend credence to her lame excuse for returning to the field. Now she stood, hidden, among the tall stalks of the last of the cane that was to be burned and cut in the morning.

She had no fear, as she normally would have had, of any creature that might be lurking in the field. She was sure the fires had driven all the animals away. But she *was* horribly afraid of her husband, afraid that he might reject her and that she would never again have the courage to try to win his heart.

She was certain that soon he would come in search of her. It was his duty to protect her; and Aurora knew that even if he had hated her—which he did not— Salvador would still have kept his word of honor to her. Ruthless he might be, but he lived by a gentleman's code nevertheless. Unlike Aurora, who had attempted to deny him on their wedding night, the visconde would never draw back from a bargain, once made.

She bit her lip, for she felt a little silly hiding in the cane, hoping to seduce her husband. She glanced down at her riding habit. Earlier she had taken off her jacket and loosened the top buttons of her blouse to reveal the creamy swell of her pale breasts. A rivulet of sweat trickled down the hollow between them. Aurora wiped it away. At the touch of her hand against her flesh, her nipples hardened of their own accord as she thought of the many times that Salvador had pressed his lips hotly to just that spot. She shivered.

Perhaps she was being too bold, too brazen. Perhaps she should put her hair, which she had unbound, back up and button her blouse. But she could not locate her hairpins, which she had tossed carelessly upon the ground; and her fingers were trembling so badly now with fear and excitement that she could not fasten the tiny pearl studs on her blouse.

At any rate, it was too late to do anything about her appearance. The thunder of Nieblo's hooves over the hard, stubbled earth warned her of the visconde's approach.

Hesitantly, taking a deep breath, Aurora stepped from the shadows to meet him.

The moon was just starting to rise in the black sky, the full silver globe shining bright and beautiful in the darkness; it seemed so close that Aurora felt she could have reached up and touched it. The shimmering haze of moonbeams that streamed down from the heavens illuminated Salvador's troubled face as he drew near. Briefly Aurora shuddered. He looked furious, and she guessed he was worried about her and angry at having to search for her. She decided that she had best act quickly, before she lost her nerve.

"I—I found my whip," she said, holding it up for his inspection and attempting to smile as though nothing were the matter.

"So I see," the visconde responded coldly, a muscle working tensely in his jaw as his eyes took in her tangled mass of hair, cascading down her back, the jacket she carried in one hand, and the open buttons on her blouse.

So . . . it *was* as Salvador had suspected! His wife had indeed been meeting a lover! The visconde glanced about surreptitiously but could spy no one else. Doubtless the man had fled at Salvador's arrival, for from the state of Aurora's appearance there obviously had been no time for the lovers to finish what they had started. The visconde had prevented them from consummating their adulterous act! He could be grateful for that much at least.

"I—I'm sorry I took so long," Aurora stammered nervously at the sight of the forbidding expression upon her husband's dark countenance. He was in a towering rage. There was no doubt about that. Perhaps she should just forget her entire plan of seduction. *Sí*, doubtless that would be best. She swallowed hard. "It—it took me a while to find the whip," she continued lamely. "I was just getting ready to return to the manor when you rode up. I'm—I'm sorry if you're mad about the delay. Would you—would you mind helping me mount Deleite?"

His face now an emotionless mask, Salvador swung down from his saddle.

"I thought your mare was coming up lame," he stated icily.

`"Oh, that." Aurora tried to shrug carelessly but somehow failed. "It—it was merely a . . . rock caught in her shoe. I pried it loose, and she's fine now.

"It's a beautiful night, isn't it?" she asked, hastily changing the subject, for there had never been anything wrong with Deleite, of course. "There's even a breeze stirring. Perhaps it's going to rain. That would be nice. It would cool things off; it was so hot today."

Aurora licked her lips anxiously, aware that she was chattering like Nicolas's monkey and unable to stop herself. She had made a mess of everything! Her plan to entice her husband had failed. He obviously was not interested in her charms this evening. In fact, Aurora thought, the visconde looked as though he wanted to murder her! She was slightly puzzled. Surely even if she had deceived him a little, compelling him to search for her, her intentions had been good; and she did not merit such ire. The way he kept slapping his riding crop against the side of one of his high black boots frightened her. Did he mean to beat her with the whip? He had never struck her before, but there was always a first time. Her upper lip beaded with sweat, and she stepped back, alarmed.

"Is—is something wrong, Salvador?" she questioned nervously.

At her words he lifted one eyebrow devilishly.

"Wrong?" he inquired, his voice low and silky, somehow threatening. "Of course not. What could possibly be wrong?"

"I—I don't know. It's just that you look so—so strange. I thought perhaps something was the matter."

"No, indeed," he rejoined coolly, barely able to repress the overwhelming desire he had to place his hands about her throat and throttle her. "Shall we return to Esplendor, señora?"

Aurora could have sworn he'd sneered the last word, but . . . why? What had she done? Why, it was as though he *hated* her. She quivered with apprehension at the notion. Things had been fine before she had come back for the riding crop; she knew they had been. What had happened between the time she'd left her husband and the time he'd appeared in the field to make him seem as though he despised the very sight of her? All of a sudden she didn't want him to touch her. She shied away as he approached her, intending to lift her into her saddle.

Salvador cursed under his breath at the skittish movement. By God! She had been too good to be taken in the shelter of the hollow log that night of the raging storm; but all the time she had been coupling in the open—in the mud—like a common *puta*, with her lover! It was too much to be borne, and the visconde would not bear it! The *ramera!* He would teach her a lesson she would not soon forget!

With a low growl, roughly, he yanked her to him, snarling his fingers in her hair, compelling her to look at him. His eyes glittered strangely as, startled, Aurora cried out in sudden fear, shrinking from him.

"*Bruja*," he muttered, placing one hand about her throat and tightening his fingers there cruelly. "You are mine, *mine*, no one else's. You belong to me—and me alone—and I shall never let you go. Never! Do you understand?"

Aurora stared at him. Why, she decided, he was jealous of his own men! She remembered how he had looked today, when he'd come to the mill and again found her laughing with some of the workers. He had said nothing more about the matter, however, and she had assumed he'd forgotten it. Now it seemed as though he had not. Once more he was filled with wrath; he looked like a demon in the darkness, she thought wildly.

"Please, Salvador," she breathed. "Let me go— You're you're hurting me and—and frightening me besides."

"You are mine to do with as I please," he replied, his mouth hard and unrelenting. "If I wish to . . . hurt you, frighten you, as you claim I am doing, that is my right. Under the law, I *own* you, Aurora, body and soul, or have you forgotten that?"

"N-no, of course not," she stammered, now utterly petrified.

He could indeed do whatever he wished to her, and she would be powerless to prevent it. According to an archaic law, he was allowed, with a stick as large as his thumb, to beat her; and if he scared her in the process, so much the better. Recalcitrant wives were a nuisance to everyone.

"I'm—I'm sorry you're upset about this afternoon," Aurora offered placatingly. "But—but the men were only teasing me. They—they meant no harm by it, I assure you."

"The men!" the visconde spat. "Do you think I care about them? I know you have no interest in them, señora. They aren't good enough for a . . . *lady* like you," he jeered. "But what of your lover, Aurora, the man whom you came out here to meet, the man whom you have been seeing all along?"

"What?" she burst out, shocked and confused. "My lover! What are you talking about, Salvador? I have no lover but you!"

"Don't you?" He shook her savagely, wanting to hurt her as she had hurt him. "Look at you! Your hair a mess! Your blouse unbuttoned! Doubtless, had I arrived a few moments later, I would have discovered you naked and locked in your lover's arms!"

"No! No!" Aurora protested, horrified. "You don't understand. You don't understand, Salvador! I can explain everything. Please give me a chance to explain. My appearance . . . I did it for you. For *you*, Salvador! Don't you understand? I—I knew you would come searching for me when I didn't return; and I—I wanted to—to seduce you. *Dios mío!* Don't you see? It was *you* I was waiting here for. I hoped that you—that you would make love to me!"

She flushed, mortified by her confession. *Santa María!* How could she have said such shameless, wanton things? How could she not have said them in light of his accusation?

"A likely story, señora," the visconde snarled, his lip curling with disgust, "when you have not given me the slightest bit of encouragement to take you before; when you, in fact, tried to deny me my rights on our wedding night and have made certain that I realized how much you have suffered during our lovemaking since!"

"Oh, no, Salvador! That's not true—"

"Don't lie to me, woman," he breathed, shaking her again. "I know you have no desire for me."

"But I do! I do!" Aurora cried desperately.

The visconde laughed, a horrible, mocking sound.

"Then in that case you shall have me," he said.

Then brutally he caught her blouse at the throat and ripped the thin material down to bare her breasts. Aurora gasped, stricken by his sudden assault. This was not the way she had meant it to happen. She had intended their lovemaking to be a joyous, beautiful, earthy act of passion, not this miserable, ugly, sordid confrontation.

"Stop it! Stop it!" she screamed, lashing out at him viciously with the riding crop she still held in one hand. "How could you do this to me? How could you?"

Again and again she struck him, slashing his shirt to ribbons. Furiously he struggled with her, finally catching her wrist in his iron grip and twisting it cruelly until she dropped the whip upon the ground and, sobbing, crumpled to her knees.

Salvador's eyes glinted in the blackness. With difficulty he restrained himself from hitting her, for the cuts she'd made upon his body stung fiercely. Had she been a man, he would have killed her. He gingerly touched a wound upon his shoulder. His fingers came away covered with blood. His anger renewed, he forced Aurora down upon the earth, paying no heed to her pleas for mercy.

Once more she fought him; but she was no match for his powerful being, and the visconde subdued her easily, pinioning her to the ground, compelling her to face him.

"You said you wanted me, *muñeca*," he growled softly through clenched teeth.

"Not like this. Not like this," she whimpered.

"I see. Your lover is perhaps more tender, no?"

"No... I—I mean I have no lover."

"Oh, but you do, *querida*," he muttered savagely. "You do."

Then he crushed his lips down on hers brutally, possessively, as though to emphasize his point. It happened so suddenly, just as she had imagined it for so many days past, that Aurora was lost.

Blindly her mind told her to break away from him, to run. But at his touch her body refused to respond to her command; with a will all its own it melded instinctively to his, yielded pliantly to his strength. Like a wild thing, she clung desperately to him, as though he might leave her if she did not hold him fast. Her sweet, vulnerable mouth trembled, parted obediently, though his kisses bruised her. He drove his searching tongue into her mouth, and her tongue answered his, fervent with longing. Though her lips felt as though they were on fire, she clung to him, smoldering with desire.

"Sweet, sweet," Salvador murmured, as Aurora gasped for air, her head spinning dizzily, her heart beating fast within her breast.

From above, the moon streamed down brilliantly, enveloping them in a silver haze that seemed to whirl about them before evanescing in the darkness. On all sides the remaining cane stood tall and proud, a sea that waved and rippled with each whisper of the cool, gentle breeze. Beneath them the good rich earth lay like a brown carpet, spreading out in all directions about them.

Of all these things Aurora was only dimly aware, however, her senses overpowered by even more pervasive images: the feel of Salvador's weight upon her body; his hands gliding sensuously, like feathers, across her flesh; the husky warmth of his breath as he whispered in her ear; the spine-tingling touch of his tongue as he probed the small, curved shell.

Anger was gone from his touch, and now she heard words of love and sex she only half understood. She shivered with delight and anticipation as he teased her ear, his teeth nibbling lightly at her lobe.

His mouth fluttered down her slender throat to take possession of that soft place upon her nape. A thrill of quicksilver excitement shot through her veins as his tongue taunted her there, and his teeth nipped her skin. His lips traveled to her naked breasts, and at their touch her areolae flushed like a rosy dawn. Her nipples

puckered, becoming twin peaks of passion that thrust
eagerly against his palms as slowly his hands cupped
the melonlike mounds and squeezed them gently, savoring
their ripe fullness. His thumbs crept up to brush tiny
circles about the hard little cherries that waited expectantly
to be touched and tasted. Bursts of sharp sensation
radiated from the buds in all directions, melting sweetly,
like warm wild honey, through Aurora's body. Involuntarily she arched upward against Salvador's hands. Her
breasts strained against his fingers, aching with desire.

Deep within the dark chasm of her womanhood, a
small spark of wanting ignited, flickered, and took
flame, burning the very core of her, setting her blood
afire. The last vestiges of her earlier resistance faded.
Her hands slid up; her fingers fumbled with the buttons
on her husband's shirt until the studs were freed from
their restraints. Wantonly she pushed the fine linen
material aside, yearning to feel his dark bronze flesh
naked against her own. Her arms slipped beneath the
fabric, tightening around his back, pulling him to her so
her breasts cradled his head.

Her fingers kneaded the muscles in his back, loving
the feel of them as they bunched and knotted beneath
her palms, then rippled free again with his movements.
His skin was damp and silky, the musky, masculine
scent of him emanating from his flesh to mingle sharply,
freshly, with the spicy fragrance of the soap and cologne
he used. His hair smelled of smoke from the thin black
cigars he occasionally enjoyed; and Aurora inhaled the
aroma deeply, liking the woodsy odor that reminded
her of fires burning in winter.

Salvador's mouth found the blushing tip of one of her
breasts and closed about it, sucking greedily, expertly
heightening her longing for him. Lightly his teeth

captured the rigid nipple, imprisoning it for his tongue, which flicked the peak rapidly, like the wings of a moth beating against a blazing candle. Aurora shuddered with pleasure and wanting as tiny electric sparks tingled through her being. Round and round, Salvador's tongue swirled about the stiff bud, bringing it to full flower. Then his lips scorched their way across her chest, seeking the other bloom that unfolded its petals just as readily beneath the nurturing caresses of his mouth and tongue.

His breath coming rapidly, impatiently he yanked away the rest of her garments, wanting to feel the length of her naked body pressed against his own, her flesh molding itself to his. Torn by his haste, his excitement, her clothes fell away to lie in ribbons about her, as though she were a long-awaited package he had eagerly unwrapped. And he—he was well pleased with the contents.

Her skin glistened with sweat beneath the moonlight, the dewy sheen pale and inviting. Languidly she stirred, her ripe lush curves beckoning him on, the black triangle between her legs a mysterious place that lured him like a siren.

His fingers continuing to fondle erotically her erect nipples, he let his lips trail languidly down her belly until they reached the soft dark forest of delight that twined between her thighs. Gently he kissed the ebony down that curled in a riotous tangle over the swells and valleys of her womanhood.

Aurora gasped, for Salvador had never done this before; and although she had to admit it felt delicious, she thought it was shocking too. She made a small whimper of protest, but her husband ignored her, his hands parting her flanks so he might explore the secret garden that enticed him.

He stroked her rhythmically until she was warm and wet with excitement, her deep rose mound pulsating with passion as he teased the tiny button that was the key to her desire. His fingers slipped inside of her, fluttering gently along the length of her, arousing her to a feverish pitch as he found that most sensitive place hidden within. Once more she felt his mouth upon her; his tongue darted out to taste her. She quivered uncontrollably as he taunted her, slowly, slowly, at first, and then faster and faster as she began to writhe sensuously beneath his lips and hands.

A low moan of surrender rose from her throat as helplessly she clutched him to her, her fingers wrapping themselves in his jet-black hair to hold him close. Her hips arched wildly against him, hungry for more, as an unbearable pressure started to build within her, seeking its sweet release. At last it came, violently, like an earthquake, sending shock waves through her body. She cried out wantonly at the ecstasy of it, wanting it to last forever. Again and again the eruptions and tremors shook her until finally they died away, leaving her limp and quivering.

Salvador raised his head and looked at her, taking in, with triumph, her half-closed, passion-darkened eyes; her bruised and swollen mouth; the lush swell of her naked breasts, covered with sweat, rising and falling languorously. Desire inflamed him, overwhelmed him.

"Now," he whispered throatily as he cast away his clothes, "you do that for me, *querida*."

If Aurora had been stunned before, she was mortified now. There was no way she could bring herself to do what he had asked of her. She couldn't. She just couldn't.

But she did. Remembering how her husband had brought her such pleasure with his mouth, she could not now refuse to reciprocate. Still, however, unsure of herself, she postponed the moment as long as possible, taking her time as she began to kiss him, her lips warm and tender upon his mouth and then, in imitation of his own advances earlier, the dark areolae that studded his chest. As her own had done previously Salvador's nipples grew rigid and excited as unwittingly she stimulated him, urging his passion to even greater heights.

Finally, gently, she let her lips slide down his bronze flesh, over the crisp black hair that curled upon his chest and trailed along his firm flat belly to the thick dark forest from which his manhood sprang. Aurora studied surreptitiously, curiously, the proud shaft, marveling at the contrast beneath the hard tumescence and the soft globes that curved beneath it.

Slowly she pressed her mouth to the spheres, felt them move in the pouch that contained them. A strange thrill unlike any she had ever experienced pervaded her being. Never had she been so intimate with her husband. Now a yearning to know every inch of his body seized her in its grasp, and she understood why Salvador had longed to explore and possess her so.

Her lips traveled the length of his bold maleness, covering it with quick hot kisses. Her tongue licked him, tentatively at first, then more brazenly as Salvador began to stir and moan. At last, hesitantly, she took him in her mouth, surprised to find it was not at all the unpleasant act she had thought it would be. His manhood was as much a part of him—the man she loved— as his lips that had kissed her or his arms that had embraced her earlier.

Instinctively her tongue swirled about him, flitting

here and there like the wings of a butterfly, searching out his most sensitive places, as he had done her own. Salvador gasped and shuddered, uncontrollably aroused and delighted.

Why, he is as helpless against me now as I am when he takes me, Aurora thought.

A surge of power rushed through her limbs at the notion, making her feel heady and awesome with its force. She had been a willing slave to her husband's desire; now he would be as much to her own. Elated, as though she had discovered the secret of how to bind him to her forever, she raised up, poising herself above him. Salvador reached out to her, intending to roll her over and press her down upon the rich earth; but, smiling strangely, she eluded his grasp. In moments she had impaled herself upon his sword, her fiery sheath encasing him in a blaze of molten glory.

Like some ancient pagan goddess—her black hair streaming, damp and wild, in a tangled cascade down her back; her pale skin shimmering with a thousand moon-touched beads of passion; her lush scarlet lips parted with feral ecstasy—she rode him.

Salvador, filled with surprise that rendered him temporarily immobile, could do nothing but submit. Was this wanton enchantress really his wife? No, it could not be. She was a witch, a sorceress, ensnaring him with her spell; and he was powerless against her.

Of their own accord his hands closed tightly about her hips, helping her with the motion, urging her on. Like a shiny snake, she held him fast, undulating against him until he believed she would drive him insane with wanting. He cried out hoarsely as his sweet release came, more forceful than any he had ever experienced.

"*Bruja. Bruja,*" he groaned.

Almost simultaneously Aurora reached her peak. She stiffened, arching her back and flinging back her head. Her eyes closed. Her face filled with rapture as a sigh of triumph and satiation escaped from her lips.

Then, as though she had indeed been momentarily possessed by some bewitching spirit, she collapsed upon his chest, grateful for the shelter of his warm embrace that hid her expression from him.

Aurora knew she ought to be shocked, horrified by her behavior. But she wasn't. She was instead quite pleased. She smiled to herself. He was hers—now and for always. She had taken him and made him so.

She did not know the magic she had conjured was ages old and known to every siren who had ever existed. She did not care. It was enough that she had woven a web of enchantment about her husband from which he would never break free, not as long as he lived. She was content.

Cradled in her husband's strong arms, she slept, a passion flower who had come to full bloom at last.

Chapter Twenty-seven

THERE was a thorn on Salvador's rose, and though he had tried to remove it, it had only pierced him deeper and deeper.

Initially he had been overcome and overjoyed by Aurora's lovemaking that night in the cane field. But then later his terrible suspicion that his wife had a lover had returned—and with more anguished certainty than ever.

She had never behaved before as she had that night. Where had she learned those things she had done with such exquisite finesse to him? Not from him, certainly! The thought made his mouth tighten whitely with anger, as it had countless times before since he had decided this was so.

That the way he had explored and caressed her own body had been Aurora's guide in arousing his, complemented by her natural instincts, her desire to please him, and her wish to win his heart, had never occurred to the visconde. No, jealous, possessive man that he was, his mind had leaped immediately to what was to him the most obvious conclusion; and he had yet to realize that it was false. A lover other than himself had taught her the skills she had plied upon him! The fickle jade! The faithless tart! Perhaps she had even betrayed him with more than one man. Did she not laugh and flirt with the laborers like a common harlot? His irrational suspicions ran rampant.

Now, as, disgusted by his spying but unable to help himself, Salvador flattened himself against the side of the house to eavesdrop on his wife and Heidi Van Klaas, he was surer than ever that he was right and that Paul Van Klaas was Aurora's lover—or at least one of them!

"I—I've got to talk to someone"—Heidi's desperate voice wafted clearly through the kitchen window—"and you're the only friend I have in the Amazon Basin, Aurora. Please, will you listen to me, try to help me sort things out? Sometimes I feel as though I'm going mad, and worst of all, I actually hope it's true, because I—I can't bear to believe what I suspect. . . ." Her voice trailed off, and she bit her lip, looking pleadingly at Aurora for a moment before turning away nervously.

"Why, Heidi," Aurora said, concerned by her friend's obvious distress, "of course, we can talk." She laid aside the knife with which she had been chopping meat to prepare hogshead cheese and wiped her hands on her apron. "Come on. Sit down, and let me pour you a cool drink." Aurora mopped her brow. "God knows, this heat is enough to drive anybody insane, and you look exhausted. I should have noticed earlier, but I guess I was just too busy." She pushed her straggling hair back into place and laughed. "I don't imagine I look much better. I must be crazy myself, thinking of cooking on a day like this. It must be well over a hundred degrees in here with that stove burning."

Aurora continued to chatter lightly, distractingly, while she poured the cold tea, grateful that a shipment of ice, packed in sawdust to keep it frozen during its long journey, had arrived just that morning. It was an expensive luxury, one she knew the icehouses in the United States were making a fortune on; but on days like today Aurora would gladly have paid her weight in gold for a single sliver of the precious ice.

She arranged the tall, already-sweating glasses on a tray along with the teapot and a tin of bonbons, which Mario had brought on his last voyage downriver, then moved to join Heidi at the table near the window, where she hoped they might catch a bit of breeze, no matter how small.

"Here. Drink this. Maybe it will make you feel better," Aurora declared as she handed Heidi one of the glasses, "and then you can tell me what's troubling you."

The girl studied her friend quietly while Heidi gulped her tea, her unladylike swallows nearly choking her and her hands shaking so badly, she could hardly hold the glass.

Aurora liked Heidi Van Klaas, who was only a few years older than she was and thus her only contemporary in the Amazon Basin, whose planters mostly numbered elderly martinets and their seemingly even more-aged wives. Most all of the latter were even sterner than their husbands or frail, wispy invalids: for the jungle either made or broke those women courageous enough to face the hardships the verdant tangle offered.

Now, as she glanced at her friend, Aurora thought it

was obvious that Heidi wasn't cut out for such a life. Though she was a pretty woman, with her dark, honey-blond hair and cornflower-blue eyes, she looked as limp and faded as a withering rose.

She's dying on the vine out here, Aurora observed silently, just like Señora de Santa Elena, Don Davíd's fragile wife. Why, oh, why do these men bring such women here? Why don't they take them home, where they belong? Heidi would be so much happier back in Holland, with her dams and windmills, her quaint houses with their half-doors, her tulips and delft china and wooden shoes and all those other things she's told me about. How much stranger Peru must be to her than to me, who was born and bred in Spain. Even now, after all this time, she barely speaks enough Spanish to get by.

Impulsively Aurora took Heidi's hands in her own.

"*Mi amiga*, what is the matter? It is something more than just the heat and the jungle, is it not?"

"Yes, oh, yes," Heidi sobbed pitifully. "It's Paul," she cried, before snatching her hands away to bury her face in her palms.

"Paul?" Aurora repeated, surprised. "Is he ill? Is it malaria?"

She asked the questions out of simple concern for a neighbor, but to Salvador, still listening from outside, it sounded as though his wife were frantic with worry for her lover. He gnashed his teeth with rage at the idea and hoped uncharitably that the Dutchman was indeed about to drop dead. Heidi's next words, however, dispelled any such notion.

"No, it's not that, although sometimes—God forgive me—I wish it were. But you know Paul. He's never sick. He's like an ox, strong and sturdy. And he's a fighter. That's why I love him so much. He's always been so brave and dependable. Even after his father disowned him Paul never despaired. He just laughed and said we'd make our own way in the world; and I—I never doubted him for an instant," Heidi claimed proudly as she brushed the tears from her eyes.

"Then I—I don't understand," Aurora remarked, puzzled. "Is all not going well at Capricho?"

"Oh, yes, as far as I know. But then Paul never tells me anything about business. Still he gives me a generous amount of pin money, and I don't think he'd do that if we were—if we were in desperate circumstances. No, I know he wouldn't. He'd make me cut back on expenses, as he did when his father threw him out. No, Aurora, it's something much worse than that. I—I wouldn't mind being poor. I never had much anyway until Paul married me. It's—it's losing *him* that I know I couldn't bear, and—and that's what's happening. I just know it! Paul is—is seeing another woman!" Heidi cried, then began once more to sob.

Aurora was stunned by this revelation.

"Are—are you sure?" she inquired, puzzled, for it did not seem to her that there was any woman in the Amazon Basin that Paul might be having an affair with.

All the possibilities that came to the girl's mind she dismissed as being too old or too infirm for the Dutchman to take an interest in; and it didn't occur to her to consider anyone who was beneath their own social class and race, because she thought Paul Van Klaas was a snob.

To Salvador, however, Aurora's perplexed query smacked of guilt; and he was certain that she had asked the question only to ascertain whether or not Heidi suspected the identity of her husband's lover. A muscle

worked furiously in the visconde's set jaw as he waited
for Heidi's reply.

"No, I'm—I'm not sure," Heidi rejoined finally. "I—I
mean, what woman ever wants to be certain of a thing
like that? But—but all the signs are there. Paul—Paul's
behavior has changed so drastically. He—he comes and
goes at all odd hours of the night—business, he says,
but I don't believe him. Not when he returns home
with his clothes all mussed and—and reeking of perfume—" She broke off abruptly, starting to weep again.

"Don't cry, Heidi," Aurora commanded soothingly,
patting her friend's hand. "After all, it might not be
true. There are a hundred explanations for something
like that. Paul might indeed be working late. As for the
state of his garments, why, you should see Salvador
when he comes in from the fields! And between the
heat, the humidity, the way he sweats when he labors,
his soap, and his cologne, sometimes I swear he smells
just like he's come from a bordello!"

Heidi's face brightened a little at this.

"Oh, Aurora, do you really think so?" she queried
tremulously, trying bravely to smile.

"Of course. Why, more often than not, Lupe makes
him wash down outside before setting foot in the house!"

Aurora laughed gaily, glad to see that Heidi was
smiling. Salvador longed to beat his wife senseless. The
callous bitch! The deceitful witch! Imagine! The nerve
of her! How cool she was, how clever, slyly allaying
Heidi's fears about her husband. No doubt as soon as
she was able Aurora would warn the Dutchman of his
wife's suspicions, and charming Paul would suddenly
become the most circumspect husband in the Amazon
Basin, causing poor Heidi to feel no end of shame about
doubting his fidelity. The visconde could barely restrain

himself from barging into the kitchen and blurting out the truth to Heidi. But he realized he would only hurt her deeply by such an action and so refrained from it, determining to help her, without her knowledge, by quietly putting an end to his wife's perfidy—if he had to throttle Aurora to do it!

Silently Salvador slipped away from the window, the ache in his heart as painful as the one in Heidi Van Klaas's own. Tormented by ire and grief, he finally managed to compose himself enough to return to his men. Even then he could discover no peace. Instead he scrutinized carefully the face of each one of his workers, wondering which of them had had a taste of his wife.

Chapter Twenty-eight

Belém, Brazil, 1850

Don Juan Rodolfo de Zaragoza y Aguilar, Marqués de Llavero, was like a bloodhound, trembling with excitement now that he had nosed out the scent. After months of diligent inquiries, the greasing of many palms with gold, and other forms of less-gentle persuasion, he had finally picked up the trails of the four people he wanted so desperately to find. They had all left Spain, from the port of Cadíz, and journeyed to the New World. Three of them, Basilio, Francisca, and Salvador, had sailed on the *Santa Cruz*. Aurora, the one whom Juan desired most, had traveled on the *San Pablo*.

To think he would never have discovered this if his secretary Tomás—fearful of losing not only his post, but his life as well, due to his continued failure to locate the refugees—had not become suspicious of the ships' passenger lists. During the months that the first three refugees, and then Aurora, had disappeared, each list bore a single page on which the signatures had been obliterated by large inkblots. Like a carrier pigeon, the marqués had homed in with wicked glee on this circumstance, certain that he was on the right track at last.

At first the captains of the vessels had merely shrugged off his questions about the partially destroyed passenger lists, claiming that such accidents happened. But Juan's evil reputation was not for naught. Relentlessly he had persisted with his soft but sharp queries.

The sly captain of the *San Pablo*, sensing a profit to be made, had wisely reconsidered his previous responses. Don Timoteo was a hard man; his rules were stringent, the man had explained. The marqués had understood and sympathized. Naturally Capitán Desvaido wished to retain his position. The breach of confidence would not, of course, be reported. Juan too was desirous of secrecy in the matter. The captain, thus reassured, his pockets jingling with coins, had been most happy to cooperate.

Sí, he had said, there had indeed been such a passenger as the marqués had described, a young, beautiful woman traveling under the name of Señorita Montoya. She had been accompanied by her younger brother, Nicolas, and a maid, Lupe. The *San Pablo* had deposited them at Belém, Brazil. Where they had gone after that the man did not know. Juan had smiled, well pleased, and left Capitán Desvaido's office.

The captain of the *Santa Cruz* had proven more difficult. He knew his duty, the man had claimed, indignant. He would not be bought off. He had done nothing wrong. The blotting of the page had been an accident. He would report the marqués's questions and attempt at bribery to Don Timoteo at once. Poor, kindly Capitán Perez!

He had been set upon in a dark alley, dragged to a dockside warehouse, and beaten unmercifully.

Sí, he had finally gasped. There had been three passengers who fit Juan's descriptions, a newly wed couple, Basilio and Francisca Montoya, and a lone man who had gone by the name of La Aguila. It had been La Aguila who had bribed Capitán Perez to blot out their signatures on the *Santa Cruz's* passenger list. The money offered had been most tempting, and the captain had seen no harm in what had been asked of him. The *Santa Cruz* had deposited all three in Cuba. The newlyweds had taken a ship to Brazil. La Aguila had embarked upon a vessel bound for *Tejas*, in *los Estados Unidos*.

Juan had smiled, slit Capitán Perez's throat, and left his body to rot in the warehouse.

The marqués had then closed up his townhouse and made preparations to sail to the New World. He had wasted considerable time in Texas and had discovered little. Four men in Laredo had recalled playing cards with La Aguila and a half-breed gunslinger named El Lobo. The two later had been spied leaving town together. Presumably they had been heading for the Llano Estacado, where El Lobo was known to have Comanche relatives.

Juan had seen no sense in risking losing his hair to the pack of red-skinned heathens he would have been forced to confront in order to locate his half brother. Salvador would wait.

So thinking, the marqués had come to Brazil.

Now he stared piercingly at the *mestizo*, Mario, who was standing upon one of Belém's many wharves, supervising the unloading of several dugout canoes.

Instinctively Mario disliked and mistrusted the scar-faced *caballero* from Spain, who was asking so many questions about the lovely Señorita Montoya, now Señora de Rodriquez.

Casually the *mestizo* shrugged. *Sí*, he said, he had indeed been approached by Señorita Montoya. She had wanted to journey to Buenos Aires, in Argentina, Mario lied. He had informed her that she would be better off to travel by an oceangoing ship to her destination rather than downriver by canoe, especially as the Iguazú Falls area was most hazardous.

"If that is the case, why did she wish to hire you in the first place?" Juan inquired suspiciously. "Surely no one in his right mind would embark on a voyage several hundred miles long and through often dangerous country in a mere canoe when a comfortable sailing ship was available for ocean transport to the same city."

Again the *mestizo* shrugged.

"She was searching for her brother Basilio and his wife," Mario began quite truthfully, then went on falsely, "and although she was sure her brother was somewhere between here and Buenos Aires, she was uncertain as to his exact whereabouts. She planned on halting at several towns along the way to look for him.

"Personally I thought the whole trip was a wild-goose chase and suggested she would do better to seek him in the coastal cities—Fortaleza, Rio de Janeiro, São Paulo, Pôrto Alegre, Montevideo—rather than the interior, where few people have settled. But she insisted that her brother was either in southern Brazil or northeastern Argentina, perhaps even as far inland as Paraguay.

"South America is a large continent, señor. Both Brazil and Argentina cover a huge amount of territory. When one throws in Paraguay—and doubtless Uruguay as well, for I have no doubt the señorita eventually would have insisted on adding it to her itinerary, once having learned its location and proximity to the rest . . ."

The *mestizo* made a clucking noise, shook his head, and spread his hands wide.

"Of course, I turned her down. I have a business to run, señor. Naturally I could not waste my time on what certainly would have proven an extensive and doubtless fruitless voyage."

"I see," the marqués said. "Nevertheless, it's very important that I find Señorita Mon . . . toya. She's . . . my betrothed. Do you know anyone else who might have undertaken such a voyage for her?"

Now Mario was more certain than ever that he had been right to mislead the Spanish *caballero*. If Señorita Montoya had been engaged to this man, she would never have married Don Salvador. She was too honorable for that, the *mestizo* thought.

"No, señor," Mario declared with veracity. "Such a man would have to have been *loco*. And though the señorita was beautiful enough for one to have lost his head over her, she did not appear to be the type who would have been a pleasant companion on such a lengthy journey, señor, if you comprehend my meaning." Mario winked and leered lewdly. "Cold, she was, or at least that was my opinion of her," the *mestizo* asserted untruthfully, "and as hard as nails. Struck me as the sort to stick a dagger in a man's back when he wasn't looking."

"*Sí,*" Juan agreed, remembering how the slut had kept her thighs closed tight against him, defending her honor with the china figurine that had marred his face forever.

The peasant was crude and ignorant, too stupid to lie, Juan reasoned, with no cause to conceal Aurora's whereabouts. The girl obviously meant nothing to the informant. With a curt nod the marqués dismissed him.

"*Adiós*, señor," Mario answered, then added softly, so he would not be heard, "*y mala suerte*."

The *mestizo* laughed heartily to himself when some days later he learned the Spanish *caballero* with the ugly scar had booked passage on *La Gaviota*, bound for Argentina.

"SEÑOR, I beg of you, please, give it up," Ijada pleaded, tears of anger and humiliation threatening to spill from her eyes.

Goddamn Paul Van Klaas! She had actually brought herself to grovel before the Dutchman, her heart's desire and her bane. Though she loved him desperately, she would yet kill him for taking not only her body, but her pride. This she knew.

Once, she had been a powerful *bruja* among the Iquitos. But ever since the handsome Indian who had hoped to marry her had followed her, discovered her mating with Paul Van Klaas, and denounced her to their tribe, she had been an outcast, mocked and scorned by her people. She had no magic, they'd said. If she did, why had she fallen prey to the Dutchman's spell? He was crazed, filled with bad medicine, and would be cursed by the ancient gods if he succeeded in finding the treasure that had been stolen from El Dorado. Ijada had lied to the Iquitos, fooled them with tricks. They were ashamed that they had believed in her powers. She was no witch. She was nothing but a lovesick idiot who would bring trouble to the Indians through her association with Paul Van Klaas. Go back to the marble tomb, the tribe had told her, and stay there. You have been tainted by its evil madness, and you will infect us all with it. Do not return to our village. So she had gone. Now all she had left was the Dutchman. She shivered at the thought. His blue eyes were wild and glazed, glittering oddly in the moonlight. He was insane, as her people had said. How could she not have seen it before?

"I have searched everywhere," she insisted. "*You* have searched everywhere, señor. There is no map. There is no fortune! You must cease looking for it—now! —before you—before you lose all sense of reason."

Paul only growled.

"It is there, I tell you. I can feel it in my bones. If I stop searching now, that arrogant Spaniard will find it. I must get to it before he does. I must!"

"Oh, señor. Don Salvador is not even looking for the treasure. He does not believe it exists."

"He is a fool, then," the Dutchman snorted.

"No." Ijada shook her head. "He has made the house come alive again. Work on the west wing is nearly finished. Soon the entire manor will be restored. The fields have been cleared and planted and are now ripe with the harvest. Don Salvador has profited from the sugarcane crop and will make even more next year. He has succeeded, I tell you, because he hasn't wasted his time searching for that accursed fortune, which has caused so many others to fail at rebuilding the plantation. In time, if it continues to progress as it has since Don Salvador's coming, Esplendor will far outstrip the other estates in wealth. If you wish to be rich, señor, you will do well to plow the earth at Capricho rather than dig up the grounds at Esplendor."

"You stupid slut!" Paul hissed, enraged by the *mestiza's* words. "I see now that you have turned against me and can no longer be trusted. I'm very sorry, my little tulip, for your body has given me much pleasure. But now—now I have no further use for you." He stepped toward her menacingly. "You have lost your nerve. I can smell the scent of fear upon you. You believe that Don Salvador possesses some magical power far greater than your own. Stupid woman! He is only a man like any other. But because you think otherwise, I must kill you, Ijada. You will betray me if I don't. You will expose the murders we committed."

"No, oh, no, señor!" the *mestiza* cried, shrinking from his threatening hulk.

"*Sí*. It is so," the Dutchman said softly before he placed his big, spatulalike hands about her throat and began to tighten them, choking her.

Ijada struggled desperately against him, terrified, unable to believe this was actually happening to her, that her lover was strangling her. She clawed wildly at his fingers, trying to rip them from her throat. But it was no use. Paul was too strong for her.

Moments later, after a last, whimpering gasp for air, her body went limp in the Dutchman's grasp. He released her, and her corpse slumped to the ground. He bent over her still figure, methodically searching for a pulse to be certain she was truly dead. He found none. He grunted, satisfied, then began to look for something that might serve as a shovel. A stout, fallen branch, partially hollow and pointed at one end, proved an adequate tool.

Sometime afterward Paul lifted the *mestiza*'s body and lowered her into the shallow grave he had dug in the soft jungle earth. Carefully he buried her, covering the spot with some rocks, dead limbs, and leaves so none would be able to tell the ground had been disturbed. Then he mounted his horse and rode back to Capricho.

Ijada's corpse was never discovered. The superstitious Iquitos, who might have pointed a suspicious finger at the Dutchman, kept silent, afraid of being tainted by his madness as their tribeswoman had been. Those at Esplendor assumed the *mestiza*, unhappy at the manor, had simply left. She had been a strange woman after all, close to none. It did not seem odd that she had told no one of her intention to depart. They discussed her absence briefly, then shrugged. They were relieved she had gone. Only Aurora was upset by the news, for she was now somehow certain that Basilio had spoken truthfully and that Ijada had had something to do with his and Francisca's deaths. Why else would the *mestiza* have disappeared without a trace? There was, in Aurora's mind, only one answer: Ijada was guilty of murder and feared to be found, lest she be tried and hanged for her perfidy.

Perhaps she assumed I had found some evidence that confirmed my suspicions, Aurora thought; maybe I unwittingly frightened her away from Esplendor. But what was it she believed I had discovered? I don't know. Still there must have been something that set her off, something that I'm overlooking. . . .

But though she racked her brain relentlessly, the girl could think of nothing she had learned that might have caused Ijada to suspect that Aurora had finally uncovered the truth about Basilio's and Francisca's deaths.

At last, like the rest, the girl shrugged and let the matter drop. If her brother and his wife had really been poisoned, there was nothing that Aurora could do about it now. The culprit responsible had vanished.

So unbeknown to all but one, the *mestiza* Ijada rotted away less than a mile from the scene of her crimes.

Chapter Twenty-nine

Aurora was filled with dismay. She had thought, after that night in the cane field, that she had won Salvador's heart. Now she was not so certain. Oh, it was true that he spent nearly every waking hour with her, as though he could not bear to let her out of his sight; and before that night this would have brought her much happiness. But the look on her husband's face, when he watched her now, gave her no joy. Though desire for her still burned in his obsidian eyes, in their depths there blazed suspicion as well . . . and something that Aurora could have sworn was hate. She knew that, despite what she had told him to the contrary, Salvador still believed she had taken a lover; and he despised her for it. The only small comfort she found in this was the fact that her husband wouldn't have been so angry and jealous if there weren't some spark of caring for her inside of him. Otherwise Aurora was miserable. How could everything have gone so awry?

Her belief that Salvador was her beloved from the past, the man of her dreams, was again shaken. If it were so, surely he too would have sensed that they

383

were destined to love, that they belonged together—
now and for always. But if he felt this, he gave no sign
of it; and Aurora was assailed by doubts. Could she be
mistaken? she asked herself once more. Was it possible
that her imagination had run away with her again? She
buried her face in her hands and wept at the thought,
for she did not think she could bear it if this were true.
She had been so certain otherwise—once. But now she
admitted that she might have been wrong, that perhaps
she had latched on to Salvador because she had needed
someone so desperately. Sometimes the notion nearly
drove her insane. Oh, God. Perhaps the jungle had
indeed driven her mad, as it had so many others before
her.

She passed many a sleepless night, eaten up by her
doubts and her misery. Mauve shadows ringed her
eyes, and she grew pale and thin from her constant
worry and unhappiness.

Her wan, anxious state did not go unobserved by her
husband. But instead of moving Salvador to pity and
concern, it only hardened his heart. Now that he
watched her so closely, she had no opportunity to slip
away from Esplendor as she had before. She was pining
away for her lover! She was indeed. But that *he* was her
lover, had always been her lover, did not occur to the
visconde. He was so obsessed by rage at what he
thought was Aurora's perfidy, so consumed by hurt at
what he believed was her deceiving of him, so stricken
by panic at the idea of losing her that he could no
longer reason logically. Blinded as he was by his inner
turmoil, he could not see that instead of binding her to
him forever his actions were in reality driving her
further and further away.

He took possession of his wife nightly, as always. But

even his lovemaking was so tainted by his jealousy that neither one of them could find any pleasure in the act. Afterward they lay silently together, Salvador stiff and cold and ravaged by guilt over his often-savage taking of her; Aurora biting her lip so hard she drew blood in an effort to keep from weeping.

Matters grew even worse, if possible, when Heidi Van Klaas drove over to visit, her face blooming radiantly, and confided to Aurora that Paul's behavior was no longer a source of distress.

"He is like a changed man," Heidi reported, blushing as she recalled how Paul had come to her bed late last night. He had been so passionate, so loving, she didn't know how she had ever doubted his fidelity. "He still works hard—and often into the wee hours of the morning—but he's . . . I don't know . . . different some- how, as though he has rediscovered my existence."

"I'm glad for you, Heidi."

Aurora tried to speak cheerfully, but her own misery over Salvador was such that she could take little joy in Heidi's happiness. To the visconde, however, once more eavesdropping on the two women, his wife's lackluster comment was further proof that she had indeed been having an affair with the Dutchman. Why else would she be so unenthusiastic over Paul's renewed interest in Heidi?

At least, Salvador thought grimly, he had managed, with his constant vigilance over his wife, to put a halt to the lovers' meetings. They would not find it so easy to cuckold him again!

Thus determined, he slipped away, his heart as heavy as a stone in his breast.

*   *   *

IT rained and rained and rained. Ceaselessly. Terrifyingly. The Amazon River rose higher and higher with each passing day until it became obvious to all that the giant waterway—no longer a slumbering serpent, but a treacherous snake poised to strike—would soon overflow its banks, flooding the terrain beyond. Of course, this happened every rainy season, when the edges of the jungle became like vast, underwater forests submerged beneath the Amazon; this was what caused the stagnant pools and swamps that remained behind long after the river had receded. But this year it was evident that the flooding would be much worse than usual, perhaps bursting past the sturdy levees that had been constructed over the years to protect the plantations. Every available hand was needed to prevent the river from claiming the estates and perhaps the very lives of those who had carved out a place for themselves by clearing the thick undergrowth. All along the Amazon, every man, woman, and child fought desperately to save what their blood and sweat built.

Salvador and Aurora, their estrangement temporarily forgotten, worked alongside the rest beneath the endless, pouring rain. Even Padre Guillermo, his sodden robes flapping wildly in the gale, took shovel in hand to help.

Under the direction of Coronel Xavier de la Palma, load after load of mud was wrested from the ground by grim-faced, strong-armed men. Burlap sacks were filled to bursting by terrified children and stitched tightly closed by white-lipped women, then positioned along the levee to reinforce the barricade against the tumultuous Amazon.

Though all labored frantically, their efforts to dam the onslaught of the giant waterway were hampered by the horrendous wind and blinding rain; so work progressed slowly. The sky was so darkened by masses of roiling thunderclouds that day and night seemed endless, without demarcation. Torches hissed and sizzled as the pelting rain drowned their light. Thunder boomed deafeningly, making it almost impossible for shouted orders to be heard. Lightning slashed its jagged way across the firmament, eerily illuminating the frenzied figures below. Exhaustion took its toll. Hungry, tired, wet, and cold, those who could carried on mindlessly, like mechanical puppets.

Accidents soon became commonplace. The injured were led away to be treated by Mayor Farolero, from the military outpost, the only doctor in the area. In the slick sea of mud that, like a wall, now strained against the levee and seeped over it, several persons slid and rolled to their deaths below as the madding waters sucked them under. There was no time to mourn. Even Padre Guillermo could do nothing more than hastily cross his breast and mutter a quick prayer to God for their departed souls.

Aurora thought she could never remember a time when she had been warm and dry, when her bones had not ached from her ceaseless exertions. Her fingers felt crippled from sewing shut the burlap sacks all hoped would prove their salvation.

Stitch. Stitch. Stitch. Make a knot. Slice off the cord of sturdy hemp. Move on to the next bag. No time for neat seams.

"Sack ready," she cried until she was hoarse.

Had anyone heard? It no longer mattered. Nothing mattered. Their struggle was utterly hopeless. The Amazon was too vast for them to try to fight it. How long could their pitiful little levee stand fast against it?

Any moment now the water would come crashing through the barricade, sweeping it away as though it were nothing. Never had the river seemed so powerful, so awesome, so overwhelming, as it did now. They were doomed, all of them. Then why did they keep on battling the elements to survive?

"Sack ready!"

Stiff and hurting all over, Aurora stood nearly thigh high in mud as she tried to stretch the kinks out of her painfully knotted back, to restore the circulation in her throbbing limbs and muscles. She was soaked to the skin; her clothes were filthy and plastered to her body; she had eaten and slept only in snatches for the past three days. Painfully she attempted to lug her burlap bag over to the levee but only succeeded in staggering in the mire and falling. She crawled to her knees, grateful—though they had always caused her such unease—for Paul Van Klaas's big strong hands that suddenly swung her to her feet. Caught off-balance, she tripped a little as she tried to gain her footing; and the Dutchman's arms closed about her to steady her.

Tiredly Aurora clung to him briefly, smiling up at him.

"*Gracias*," she said. "I don't think I could have managed alone."

"Think nothing of it," Paul replied as easily he hefted her sack to his shoulder and moved on.

Scarcely a moment later Salvador stood before his wife, glowering at her ominously.

"Isn't it bad enough that you consort shamelessly with that goddamned Dutchman in private?" the visconde yelled at her, snarling as he shook her wrathfully. "Must you make eyes at the bastard in public as well?"

"He did nothing but help me to my feet," Aurora

protested, hurt and angered by her husband's hateful and unjust remarks. "Leave me alone, Salvador. I'm exhausted and in no mood for your ridiculous accusations!"

"No doubt," he sneered, unable to stop the ugly words that rose to his lips. "I'd be weary too if I'd been coupling in the mud like a common *puta!*"

At that Aurora cracked. Her eyes snapping sparks, she slapped the visconde as hard as she could, her hand leaving a bright red palm print upon his face. Then she turned her back on him and, blinded by tears, stumbled toward the house.

It was perhaps a mercy that she did so, for she never saw the brilliant flash of lightning that cut a crooked path down from the heavens to strike a nearby tree. With a crash that rose above the roar of the storm, the gnarled old trunk split with such awesome force that the ground shook. Branches splintered away, flying in all directions. The pungent, acrid smell of burning wood filled the air.

Aurora reeled as though the earth had suddenly dropped from beneath her feet. Tiny tingles of electricity blazed through her body. She knew a ghastly moment of absolute terror—then all was blackness.

There was no time for anyone to warn her. They were all stunned and frozen with horror as they watched the heavy, shattered limb that hurtled toward her, smashed sickeningly against the back of her head, and felled her instantly.

"Aurora! Aurora!" Salvador shouted as he raced toward her inert form lying prostrate upon the ground. "Oh, my God, Aurora!"

His heart pounding with sick fear, he bent over her, searching desperately for some sign of a pulse. It was there. Barely. She lived. Somehow she yet lived. Fran-

tically he ripped off his drenched shirt, trying to staunch
the flow of blood that gushed from the ugly wound on
the back of her head. He lifted her up, cradled her
broken body tenderly in his arms, and staggered toward
Esplendor, terror-stricken, calling all the while for Mayor
Farolero.

Oh, God. Where was he? Didn't the doctor understand that every minute, every *second*, was precious?

Salvador held the light of his life in his warm embrace, and though the flame flickered faintly, he knew it
was very near to being extinguished forever. Feverishly,
as though he could somehow keep her alive by his will
alone, he kissed Aurora's pale still countenance again
and again as he staggered toward the manor.

It was not until he tasted the salt, bittersweet upon
his lips, that the visconde realized that tears of anguish
and remorse were streaming down his cheeks, falling
upon the deathly white face of his beloved.

BOOK FOUR

Hold Fast

Chapter Thirty

Esplendor, Peru, 1850

"WILL she—will she live?"

Mayor Farolero sighed and shook his head as he gazed at the tormented man standing before him.

"I must be honest with you, Don Salvador," the doctor replied quietly. "I don't know. I have done all I know to do, but the blow was very severe. It is a wonder her neck was not broken. However, the laceration, while very nasty, does not appear to have punctured the brain. I am therefore at a loss to explain your wife's coma. Under the usual circumstances she ought to have regained consciousness by now. It's most puzzling to me why she has not. I'm afraid there may be some damage to the brain."

Turning aside to allow the stunned and grieving visconde a few moments of privacy in which to regain his composure, the weary Mayor Farolero dropped into his bag the complicated medical instruments of his profession. Then, slowly, glad of a brief respite from his recently endless labors, he removed his wire-rimmed spectacles and polished them clean with his handkerchief. Like everyone else, he was exhausted; and he had seen too many horrible injuries—fingerless hands, mangled arms, crushed legs, punctured lungs—these past few days to be moved by one more.

"There is more, Don Salvador," the physician went on, hating to burden the visconde further but realizing the truth had to be told. "If my analysis is correct—and I feel certain that it is—I must warn you that if Doña Aurora *does* recover, she may no longer be the woman you knew. Head injuries are unpredictable and most difficult to treat. At best, the victim sustains nothing more than a simple concussion. At worst, the victim survives but as little more than a vegetable. The majority of cases that do not end in death usually fall somewhere in between; that is, there may be a skull fracture—extremely likely in your wife's case, I should think. There may be some degree of cerebral edema, which puts pressure on the brain—in this case, very probably a subarachnoid hemorrhage. However, generally speaking, the blood clot will be spontaneously absorbed and need not concern us. What is more important is that various nerve centers of the brain may be affected, causing certain impairments to both the mind and the body. I will not know for sure until your wife comes out of her coma, but one or all of her faculties may have been damaged extensively—perhaps permanently—by the blow.

"Part or all of her memory may have been wiped clean. There will probably be pre- and post-traumatic amnesia; that is, your wife will not recall the events immediately prior to her injury and following her regaining of consciousness. She will have headaches and dizziness for several weeks and may also prove irritable, restless, and extremely depressed. She may be prey to recurring, convulsive seizures. She may be unable to concentrate and therefore unable to comprehend anything said to her. She may have trouble speaking. She may suffer from some form of paralysis.

"If Doña Aurora does come out of her coma, and such localized damage as I have described has occurred, it may be—and we must hope it indeed will be—only temporary. Your wife may be like a child for a few months or perhaps for years. She will have to relearn such basic accomplishments as walking, talking, et cetera; and she will need the utmost of care and patience in order to achieve this.

"In the unlikely but fortunate event that there is no impairment whatsoever, she will still require the same treatment accorded any person who has suffered a traumatic shock: absolute quiet; extensive bed rest; lots of liquids; light, nourishing broths and then gradually more substantial meals as she is able to consume them; no activity at first, but then a little exercise, such as a short walk each day until she is completely well.

"Other than this, I know of nothing more to tell you, Don Salvador. I'm sorry. As for the rest, I'm afraid we must take a 'wait and see' attitude. As I said, Doña Aurora may not even regain consciousness. The thread that holds a comatose person suspended between life and death is a slender one indeed."

"I understand, Mayor Farolero," replied the visconde gravely but calmly, having attained some mastery over his emotions. "Thank you for coming. I know these past few days have not—have not been easy for you—for any of us."

"Sí, that is so," the doctor agreed. "We must thank God that the rain appears to be diminishing, and that, so far, the levee is holding. There has been some flooding, of course, but not nearly what we would have sustained otherwise. God has indeed been merciful."

"*Sí*," Salvador responded, but his tone was bitter.

If God had not sent the relentless rain to begin with, the Amazon River would not have overflowed its banks so much farther than usual, and there would have been no need to reinforce the protective levee; no need for Aurora to be breathing so shallowly, to be lying so still, to be hovering so heartbreakingly close to death.

A pall hung over Esplendor. Work on the great house had ceased, for Salvador had insisted on absolute quiet for his beloved. Those at the manor spoke in hushed whispers, when they spoke at all—for none dared to disturb *el patrón*, who had been like a madman since his wife's terrible accident.

Those who had witnessed the violent argument between the couple right before Aurora had been struck down suspected—and quite rightly so—that the visconde was eaten up with guilt and sorrow. Private scenes were bad enough—and every couple suffered them after all—but to wash one's dirty laundry in public . . . *ay, caramba!* What a disgrace! How could *el patrón* have been so tactless, so cruel? No one knew—least of all Salvador. Something inside of him had snapped when he'd seen his wife in the arms of Paul Van Klaas. A *common* puta, the visconde had called her. To think that if she died, those were the last words he would ever have spoken to her.

Oh, God. Truly he was accursed—and, what was even worse, he was accursed by his own hand. For once, Salvador did not blame misfortune on the black

cloud of foreboding that he felt hung over him. No, the
fault was his—and his alone; and his self-recrimination at
the thought was bitter indeed. Aurora had been safe and
well until his ugly suspicions had gotten the better of
him. Had he not stood there, angrily shouting those
horrible accusations at her, she would not have run into
danger.

Though Lupe and Nicolas both had offered to assist
him in his constant vigil at Aurora's bedside, the visconde
would have none of it. Almost superstitiously he feared
that if he were not with her every minute, his wife's
tenuous hold on life would loosen, and she would slip
away.

Once each morning and evening Salvador raised her
comatose body, propped her up among the pillows, and
carefully cleaned the ghastly wound at the back of her
head, terrified that otherwise gangrene might set in, as
it so often did in the awful tropical heat. And each time,
as the visconde unwrapped the bandages that protected
the gash, his heart thudded in his breast, for he was
afraid he would see the telltale, rotting flesh that heralded
the onslaught of the infection. To Salvador's relief,
however, the wound appeared to be healing properly.
The angry red streaks and pus that had marked it
earlier were gone, leaving an encrusted scab, hard and
dark against the soft white of Aurora's scalp, which
shone in a little circle where they had cut away her hair.

The physician, Mayor Farolero, had wanted to shave
her entire head. But the visconde had refused permission for this, certain that if Aurora did awaken, she
would be appalled by the loss of her ebony tresses, for
he knew her thick, glossy black hair was his wife's one
secret vanity. Salvador diligently kept the strands pulled
away from the gash, brushing and braiding the locks

tightly each day. If she recovered, Aurora would be able to hide the bald spot until her hair grew back there.

Knowing how she valued cleanliness, the visconde himself bathed Aurora daily and lightly scented her temples and wrists with her jasmine perfume.

He kept a pitcher of cool water by her bed as well; and every so often he laid a soothing cloth upon her forehead or pressed one to her lips to keep them moist in hopes that a little of the water might find its way into her body and prevent her from dying of thirst. She was not allowed to drink anything, of course. In her comatose state she might easily choke to death.

And all the while, Salvador talked to the unconscious girl, carrying on conversations with her as though she could hear and understand and reply.

"Do you know the first time I ever saw you, *querida?*" he asked. "It was aboard the *Santa Cruz*. I was fleeing from Spain, from our homeland, as were your brother Basilio and his wife, Francisca. They did not have enough money to pay for first-class passage on the ship, so I purchased Basilio's pocket watch from him. Later in my cabin I opened the timepiece so I might hear the chimes once more, and there you were, gazing out at me with your sapphire-blue eyes. I thought you were the most beautiful woman I had ever seen; and in that moment I knew I loved you, *muñeca mía*. I have never stopped loving you since.

"Listen." The visconde sprung the clasp of the watch so it began to play the sad, haunting melody that had always moved him so. "It is a song of love, is it not? If the tune had words, this is what it would say."

Quietly Salvador started to sing. His voice broke with heartache at first, but gradually he controlled it and

went on, his tone filled with all the love and longing he
had for his wife.

> *"Te amo, mi alma, ahora y siempre.*
> *Aunque separado en esta vida,*
> *A los muertes, seremos libre*
> *Reunirnos. Mi corazón, recuerda."*

> I love you, my soul, now and always.
> Though separate in this life,
> At death, we will be free
> To reunite. My heart, remember.

Slowly the visconde closed the timepiece, then checked
to be certain the mosquito net was still securely fastened
about Aurora's helpless figure. He continued to talk to
her, sure that the sound of his voice penetrated some
dark recess of her unconscious mind, giving her the
strength and will to survive.

In the evenings, he lay beside her, cradling her
tenderly against his body, turning her still form several
times during the night so she would not develop bedsores.

Naturally his prolonged watchfulness over Aurora
took its toll on Salvador. He slept only in snatches,
jerking into wakefulness the minute he realized his eyes
had closed. Immediately he would bend over his wife,
listening intently for the sound of her shallow breathing, afraid she had died while he'd slumbered; and each
time, he sighed with relief upon finding she yet lived.

Mauve shadows ringed his eyes. He had not bathed
or shaved for days; and he had grown gaunt and thin as
well, eating mechanically and only when Lupe towered
over him, glowering with concern, practically forcing
each bite into his mouth.

Over and over, constantly, he prayed to God to spare Aurora's life.

"I will release her from her marriage vows; I will stand aside and let her go to the Dutchman, if that is what will bring her happiness. I will do anything, God, if only you will let her live. I lost her once, to death, in another life. Was that not punishment enough for my sins?"

For some way, in his tortured, grieving mind, the visconde had arrived at the conclusion that he had lived once before as Don Santiago Roque y Avilés, that in some past life he had been the accursed madman who had built Esplendor as a monument to his beloved Doña Arabela . . . Aurora. Why else had Salvador felt as though he had come home when first he'd seen the manor? Why else had he known his way unerringly about the house? Why else was the visconde so sure the madman's treasure was not buried on the plantation grounds, but was instead an intangible thing, a secret of the heart waiting to be revealed only to those worthy of the knowledge?

I could learn the answer, Salvador thought, but only with Aurora. . . .

"Aurora. *Aurora*," he cried.

As though he had somehow reached her at last with his anguished wail, the girl's eyes fluttered open. She thought she must be dreaming, for all was darkness, and it sounded as though her husband spoke to her from far away.

"Sal—Salvador," she murmured, dizzy and confused.

His heart leaped with incredible joy at the sound of her voice. Scarcely daring to believe she had regained consciousness, the visconde jumped to his feet and pushed back the mosquito net to take her into his arms.

"Aurora! Thank God. Aurora!" He laughed and wept as he hugged her near, as though fearing that if he let her go, he would lose her forever. "You're awake! You're alive!" Then, more gently, "Oh, *querida*, how do you feel?"

"My—my head aches," she stammered, still highly disoriented.

She could speak at least. That was something, and she appeared to be able to move. Hope that she was undamaged soared in the visconde's breast.

"*Sí*, there was an accident," he explained. "It was storming, and we feared the Amazon would overflow, flooding the terrain beyond more than usual. We were working, trying to reinforce the levee. A bolt of lightning struck a nearby tree. It . . . shattered; branches flew everywhere. One of them—one of them . . . hit you. You don't remember? Of course, the doctor said you would not."

"No." Dazedly, Aurora put her hand to her head, feeling gingerly the bandages wrapped about her. "It just seems like all of a sudden everything went—went dark," she said, "so dark. Salvador, my husband, light a lamp so I can see you. . . ."

At her words his heart suddenly stopped beating, then lurched on. His high hopes for her well-being splintered into a million pieces. How could he tell her? Oh, God, how could he tell her? Silently Salvador gazed at the brilliant sunlight streaming in through the bedroom's open French doors, softly illuminating his wife's pale, lovely countenance; her wide deep-blue eyes.

"Oh, *querida*," the visconde breathed, then broke off abruptly, his heart aching with hurt and pity for her. "Oh, *querida* . . ."

Aurora, his beautiful, beloved Aurora, was blind.

Chapter Thirty-one

THE physician, Mayor Farolero, sighed as he held the lighted candle close to Aurora's eyes, then moved it away, then back. It was as he feared. There was no contracting or dilating of the girl's black pupils in response to the flame.

He licked his fingers, pinched the wick, then set the brass candlestick down upon a nearby table.

"Well?" Aurora asked, already knowing and dreading the answer to her question.

"It is, as I surmised, one of two things," the doctor said. "You may be suffering from hysterical blindness, something that usually occurs after the victim has witnessed a horrifying episode with which he or she mentally cannot cope and therefore attempts to block out of his or her mind by not being able to see anything at all. The condition is treatable; and the victim usually recovers with no difficulty once he or she is brought to face up to and deal with the terrifying scene viewed.

"However, it is my own opinion that hysterical blindness does not apply in this case, as the sight of a lightning bolt striking a tree is hardly a traumatic visual experience, which leads me to my second theory.

"I am sorry to tell you this, Doña Aurora, but I think it is far more likely that there has been some sort of damage done either to your optic nerve or to your visual cortex. How much impairment there is, in that case, I don't know. It may be only a very slow-healing contusion, and your blindness will thus be temporary. On the other hand, the damage may well be extensive, and your blindness will therefore prove permanent.

"It is too early, of course, to know anything for certain. However, in all fairness and kindness to you, Doña Aurora, I feel that you should, while naturally hoping for the best, prepare yourself for the worst; that is, that you will never be able to see again."

"I . . . see." Aurora spoke slowly, without thinking, then, upon realizing what she had said, gave a small, brittle laugh. "I guess I should have said, 'I understand,'" she intoned bitterly. "Well, thank you for your honesty, Mayor Farolero. If you—if you don't mind, I'd like to be alone now."

"Of course. I'll stop by in a few days or so to check on your progress. *Buenos días,* señora."

After the physician had departed Aurora sat silently for a very long time, absolutely devastated by the news she had just received. It wasn't true. It just couldn't be true!

Blind. She was totally blind—perhaps permanently. She stared at the darkness that engulfed her. Perhaps that stark, utter blackness was all she would ever see from now on. It just didn't seem possible. It just didn't seem real. Surely it was all just some abominable mistake. Surely God couldn't have been so cruel, so unfair, as to have robbed her of her sight!

A thousand memories overwhelmed her: images of the brown-and-ocher plains of the Spanish *meseta* stretching out in all directions, the splashes of color that were the gardens at Aranjuez, the brilliant costumes of the *toreros*, the grey-green of the Atlantic Ocean beneath an endless azure sky, the verdant tangle of the jungle threaded with exotic tropical flowers of every hue and animals of every kind, the muddy yellow of the vast Amazon River that had inadvertently caused the loss of her vision.

Oh, God, never to see any of it again. It just couldn't be true! It was too painful to be endured. Surely the darkness would lighten soon, and Aurora would be able to see again. Yes, in a few moments she would be fine. What did that poor excuse for a doctor know anyway? He couldn't be any good at his profession, or the military would never have posted him to such a remote area of Peru.

She would close her eyes and sit quietly for a minute, taking slow deep breaths; and when after a time she once more opened her sapphire-blue orbs, the blackness would be gone, and she would be able to see again.

But it was not so.

After a while, still unable to believe, to accept, what had happened to her, Aurora pulled herself to her feet. Her head ached horribly. She felt dizzy, and she wanted to lie down again. She moved from the chair by the French doors, to which Salvador had carried her earlier, and bumped into a small occasional table. She stumbled and fell, bringing the table crashing down with her. The porcelain bric-a-brac that had sat upon the table smashed upon the floor. She groped for something to hold on to, to pull herself back up with, and only succeeded in toppling over the fallen table and cutting herself on a shard of china. Utterly overwhelmed and defeated, she sank to her knees and wept bitterly at the terrible reality of her blindness, so cruelly brought home to her.

Aurora could only imagine the awful, pitiful spectacle she presented; and when Salvador, upon hearing the commotion, rushed into the chamber to help her, she shouted at him hysterically.

"Get out! Get out!" she screamed and, with her fists, lashed out at him wildly as he tried to raise her to her feet. "Get out, and leave me alone!"

The visconde, his heart wrenched by the sight of her, did not know what to do. Although Mayor Farolero had prepared him for this, still somehow he had not expected it. At last, overcome by his own helplessness in the matter, he left the room, quietly closing the door behind him.

Aurora, feeling that her young life was at an end, cried herself to sleep upon the floor.

ONCE the initial shock of her blindness had lessened, Aurora did not, as Salvador had hoped, make any effort at accepting and coping with her condition. Instead, severely depressed, she lay in bed, totally consumed by self-pity. Other than her short, necessary walks to the chamber pot, which she had had Lupe move as close to the bed as possible, Aurora made no attempt to rise, to bathe, or to dress. After all, she asked herself, what was the use? She could not see herself, and she didn't want anyone else to see her either. After her first disastrous try at eating she subsisted totally on cups of soup and slices of toast, for neither required that she manage any silverware. She had become, the visconde thought, like an animal, for he scarcely recognized the alternately wild and withdrawn woman who was his wife.

Always so clean before, Aurora was now filthy. Her

once-shining mass of black hair was a dull, tangled mess of snarls. The nightgown she wore constantly was dirty, stained with spilled soup and reeking of sweat, for, as an aftereffect of her accident, she perspired even more profusely than normal in the tropical heat.

The bed where she and Salvador had once made love was just as repugnant. The sheets had not been changed in weeks. The mosquito net was clotted with insect dung.

Frustrated and miserable because he could not help the woman he loved, the visconde paced restlessly, ceaselessly, in the room across the hall, into which he had been forced to move, Aurora having made it clear that she did not desire his presence. He racked his brain endlessly for an answer to the dilemma posed by his wife's behavior. There must be some way to aid her. What was he doing wrong?

Although Salvador understood and sympathized with Aurora's plight, he felt in his heart that it was wrong and cowardly of her not to face her blindness, to learn to deal with it. For over a month he had tried being kind and patient with her, and he had failed. Today the visconde decided grimly that he would attempt another way.

Determinedly he opened the door of her chamber. As usual, upon discovering that it was he who stood there, Aurora greeted him with a barrage of vituperative remarks. This time, however, Salvador refused to bend to her demands that he leave her alone. Though it took all of his strength and willpower to be hateful to her when he loved her so, nevertheless, he remained adamant about his intention.

"No, I will not go," he announced coolly, meanly, "not today, not ever again. I am tired of your childish sulks and your self-pity, and I do not intend to endure either another minute. You have upset the entire household long enough."

"They're upset! *They're* upset! What do they know about it?" Aurora spat. "They're not the ones who are blind. Blind, do you hear? B-l-i-n-d!"

His heart ached for her. Despite the decision he had reached earlier, it was all the visconde could do to bring himself to continue. But he did, coldly, as though she were indeed a bad-mannered child indulging in a tantrum.

"This sarcasm ill becomes you, Aurora. I can spell as well as the next person. *Sí.* You are blind, perhaps permanently. We all know it; you have made certain of that. But you are not dead, and I will not allow you to bury yourself alive in this room simply because you do not have the courage to go on living!"

If her husband had slapped her, Aurora couldn't have been more stunned. She had known him to be ruthless, but she had never believed he could be so cruel.

"Oh! How can you say such despicable things to me?" she wailed, deeply hurt, unable to see the pain etched plainly upon his own face at having to wound her so.

Salvador decided then and there to tell her the truth about his feelings for her. Perhaps if he had told her before, explaining his fears about being accursed and not caring whether or not she scorned him and thought him mad, Aurora would not have reached this terrible impasse. Secure in the knowledge of his love for her, she might have held out her hand to him and asked for his help. Together they might have been able to overcome the tragedy that had befallen them.

"I say such things because I love you, *querida,*" the visconde informed his wife softly, "and you are killing me inside."

Aurora's heart lurched queerly at his confession. For a moment she could not believe she had heard him correctly. Oh, God. The man was a monster! More hateful than she had ever imagined! How dare he come here and mock her so, she, who was helpless? What she would have given once to hear those words! Now—now they sounded as bitter as the relentless thudding of her heart, which for some strange reason went on beating, even though she knew her life was over. Salvador loved her? No, it was not so. He had insulted and humiliated her with the very suggestion. He only felt sorry for her—and she did not want his pity.

"What perverse cruelty makes you taunt me so?" she asked miserably, injured to the very core of her being by what once she would have given her very life to know. "Get out, and leave me alone. I hate you!"

Oh, if only she could have seen how her husband's dark face twisted with agony at that. But she could not.

Salvador inhaled sharply. It was as he had feared. His wife did not care about him. She never had.

"I—I'm well aware that you do not love me, Aurora," the visconde managed to say calmly so she would not suspect how she had hurt him. "I know it is the Dutchman, Paul Van Klaas, who holds your heart. If—if he is what you desire, I will release you from your marriage vows to me, and you can go to him, if that is what you want. I will do anything you ask, if only you will get out of that bed, and start living again."

Aurora turned her sightless eyes toward her husband, incredulous. *Madre de Dios.* He truly believed that awful accusation he had made that night in the cane field—and again the day of her accident. That she had a lover. The Dutchman, Paul Van Klaas. The man whose hands had always evoked such unease in her.

The thought of those hands ever caressing her body was so ludicrous to her that she started, to Salvador's surprise, both to laugh and to cry.

"You fool," she choked out bitterly. "You utterly stupid, stupid fool."

Whatever the visconde had expected, it certainly was not this. He shifted uncomfortably on his feet, as though he had in some way made some dreadful faux pas. He flushed at the notion.

"If I have made a mistake—" he began, only to be interrupted by Aurora.

"Oh, *sí*, you have indeed," she claimed, jeering at herself as well as him, "but don't worry, Salvador. Your precious pride is still intact, for I have been an even bigger fool than you." What did it matter if she told him the truth now? He could hurt and humiliate her no worse than he already had. "You see," she declared, "I have given my heart to a man who thinks I am no better than a dishonorable, lying trollop; a man who believes I have adulterously deceived him with my best friend's husband!"

Then she flung herself onto her pillow, crying out her heart and soul.

Now it was the visconde's turn to stare, for he could not believe what he had just heard. Was it possible that his wife had spoken the truth, that he had been mistaken about her having an affair with Paul Van Klaas? Dear Lord. Salvador's heart leaped in his breast. Aurora had just told him that she loved him! She loved *him!*

"Aurora, *querida*, please don't weep." He moved to take her in his arms, filled with joy and yet stricken with remorse. God in heaven, what must she be thinking of him? No wonder she hadn't believed his profession of love for her. "I'm sorry. Oh, God, you don't know how sorry I am that I ever suspected you of being unfaithful to me. I didn't know. I didn't know," he reiterated lamely in the face of her rejection of him.

"Go away!" she ordered curtly, not caring that she had bared her true feelings for him at last. What did it matter what he thought? she asked herself again. Her life was in ruins anyway. "I don't want your pity! *Sangre de Cristo!* What a fool indeed I have been!" She gave another harsh, brittle laugh, then went on feverishly. "Do you know that in Spain I had but to look at a man to know he was not for me? That, much to my family's despair, I turned away every rich, handsome young *caballero* who courted me, cut them all off without a single explanation? I couldn't tell them, you see, that I dreamed of but one man, a lover from a past life, who haunted me still.

"You didn't know you had wed a heretic, did you? Oh, *sí*, I am certain my soul is mortally damned for such a belief. But I don't care. I don't care!" Aurora whispered fiercely. "I would have braved even the flames of hell for the man I loved!

"That day I came back to Esplendor and saw you standing on the steps, I knew you were my beloved from the past, the man of my dreams. I loved you then, and I love you now. The very idea of another man, especially Paul Van Klaas, touching me makes me ill. There has never been anyone for me but you, Salvador. I thought—I thought you felt it too, that we belonged together, that we were . . . soul mates, if you like. But I was wrong. I searched a hundred lifetimes for you, and you didn't even recognize me! Now, please. Go away, and leave me alone. And take your pity with you. I hope—I hope you choke on it!"

A joy such as he had never known in his life took hold

of Salvador. His heart soared so high, he thought it must have wings.

"Oh, Aurora, Aurora. *Mi corazón. Mi vida. Mi alma.* How could I ever have doubted you? What a mess we have made of things. Don't you understand? We have been at cross purposes all the while. I have loved you since time's beginning, and I will go on loving you until its end. You see, *querida,* I did feel it too. Only I thought you did not, that you would think me mad if I spoke what was in my heart and soul; and I—I feared to love you as well because—because I thought I was accursed. Everyone I've ever cared for has been torn from me, and I—I did not want to lose you in this life as I had before. . . . Oh, *muñeca mía,* I pity you, *sí,* for your blindness is a tragic thing. But, more than this, I love you. *I love you,* do you hear? Oh, *querida.* We have waited so long to find each other. Do not now turn me away. You are the very light of my life. Without you my world would be as dark as the one you now see."

He had spoken so earnestly that Aurora could not now doubt him. She was appalled by her own previous silence. Oh, God. If only she had not been so proud. Time was so precious, and they had wasted so much of it.

"Oh, Salvador," she whimpered pitifully, torn between the overwhelming joy he had brought to her and the belief that now she could be nothing but a terrible burden to him, a millstone about his neck for the rest of his life. "Why do you tell me this now, when I am blind? *Blind!*" she sobbed, turning away, suddenly horrified by her filthy being and ashamed of the way she must look and smell to him.

The visconde took a slow deep breath. Whether or not the rest of his life would prove an empty, barren wasteland or a rich garden of love depended on what he did in the next few minutes—and he knew it.

"Give me your hand," he commanded quietly, knowing his wife's thoughts in that moment as well as he did his own. His palm closed tightly about her own. Gently, he led her to stand before the French doors that opened out onto the gallery. "The rain has stopped, *querida*," he said, his voice like a paintbrush sweeping across a canvas. "The sky is washed clean and blue by the gold of the sun and filled with clouds so white and soft they make you long to reach up and sink your hand down into them. In the distance, where the heavens meet the earth, the jungle stretches out endlessly in all directions, a lush green forest ablaze with glorious colors, enough to rival a rainbow—and more. The muddy yellow Amazon, still swollen, winds its vast way, like a giant anaconda, through the basin, rippling like a sea against the shore. The cane fields gleam black and stark against the horizon, waiting to be plowed and strewn once more with tall sweet stalks that waft gently in the sultry tropical breeze. The coffee plants grow rich, their leaves whispering to the banana and pineapple trees that shade them." He paused, waiting for her to absorb this, then asked softly, "Can you see it, Aurora?"

Her heart swelled with happiness, understanding his intent. He could not bring back her sight, but he was offering her the gift of his own. Aurora had never loved her husband more than she did now in this precious, intimate moment, which she knew she would treasure as long as she lived.

"*Sí*. Oh, *sí*, Salvador! I can see it all, as though I gazed upon it myself."

The visconde turned and kissed her passionately, with all the love for her that filled his heart and soul.

"You are not blind, *querida*," he breathed, "for as you are the very light of my life, so I will be yours, now and for always."

Chapter Thirty-two

"No. Try it again, and this time, walk normally, *querida*. That is the whole point. Otherwise, as you gain confidence in yourself and your ability, you will revert to your usual stride anyway, and the count will be wrong. Besides, taking those tiny steps makes you look like one of those mincing fops who used to prance about the Spanish court."

Aurora giggled, her face beaming with joy that was reflected on Salvador's own. How strange to think that out of her blindness had been born more happiness than either of them had ever known. It did not seem possible; but it was so.

"Oh, no!" she wailed with mock indignation, still laughing. "Do I really?"

"Indeed you do, *muñeca*," the visconde responded, grinning. "*Bruja!* Stop dallying, and try it once more."

"Oh, all right. But I warn you: If I topple into the bathtub again, it will be all your fault!"

"Agreed," Salvador answered, glad and grateful that his wife had at last come to terms with her blindness and was even able to joke about it occasionally. "Count," he ordered as she began to walk toward the hammered-brass bathtub that sat to one side in the bedroom, which they once more shared.

"One, two, three... seven steps!" she crowed triumphantly, her lovely countenance flushed and glowing with pleasure as she bent down, and her hands found the edge of the bathtub, positioned exactly where she had guessed it was. "I could sense it, Salvador!" she exclaimed excitedly. "I could sense it was there, before me."

"*Bueno!*" he praised and applauded her. "Now let's see how good you are at taking off that nightgown and bathing yourself, ragamuffin."

"Oh, señor," Aurora tittered, fluttering her eyelashes like an innocent maiden. "I'm afraid, after that remark, I must ask you your intentions toward me, for I fear they are not at all honorable."

"I'll turn my back," the visconde promised with false solemnity, a willing participant in her game.

"Liar!" the girl accused, blushing as she began to remove her negligee. "I can already feel your eyes upon me, wicked man! And, believe it or not, I even know the expression on your face."

"You do, eh?"

"*Sí*, I do," Aurora claimed, most emphatic. "You are smiling that lopsided grin of yours, and your black eyes are dancing and yet blazing at the same time with that flame of desire that always makes them look as though they are smoldering embers."

"Such poetic thoughts you have," Salvador mused as he lit a thin black cigar. "Have you ever considered becoming a writer? You might even rival Miguel de Cervantes. You could create a female Don Quixote."

"No. No tilting at windmills for me," Aurora replied

cheerfully as she stepped into the bathtub and carefully lowered herself to a sitting position in the water. "You are a far more likely candidate for that. In fact, Pancho has always reminded me of fat Sancho Panza."

"My valet would be delighted to hear that, for I do believe he has always fancied the role," the visconde announced. "Dear Dulcinea, say you will be mine, and we will mount my faithful steed, Rosinante, and ride off together in search of adventure."

"I have enough of that right here," Aurora asserted as she reached hesitantly toward the special shelf that Salvador had had one of his men build for her. It fastened right onto the edge of the bathtub, so all her toiletry essentials were close at hand.

Gingerly her fingers wrapped about her flacon of perfume. She unstoppered the bottle, tilting it slowly so a small amount of the fragrant jasmine scent flowed into her bath water. Then she recapped the bottle and replaced it upon the shelf. Next she groped for her sponge and a cake of soap, cursing under her breath as the bar slipped from her grasp and fell with a loud plop into the water.

"Damn!" she said, biting her lip as she began to search for the elusive cake.

"Patience, *querida*," the visconde reminded her quietly. "It takes time to learn and adjust to new ways."

"I know," she replied. "It's just that I—I get so depressed sometimes."

With difficulty she blinked back the sudden tears that had started in her eyes. Salvador, accustomed now to the lightning changes of mood that were part of the aftereffects of her accident and hard for her to control, made light of the mishap.

"You will find the soap in a minute, *muñeca*," he said

calmly, restraining the urge he had to go and help her look for it. "Just remember that you didn't drop it because you are blind. The cake was still wet from my own bath and slippery. Even a person who can see finds it difficult to hang on to such a bar and just as hard to locate beneath the water."

"I know. Still . . . ah." Aurora smiled, brightening. "Here it is."

The visconde relaxed as she began to lather herself vigorously. Sometimes just watching her struggle with small things that he himself took for granted, didn't even have to think about, was more than he could bear. On more than one occasion he had had to prevent himself from rushing to her aid. Still he knew in his heart that, for her own sense of well-being, pride, and self-esteem, it was vital that Aurora learn to care for herself. Together, slowly but surely, they were making progress toward that end.

They had discovered, only a week ago, that once Aurora had memorized the exact placement of furniture in a room, nothing could be added, changed, or removed. This had been driven home to them when she, having learned the layout of the bedroom well enough to maneuver her way about rather well, had nearly died because they had overlooked the fact that the bathtub was not normally present in the chamber. Lupe, not realizing this any more than they had, had gotten it out and filled it for Salvador. Aurora, not knowing it was there, had walked right into it, stumbled, and fallen into the water. Still subject to periodic bouts of dizziness, she had fainted. Had the visconde not been there to save her, she would have drowned. Now the bathtub was a permanent fixture of their bedroom, and she had had to learn the number of steps she must take until she reached it.

The bed was her main focal point, for she still did not

leave their chamber unless Salvador was there to guide her and direct her movements. It was, they both felt, too difficult for her to attempt to memorize all the rooms in the house at once. Eventually, though, she would know them all. Now that she had conquered the bedroom, they had started on the small salon and the dining room. More hazardous was the grand staircase leading to the lower level. Though her husband had taken her up and down it several times, Aurora still did not trust her ability to manage it on her own, especially as long as her dizzy spells persisted.

Today was the first time she had bathed herself, and the visconde had insisted on being present, fearful that she might faint again; tonight she would make her first attempt at eating without assistance, though they had practiced her meals together for several days now. Aurora had only to imagine that her plate was like the face of a clock. White vegetables, such as potatoes, rice, or cauliflower, were placed at nine o'clock; yellow or orange vegetables, generally carrots, squash, or corn, were at twelve o'clock; green vegetables, like beans, zucchini, or brussels sprouts, were in the three o'clock position; and meat was always at six o'clock. Asides, such as salad, sliced tomatoes, and bread, were put alone on smaller plates, as was dessert.

Cocido—stew—was especially difficult to manage, because it was usually made with chickpeas, which were hard to keep on a fork. But on nights when they had such one-pot meals as *paella* or *cazuela*, it was easier. When they ate *chorizos*—sausages—Aurora sometimes cheated, picking them up by hand until Salvador saw and admonished her.

Tonight they were having saffron beef, which was a casserole served with rice and which Aurora hoped would not prove hard to cope with. For dessert there was to be caramel custard, Aurora's favorite.

"You're sure I look all right when I eat?" she asked her husband anxiously as she stepped from the bathtub and reached for the towel that hung on a nearby stand, which the visconde had also had one of his men construct.

"No worse than Bribón," Salvador commented, trying hard not to laugh.

"Oh, you!" Aurora cried, throwing the towel in his direction. "How dare you compare my manners to those of Nicolas's monkey?"

"Well, other than Nicolito himself, Bribón is the only member of this household likely to be joining us for supper. So I thought perhaps it was he whom you were worried about impressing."

"Salvador, are you teasing me again? Surely you cannot mean to allow that abominable creature to eat with us."

"Well, while we have been dining up here alone for some days now, Nicolas, lonesome for company, has been downstairs supping with his pet; and he assures me that Bribón's manners are quite improved."

"You are joking, of course," Aurora sniffed as she counted out the steps to her armoire and opened its doors. "I want my fuchsia gown, Salvador, the one with the gold lace trim."

"Third dress from the right," he directed as he admired her naked figure. "You are truly beautiful, you know," he remarked softly.

Aurora blushed.

"Now don't go getting any ideas," she uttered sternly. "It's already past noon, and it's going to take me a long time to get ready for dinner, since you insist I perform my toilet myself."

"How do you know it is after noon?" Salvador questioned curiously, for though he could tell at a glance at the small clock that sat upon the dresser what time it was, he knew that Aurora could not.

"Why, I don't know," she confessed, shrugging. "It's just something about the warmth of the room and the sounds coming from the jungle in the distance, I guess. It's quiet now, *siesta* time."

"That's good, *querida*. You are starting to develop your other senses to compensate for your blindness. Mayor Farolero said that was very important to your progress."

"*Sí*." Aurora nodded as she carefully located and slipped into her undergarments, then sat down before the dresser to do her hair.

Deftly she parted the shiny black mass, bringing the silver comb on down vertically along her face so the comb's top teeth lined up straight with her nose. That way she could be certain the part was even. Then she brushed the thick cascade until it gleamed even more glossily. After that she wound the tresses into a smooth chignon at the nape of her neck. She felt for her box of hairpins, opened it, and pinned her hair into place.

Once finished with that, she began to dress.

Salvador watched silently, marveling at how well she was starting to adjust to her blindness. Her movements were still tentative, as yet unsure. But eventually she would gain confidence in herself. Time was all she needed now.

Aurora lifted the lid of her jewelry box, searching for the amethyst necklace and earrings that the visconde had given her this year for her birthday. Her hands examined each piece of jewelry carefully. Finally she located the pear-shaped gems set in an ornate gold collar. She smiled to herself, pleased that she had not needed to ask for assistance. She was learning. Slowly but surely she was learning.

She scented herself lightly with her jasmine perfume, then picked up her fan, turned, and held out her hand to Salvadore.

"I'm ready," she announced. "How do I look?"

He knew she was not just fishing for a compliment, as most women would have been doing by asking such a question. Aurora genuinely needed to know that there was nothing wrong with her appearance.

"Beautiful beyond compare," he reassured her. "Shall we go, señora?"

"*Sí.*"

Dinner went well, despite the fact that Nicolas did indeed attempt to persuade the visconde to allow Bribón to join them. Finally, after much cajoling, Salvador relented, saying that only this once the boy might permit his pet to give a demonstration of his "improved manners."

To everyone's surprise the monkey actually sat up at the table and ate like a little gentleman, even managing a knife and fork and blotting his lips with a napkin after finishing. Everyone applauded, and Nicolas was quite pleased with Bribón's performance—that is, until the mischievous animal settled back in his chair, produced a cigar he had stolen from the visconde's study, and proceeded to light it and give a fair imitation of Salvador smoking.

The visconde was not amused.

Nicolas, however, laughed so hard tears streamed down his face. Between gasps for breath he informed Aurora of what was happening, describing Bribón's comical actions so aptly that the girl too began to giggle.

Salvador stood.

"Out," he commanded the roguish creature, who shrieked and cackled, then started to prance about the dining room, waving the cigar mockingly.

"Oh, Salvador," Nicolas choked out between guffaws, "he looks just like you giving orders to the men."

As this was indeed the case the visconde grew even more annoyed at the monkey, though secretly Salvador was having a hard time restraining his own laughter at Bribón's antics.

"You taught him this!" the visconde, trying to look stern, accused Nicolas.

But the boy was not fooled. He saw Salvador's black eyes dancing and knew the visconde was not truly angry.

"No," Nicolas protested his innocence vigorously. "What can I say? Monkey see, monkey do. You should see him imitating Lupe. I wish I had a rolling pin handy. I'd get him to show you."

It seemed almost as though she had been waiting for just that moment, for after hearing the commotion and coming to investigate, Lupe herself barged into the dining room, wielding the device that Nicolas had wished for. Bribón took one look, screamed, threw away his cigar, and scampered off as fast as he could, Lupe hard on his heels and grumbling all the while.

"Horrid beast!" the maid shouted, waving her rolling pin as she ran. "I'll teach you to upset *el patrón*'s supper!"

No one waited around to see whether or not Lupe caught the unfortunate Bribón. They too hurried from the dining room, not wanting to face the irate maid if she failed in her attempt to capture the creature. Presently both Bribón's chuckling and Lupe's outraged replies faded into the distance. Slyly Nicolas slipped away, no doubt to rescue his pet, leaving Salvador and Aurora alone on the veranda.

Above in the twilight sky the moon was just rising, a silver crescent that heralded the arrival of the night. A breeze stirred gently, whispering to the forever-green leaves of the jungle. The evening air was sultry, filling up Aurora's senses with the heady aromas that wafted from the thick undergrowth in the distance. The scents of rich mahogany and pungent cedar mingled sweetly with that of spicy cinnamon and fragrant rosewood, tinged with the smells of countless multicolored flowers, which bloomed in exotic profusion now that the rainy season had ended.

It was a quiet time—a time for standing close together. Salvador's arms wrapped contentedly about his wife as he gazed out over the vast plantation, lost in his reflections, as she was her own.

It was hard to believe that out of the savage jungle one man had carved this glorious creation that was Esplendor. The visconde felt a sense of pride in the estate, almost as though he had built it himself. Its restoration was nearly finished. The west wing was almost completed at last, lacking only a few touches here and there, work that had been postponed due to Aurora's accident. Then only the attic, the widow's walk, and the cupola would remain. The last thing they would do would be to hang the angelus bell in its rightful place. Once that was done, Esplendor would be as it had been in the beginning.

No, Salvador thought. It would be more than it had been before: for it would be a place not of sadness and death, but of love and life. Here he and Aurora would live out their lives together. Here their children would be born, would grow to adulthood, and make lives of their own. They might choose to stay or to go, as they pleased. But Salvador and Aurora would never leave Esplendor. They belonged here, now and always.

Someday, the visconde mused, if God lets me live that long, I shall build two rocking chairs for this veranda; and when Aurora and I are very old we will sit upon them in the evenings and know that, for all the hardships we have endured, we have lived life to the fullest.

"What are you thinking, *mi corazón?*" the girl asked softly, bringing her husband back to the present.

He smiled down at her, his arms tightening around her.

"I was thinking that someday I shall be a very old man sitting on a rocking chair out here. And you know what?"

"What?" Aurora queried curiously.

"I want to look over and see you sitting right there beside me and know my life was the richer for having shared it with you."

"Oh, Salvador."

Tears of overwhelming emotion started in Aurora's eyes. How beautiful, how utterly beautiful to be loved like that. Surely she was the luckiest woman alive! God had taken away her eyesight—perhaps permanently— and that was a tragic thing; but He had also given her Salvador to fill her world with light and love. She knew if she were suddenly offered a chance to trade her husband for the other, she would say no. Her world would never be totally dark, not as long as it had Salvador in it.

"Listen!" she said suddenly, her ears straining to hear the sound carried on the wind. "Do you hear it?"

"Hear what, *querida?*" the visconde inquired, listening intently.

"There . . . no . . . it's gone now. For a moment I—I could have sworn the angelus bell was ringing."

"Then you hear it too," Salvador stated quietly, shivering a little. "I know it's not possible, that the story is only an old Indian tale; but sometimes I would stake my life that that bell is chiming. It's eerie, almost as though it's trying to tell us something. . . ."

"I wonder what it could be?"

"I don't know." The visconde shook his head. "Come, let's go in now, *muñeca*. It's getting late."

AURORA dreamed that night as she had not dreamed in a very long time, visions of blurred images and distorted sound, fleeting impressions of only half-remembered faces, places. . . .

It was dark at first in her dream, as though she were in a cave; and gradually, as a flickering light began to illuminate the hollow, she saw that it was indeed a grotto. She was alone, curled up in a black corner, upon some kind of furry, animal-skin rug. She was naked except for several other pelts wrapped about her for warmth. A fire burned in the center of the cave. On the walls were primitive paintings; on the floor were crude bowls and utensils.

Beyond the hollow of the opening she could see that it was snowing, and a sharp wind was blowing, bitterly freezing. Her teeth chattered. She was cold and hungry.

Presently the grotto was filled with the looming shadow of a man. In the beginning she was frightened as he lurched toward her, his frozen feet making him unsteady. Then she seemed to recognize him and scurried to his aid, pulling away the ice encrusted furs that encompassed him, trying to warm his flesh by drawing him near to her, sharing the heat of her own body with him.

It was hopeless. Her lover, her protector, her provider, was beyond help. Soon she became aware that he was dead. Not wanting to believe it, she huddled close to him, by the light of the dying fire, until she too was stiff and lifeless.

All grew dark once more, then a splendidly shining luminescence filled the air, blinding her. Shapeless forms appeared to embrace her, to draw her into their midst. She felt warm and safe.

She was sorry to leave the strange, hazy place of light and happiness. But she understood why she must go. Her time to join the others there had not yet come. They must send her back.

Aurora felt herself rushing through a timeless black tunnel, then all was again darkness. She was floating, as though adrift in a sea-filled bubble. When she could once more see, she was overwhelmed by her surroundings.

It was hot, very hot. In the distance endless desert sands spread out to touch the horizon, where the azure sky bent to kiss the earth. The sun shone brightly, piercingly, a ball of flame in the firmament.

In sharp contrast to the golden-brown desert sands was the place where she now stood. It was a garden-filled terrace, ingeniously designed and constructed, and irrigated by water from the Euphrates River below. Trees and flowers of every kind bloomed in gay profusion, their riotous tangle cascading over the walls, so the gardens seemed to hang.

A sound behind Aurora made her turn. Laughing,

she stretched out her arms, running to greet the tall, handsome man striding toward her.

As before, the scene faded, to be replaced by yet another.

Once more Aurora was floating, but this time it was because she sat in an ornate barge traveling slowly down the Nile River, even more vast, if that were possible, than the mighty Amazon. It was flood season, and here at the magnificent stone dock some twelve miles downriver from Memphis, the Nile was four miles wide.

Slowly the barge edged near to the wharf. Her head bent humbly, as befitted a slave, Aurora followed the princess, whom she served, across the raised stone road that ended in a beautiful temple. There the priests were praying. Aurora tried hard to concentrate on the ceremony, but she could not, for her eyes kept straying to the three omnipotent, triangular tombs that towered over her, massive and awesome. Made of limestone, they were smooth and white and so tall they seemed to soar almost to the heavens. The greatest one of all, built by King Kheops, looked like a mountain perched upon the desert plateau.

She wondered what it would be like to stand at the very summit of one of the pyramids; but this was not possible, for there were no steps by which one might climb to the peaks.

In the distance she could see the crouching, lionlike statue of King Khephren. It had been cut from solid rock; only its front paws were of brick. She would have liked to study it more closely as well. Perhaps the princess would hire a guide to take them by camel to view the figure.

Aurora liked the humpbacked beasts, with their brilliant, multicolored silk trappings and their ornate, silver-adorned saddles. When the animals moved, little bells on their harnesses chimed, filling the air with a gay, tinkling noise.

Her attention was caught by one of the camel drivers.

He was dark and swarthy. To her surprise his eyes met hers through one of the open windows of the temple. A flash of sudden recognition seized her and she lowered her head to hide the quick tears of sorrow that trickled from her eyes.

As she followed the princess from the temple, Aurora's heart ached with sadness in her breast, for she knew she would never see the man again. Their paths were too different this time. . . .

The sudden, abrupt change of scene, accompanied by raucous revelry, startled Aurora so badly that for a moment she was nearly jolted awake. But though she stirred restlessly, sleep once more enveloped her.

A long marble pool surrounded by tall columns rippled before her. Through the steam that was rising from the bath, she saw a tall man, wearing a white toga, bending over her, offering her purple grapes. Reclining lazily upon satin cushions, Aurora laughed huskily and parted her scarlet lips to pluck a single berry from the bunch.

Then the man's hands were upon her gown, pulling it down to bare her breasts. His palms closed about them, while she, heedless of the others in the room, reached up to draw him near. With a low growl he swooped her up, carrying her away to a quieter place, where they made love feverishly, mating like animals.

Now, one after another, images flashed before her so rapidly there was no time for Aurora to absorb them all. Once, wearing a metal, horned helmet, she raced forth eagerly, thigh high in cold, swirling water, to pull a long, dragon-headed ship to shore, then found herself keening sorrowfully along with the rest who marched on to the snow-covered beach, carrying a shield that bore a slain warrior.

Once, garbed in a strange, gold-braided satin halter top and sheer gauze pants, she felt herself dancing sensuously, her heavily lidded, kohl-darkened eyes black and drugged with passion as she performed for the hawk-faced man watching her.

Once, she stood again at Aranjuez, as she so often had before.

There were twelve scenes in all, though Aurora did not know how she knew this.

It was the last one she found most disturbing, however, for it was not of the past, but rather a twisted revelation of her own dark fear that her happiness now was too good to be true. In the nightmare the jungle had swallowed her up, engulfing her in its black core; and she was lost . . . lost. The angelus bell of Esplendor was ringing, louder and louder, dinning in her ears. . . .

With a start Aurora was jarred into wakefulness as she realized that this was no longer a dream, but real—for the bell was somehow truly ringing! Salvador must have heard it, for he no longer lay beside her but was already upon his feet, cursing the darkness as he fumbled for his pants and only succeeded in stumbling into a table. Half smiling to herself because she experienced no such difficulty as she moved confidently in the blackness, Aurora pulled on her robe and lit an oil lamp so her husband might see.

"It's the bell, isn't it?" she asked. "It's not just my imagination, is it? The angelus bell is really ringing."

"*Sí.* I don't know how, but it is," Salvador said. "Wait here, *querida*. I'll be back in a moment."

He grabbed up his rapier and the lamp and hurried from their chamber. The long corridors of Esplendor seemed eerie in the darkness. Shadows cast by the flickering light he held in one hand danced upon the walls like mocking specters. But the visconde was not afraid. This was his home. Briefly he wondered why no one else had joined him to investigate the bell's deep, erratic chiming. Then he realized that even if those at the manor had heard the angelus, they were probably too terrified to examine the cause of its ringing. No doubt they lay in their beds, paralyzed by superstitious fear.

Cautiously, because this was a part of the house that had not yet been restored, and the floorboards were rotten, Salvador climbed the steps leading to the attic. Slowly he opened the attic door and peered inside. There was no sign of anyone or anything. Nevertheless, the visconde moved warily as he began to search the many rooms that filled the top story of the manor. Originally these had been the servants' quarters, so the chambers were small.

Here and there were old, forgotten pieces of furniture, doubtless left by previous owners of the house and of no use to anyone. The dusty pieces had been warped by the heat and humidity of the jungle and were infested with termites besides. The army ants had done a thorough job of ridding the house of bugs. Salvador didn't know how these had gotten back inside. He made a mental note to have some of the men come up here tomorrow and remove the furniture, lest the rest of the manor be invaded by the crawling white insects.

There seemed to be an awful lot of fine dirt floating around. The visconde coughed slightly and wished he had thought to bring a handkerchief to protect his nostrils from the clouds of dust that were being stirred up by his passage. Where was it all coming from? he wondered. Surely he had not caused this much of a disturbance.

Suddenly an uneasy feeling that he was being watched crept chillingly up Salvador's spine. He shivered, momentarily alarmed. Then he laughed and forced himself to continue with his search. Surely the idea was ridiculous. Who on earth would be prowling about the attic at this hour? He held the lamp higher, so the light would cast a more revealing glow as he pushed his way past the cobwebs that were strung from rafter to rafter.

Yes, someone had definitely been up here, for now the visconde could see footprints in the dirt that had settled over the years on the floor. Faint, smaller marks that were obviously much older mingled with much larger, newer tracks that looked as though they had been made by a big man . . . Paul Van Klaas! Was it possible that the Dutchman was the intruder?

How dare he? Salvador thought, a muscle working tensely in his jaw at the notion. How dare Paul Van Klaas break into our home in the dead of night?

By now the visconde had reached the room wherein the angelus bell lay. Slowly he pushed open the door to the chamber, wincing as the sound of rusty hinges grated on his ears. The bell had been moved, and the dust upon the floor was streaked with footprints and handprints too, as though someone had stumbled over the angelus in the darkness and fallen, sending the bell rolling. Yes, that would account for angelus's erratic ringing.

Now Salvador was more certain than ever that the Dutchman was the intruder, for it would have taken a giant hulk of a man to have moved the angelus. It was so heavy no thief had been able to carry it away. The visconde couldn't imagine how Don Santiago had ever gotten it up to the cupola to begin with. No doubt a system of rope and pulleys had been devised to haul the bell up to the roof.

Salvador paused, once more uneasy. He wanted to examine the angelus to be certain it was undamaged, but some instinct prevented him from bending over the bell to inspect it. The attic was quiet, almost too quiet. It reminded him of when he and Rafael, as children in Spain, had played hide and seek together. The visconde had always known when he'd been close to his cousin's hiding place, for Rafael had never failed to make some slight, almost imperceptible movement before stiffening with excitement, holding his breath, waiting for a chance to run.

Salvador wheeled about just in time to avoid having his head bashed in as a huge dark figure wielding a heavy, broken bedpost suddenly lunged at him from the shadows, striking at him powerfully, viciously. The attack caught the visconde on the shoulder. Pain ripped through his flesh as he staggered backward from the force of the blow. He tripped over the angelus bell and fell, his rapier rolling to one side, the oil lamp smashing upon the floor. He ducked instinctively as the bedpost came hurtling toward him and crashed against the far wall. Before Salvador could recover his wits and jump to his feet, the intruder raced from the chamber, slamming the door shut behind him.

Swearing mightily, the visconde righted himself, wrenched open the door, and rushed after his rapidly fleeing assailant.

As she had not done in many long weeks Aurora now cursed her blindness, her helplessness to assist her husband. She paced their bedroom nervously as she waited for him to return to her. Since she could not see the clock that sat upon the dresser, she did not know how long he had been gone from her; but to her it seemed like forever. As time passed, and Salvador still did not appear, Aurora grew more and more worried about him. What had become of him? The angelus bell had stopped ringing. Why had her husband not come back?

Something was wrong. She was sure of it. When she heard the loud crash from above, she decided to wait no longer. The floorboards in the attic were rotten, and it sounded as though Salvador had fallen through one of them. He might be hurt, unable to call for help.

Yanking open the door to their chamber, Aurora hurried out into the hall. There she paused for a moment, trying to orient herself, to remember the layout of Esplendor. Were the stairs leading to the attic to the right or the left of her? Oh, goddamn it! Why must she be blind, unable to see where she was going, when Salvador needed her?

"Nicolas! Lupe!" she cried. "Wake up! Wake up!"

Thank God, someone was coming to her aid, for now she could hear footsteps pounding along the corridor.

"Nicolas?"

Whoever was there, it was not Nicolas. Someone big and heavy ran straight into her in the darkness, swore, and then flung her brutally against the wall. Stumbling to her feet, she called frantically, "Who's there? Nicolas! Lupe!"

There was no answer. Whoever had been there was gone, thudding furiously, as though half jumping, down the grand staircase to escape through the front doors of the house. Moments later there came the sound of hoofbeats fading into the distance.

Then suddenly her husband was there, enveloping Aurora in his warm embrace; and all was once more right in her world.

"Aurora! Are you all right?" he questioned sharply.

"Salvador! *Sí, sí.* I'm fine, just scared; that's all," she said as she nestled her trembling body close to his strong one. "*Madre de Dios,* my husband! What is happening? Who was that? *Heridas de Cristo!* Smoke! I smell smoke! There's something burning. . . ."

"*Mierda!* The oil lamp!" the visconde gasped. The glass lamp had smashed when he'd fallen, and in his determination to catch the intruder he'd paid no heed to the spilled whale oil, the licking flames that, freed from restraint, had begun to spread along the floor. "I forgot the oil lamp! I'll be right back, *querida.* I promise. Nicolas. Lupe. Thank God. You two certainly took your time about getting here. Where have you been? Never mind. Nicolas, fetch some blankets, and come upstairs to the attic with me immediately. Lupe, take your mistress back to bed, and examine her to be certain she has suffered no injury," he shouted over his shoulder as he and his young brother-in-law started toward the attic.

The maid, though still half-asleep and confused, did not question Salvador's orders but led the protesting Aurora away firmly.

"You heard *el patrón,*" Lupe stated. "Come, señora. Look! Already you are dizzy. You must lie down before you faint."

"No. I'll be all right in a minute," Aurora claimed weakly, though her head, where she had struck it against the wall, was starting to ache.

She was fast asleep when Salvador finally returned to their chamber. Nevertheless, some part of her being was listening for his arrival; and at the sound of his entrance she sat up immediately.

"Salvador?"

"Sí, it is I, *muñeca*. What are you doing up?"

"I—I wanted to be awake when you came back. Is—is the fire out?"

"Sí. No thanks to my stupidity, it had just begun to take hold when Nicolas and I reached it. I shudder to think what would have occurred otherwise. There was some damage done, but it was minor, and fortunately we have not yet started the restoration on that part of the manor anyway."

He finished washing off the soot, then came to sit beside her on the bed, a damp towel flung over his shoulder.

"Oh, Salvador, what happened tonight? Did someone break into our home again? No. Don't try to spare me, to protect me, because I'm blind."

The visconde smiled wryly.

"How well you are learning to read my mind, *querida*," he remarked. "However, I wasn't going to hide anything from you. I just didn't want you to worry; that's all. But, *sí*. There was an intruder—up in the attic. He must have climbed up a trellis on to the widow's walk and come down through the cupola. In the darkness he stumbled over the angelus bell. That's why we heard it ringing."

"But . . . Salvador," Aurora mused aloud, "that bell is so heavy. Even two or three men have difficulty lifting it. For one man to move it . . ."

"Sí, I know. He was very large and very strong," the visconde declared. "Unfortunately I didn't get a good look at him, so I can't be certain of his identity," Salvador told her. He didn't want to upset his wife further by informing her that Paul Van Klaas had been prowling about their home. Aurora was so sensitive, especially now. She might believe that he was reviving his old suspicions about her having an affair with the Dutchman. Salvador didn't want to open up any past wounds and have his wife stubbornly decide, despite his protests to the contrary, that he was accusing her of any wrongdoing. "When I surprised the man," he continued, "he raced down here and escaped."

"I know," Aurora said. "He ran right into me. Oh, if only I could have seen who it was. That accursed treasure!" she asserted. "Someone truly thinks it exists. That's why they keep breaking in here! They're searching our home, trying to find the treasure—or possibly a map. Oh, I wish we could catch whoever it is!"

"So do I," Salvador agreed. "So do I. I'm going to post guards around the house again, until we can solve the problem. Perhaps that will prove a deterrent to any would-be treasure seekers in the future."

What the visconde really wanted to do was to ride over to Capricho, now, and accuse Paul Van Klaas outright of breaking into Esplendor, but he realized the notion was ridiculous. If he were wrong about the Dutchman being the intruder, and Paul Van Klaas had been in bed all night, Salvador would look like a fool—or worse. No, he was simply going to have to catch the man in the act.

He pulled Aurora's indignant, quivering form into his arms. What a little termagant she was sometimes! Had she been able to see, he had no doubt that she would have chased their prowler herself, hurling abuse at him all the way.

He laughed softly at the idea.

"What's so funny?" Aurora inquired, bristling.

"You are," Salvador remarked teasingly, kissing her on the tip of her nose. "Are you tired?"

"No, why?"

"Oh, I thought I might do a little treasure seeking of my own," the visconde told her, nuzzling her ear and slipping one hand inside her robe to fondle her breasts beneath the thin material of her negligee.

Aurora smiled.

"Search on, señor," she said. "You are one intruder I shan't try to drive away."

"You'd better not," he announced with mock anger, "for I love you too much ever to let you succeed in such an attempt, *querida*."

"*Bueno,*" Aurora whispered. "*Bueno, mi corazón.*"

Then she gave herself up to his all-consuming embrace.

Salvador's lips found hers in the darkness, feverishly, possessively, as though to drive all thoughts but those of him from her mind. He would wipe away the last, unhappy vestiges that remained of the evening's terrors, replacing them with joy and love.

Aurora refused to dwell on thoughts of the man who had invaded their private sanctuary. Salvador would protect them both; she felt secure in that knowledge. She sighed with longing and held her husband even more tightly.

The visconde's tongue traced lingeringly the outline of her lips, as though memorizing their delicately curved shape, almost childlike as they parted for him, so soft, so vulnerable. Still there was nothing childish about their response. All woman Aurora was as she kissed him back, fervently answering the desires of his mouth. Hotly, eagerly, he explored her, tasted of the sweetness that waited within her lips, like wild honey, warm and melting on his tongue.

Her tongue was like a wisp of a cloud in reply, trailing gently here and there, twining about his own like mist, engulfing him. Her mouth and teeth erotically nuzzled his lips, nibbling at him as though she meant to devour him with her kisses.

Salvador was thrilled by her obvious yearning for him. Her wanting him made him feel proud and special. Aurora was a beautiful woman. She might have had any number of men. But she had chosen him.

She will never regret it, he thought. I shall never again give her cause to regret it.

He cradled her head in his hands, his fingers tangled in the long, silky strands of her ebony tresses, as though to imprison her, to prevent her from escaping from him. His mustache tickled her; his lips burned like a molten ore across her face. He kissed her cheeks, her eyelids, her temples, her hair. He caught the shiny black cascade and drew its threads through his fingers, marveling at its luster, its softness. How he loved the feel of it, like satin as it slid and shimmered through his grasp. With a sigh of pleasure he buried his face in the jasmine-scented locks and wrapped them about his throat.

"*Querida*," Salvador whispered. "*Mi amor, mi alma, mi corazón.*"

Aurora shivered as he blew gently in her ear. His breath felt warm upon her face and smelled of good whiskey and tobacco, masculine scents she found intoxicating. His tongue darted forth to lick the contours of the small, curved shell into which he muttered words of love and sex, words that Aurora only half heard, only dimly comprehended: for the roar of her heart was like that of an ocean, so loud it filled her ears with every throbbing wave.

A tide of emotion whirled up to seize her in its grip, carry her out to sea and beyond. She loved him so.

"Salvador," she murmured, catching his face between her hands and kissing him again and again. "Oh, Salvador."

Beneath his hands her nightgown fell away as though it were nothing, the barest of hindrances to their passion— and soon conquered. Greedily his palms cupped her breasts; his thumbs circled her areolae and then brushed her nipples, which sprang to attention at his touch. He fondled lightly the rigid buds, taunting them to even greater heights before he took each one, in turn, into his mouth. His tongue flicked quickly, delightfully, the tiny buttons before trailing its way down her belly to tease her navel while she laughed and writhed beneath him, trying playfully to escape.

At last Aurora wriggled free, then turned to weave a web of magic about her husband. She could not see him, and though she mourned that loss, she discovered there were other compensations for her blindness. Her remaining senses had grown so dramatically sensitive that with just the slightest touch of her lips or hands, she drove Salvador wild. She did not have to look up, as she had before her accident, to discern the expression on his face to find out if she were giving him pleasure. Now she could feel unerringly the smallest tremor of his body in response to her movements.

She smiled.

"You are like sugar, my husband," she bantered, "and I feel that it is time to strike."

Once, Salvador would have been angered by her remark, for it recalled the sugarcane harvest and how she had laughed and joked with his men—the men he had once eyed so suspiciously, wondering which, if any, had shared his wife's bed. Now the visconde knew how irrational his jealousy had been, and he was able to smile at Aurora's double entendre.

"Then strike, *muñeca*," he murmured, "for I am in your hands."

They made love, joyously, passionately; and somehow, even before she knew for certain that it was so, Aurora was sure that on this night Salvador had given her a child.

Chapter Thirty-three

As he rode furiously toward Capricho, Paul Van Klaas was shaking with rage and frustration. Damn it! He was never going to get his hands on the treasure at this rate! He had bungled everything—again! Worse yet was the fact that even though it had been dark in the attic at Esplendor, Salvador still might have recognized him. If only he had killed the visconde! But some way the Spaniard had sensed his presence and turned in time to avoid being struck fatally by the broken bedpost that Paul had wielded so brutally. He gritted his teeth wrathfully at the thought.

Twice he had tried to murder Salvador, and twice the Spaniard had escaped death. Paul shook his fist savagely at the heavens. Somewhere up there in the black firmament a lucky star shone down upon Don Salvador Rodriquez y Aguilar. Curse the man!

Stealthily, so as not to waken the grooms, Paul eased his horse into the stables and quietly relieved the beast of its trappings. He didn't want anyone to know he'd been absent from Capricho this night—or any other night. He'd already been forced to strangle one Indian slave who'd watched him too closely for comfort, as well as Ijada, who had lost her nerve in their hunt for the treasure. Paul had not wanted to kill the *mestiza*, but he had had no choice. He had seen the look of fear in her eyes. She would have confessed to Salvador about the murders of Don Basilio and Doña Francisca, and Paul would have been tried and hanged for his crimes. Coronel de la Palma might be old and fat, but he kept order in the Amazon Basin.

Once inside the house, Paul crept upstairs to his dressing room, where he disrobed, washed, and carefully cleaned his boots. Then he sneaked into his wife's room and slipped into bed beside her. Heidi stirred but did not awaken, and Paul breathed a small sigh of relief. If he had to use the chamber pot as the excuse for his absence from her one more time, he was certain she was either going to become suspicious of him—or start thinking his bladder was ailing and send for Mayor Farolero. Paul wouldn't have slept with Heidi at all on these nights except for the fact that he might need her to substantiate his alibi.

Should Salvador dare to accuse him of invading Esplendor tonight, Heidi would swear that Paul had been in bed with her all evening. She was so enamored of him she would have done almost anything for him; but she also had a strong sense of religious duty, and despite her love for him, her conscience would force her to expose his crimes, should she ever learn of them. Yes, she would weep painfully all the while, but she would report him to Coronel de la Palma all the same.

Perhaps, Paul thought, it would be best if he got out of the Amazon Basin for a time and gave things a chance to cool down. He could pay one of his men to go over to Esplendor every so often during his absence and dig a few holes to confuse Salvador—should he have recognized Paul as the intruder there this evening. Then the Spaniard would not be certain that it really had been Paul who had broken into Esplendor tonight. Yes, that was a fine plan. The incidents at Esplendor would continue, but if Salvador tried to blame *him* for them, Paul could truthfully say he had been out of town when they'd occurred. Yes, that would indeed do nicely. He would go to Belém—on the pretext of needing supplies—and while he was gone one of his men would take his place in the search for the treasure. Not that the man would know that, of course. Paul would make sure of that. He would say it was all just a joke—a joke on his friend Salvador—and if the man should become suspicious, he would be killed and buried beside the overly inquisitive Indian slave who was rotting away beneath a pile of manure in the north forty.

THE following morning over breakfast Heidi commented that Paul looked tired and inquired somewhat anxiously whether or not he had slept well. Since Heidi always asked this after his forays to Esplendor, Paul was prepared for the question and easily informed his wife that her tossing and turning (although in reality she'd lain quite still) had kept him awake all evening.

"I'm sorry, dearest," Heidi apologized. "I must really be a restless sleeper, for you always have bags under your eyes after a night with me. I hate to think I'm keeping you up, dearest. Why don't you go back to your own room after we—after we . . . after I fall asleep?"

"You know I love holding you, Heidi," Paul professed as his wife blushed. "What are a few dark circles when I have you to console me? Besides, I have to leave for

Belém shortly, and I want to spend as much time with you as I can before I go."

"You're leaving? To go to Belém? But . . . why? Manaus is so much closer, and besides, the traders are due here any day now."

"I know," Paul mumbled as he stuffed a hot sweet roll into his mouth, "but . . . well, your birthday *is* coming up, sweetheart; and I want to get you something special," he explained, smiling smugly at his sudden inspiration.

Heidi smiled back shyly.

"Oh, Paul, you're so good to me," she said. "I can't think why I ever—why I ever—" She broke off abruptly, biting her lip at what she had almost confessed to him.

"Why you ever what, sweetheart?" Paul queried casually, although his body had grown suddenly tense and wary.

Heidi reddened, mortified and embarrassed over her slip. Now she would be forced to disclose her suspicions to him, and she had never wanted him to know about them, especially now, when he loved her so much he was traveling all the way downriver to Belém just to buy her a birthday present!

"Oh, Paul, I—I feel so silly and so—so ashamed," she stammered. "It's just that for a while you—you were gone so often and—and working so hard and so late that I—I thought you had taken a mistress."

Paul exhaled softly with relief.

"You're right, Heidi," he told her, causing her heart to lurch sickeningly momentarily before he went on. "You *were* silly. Why would I look elsewhere when I have you, sweetheart? Besides, who could I have been carrying on with anyway? Outside of Aurora de Rodriquez, I can't think of another woman in the Amazon Basin even remotely interesting," Paul protested. "They're all either too old or too infirm. And if you believe for one minute that I would risk incurring Salvador's wrath by attempting to steal his wife, you're crazy. You saw how the jealous idiot behaved right before her accident— when I just helped her to her feet. Can you imagine what he'd do to a man actually having an affair with her?"

"Oh, Paul." Heidi laughed. "I never thought of that; and I never once suspected Aurora besides. She's much too loyal to Salvador."

For a moment, as he gazed at his wife's sweet, trusting face, Paul was stricken with remorse. He had loved her once, and she still loved him. Where had he gone so wrong? How could he have committed such ghastly crimes—all in the name of greed? How horrible Heidi would feel if she ever found out what he'd done, how the hands that wakened such passion in her had choked the life from others. Briefly Paul closed his eyes tightly at the notion and wished fervently that he might undo the awful carnage he'd wrought. But he could not. It was too late. He had set his feet upon a path from which there was no turning back. He could only go forward. The legend of the buried treasure of Esplendor had obsessed him. He must find the fortune. He simply had to. Otherwise everything he had done would be for nothing.

Don Juan Rodolfo de Zaragoza y Aguilar beat his head against the side of his cabin and tore at his hair in a frenzy. He had never been so enraged in all his life! He had been tricked! So cleverly and thoroughly fooled that he feared he would have a stroke if he continued to dwell on the idea. That stupid, half-breed peasant

Mario had sent him on a wild-goose chase that had cost him untold time and money. If he got his hands on the trader, Juan would slit Mario's lying throat!

The marqués had traveled down the coast of Brazil. He had called at every port in Uruguay. He had journeyed the length of Argentina and ventured inland to Paraguay—and all for nothing! No one had seen or heard of Basilio, Francisca, or Aurora. All that Juan had gotten for his pains was the dreadful malaria that continued to attack him, leaving him alternately burning up with fever and racked by chills. He had, of course, refused the white crystals the natives had told him would keep the disease at bay. Ignorant Indians. What did they know? Doubtless they'd only been trying to poison him so they could rob him of his riches. Well, they had not found him so easy a mark.

Now he must return to Belém, battling not only the malaria, but sea sickness as well. The marqués gasped, then gagged as the *Angel de Venganzo* rolled upon the waves. Then he staggered toward his chamber pot and retched violently into the basin. Exhausted, he lay down again upon his bunk and cursed bitterly all those who had brought him to this vile pass.

Chapter Thirty-four

AURORA hugged the chamber pot tightly as the contents of the breakfast she'd eaten earlier now came right back up. Her body felt wretched, but her mind was soaring with joy. She was pregnant. She was absolutely certain of it now.

"Have you told *el patrón* yet?" Lupe asked as she handed Aurora a damp cloth with which to wipe her face.

"No. I wanted to be sure first. Oh, Lupe. He'll be so happy. *I'm* so happy! I want to sing and dance and shout it to the world. I'm going to have a child! I'm going to have a child!" She stood, her arms wrapped about herself as she whirled around the room. At last she stopped, swaying a little at the dizziness that assailed her. After steadying herself she went on. "I've got to go and find Salvador and tell him—now. He's been so worried, thinking I was really sick. It was all I could do yesterday to prevent him from sending for Mayor Farolero. Where is my husband, Lupe? Do you know?"

The maid nodded, then replied, "*Sí,* he is at the

stables," as she realized that Aurora could not see her nonverbal gesture.

It was so difficult these days to remember that Aurora was blind; she managed so well now. She even rode her horse, Deleite, once more. More often than not, Salvador led the mare. But if he were not there, Aurora cantered Deleite slowly over a special bridle path her husband had had his men clear for her. It was out in the open, so there were no tree limbs to endanger her; and two young boys kept it free of rocks, holes—into which the horse might stumble—and other debris. Each time that Aurora rode the trail the children also stood guard, warning her when she had reached the end of the path and must turn around.

More than anything, Aurora loved Salvador for giving her this freedom, for the thought that she might never ride again had been especially painful to her. Now, knowing that she had the trail to traverse alone, she did not mind when her husband led her over the rough terrain of the rest of the plantation.

She gave Lupe a quick hug, then hurried downstairs, leaving the maid smiling with wonder over her mistress's many accomplishments.

At the front doors of the manor Aurora paused to pick up the walking stick that Salvador had fashioned for her and that was kept always in the entry. Then she went outside, tapping her way to the stables. Behind her she heard quiet footsteps, but she felt no alarm. It was only one of the youngsters her husband had ordered to follow her wherever she went. The child would not intrude upon her privacy unless she needed help.

When she had reached the stables Aurora went inside and called out for Salvador.

"Here, *querida*," he responded, "in Incendio's stall."

Without hesitation Aurora made her way to the gelding's box.

"Is something wrong with Incendio?" she asked, concerned.

"No," Salvador said, then laughed wryly. "It's one of those damned dogs of yours. She decided to have her litter in here, and now she won't let us move her or the puppies. We've managed to get two of them out, but Pepe's nursing a bloody thumb, and Jim's leg will never be the same!"

Aurora giggled brightly.

"Jim," she declared, "you and Pepe had better go on up to the house, and let your fiancée take a look at your wounds. Lupe's liable to take her infamous rolling pin to me if I let anything happen to you before your wedding."

The Texan, Jim Rawlings, had finally asked the maid to marry him, and she had agreed. They planned to hold the ceremony sometime after the spring planting. Now, at Aurora's teasing, Jim smiled sheepishly and shuffled his feet.

"Aw, shucks, Miz Rodriquez, my Lupe thinks the world of you, and you know it. It's *my* ears she's gonna box, more 'n likely, when she finds out how I let that critter take a chunk outta my leg. Heck. She ain't yet fergive me fer allowin' that monkey to git the best of me the other day—the durned pest! If I didn't like Nicolas so much, I swear I'd blast that rascal of his with my shootin' iron. Miz Rodriquez, do you know that durned monkey actually locked me in the cannin' shed? I thought Lupe was inside, puttin' up some preserves;

and when I went in to talk to her that sly ole Bribón scampered out quicker 'n a rattler kin strike, pushed the door shut, 'n' slammed the bolt home. I hollered fer over an hour 'fer somebody showed up to let me out. I tell you, I never felt like sech a fool in my life.

"Well, you'll be wantin' to speak to the boss, more 'n likely, so me 'n' Pepe'll jest mosey on up to the house, like you said. Good day, Miz Rodriquez, Boss. Come on, Pepe. Let's vamoose."

"It's *vamanos*, Jeem, *vamanos*," Pepe uttered with mock exasperation and rolled his eyes. "You been here more dan two years now, 'n' still you doan learn. I tink you ain't never gonna speak de Spanish properly."

"What're you talkin' about, you yahoo?" Jim grinned. "My Spanish is a durned sight better 'n yore English, 'n' that's a fact. 'Sides, Lupe understands me jest fine."

"Shore," Pepe drawled, nodding and making another face, "'n' why not? I heerd you whisperin' to her. You doan say nothin' but '*Te quiero; te quiero.*' What woman doan understand that?"

Continuing their friendly argument, the two men left the stables, leaving Aurora alone with Salvador. Still chuckling, she turned to her husband.

"I don't know about you, but I'd say it was a toss-up as to who speaks the other's language best. I don't think either one speaks the queen's Spanish—or English, for that matter. Stand aside, Salvador, and let me get that dog and her puppies out here. It's Jengibre, isn't it?"

"*Sí,*" the visconde answered, "but I really don't think you ought to try to move her, *muñeca*. She's being very protective of her litter."

"Well, I can certainly understand that," Aurora claimed with a smile, thinking of the happy news she had to tell her husband.

Perhaps Jengibre sensed the girl's condition, for the dog gave her no trouble whatsoever but, whining anxiously, permitted Aurora to move both her and her puppies to a box that Salvador had prepared for them in another corner of the stables. After she had transported them to their new home, Aurora knelt down, carefully lifted up one of the puppies, and tenderly pressed it to her check.

"Oh, Lord," the visconde groaned as another dog came bounding inside the stables, "here comes the proud *padre* to defend his family. You better put that puppy back in the box, *querida*. I don't want to lose a chunk out of my leg too."

"You don't, eh?" Aurora asked as she returned the puppy to its mother. "Well, how would you like to be a proud *padre* yourself instead?"

For a moment Salvador stood absolutely motionless, not certain he had heard his wife correctly.

Then he spoke hesitantly, "Aurora, do you mean . . . are you sure . . ."

"*Sí*," she replied, her countenance glowing. "I am sure. We're going to have a child."

"*Madre de Dios!* I'm going to be a father. I'm going to be a father!" the visconde shouted.

Then he swung his wife to her feet and, hugging her near, whirled her about madly with delight, kissing her again and again. Just as suddenly he stopped and gently set her down.

"Oh, *muñeca mía*, I was so excited I didn't think. Are you all right?"

"Of course," Aurora informed him, laughing as she considered the expression she knew he must have upon his face. "Except for a few bouts with morning sickness, I've never felt better in my life."

"But the baby—"

"Is fine. Don't worry, Salvador," she reassured him. "I'm not as fragile as you think. I won't break. But I will need a lot more rest now, and there are certain things I won't be able to do, like lifting heavy objects."

"You shall lift nothing whatsoever, not even a feather. Come. Are you tired? Do you wish to lie down now? Can I do anything for you?"

"*Sí, sí,* my husband."

"What? Just name it, *querida,* and it is yours," the visconde stated earnestly, anxiously. "What can I do for you?"

"Tell me that you love me," Aurora said softly.

Salvador's eyes filled with overwhelming emotion at her words. He did not know what he had ever done to deserve her, but he thanked God that she was his.

"I love you, Doña Aurora Leila Gitana María Raquel Montalbán de Rodriquez. Now—and forever."

Then he wrapped his arms about her tightly, as though he would never let her go.

Chapter Thirty-five

SALVADOR was more than a little confused. He had been so certain that Paul Van Klaas was the intruder at Esplendor. Now the visconde was not so sure. Despite the fact that guards patrolled the plantation nightly, someone was still slipping on to the estate and digging up the grounds. It could not be Paul. This Salvador knew. The Dutchman had gone to Belém—or so Heidi had reported to Aurora when visiting the other day. But then Heidi could have been lying or truly unaware of her husband's real whereabouts. Perhaps the story of his being out of town was just a ruse on Paul's part to allay Salvador's suspicions. But, no, too many people had seen the Dutchman set out on his journey, in a dugout canoe filled with his illegal Indian slaves and a hired peasant to guard them. Paul would hardly have taken them along if he really weren't leaving the area.

Damn! the visconde swore silently to himself. Just when it seemed he had everything all figured out, it went awry. Now he did not know what to think. There was only one explanation that appeared to make any sense: The Dutchman had someone else working with him. But who could it be? Salvador could not imagine Heidi sneaking around Esplendor at night, and Paul would have to be using some powerful means of persuasion to convince one of his Indian slaves to set foot on the place.

At last the visconde shrugged. He would just have to go on waiting and hope he could catch the intruder in the act of prowling about the plantation. Whoever it was was growing bolder. Sooner or later he would slip up; and Salvador would be there to capture him.

Mario and the rest of the traders broke into smiles as they drew near to Esplendor, and the Indians began to chatter brightly to each other at the sight of the estate.

It was a miracle, they said. Don Salvador was truly a powerful *brujo* with much magic. Just look at how Esplendor had been transformed. It stood like a shining, white marble jewel in the midst of the evergreen jungle, rising up tall and proud and, for all its restoration, somehow as mysterious as ever. Work on the manor was nearly completed. All that remained was the finishing of the widow's walk and the cupola. Then Esplendor would be complete.

Eagerly Mario climbed onto the boat dock, along with the others, to greet Don Salvador and Doña Aurora. The *mestizo* was most anxious to see *la señora* again. He had letters for both her and Don Salvador, from Spain; and besides, he wanted to tell her about the strange, scar-faced man who was searching for her. Mario walked toward the girl, his hands outstretched warmly.

"Doña Aurora," he said, beaming, "how delighted I am to be welcomed once more to your home. You are looking even more radiant than usual. Can it be that

you and Don Salvador are expecting a happy event?"
His eyes took in her blossoming figure.

Aurora blushed and smiled as she instinctively
extended her hand, and the *mestizo* took it in his
own.

"*Sí*," she told him. "Our child will be born sometime
next year."

"Ah, my congratulations to you both. So, Don Salvador,
you are to be a proud *padre*, no?"

"*Sí*," the visconde replied, grinning. "I know it's a
little early yet, but have a cigar, Mario." Salvador
handed the *mestizo* a thin black cigar, then shook his
hand and clapped him upon the back. "Come, let us go
up to the house. The men will take care of things here."

So well had Aurora now adjusted to her blindness
that it was not until Mario saw the girl had already
started back to the manor, ahead of them, and was
tapping with her cane upon the path, that he realized
she could no longer see. He stopped dead in his tracks,
his face filling with disbelief and sympathy for her.

"Oh, Don Salvador, what has happened? Can it be—
can it be that..." His voice trailed off questioningly.

"*Sí*," the visconde answered the unspoken query.
"There was a terrible accident during the last rainy
season. A bolt of lightning struck a large tree. One of its
shattered limbs hit my wife in the back of the head,
blinding her. We had hoped her sight would return, but
now we fear her loss will be permanent. However,
Aurora is coping magnificently. Do not be afraid you
will make any inadvertent slip to remind her of her blindness, Mario. My wife will be much more at her ease
with you, I assure you, if you continue to treat her as
you always have."

"Of course. I understand. But perhaps, señor, you

will stop here for a moment with me, eh? I had something of importance to tell Doña Aurora; but now I think perhaps it is best if I tell you instead. Under the circumstances I do not wish to worry *la señora*." The *mestizo* paused briefly, then continued. "Some time ago a man came to Belém, a strange, scar-faced man who was searching for Doña Aurora."

Salvador tensed and inhaled sharply at the news.

"Did he give his name—this man?" he asked.

Mario shook his head.

"No, señor. He said only that *la señora* was his betrothed, and he must find her. Forgive me, Don Salvador, if I erred, but . . . I did not like or trust the man, and I did not believe his story. I thought that Doña Aurora was too honorable to have married you if she were betrothed to another. When the man questioned me about her whereabouts, I lied to him. I told him that she had traveled down the coast of Brazil to Argentina, looking for her brother. The man booked passage on *La Gaviota* and sailed away. Did I—did I do the right thing, señor?" the *mestizo* asked somewhat nervously.

"You did indeed, *mi amigo*," the visconde responded, much to Mario's relief. Then Salvador's mouth tightened. "The man was my half brother, Don Juan. I am sure of it. He is quite mad. If he can get his hands on her, he means to harm my wife, for it was she who gave him the scar he now bears upon his face. He did not ask about me?"

"No, Don Salvador."

"*Bueno*. Then he is as yet unaware that I am here and with Aurora. Once he learns that, I have no doubt that my half brother will wish more than ever to kill me."

"To kill you, señor!" Mario gasped.

"*Sí*." The visconde nodded grimly. "Juan hates me. He will stop at nothing to see me dead; and if by some chance he should succeed in murdering me, my wife will be powerless in his hands—especially now."

Salvador's heart jerked sickeningly at the idea the *mestizo* voiced aloud.

"Oh, señor, to think of Doña Aurora, blind and with child, in the clutches of a madman . . . *Dios mío*." Mario crossed his breast hastily. "Then there is more, Don Salvador, that you should know. By now your half brother will have realized that I tricked him. Even as we speak he is probably on his way back to Belém."

"Then you must take great care, *mi amigo*," the visconde warned the *mestizo*, "for Juan is not a man to take lightly being fooled. He is eaten alive by his desire for revenge, and now he will be searching for you also. Tread warily, that you do not wind up with a knife in your back!"

Mario smiled again, but this time his grin was spine-chilling; and his black eyes were narrowed.

"Do not fear for me, Don Salvador," he declared. "I have not lived all my life in this savage jungle and on the wharves of Belém for naught. If Don Juan crosses my path again, I shall know how to deal with him."

He laid one hand upon the blade at his waist, as though to emphasize his point.

"Come," Salvador said. "Aurora will wonder where we are if we linger too long here, and she will sense that something is wrong. Even if she questions you, Mario, say nothing to her about this matter. This is a delicate and emotional time in her life, and I do not want her upset."

"No, señor. I understand. I will protect her—with my own life if necessary—for though I am not much, you and Doña Aurora have always treated me with the utmost respect and friendship. I, Mario, do not forget this, Don Salvador."

PAUL Van Klaas stared morosely at the whiskey in his half-full glass. Since his arrival in Belém he had done nothing but drink himself into a stupor each night, for no matter how hard he tried, he could not get the thought of Esplendor's buried treasure out of his mind. Everywhere he turned the fortune glittered before him, enticing him on with its golden splendor. He could almost feel the shimmering coins and shining jewels running through his fingers, an endless stream of riches. There would be bricks of solid gold, with which the natives of El Dorado had paved the lost city. There would be gem-studded collars so heavy a man could wear no more than one at a time. There would be lavish wine cups and dinner plates, ornate bracelets and rings—a king's ransom and more. Yes, Paul could see it all, and he meant to have it, whatever the cost. He could not allow it to slip through his grasp, not now, not after all he'd done to obtain it.

He lifted his glass and downed its remaining contents, then ordered another drink.

"Oh, and, bartender," he called drunkenly as he pounded his fist upon the table, "this time leave the bottle. I've come all the way from the Amazon Basin, and I've been thirsty a long time."

The bartender grimaced with disgust as he refilled the Dutchman's glass and thumped the bottle down in front of Paul. Already, in the bartender's opinion, the big blond man had had more than enough. His blue eyes were bloodshot and mean. He was just the type, the bartender thought, to start trouble.

"Pardon me, señor"—a smooth, cultured voice spoke politely in Paul's ear, startling him—"but did I understand you to say you have come from the Amazon Basin?"

The Dutchman glanced up hostilely at the stranger who had accosted him.

"What's it to you?" he asked, his tone surly.

"Nothing señor, except that I am searching for a woman who may perhaps be in the region you mentioned. I thought, in that case, that you might know of her."

Paul shrugged, uninterested.

"I might, but then again, I might not," he remarked. "What's her name?"

"Do you mind if I sit down, señor?" the man inquired. "It would be better perhaps if our conversation were to be a private one."

Again the Dutchman shrugged.

"Suit yourself," he responded tersely.

"The woman's name is Doña Aurora Mon . . . toya," the man said, once he had pulled out a chair and seated himself. "If you know her, señor, we may have a most profitable discussion. If you do not, then I shall not waste any more of your time. *Do* you know her, señor?"

"That depends," Paul replied slowly, wondering if the stranger were yet another relative who must be dealt with before he could get his hands on the fortune at Esplendor. "What's she to you?"

"My . . . betrothed, señor. We . . . quarreled—a silly argument—and she ran away from me. So, you see, it's very important to me that I locate her. I would pay a great deal to anyone who might be able to help me do that," the man asserted as he laid a fat purse upon the table and opened it to reveal the wad of pesetas inside.

The Dutchman took a long swallow of his drink, then wiped his mouth off with his sleeve and laughed shortly.

"I'd say you're a little too late to patch things up, señor. I *do* know Señorita Montoya, and she got married last year. You weren't in too much of a hurry to find her, now, were you?"

"No!" the man gasped. "That cannot be!" Then, recovering quickly from the shock of the information just imparted to him, he uttered rapidly, "No, don't go, señor. *Por favor.* I want to know everything—everything about Doña Aurora that you can possibly tell me. You have seen the color of my money. Does it not interest you? Bartender! Another bottle for *mi amigo* here."

Though outwardly the stranger had regained control of his emotions masterfully, Paul could tell the man was still highly agitated. Further, there burned in his eyes such hatred and fury as the Dutchman had never seen. Sensing a situation that might be turned to his advantage, Paul settled back in his chair, deciding to hear what else the stranger had to say.

"Forgive me, señor," the man said again once the bartender had served them, then departed. "I have not even told you my name. Allow me to introduce myself. I am Don Juan Rodolfo de Zaragoza y Aguilar, Marqués de Llavero, de España. And you, señor?"

"Paul Van Klaas, of Capricho."

"I am pleased to meet you, señor. You must excuse my earlier behavior, but your news stunned me so badly. . . . *Ay caramba!* To think I have searched for my betrothed all this time, only to find her wed to another! Who is this man, señor, who has stolen Doña Aurora from me?"

"He calls himself the Visconde Poniente, Don Salvador Rodriquez y Aguilar."

"No!" Juan gasped again. "It is too much! I will not bear it! *Heridas de Cristo!* The swine! Here. Married to Aurora. I shall kill him!"

As this was exactly what the Dutchman himself wished to do, he was gratified beyond measure that he had determined to listen to the marqués.

"Do you know Don Salvador, then señor?" Paul queried.

"Know him!" Juan spat. "He's my half brother, and a more black-hearted creature never walked the face of this earth! He is wanted in Spain for both murder and treason, the foul *bastardo*, and I have searched ceaselessly for him since the night he killed my father."

At these words Paul's eyes gleamed with triumph and satisfaction. At last perhaps he had found a way to rid himself of the visconde once and for all, leaving him free to claim the treasure of Esplendor for his own.

"Have another drink, señor," he suggested to the marqués, pushing the bottle toward Juan and smiling wolfishly, "for I think that you and I are indeed going to have a most profitable discussion."

Chapter Thirty-six

AURORA sang joyfully to herself as she arranged, inside the cradle that Salvador had fashioned for their coming child, the bedding she had sewn. The letters that Mario had brought had been from her parents and the visconde's mother. The Montalbáns and the Yerbabuenas were delighted with Aurora and Salvador's marriage. Both families claimed it could not have been better if they had planned it themselves, for since banding together against Juan they had become the dearest of friends. Doña Catalina, in her letter to Salvador, had also enclosed a note to Aurora. It had read, in part: *Once, I wished you were my daughter, and now you are. Watch over my beloved Salvador, and know that you too hold a special place in my heart. God keep you until we meet again.*

How touched Aurora had been by Catalina's words. The girl had refolded the note carefully and locked it tightly away in a small chest to prevent it from growing rotten with the mildew that encroached upon almost everything in the jungle.

Perhaps the most thrilling news of all had been that

both the Montalbáns and the Yerbabuenas were planning, if the estate were now well enough restored to accommodate them, to journey to Peru, to Esplendor.

"Only think, Salvador"—Aurora's face shone as she turned to her husband—"both my mother and yours will be here when our child is born. We must write to them right away, telling them of our expectations. You cannot know how much it will mean to me to have them present at the birthing. I have been . . . so afraid, having no one to advise me, for Lupe has never borne a child either. Now I will have someone to talk to, to guide me and ease my fears—not that you do not, my husband, but . . ."

"There are times when you wish for another woman's company, especially your mother's, no?" the visconde ended, understandingly, the sentence that Aurora had left unfinished. "I know that though you love them both dearly, Lupe and Heidi are not the same as family."

"Sí." Aurora sighed, then smiled wistfully. "It is so. How well you know me, *mi corazón*. I am indeed the luckiest woman alive to be your wife."

A brief shadow of pain clouded Salvador's countenance at her words, for no matter how hard he had tried he still had not been able to rid himself totally of the notion that he was accursed. In a moment of weakness he had given in to his desires and allowed himself to love Aurora. Now she was blind. More than ever he watched her protectively, fearing that if he did not, something even worse would befall her, would wrest her from him—and he would lose her, as he had lost so many others in his past. Somehow the love and joy they shared was so beautiful, so precious, that the visconde was afraid it was too good to be true. He feared something horrible would occur to destroy it, to punish them both for daring to grasp what others only dreamed of.

Once, he spoke of his feeling of foreboding to Aurora. She did not laugh and dismiss it, as he had half suspected she would. Instead she took his hand comfortingly and pressed it to her cheek.

"I too have felt such a presentiment, *mi vida,*" she confessed. "But I do not believe, as you do, that I am accursed, though, like your loved ones, bad things have happened to those I cared for as well. No, Salvador. I think it is because most people, in their hearts, feel as you do. They are afraid that if they are too happy, God will smite them down for daring to attain here on earth that which is promised only in heaven. And, oh, *mi amor,* perhaps it is true, for there are times when I know such heaven in your arms I have no need of another. I know it is wrong of me, and I know too that God can see into my heart and soul, that I have no secrets from Him; and I tremble to think of His wrath at my impertinence. But then I ask myself: If God did not mean me to know such happiness, why did He send you to me in the first place? So you see, Salvador, I do not believe that God will punish us for loving so. I think if we suffer, it is but His way of testing us, to be certain we are truly worthy of such a love."

"Ah, *querida,* how I wish I had your faith, but I do not," the visconde said.

"You have something else instead, my husband. God gave you strength. Perhaps between the two we will endure."

It was Lupe's wedding day. All week long the women of the household had been cooking and cleaning in anticipation of the happy event; and the men had been building long picnic tables, benches, and canopies for the *fiesta* that would follow the ceremony. All of Esplendor rang with laughter and activity. It was indeed as though the manor had come alive.

Upstairs, Aurora sat quietly, listening to the gay chatter of the women about her as they fussed over Lupe's wedding dress and veil, tugging the satin and lace this way and that until at last they were satisfied with the maid's appearance. When they had finally finished they described, for their mistress's benefit, the gown and how beautiful Lupe looked in it.

"Oh, Lupe," Aurora declared, as she rose and took the maid's hands in her own, "I know you are lovely. Jim is indeed a lucky *caballero*. Come. It is time. Already I can hear everyone calling for you."

Once all had gathered outside on the lawn in back of the house, those men who could play the guitar began to serenade the wedding couple; and Lupe, escorted by Salvador, walked slowly down the flower-strewn path to where Padre Guillermo and her fiancée, Jim Rawlings, awaited her. Aurora's sightless eyes shone with tears as the couple knelt and repeated their vows, for the words reminded her of her own promise to Salvador the day of their own marriage. As though sensing his wife's thoughts the visconde, after giving Lupe away, took Aurora's hand in his, holding it tightly throughout the ceremony.

At last the service ended. Amid the cheers and applause, Jim kissed his blushing bride; and all rushed to break open the wine and toast the newlyweds. After that the dancing began; and Aurora found herself whirled from one pair of arms to another as the men of Esplendor claimed the honor of dancing with *la patrona*.

Finally, breathless, the girl excused herself and, realizing that in all the excitement she had forgotten her fan, went back to the house to retrieve it. She was just descending the grand staircase to return to the festivities when one of the children of the estate approached her.

"Señora de Rodriquez, it's Fernando," the boy announced as he stepped forward into the entry. "I did not want to disturb you, señora, because of the *fiesta;* but there are some men at the boat dock, and they say they must speak to you. Will you come, or should I tell them to return another day?"

"No, I'll come," Aurora replied; then, smiling as she heard the boy's feet shuffling anxiously, she insisted, "You run on back to the festivities, Fernando. I know you don't want to miss a moment of them."

"No, señora. *Gracias*, señora. But I must accompany you. *El patrón* would be very angry if he found out I allowed you to go alone."

"Well, just this once I think you may be excused. Go on now. Hurry!"

"Are you—are you sure, señora?"

"*Sí*. I will explain things to Don Salvador."

"Oh, *muchas gracias*, señora!" the boy exclaimed before, his face beaming, he scampered toward the music and laughter.

Wondering idly who could be at the boat dock, Aurora went out through the front doors of the manor and started to tap her way, with her cane, down the road leading to the river.

At the boat dock four rough men stood, watching her coming.

"*Mierda!*" one of them, named Ricardo, swore when he saw the girl. Then he turned accusingly to Paul Van Klaas sitting in a dugout canoe below. "Señor, you said nothing about the woman being blind—and with child

as well! I have done many terrible things in the past;
but this I do not like. I do not like it at all."

The Dutchman was startled by the man's words.
Aurora pregnant? Paul had not known that when he'd
agreed to Don Juan's wicked plot. Nevertheless, their
scheme must be carried out as planned. It was the only
way that Paul was ever going to get his hands on the
treasure.

"Blind. With child. What difference does it make?"
he growled curtly to Ricardo. "You're being paid enough
to kidnap the Madonna herself. Now shut up, and get
on with it! Otherwise I shall have to report your
dilatory attitude to señor el Marqués."

That thought silenced any further protests that Ricardo
might have made. He was *muy macho*, but even he was
afraid of the scar-faced Spaniard.

"As you wish, señor," Ricardo uttered, grumbling
under his breath.

"*Hola*," Aurora called out as her cane left the dirt
road to tap more firmly upon the wood of the boat
dock. "Who's there, please? *Hola*. Is anyone there?"

Aurora never even had a chance to fight. She had
only an instant of sudden premonition before two of the
men grabbed her, one of them pressing a sickly sweet-
smelling cloth over her face. Moments later she knew
nothing more.

"Hurry up, *hombres!*" Paul ordered, standing up in
the dugout canoe, carefully, so it would not tip over, as
the men handed down to him the girl's limp, unconscious body.

Slowly, as the men untied the ropes that bound the
vessel to the boat dock, Paul sat back down in the craft.
Beneath the shelter of the thatched roof over the center
of the dugout, he propped Aurora up beside him, one

arm about her tightly to keep her inert figure from falling over. Her head lolled against his shoulder, and his nostrils twitched as he inhaled the sultry scent of her. Jasmine. Paul detested jasmine. It was too thick and cloying for his taste; but no doubt her husband, a hot-blooded Spaniard, preferred it to the light, citrus aromas the Dutchman liked. As far as he could and still manage to keep her upright, Paul edged Aurora away from him.

"Paddle, you bastards! Paddle!" he hissed as the men jumped into the canoe and shoved off. "The effects of the drug don't last more than ten or fifteen minutes. We've got to be well away from here before then, or the girl's liable to wake up and start screaming and struggling and attract somebody's attention."

"Tie her up, then, and gag her, now, while she's still out," one of the men, Andrés, suggested.

"No!" another man, called Ernesto, dissented sharply. "It will be obvious, then, to anyone who might be watching, that we are abducting her. As it is it only appears as though she and Señor Van Klaas are lovers. Hold her a little nearer, señor. *Sí.* That's it."

Ernesto nodded as the Dutchman again pulled Aurora's still form close and then, with his free hand, cupped one of her breasts. To make the scene even more convincing Paul pressed his lips caressingly against her hair, as though he were murmuring in her ear.

The fourth man, César, sniggered.

"If you find the woman is too heavy, señor, I will be happy to trade places with you," he bantered slyly.

"Shut up and paddle, you *cabrón!*" Ricardo snapped, his conscience still bothering him. "Would you rape a woman who is blind—and with child besides?"

"*Mi amigo*, I would rape your ugly sister if I thought it would give me pleasure."

At that the two men nearly came to blows before the Dutchman, with a terse command and another sharp reminder about reporting their behavior to señor el Marqués, sent them sullenly back to work. After that they paddled silently, intent on putting as much distance between themselves and Esplendor as possible.

In the bushes along the bank of the river, the boy Fernando crouched, shaking, tears of fright streaming down his face. Despite Aurora's assurance to the contrary, after he had returned to the *fiesta* he had again grown worried that *el patrón* would be angry with him for not keeping guard over *la patrona*. When she did not return from the boat dock, Fernando decided he had best go and check on her. Now he did not know what to do. He had arrived too late to see the men drug Aurora and lower her unconscious body into the dugout. All that Fernando had spied was his seemingly willing mistress in the arms of the Dutchman, Señor Van Klaas. The boy was afraid to go and tell Don Salvador what he had witnessed. *El patrón* was very jealous when it came to his wife. He would not be pleased with the person who informed him that *la patrona* had run off with another man. At last Fernando determined that he would keep silent for now. After the festivities he would ask his mother what he should do.

NATIVIDAD wrung her hands nervously as she stood, her eyes downcast, before Salvador. Behind her skirts her son Fernando trembled with fear as hesitantly he peeped around his mother to get a better view of *el patrón*.

The visconde did not look angry, only worried sick, for by now it had been discovered that Aurora was missing. Salvador was even now in the process of questioning everyone and organizing his men into search parties to look for *la patrona*. They would prove fruitless, the boy knew, then he quivered uncontrollably again at the thought of the visconde's wrath when Natividad revealed what Fernando had told her only moments before in their small cabin. How she had wailed and raved at the news! For a minute Fernando had feared she would strike him for not reporting the matter to *el patrón* at once. Then she had hugged him close; and he had realized that his mother understood why he had not—that she was as afraid of Don Salvador as he was. She had barely managed to put one foot in front of the other as, dragging Fernando behind her, she had crept up to the great house and asked to see the visconde.

Now she licked her lips anxiously before beginning to speak.

"Don—Don Salvador," she stammered, "I—I am sorry to disturb you, especially with Esplendor in such an uproar over *la patrona*'s disappearance. But I—I think, señor, that there is—there is no need to send out search parties for your wife."

"Why? What do you know, Natividad?" Salvador queried sharply. "Tell me. Quickly!"

"Oh, señor!" the woman cried. "Do not blame Fernando! Please. He's only a boy, and he was so frightened. . . ." Her voice trailed off as she started miserably to weep.

More quietly, realizing that Natividad was almost hysterical, the visconde continued, laying his hands upon the woman's shoulders to soothe her.

"Natividad, I blame no one as yet for my wife's disappearance. I am merely concerned about her safety.

She is blind and with child. She might be lost or hurt, unable to call for help. Whatever you know, Natividad, no matter how bad it is, you must tell me at once. Do you understand?"

"Sí, Sí, señor." The woman sniffed tearfully as, with one corner of her *rebozo*, she attempted to dry her eyes. She took a deep breath, then continued. "Some men came to Esplendor during the *fiesta*, and they asked Fernando to take a message to Doña Aurora. Would she come to the boat dock? they asked. They needed to speak to her. Fernando, remembering your orders, señor, told *la patrona* that he would accompany her when she went to talk to the men. But she—she said he shouldn't miss any of the *fiesta*, and she sent him away. She said—she said she would tell you it was all right, señor, so that Fernando would not be blamed for shirking his duties."

"I understand," Salvador stated. Of course, Aurora had thought of Fernando before herself. "Please go on, Natividad."

"Though Doña Aurora had reassured him, still, once he returned to the *fiesta*, Fernando worried. He watched for her to return, and when she did not, he went to look for her. He spied her sitting in a dugout canoe that was pulling away from the boat dock. Oh, señor! *La patrona*—*la patrona* has run away with Señor Van Klaas!"

"That's a lie!" the visconde spat, causing Natividad to cringe.

"No, no, señor! It is the truth!" Fernando insisted as he stepped forward manfully to defend his mother. "The Dutchman had his arm around Doña Aurora's waist; and she had her head against his shoulder; and he was—he was kissing her, señor!"

"No! I don't believe it," Salvador declared flatly. Not for a single moment would he allow himself to believe what he had just been told. He had been suspicious of Aurora once, and now, because of it, she was blind. He would not doubt her again. "If you did indeed see Señor Van Klaas taking my wife away—and I *do* believe that," the visconde said, his voice softening as his eyes took in the scared faces of Natividad and her son, "then things were not truly as they appeared. This I know. He has kidnapped her! For some purpose of his own, he has kidnapped my wife."

Sí, Salvador thought. That is it! Twice the Dutchman tried to kill me, and twice he failed. Perhaps he means to hold Aurora for ransom so he can get his hands on Esplendor. It's the plantation he wants, so he can search without hindrance for the treasure he thinks is buried here.

"Fernando, you are not to blame for what has happened," the visconde told the frightened boy. "You ought to have reported to me at once what you saw, but I understand why you did not. Go, and tell Daniel to saddle Nieblo. I am going to ride over to Capricho to see what I can learn."

Salvador returned more dispirited than ever to Esplendor. He had discovered little from Heidi Van Klaas. As far as she knew, she'd told him, Paul was still in Belém, although she expected him any day, one of his Indian slaves having brought her a message to that effect.

The visconde, not wanting to upset her, had said nothing to her of his suspicions about her husband. He'd simply informed her about Aurora's disappearance and asked her to keep an eye out for his wife. Then he had left.

Now, thoroughly downcast, he sat alone in the bedroom he shared with Aurora. She had not gone willingly with the Dutchman. Of this Salvador was sure. Stoutly he crushed the small, niggling doubt that pricked his heart. Aurora had *not* betrayed him. She loved him.

And I love her, Salvador thought. And now the black cloud of accursedness that hangs over me has enveloped my beloved. Well, it shall not have her! I will find her. I must. My life is nothing without her. I will *not* allow her to be torn from me.

Thus determined, the visconde summoned his men to begin making arrangements to travel down the vast Amazon River after Aurora.

UPON coming to her senses Aurora had screamed and struggled and demanded to know the reason for her abduction—all to no avail. With his big, spatulalike hands that had always caused her such unease, Paul Van Klaas had nearly choked her to death, threatening to kill her if she didn't shut up and stop fighting him.

Now, frozen with fear, she huddled on her seat in the dugout canoe that was taking her away from Salvador. Where was she going—and why? She did not know; she could not even see the landmarks that might have told her. She knew only that she was aboard a small vessel journeying down the Amazon River to a destination that might, she realized with horror, be final in more ways than one.

Did the brutal men who'd kidnapped her mean to murder her? Or would they only use her, then hold her for ransom? And why, oh, why had Paul Van Klaas been a party to her abduction? What could he possibly hope to gain by such an act?

Aurora had no answers to her questions, though she had pleaded endlessly with the Dutchman to allay her fears. But he had not. She had learned nothing except that she was defenseless, powerless against the men who'd taken her captive. Most terrifying of all was the fact that she was blind and with child. Even if somehow there were a chance of escaping from her kidnappers, she could not take it: for how far would she get, unable to see and burdened by her pregnancy?

No, there was nothing she could do to save herself. She was utterly at the mercy of the men who had abducted her.

Aurora had never felt so alone, so helpless, so frightened in all her life.

BOOK FIVE

And Gold Was Ours

Chapter Thirty-seven

Belém, Brazil, 1851

MARIO ran on in the darkness, stumbling a little over the uneven cobblestones of the alleys that twisted between the sprawling buildings lining the waterfront of Belém.

Presently he could no longer hear the sound of pounding feet behind him; and, realizing that the men so hotly pursuing him had given up the chase at last, he paused, leaning against a nearby wall for support as he gasped for breath.

Finally the furious thudding of his heart slowed. With the back of his hand he mopped the sweat from his brow. *Mãe de Deus!* That had been close, too close for comfort. The Marqués de Llavero was indeed a man to be reckoned with if one crossed him—as Mario had. He could only be grateful that, thanks to Don Salvador, he had been warned in time about Don Juan's mad penchant for vengeance.

The first thing that Mario had done when he'd returned to Belém had been to check the passenger lists of the ships anchored in the port's harbor. He had found the marqués's signature scrawled upon a page in the *Angel de Venganzo*'s record book, and he'd known that Don Juan would be looking for him. Instead of going to his lodgings Mario had taken up residence with a friend whose life he had once saved and who could thus be counted on not to betray his whereabouts. Then he had begun spying on the tenement building in which he actually lived. Sure enough, rough-looking strangers had shown up, asking questions about him. They had poked about the waterfront as well; but the men who worked the docks were close-mouthed and the marqués's hirelings had learned nothing. It was simply by chance that they had seen Mario tonight and tried to catch him. Fortunately he had escaped.

Now, he decided, it was time to turn the tables. He had discovered in which hotel Don Juan was staying, and Mario thought he would start to do a little stalking of his own. *Sím*. The marqués would soon learn that he, Mario Nunes, could be just as dangerous as Don Juan!

"PULL over here," Paul Van Klaas directed to the others in the dugout canoe as he caught sight of the camp, some distance from Manaus, where he had left his illegal Indian slaves and the hired peasant in charge of them. As the vessel neared the shore the Dutchman turned to Aurora. "This is where I leave you, señora," he told the terrified girl. "*Adiós*, and *bueno viaje*."

"No, wait!" Aurora cried. "Don't go! Oh, please, Paul—" She broke off abruptly, biting her lip. Then she went on more quietly. "I know you must have a reason for becoming a party to this plot against me; but whatever it is, whatever is wrong, we can work it out. Somehow. Salvador will help. I know he will. You and

Heidi were our friends, Paul. How can you do this to me? Take me with you. Oh, please. Don't leave me here alone with these men!"

"It's too late, Aurora," the Dutchman replied flatly, dashing her last hope that she might yet prevail upon him to change his mind and return her to Esplendor. "What's done is done. I've gone too far now to draw back. If only you had left Esplendor when Ijada tried to drive you away! All of this would have been avoided. But you persisted in staying, foiling my attempts to get my hands on the—" Paul snapped his mouth shut in midsentence, remembering just in time that he had revealed nothing about the buried treasure to Don Juan or the marqués's henchmen, who were now listening intently to his conversation with Aurora. When Don Juan had questioned him about his reasons for also wishing to kill Salvador, Paul had merely stated that he too held a deep grudge against the marqués's half brother. "Foiling my attempts to get my hands on the plantation," the Dutchman ended untruthfully to satisfy the curiosity on the faces of Don Juan's hirelings. "I always wanted Esplendor, you know. And I would have had it too, had your brother Basilio not deeded it to your husband."

But Aurora knew it was not the estate that Paul wanted. It was the fortune he believed was buried on the grounds. He had become obsessed by it, and his greed had driven him insane, just like so many before him.

"It—it was you who tried to murder Salvador, wasn't it?" Aurora began at last to fit together the pieces of the puzzle. "And—and Ijada . . . she was in on it with you, wasn't she? That's why she tried to get rid of me and Nicolas. It was as Basilio told me. She poisoned him—

and Francisca too, didn't she? Oh, Paul! Don't you see? It's all been for nothing! What you're looking for doesn't exist. It never did. Take me home. Please," Aurora begged.

"I can't. Especially now," he told her. "You know too much. But I'll tell you what I will do: I'll put up a tombstone for you at Esplendor, right next to Salvador's, once he's dead." Then he laughed. "Take her away, *hombres*. I'm sure that Don Juan is anxiously awaiting her arrival."

If the Dutchman's parting shot had been meant to strike terror into Aurora's heart, it had certainly done so. She stiffened will all-consuming fear at his words. The marqués was here in South America and waiting for her when they reached their final destination! No! It could not be! It could not be! Salvador. *Salvador!*

"No!" she gasped. "No!"

Then, before any of the men realized what she intended to do, she tried to throw herself overboard. Only the fact that César had edged his way up to take Paul's place by her side saved her from the murky depths of the Amazon River. César lunged toward her like a jungle cat, his arm like an iron band about her waist as he restrained her. Savagely Aurora fought him, rocking the dugout so violently the others feared it would tip over. At last César held the girl prisoner. Crudely he fondled her before the eyes of the others, taunting her with lewd remarks about what he meant to do to her now that Paul Van Klaas no longer served as her protector. Both Andrés and Ernesto sniggered. Ricardo, however, scowled ominously.

"Leave her alone," he ordered. "Señor el Marqués said he would kill any man who touched her—or have you forgotten that? He wants the woman himself—and undefiled by your stinking seed. Can it be, César, that your brains have gone to your *calzones* that you would risk your life for something that might be had from any *puta?*"

César shrugged, then grinned craftily.

"What Don Juan does not know, he cannot punish a man for. Who is to tell him if I take the woman? You, Ricardo? *Ay, caramba, amigo!* Forget your conscience. Have you looked at the woman?" He suddenly caught Aurora's cheeks and, pinching them between his fingers, jerked her face up so the others might view it. "She is indeed a beauty, no? When was the last time you had a piece of *culo* like that, eh? We will take turns, all four of us. If we keep silent, the marqués will be none the wiser."

Aurora's heart beat frantically in her breast as she waited for Ricardo's answer. The thought of being brutally gang-raped filled her with sick horror. The idea of being viciously assaulted by men whose faces she could not even see made her want to die. If she survived, she would never be able to speak to a man again without wondering: Was he one of them? Oh, God. *Was he one of them?* As the ghastly notion took hold of her, her stomach roiled. Without warning she leaned to one side of the canoe and vomited violently.

"You see?" Ricardo crowed triumphantly. "What you suggest is impossible, César. The woman is with child. Already she is ill. If you rape her, she is liable to suffer a miscarriage and bleed to death. Then what will you tell Don Juan? Leave her alone, I say. She is not worth your life."

Disgusted, César swore, then roughly shoved Aurora to the floor of the vessel. Still cursing her, he flung an old rag in her face.

"Clean up that mess you made, *ramera!*" he snarled.

"I'm not traveling all the way to Belém with stinking puke at my feet."

Shaking horribly, Aurora did her best to comply with César's demand. Then she crouched upon the floor of the craft, weeping quietly as she tried hard not to attract any further attention to herself.

The dugout once more got under way, carrying her farther and farther from Esplendor—and her beloved.

"Nicolas! Where have you been?" Salvador asked, his voice sharp with anger and concern. "Isn't it bad enough that Aurora has been kidnapped, without your disappearing as well?"

"I know how to take care of myself. There was no need for you to worry. Besides, I told Jim that I was going to do some scouting around the area."

"That's not the point. I *knew* I should have left you behind at Esplendor."

"Well, when I tell you what I found you'll be glad you didn't. That *bastardo* of a Dutchman is camped not more than a mile away from here."

"Nicolas, are you sure?" Salvador's voice rang with sudden hope, excitement, and grim satisfaction.

"As sure as I'm sitting here. I crawled up as close as I could to the edge of the camp to get a better look, but I didn't see Aurora anywhere. If the *hijo de la chingarra* took her, she's not with him now."

"How can you be so certain of that? The Dutchman's no fool. He's probably got her well hidden."

"She's not there, I tell you," Nicolas insisted. "I sent Bribón in to find her. He caused a devil of a stir, but I knew they wouldn't catch him. If she had been there, Bribón would have tried to lead me to her."

"Goddamn Paul Van Klaas!" the visconde swore, realizing the boy was right.

The monkey was so clever that Salvador sometimes wondered if the creature were half human. If Bribón had not found Aurora at the Dutchman's camp, then she wasn't there. That was all there was to it.

"What do you suppose he's done with her?" Nicolas questioned, his dark eyes suddenly anxious.

"I don't know," Salvador rejoined soberly, his voice filled with determination, "but I intend to find out. Show me where the *cabrón* is camped."

THE moon was a hazy halo in the midnight sky as Nicolas quietly led the way to the place where Paul Van Klaas was camped. The wind whispered through the trees, filling the jungle with an eerie sigh. Here and there an animal darted, eyes glowing in the darkness; and occasionally from the distance there came the hoot of an owl or the screech of a bat.

On softly padding boots Salvador and his young brother-in-law traversed the overgrown terrain, cursing under their breaths when the verdant tangle barred their path and must be cleared with machetes. Each whack of the blades rang in the stillness of the rain forest; and the visconde was sure that Paul Van Klaas must hear and be warned of their approach. But he was not, and they were able to sneak stealthily up to the edge of the encampment.

Hatred burned in the visconde's heart as he spied Paul Van Klaas's tent at last.

"I've got to get him away from the others," Salvador murmured, thinking aloud. "Somehow I've got to get him alone."

"No problem," Nicolas said, flashing a mischievous smile. "I'll just spook the natives."

With that, before the visconde could protest, the boy released a bloodcurdling scream, simultaneously rattling the undergrowth by swinging his machete.

To Salvador's amazement the five Indian slaves seated about the campfire jumped to their feet, yelling, and began to run, scattering in all directions. The peasant guarding them shouted frantically for them to come back, but they ignored him. Firing his carbine, he raced off after the last native just now disappearing into the brush. The Dutchman, roused by all the commotion, pushed open his tent flap and took after them.

"Sweet *Jesús*." Salvador whistled, gazing with surprise and admiration at Nicolas. "How did you manage to accomplish all that?"

Once more the boy grinned.

"They thought we were Jívaros—a tribe of headhunters. Mario used to tease Aurora about them. It was he who showed me how to make that dreadful noise. It's just awful, isn't it?"

"*Sí*, but it worked, and for that I am most grateful. You stay here, Nicolas. I'm going after Van Klaas."

JUAN could not believe it. He had been cheated. Cruelly, vilely cheated. He had waited forever, it seemed, for this moment; and, now that it had come, its triumph was sour. Doña Aurora Montalbán de Rodriquez, Viscondesa Poniente, was blind. She could not see the terrible scar that she had left upon his face. The marqués was so angry he struck Aurora viciously, knocking her to her knees. How dare she be blind? Unable to view the ugly, twisted gash she had inflicted upon him? Juan wanted her to see it. He wanted her eyes fastened upon it as he leered down at her, raped her, tortured her. He wanted her to know what she was paying for. Goddamn the Dutchman! Why hadn't he mentioned the fact that the girl was now blind? And pregnant as well? Salvador was to have an heir, while he, the Marqués de Llavero, had none. Basilio, Aurora's brother, had stolen the woman whom Juan had coveted, who might have borne his child. Now Basilio and Francisca were dead, thanks to the Dutchman and his mistress. But Salvador and Aurora were alive. They would pay for what they had done.

"Get up, you whore," the marqués ordered curtly as savagely he kicked Aurora in the ribs. "Get up!"

Trying desperately to conquer the waves of dizziness and nausea that assailed her, Aurora staggered to her feet, groping for something, anything, that might help to support her. Her hands found the edge of a table, and she leaned against it gratefully, fearing she would fall otherwise.

Juan laughed wickedly at her obvious fright and distress.

"You're not so high and mighty now, are you, bitch?" he jeered. "*Dios!* How I have waited to see you brought down—as Salvador, your husband, shall be when I am finished. How did you ever get together with my half brother, I wonder? No matter. It is even better than I had planned. I will write him a note, of course, telling him of your whereabouts. No, don't begin to hope, my dear. I'm afraid that by the time that Salvador arrives in Belém, we shall be gone. Oh, I shall lead him a merry chase, the *bastardo!* And all the while you will be at my mercy; and my half brother shall know it. It will drive him insane, for the Dutchman told me that Salvador is quite enamored of you. Is he, my dear?" the marqués inquired, reaching out with one hand to caress her cheek.

Aurora shuddered, overcome by loathing, and jerked away. Once more Juan chuckled evilly.

"You foolish child! Do you really believe you can escape from me so easily? I can take you whenever I wish, and you will be powerless to prevent it. Oh, how Salvador will suffer when he learns that! And he will go on suffering until I decide to kill him and put him out of his misery! However, right now I have further arrangements to make for our journey; so I will leave you alone—to contemplate our joining. Do not fear, my dear. It will be soon, very soon. This I promise."

Then, as though to emphasize his words, the marqués cupped one of Aurora's breasts and squeezed it tightly.

"I can hardly wait," he chortled. "But first"—he poked her rounding belly—"this must go. I dislike the idea of sharing you with Salvador's child."

Aurora gasped, horrified. What did Juan mean? No! Oh, no! He couldn't possibly intend to murder her baby. Surely not even the marqués could be such a monster!

"You *bastardo!*" she hissed, her voice a whimper of agony and rage. "If you dare to touch me, to harm me or my child, Salvador will kill you!"

"You think so, eh? Well, we shall see, my dear. We shall see."

Once the marqués had gone, locking the door behind him, Aurora sank to the floor, sobbing with terror and despair. The long journey to Belém had been a nightmare of verbal and physical abuse. Constantly she had been forced to endure not only César's lewd remarks and groping hands, but those of Ernesto and Andrés as well. How they had delighted in torturing and humiliating her! Only Ricardo had prevented Aurora from being raped by his brutal comrades. He had guarded her protectively and even had apologized for his part in her abduction.

Still the peril-ridden trip had taken its toll on her. She was exhausted; her mind was numb from ceaseless fear; her body, burdened by her pregnancy, ached for rest.

Slowly and with difficulty Aurora stood, one hand pressed against the small of her back, where a dull pain throbbed. It was a miracle that she had not lost her child from the torment she had suffered. Now Juan proposed to take her baby from her forcibly. She would die before she would let that happen.

She was no longer in the savage jungle, but the city of Belém. Here there would be people to help her—if only she could escape. Aurora did not know for certain where she was being held captive; but from the sounds that reached her ears from the outside world, she guessed that she was someplace on the waterfront.

Feeling her way about, she began to search carefully the tiny room in which she was imprisoned. If there were a means to escape from her cell, she must find it—and soon.

QUIETLY Salvador crept up on Paul Van Klaas, circling about to get behind the big blond man, for the visconde did not delude himself as to his chances of prevailing over the Dutchman in hand-to-hand combat. Paul was much larger and more powerful than Salvador, though the visconde was a tall and muscular man. The Dutchman, however, was not only four inches taller than Salvador, but fifty pounds heavier as well.

Slowly the visconde drew the black-barreled dragoon

Colt revolver at his waist and sneaked forward until the gun was pressed against Paul's back.

"Don't move, and don't make a sound," Salvador commanded softly as the Dutchman tensed warily. "I bought this pistol in *Tejas*, in *los Estados Unidos*. It fires six shots, and at this range I can hardly miss. Toss away that carbine, as far into the jungle as you can. That's right," the visconde went on as, cursing at being taken unawares, Paul threw away his gun. "Now, with your left hand, reach into your belt, and get rid of that knife in the same fashion. Then put your hands on top of your head, and turn around. *Bueno*. You're doing real well, Van Klaas. Back off, slowly. That's far enough. Now," Salvador snarled, "tell me what you've done with my wife, you *hijo de la chingarra!*"

Paul saw no reason to lie.

"I left her with four hired men, who were taking her down the Amazon to Belém."

"But . . . why?" the visconde asked, puzzled. "Why didn't you just ransom her back to me for the deed to Esplendor? That's what you want, isn't it? Possession of the plantation, so you'll be free to search wherever you please for that damned nonexistent treasure? So why did you send her to Belém?"

The Dutchman smiled, a gruesome grin that sent chills down Salvador's spine.

"Because your half brother, Don Juan, is in Belém," Paul informed the visconde.

"*Santa María!*" Salvador gasped, stricken. "You bastard! You utter bastard! I ought to shoot you where you stand!"

Perhaps the Dutchman feared that the visconde was so enraged he would actually do this. Whatever the reason, Paul suddenly lunged at Salvador, knocking him to the ground, sending his revolver flying. Over and over the two men rolled, pummeling each other viciously, paying no heed to the fact that their desperate struggle had brought them to the edge of a stagnant forest pool.

The visconde was breathing heavily now, for the fight with the bigger man was taking its toll on him. Already he felt certain that several of his ribs were cracked; and one of his eyes had been blackened. Blood from a gash on his brow dripped into the swelling orb, blinding him. His jaw felt as though it would never be the same. Still he battled on, knowing that his life—and Aurora's—depended on his winning.

He wriggled from beneath the Dutchman and staggered to his feet. But before Salvador could get his bearings, Paul, with his head, rammed into the visconde's stomach. Once more Salvador went down, his arms flailing frantically for support as he fell into the swamp. He inhaled raggedly for air as his head went underwater, and he felt the Dutchman's hands close tightly around his throat, choking him. Grimly, with every ounce of strength he could muster, the visconde managed to surface, gasping for breath before Paul pushed him under again, continuing to strangle him.

Then suddenly, inexplicably, Salvador was free. Panting, gulping for air, he stumbled from the pond, shaking his head to clear it, wiping the water from his eyes and feeling gingerly his horribly bruised throat. After recovering somewhat he glanced around, searching the darkness for the Dutchman.

Though the visconde had wished for his enemy's death, even he was appalled by what he saw. Paul was screaming soundlessly for help; his eyes were bulging from their sockets; his arms were waving about spastically as he tried to escape from the dreadful thing that held him fast.

The two men thrashing about in the pool had disturbed a deadly giant anaconda. Slithering from its resting place in the shallow water, it had coiled itself crushingly about the Dutchman. The snake was huge, almost forty feet long, and so powerful not even Paul could overcome it. Its beautiful, multicolored skin glistened in the moonlight, providing a sharp contrast to its murderous intent. Salvador could see the serpent's beady eyes gleaming as it continued to squeeze its powerless victim to death.

The visconde staggered to firmer earth, searching for his pistol. *Heridas de Cristo!* Where was it? Where was it? There!

Before he could reach the gun, however, the Dutchman's hired peasant suddenly appeared without warning from the shadows, his carbine aimed right at Salvador. Slowly, grinning, the peasant cocked the hammer on the weapon, and the visconde knew he was a dead man.

He thought fleetingly of Aurora, his beloved, then closed his eyes to deliver a silent prayer to God as he waited for the shot that would kill him.

There came a rapid, *whoosh*ing noise—but no report. Startled, bewildered to find himself alive and well, Salvador opened his lids. The peasant lay sprawled on the ground, and Nicolas was striding forward, asking anxiously if his brother-in-law were all right.

"I—I think so," the visconde panted as, still dazed and confused, he leaned against a tree for support, one arm about his ribs, which were paining him badly now. "What—what happened?" he asked, gesturing toward the peasant's fallen body.

"I killed him," Nicolas stated calmly, replacing the

weapon at his belt, "with my blowgun." Then the boy exclaimed, "*Madre de Dios! Look at that!*"

Salvador turned. Paul Van Klaas was dead; and now the snake was uncoiling itself from the Dutchman's corpse. Awe-struck, the visconde and his young brother-in-law stared as slowly the serpent unhinged its jaws and began to devour the body.

"It'll never be able to swallow him," Nicolas whispered. "He's too big! The Indians who brought Aurora and me to Esplendor told us that even the largest of anacondas can't consume anything weighing more than a hundred and fifty pounds at the most—at least," the boy amended, troubled, "there haven't ever been any reports of them eating anything larger than that."

"Well, at any rate, there's nothing we can do for him now," Salvador said as he turned his gaze away from the unfortunate Paul. "Help me drag that peasant's corpse over there too. I want to dump it in the swamp as well."

"Why?" the boy inquired, slightly baffled. "No one will accuse us of murder. He was going to shoot you."

"I know, but even so, I don't want any traces left of what happened here tonight," the visconde explained, grunting as he bent his aching body to grab hold of the peasant's arm. "There'll be an investigation otherwise, and I don't want Heidi Van Klaas to learn about her husband's true nature. She's a good woman, and she'd be horrified if she ever discovered that Paul was a crazed murderer.

"When we get back to Esplendor, I'll tell Coronel de la Palma that we came upon Van Klaas's camp, that it had been attacked by Jívaros—which the Indians, if any of them return to Capricho, will bear out—and that both Van Klaas and the peasant died trying to defend themselves. Then the coronel and I will tell Heidi the same story and explain to her that it was impossible to bring the bodies back, that you and I buried them in the jungle. Do you understand, Nicolas?"

"*Sí*." The boy nodded.

"Oh, and Nicolas," Salvador said gravely as he extended his hand to shake the boy's own, "I want to thank you for saving my life. You ought to have stayed put, as I told you to do; but I'm awfully glad you didn't. *Muchas gracias para todo el mundo, mi amigo*. This night you have become a man."

Nicolas grinned shyly and glanced away, overcome by emotion.

"It was nothing," he said.

"No," the visconde replied softly. "It was more than I can ever repay. If I had been killed, Aurora would most certainly have been murdered too, for she is being held prisoner by my half brother, who hates me and wishes me dead. Now . . . I have a chance to rescue her. You gave me that, Nicolito, and for that I am more grateful than I can ever express."

MARIO stayed well back in the shadows as he watched Juan and his hirelings hustling Aurora up the gangplank to board the *Rosa de España*. For days the *mestizo* had been curious as to what the marqués was keeping so carefully hidden, under lock and key, and vigilantly guarded in the building on the waterfront. Now Mario knew. It was Doña Aurora.

"*Sangue de Deus*," he swore softly to himself in the darkness. "The *porco* has Dom Salvador's wife!"

How ill and terrified she looked! By the light of the moon Mario could see how white and strained her face was, the mauve circles that ringed her eyes and the bruise she bore upon one cheek, where Juan had struck her viciously. She needed help desperately.

Quickly Mario slipped away, racing to the rooms in the tenement building where he had been staying with his trusted friend Bernardo.

"Bernardo," the *mestizo* asked as he began to scribble some words on a piece of paper, "how well do you speak Spanish? Castilian Spanish, I mean, not just the mixed dialect of the waterfront."

"Pretty good, *meu amigo*. Well enough to make myself understood, I think. But . . . why?"

"I want you to do me a favor—one that you'll be well paid for, if I know Dom Salvador. I want you to take this note to him at Esplendor. His wife, Dona Aurora, has been kidnapped by his half brother, Dom Juan. The evil *cobra* has taken her aboard the *Rosa da Espanha*, which is bound for *México*. I would go to Dom Salvador myself, but it is more important that I find some means of accompanying *a senhora*, else *o senhor* will not know where to search for her. *México* is a big country. Will you do this for me, *meu amigo*?"

"But of course," Bernardo said. "I will do whatever I can to help, Mario."

"*Bom*. I knew I could count on you. Let us go, *meu amigo*, before it is too late!"

AURORA huddled in terror on her cramped bunk aboard the *Rosa de España*, which was taking her to some unknown destination in Mexico. Mexico! Her heart sank at the name, which she had managed earlier to overhear. Salvador, if he were still alive, would never find her there. He would assume that Juan had returned to Spain, taking her with him; and while her husband risked his life to go back to their homeland, Juan would be holding her captive thousands of miles away.

Oh, God. Aurora wept into her pillow. She could not bear it. She could not! Salvador would be caught and hanged for murder and treason, and she would be helpless in Juan's grasp for the rest of her life! Even more horrifying than this was the thought that Juan meant to kill her child too, the only part of Salvador that she would have left to her.

Aurora shuddered with revulsion as she remembered the ghastly man whom the marqués had brought to her cell on Belém's waterfront. Doctor Perez, the man had called himself, but she'd doubted if he'd ever been to medical school. While Juan's hirelings had restrained her, Doctor Perez had shoved up her skirts to examine her with his dirty hands, poking and prodding her, making her long to retch.

At last he had turned to the marqués.

"I can perform the operation that you desire, señor," he had said, "but I must tell you that it is my opinion that the woman is too far along in her pregnancy to successfully abort the baby. Doubtless the mother will die also. If you wish to take that chance, however, I shall get started."

"No," Juan had replied, much to Aurora's overwhelming relief. "I want the woman to live—and suffer. I will wait until the child is born, then I will strangle it at birth."

Now, as she recalled the marqués's evil announcement, Aurora's blood ran cold. Juan was not only insane, but inhuman. She could only be grateful that he found the idea of sharing her with Salvador's baby repugnant and did not want to risk killing her by causing her to miscarry the child. So far, though he continued to taunt her ceaselessly with the notion, the marqués had not forced himself upon her. Still any day now Aurora imagined that he would overcome his revulsion and desire to keep her alive and would come to her cabin to rape her. She was puzzled as to why he had not.

She stiffened with fear as there came a sudden, stealthy knock upon her door.

"Doña Aurora?" Mario whispered, glancing warily over his shoulder down the corridor of the ship. "Doña Aurora, are you in there?"

"Ma—Mario?" she breathed hesitantly, stunned.

"Sí, it is I, señora. Are you all right? Come closer, so we can talk."

"Mario! Oh, thank God!" Aurora cried as she stumbled to the door and pressed her ear against it. "Sí, I am holding up as well as can be expected. What are you doing here? How did you find me? Is Salvador with you?"

"No," he answered this last, dashing the sudden hope that had soared in her breast. "As to the rest, it is a long story, and I may not have much time. I do not know how long the guard will be absent from his post. Listen to me, señora: I have sent word to your husband. Even now he is doubtless on his way to rescue you, so do not despair. In the meantime I will come to you as often as I can."

"But—but how did you find me?"

"I spied Don Juan sneaking you aboard and followed. I have hired on as one of the crew. I would report your abduction to the captain, but unfortunately I doubt that the word of a *mestizo* peasant would be taken over that of the marqués. Besides, he has already informed the captain that you are unwell, suffering from a tropical illness and subject to periodic fits of delusion, during which you claim he has kidnapped you. So your word too is useless against him, señora."

"*Mierda!*" Aurora swore. "The swine! Oh, Mario, I'm so afraid. Does Juan know who you are? Is there a chance that he may recognize you?"

"No, I have disguised my appearance. Even you would not know me, señora. In addition to this, the marqués has been stricken with sea sickness—and malaria as well. He has not set foot out of his cabin since the beginning of our voyage. Señora, I hesitate to ask this, but he has not—he has not—"

"Molested me?" Aurora finished, flushing with embarrassment. "No, thank God. Not yet."

"*Bueno.* And your child?"

"Is still safe within me."

"Then you may rest easier, señora, for I believe that Don Juan will be incapacitated for our entire journey. I must go now. Someone is coming. Have courage, señora. You are no longer alone. I, Mario, am with you."

After the *mestizo* had gone Aurora sank to the floor, trembling, and began to weep with relief. She was not alone. She was not alone! Still sobbing and yet starting to laugh too, she hugged herself tightly, realizing that she was perilously close to hysteria. As though sensing its mother's distress her baby kicked within her. Almost immediately Aurora stopped crying and, marveling at this miracle of life, placed her hands over her belly to soothe her agitated child. Presently the fluttering of movement settled to a more peaceful stirring.

Now more than ever Aurora cursed Juan. To think he would destroy the seed born of her and Salvador's love!

"Do not worry, little one," she murmured to her

baby. "Your father is coming. Soon—soon he will be with us. Have faith, little one. Salvador's love for us will prevail over the monster's evil. This I believe. I *must* believe it, else I am lost . . . lost—" Aurora broke off abruptly, biting her lip.

Though Mario had given her strength and hope, still her world was a dark place indeed without the light of her life.

"Hurry, my beloved Salvador. Hurry," she whispered to the empty room, "for I do not know how much longer I can go on."

Chapter Thirty-eight

Matamoros, Mexico, 1851

"More rice, Maman. Want more rice!" the boy Chance squealed as he beat, with his spoon, upon the edge of his plate, then, at his mother's admonition about the noise, waved the utensil about in the air, laughing with delight.

"Hush, Chance, hush!" Storm Lesconflair reproved her nearly two-year-old son. "People are staring."

Then she smiled and began to ladle more steaming Spanish rice onto his plate as the others seated outside in the open courtyard of the hotel looked on with amusement.

"He is a handful, no?" an elderly dowager a few tables over commented, her rheumy blue eyes twinkling at the boy.

"*Sí,*" Storm replied in Spanish tinged with a slight French accent. "But I love him all the same."

"Of course," the beldam observed, then sighed. "That is what mothers are for, is it not? Julio! My check, *por favor.* Ah, this must be the proud *padre,* eh?"

"*Sí*," Storm declared as she glanced up to see her tall dark husband, Wolf, striding toward her.

Her keen grey eyes shone with love as she gazed at him, noting the stares of admiration that followed his lithe handsome figure as he moved across the courtyard, his silver spurs jingling. Any woman would have been proud to call him hers—and Storm was prouder than most.

She was a Southern belle, born and reared in the French Quarter of New Orleans. A few years ago, when she'd been a sixteen-year-old orphan, her wastrel uncle had gambled away her inheritance, leaving her penniless. Then he had wagered away Storm herself to a horrid rancher, Gabriel North, the man who had murdered Wolf's parents. While she'd been en route to Texas to wed the rancher, Storm's stagecoach had been attacked by a notorious gang of outlaws, the Barlow brothers, who'd taken her captive. Fortunately, before they could force themselves upon her, the youngest of them, Billy Barlow, had lost her to Wolf in a card game. Wolf had fallen in love with her and married her.

For a time they had made their home with his adopted Comanche family in the Llano Estacado; but after an outbreak of cholera had decimated the Indians, they'd moved on. Their son, Chance, had been born on the Great Plains of Texas. After the boy's birth Storm had prevailed upon her husband to come to Mexico and settle down. Today they had journeyed the distance from their farm, Fin Terre, to Matamoros for supplies.

Eagerly Storm lifted her lips for Wolf's kiss and smiled as he affectionately ruffled their son's hair before pulling out a chair and sitting down.

"*Dos enchiladas y frijoles y arroz,*" Wolf told the waiter who hurried over to take his order, "and a bottle of mescal. So"—he leaned back in his seat and lit a thin black cigar, blowing a cloud of smoke in the air—"what have you two done with yourselves today?"

"*Maman* take me to see boats, Ap', boats *muy grandes*," Chance mumbled—after stuffing himself with more rice—speaking his own peculiar mixture of French, English, Comanche, and Spanish, the four languages in which his parents conversed, depending upon their moods.

"Don't talk with food in your mouth," Storm reminded the boy, "and they are called ships—*buques*—not boats." Then she explained to her husband, "I hired a carriage to take us down to the waterfront, so that Chance could see the Gulf."

"Did you have a good time?"

"*Sí*, but . . . Oh, Wolf. There's something that's been troubling me ever since."

"Yeah? What's that, baby?"

"I saw a woman there. She was blind, and with child besides; and the most horrible-looking, scar-faced man was dragging her along the dock, swearing at her something awful. He even struck her once or twice before he pushed her into a hired carriage. I just couldn't believe it! I wanted so much to help her, but I didn't dare to intervene. I had Chance with me, and the man was accompanied by several rough guards as well. . . ."

"Yeah, so?"

"Oh, Wolf, it's the strangest thing, but I can't get out of my mind the idea that I've seen the woman someplace before. I can't remember where, but I feel terrible, as though I ought to have done something, anything, to aid her. It was obvious that she was absolutely scared to death of the scar-faced man. In fact, I wondered if he weren't holding her prisoner or something.

She seemed so unwilling to go with him. *Sainte Marie!* Wolf, look! There they are now! See what I mean. Just look how hateful he's being to her!"

Wolf turned and tipped back his black, flat-brimmed *sombrero* to get a better view of the couple just now entering the courtyard and taking a table some distance away. It was as Wolf's wife had told him so indignantly. The scar-faced man was treating the blind woman as though she were a dog—or worse—cruelly yanking her along and cursing her when she stumbled, heedless of the sharp frowns he was attracting by his actions toward her. At the sight of them Wolf suddenly stiffened. Then, casually—or so the unobservant would have said—he turned back to Storm.

"Stop staring, *paraibo*," he ordered softly, "and do nothing to draw attention to us."

"But . . . why?" she asked, baffled.

"I know who the woman is."

"Who?"

"Doña Aurora Montoya—"

"Aguila's *novia?* The one whose portrait he had in his watch? Of course! Oh, I just knew I'd seen her someplace before!" Storm insisted. "And the man?"

"I don't know." Wolf shook his head. "He's a stranger to me. But I think you're right, baby, and there's something wrong. The woman *does* look terrified. I want you to go over there, and find out what you can. Pretend you're an old friend of the family or something."

"All right," Storm agreed. She stood and, assuming a nonchalant manner, started toward the couple's table. When she was almost past it she stopped and, as though quite startled, gave an exclamation of delight. "Why, Doña Aurora!" she cried, smiling as she bent forward to hug the bewildered woman. "Doña Aurora!

What a surprise!" Rapidly, as she kissed the woman on both cheeks, Continental fashion, Storm whispered in Aurora's ear, "I'm a friend, here to help—if you need it. Pretend you know me." Then more loudly Storm continued. "Dear Doña Aurora. It's been ages! What are you doing here in *Méjico?* How is your family?" Quickly Storm searched her memory for the names of the woman's brother and his wife, from whom Aguila had purchased the timepiece; then she went on. "Your brother Basilio and his wife, Francisca, they are well?"

"No, alas, no," Aurora murmured, still highly confused. Who was this strange woman who knew her name—and her brother's and his wife's names as well— and was offering to help her? How did she know that Aurora desperately needed assistance? "I am sorry to tell you this, señora, but Basilio and Francisca are dead. They passed away some time ago."

"*Dios mío,* how sorry I am to hear that. My deepest sympathy, Doña Aurora, on your loss. No wonder you seem so pale and—and ill. I thought perhaps you'd had an accident, for . . ." Here Storm floundered, not knowing whether or not to mention the woman's blindness, for Aguila had not spoken of it.

Had the woman always been unable to see? Or was this a recent occurrence?

"*Sí,* señora," Aurora uttered hastily, sensing that Storm was hesitantly feeling her way in their conversation. "It was that which caused the loss of my sight."

"How awful for you," Storm observed, then went on. "But you must forgive me, Doña Aurora. I—I was not aware at first of your blindness," she lied. "No doubt you are wondering who I am. It is Storm—Storm Lesconflair—from—from Paris," she improvised, for she had never been to Paris in her life. "We met one summer in Spain while I was on holiday."

"*Sí*, oh, *sí*, Storm. I remember now." Aurora deftly picked up the threads of the fabrication. "It was the summer I spent with my grandmother in Barcelona. Please. Allow me to present you to my . . . brother-in-law, señor el Marqués de Llavero, Don Juan Rodolfo de Zaragoza y Aguilar."

"*Mucho gusto,* señor· el Marqués," Storm stated politely as she extended her hand, but inwardly she shivered as the scar-faced man stood and bent to kiss her fingers.

"*El gusto es mío,* señora," he responded courteously, though his dark eyes pierced her like a hot iron poker, as though to determine whether or not she posed a threat to him.

Coolly, knowing that Wolf was watching and would kill Juan instantly, should he dare to lay a hand upon her, Storm ignored the marqués and turned back to Aurora.

"Your husband is not with you, then, señora?" she inquired, her eyes taking in the woman's thin figure, heavy with child.

"No. Salvador was . . . unavoidably detained," Aurora answered carefully, feeling Juan's· burning eyes upon her.

"I . . . see," Storm intoned thoughtfully, for she had not failed to notice the woman's imperceptible pause before explaining that her husband was not with her. "But, come. You still have not told me what you're doing in *Méjico.* How long are you staying? Shall we have time to get together for lunch?"

"I doubt that, señora," Juan remarked smoothly before Aurora could reply. "We are here on business—and for a short while only. It has been a pleasure meeting you, señora. *Buenos días.*"

Then, without even waiting for the meal they had ordered, he hustled Aurora away.

Now more convinced than ever that the blind woman was an unwilling captive of her brother-in-law, Storm returned to her own table and leaned forward surreptitiously to report to Wolf. Noting, from the corner of one eye, two of Juan's henchmen sidling nearer in an attempt to overhear what she was saying, Storm spoke rapidly in Comanche to her husband.

"It *is* Doña Aurora! And I definitely think there's something wrong. Her brother Basilio and his wife, Francisca, are dead; and when I asked about her husband she told me he wasn't with her, that he'd been unavoidably detained. Something about the way she said it made me think there was more to it than that. She claimed the man with her was her brother-in-law, but even if he is, I still believe he's holding her prisoner! When I asked if she could have lunch with me, he cut in rudely, practically snapping my head off, and said no, she couldn't. Then he carted her off before I could question her further. What do you think, Wolf?"

"Did she mention her husband's name—or that of her brother-in-law?"

"*Sí.* She's married to a man called Salvador—what a blow to Aguila! And her brother-in-law is the Marqués de Llavero, Don Juan Rodolfo de Zaragoza y Aguilar."

"What?" Wolf burst out, tossing away his cigar and leaning across the table to take Storm's hands tightly in his own. "*Paraibo*, are you sure?"

"Of course. Why?"

"Jesus Christ! Salvador is my cousin Aguila's true name, and Don Juan is his half brother!"

"What?"

"*Sí*, it's a long story, but suffice to say that Juan hates Salvador and has always wished him dead. *Por Dios*, Storm! Juan has kidnapped Doña Aurora; I'm certain of it! You take Chance, and go on back to our hotel room. I'll be up shortly."

"All right," Storm assented, though she was eaten up with curiosity.

Still she had learned a long time ago that it did no good to argue with her husband, especially when his dark visage wore the deadly expression it bore now. She wiped Chance's face and hands with his napkin, then led him away. Already it was past time for his nap, and he was yawning, barely able to keep his eyes open.

I'll put him to bed, Storm thought, then I'll ask one of the bellboys to take that poor woman something to eat. She looked, as though she were starving.

Thoroughly outraged by the notion, Storm stalked up to her hotel room and yanked indignantly on her bell rope.

It was easy for Wolf to give Juan's hirelings the slip. The gunslinger had, in the past, outsmarted many men more clever than they were. As their confused shouts rang out behind him, he hoisted himself up to the balcony, which ran all the way about the hotel, and, pressed flat against the wall, he inched himself toward the room where he'd spied Juan taking Aurora.

Through the open windows Wolf heard his cousin interrogating the helpless blind woman about Storm.

"It was just as she said," Aurora whimpered piteously. "I met her one summer in Barcelona while she was on holiday from her school in Paris. I don't know her that well, and I certainly have no idea what she's doing in

Méjico. It doesn't matter how much you beat me, Juan; I can't tell you anything more than that."

A sharp cry followed this statement, as though the marqués had indeed struck Aurora. Wolf's eyes narrowed at the sound. It was all he could do to keep from barging in then and there and rescuing Salvador's wife. But the gunslinger restrained himself. He did not want to kill Juan just yet—at least not until Wolf had discovered whether or not Salvador was still alive. If the marqués had murdered his half brother, he would pay dearly for the crime. The gunslinger would see to that, and Juan would not find it pleasant. Wolf had learned many things besides stealth from the Comanches. But he must be cautious now. If he shot his way into the room, Doña Aurora, unable to see and take cover, might be hit by a stray bullet in the confusion. Even so, in light of her suffering, Wolf might have taken this risk, had it not been for the child the blind woman carried. Hardened though he was, he could not bring himself to endanger the life of an unborn infant.

"Don Salvador?"

The gunslinger whirled quickly, both his black-barreled pistols drawn and ready and aimed straight at the heart of the man standing there before him, for Wolf had not been taken unawares. Ever-alert, he had heard the approaching footsteps of the man who now backed away from him, empty hands raised high.

"Forgive me, señor." The stranger warily eyed the gunslinger's deadly revolvers. "My mistake. I thought—I thought you were someone else."

"Don Salvador," Wolf breathed. "That was what you called me, wasn't it? Does that make you my friend or my foe, mister?"

"Your friend, señor, if you are as much to Don

Salvador," the man stated. "Your foe, if you are the *compadre* of that black heart inside, who is torturing sweet Doña Aurora."

"They are both my cousins," Wolf uttered tersely, "but Don Juan is no *amigo* of mine."

"Your cousins! *Sangre de Cristo!* Then allow me to introduce myself, señor. I am Mario Nunes, friend of Don Salvador, at your service. You are the one called El Lobo, are you not? No wonder I mistook you for Don Salvador. Except for the eyes there is much resemblance between you. He has spoken often of you to me, señor. He told me it was you who gave him the pistol that he carries always at his waist. He showed me, one day, how to load and fire the revolver. I thought he was fast with it, señor. I did not believe him when he said you made him look like an amateur. Now I see that it is so."

Slowly Wolf lowered his guns and dropped them back into their holsters. Then he extended his hand to the *mestizo*.

"Come," he said. "I think there is much that you and I must discuss."

WHEN Mario had finished his tale, Wolf was silent for such a long time that at last the *mestizo* cleared his throat and spoke again.

"Do we—do we move in, señor?" he asked.

"No." Wolf shook his head. "Much as I hate the idea of Doña Aurora spending another minute with that madman, I think we owe it to Salvador to wait for his arrival. From what you say he should be here any day now—if your friend Bernardo got your message to him."

"Oh, I am certain that he did, señor. Bernardo is a true *amigo*. He would not have failed me."

"Then we will wait," Wolf repeated. "It is Salvador's vendetta. I will not rob him of his triumph. Besides, right now Juan is too closely guarded for us to assault him en masse—especially as long as he keeps Doña Aurora nearby; she might be killed accidentally in the process. And if we attack him and fail, Juan's liable to murder the woman outright. I don't want to be the man responsible for causing the death of Salvador's wife."

"I understand, señor."

"In the meantime we will keep careful watch that Doña Aurora's situation does not worsen," the gunslinger continued, smiling in a way that sent chills up Mario's spine, "and we will give my cousin's half brother something to think about, no?"

Juan peered nervously down the long corridor of the private house that he had rented and into which he had moved Aurora. The hotel had been too public for his purposes and too crowded besides. Always, people had stared at him, suspicious of his treatment of the girl; and that bitch Storm Lesconflair had poked and pried into his affairs until the marqués had thought he would lose his restraint and strangle her.

Finally, though it was a lie, he had informed her that they were leaving Matamoros; and he had rented the private house.

Now he tried to tell himself that his shaking was due to another onslaught of the malaria that continued to plague him. But this was only partially true. More than anything Juan trembled with fear. Though the private house was like a fortress, with guards posted everywhere, still someone had managed to invade it. Andrés was dead. They had found his body two days ago on the doorstep. His throat had been slit. Now, this morning, the corpse of Ernesto had been discovered hanging from a tree in the courtyard.

It is Salvador, Juan thought for the hundredth time. It is Salvador who is murdering my men, taunting me, goading me. Why doesn't he show himself? The *bastardo!* Why doesn't he come and get his wife?

But there was no answer; and the more that Juan thought about it, the more perplexing it became.

How had Salvador discovered his whereabouts? he wondered. In the letter that he had written to his half brother, just before leaving Belém, the marqués had told the visconde to wait at the Caiman's Tooth Inn, a shabby hotel on the waterfront, until he received further notice. To do otherwise—Juan had underlined these words twice—would be to seal the fate of his beloved Aurora. Was it possible that Salvador had ignored him, had somehow discovered he was bound for Mexico instead of Spain?

No!

But then who was killing Juan's men? He did not know; and the thought filled him with apprehension, for, like all bullies, he was a coward at heart. He shivered involuntarily. It was almost as though a phantom were at work, for the guards had seen no one, heard no one. Surely no human could move so invisibly, so soundlessly, in the darkness!

Still anxious, the marqués went into his bedroom, carefully locked the door, and sank to his bed, racked by the quivering of his limbs that heralded another malaria attack. Curse the disease! Despite the medication that Juan was now taking for the tropical illness, his condition appeared to be worsening. He was having difficulty both hearing and seeing; several times his skin had broken out in a hideous rash; and his stomach troubled him. He was so debilitated that he could not even force himself on Aurora, his prisoner. The last time he had tried he had been so weak that when the girl had fought him he had fallen to the floor and had scarcely been able to pull himself to his feet again.

Everything had gone so awry that for a moment Juan wished he were dead.

"You're sure the *hijo de la chingarra* is in there?" Salvador asked as he stared grimly at the private house that Juan had rented in Matamoros.

"Yeah, I'm sure," Wolf drawled, "and except for Aurora he's all by his lonesome self. While we were waiting for you to get here, Mario and I took care of all his men—one by one."

The visconde shuddered a little at that, for he knew how his cousin "took care of" people, and it wasn't pleasant. Nevertheless, he felt that no treatment was too cruel for the men who'd kidnapped Aurora, and he yearned to deal Juan an even worse fate.

How Salvador had waited for this moment, had longed for it ever since Mario's friend Bernardo had found him on the Amazon River and delivered to him the *mestizo*'s note. The letter that Juan had sent to him the visconde had never received. He had paddled downriver so furiously in order to catch up with his half brother and Aurora that the marqués's messenger had missed him.

In Belém, Salvador had boarded another ship bound for Mexico. He had arrived this morning to find Mario waiting on the coast to transport him into Matamoros.

Now the visconde must learn every detail of Aurora's

imprisonment. In his battle against his half brother his beloved's life was at stake.

"You're certain that my wife's all right?" he inquired again.

"As far as we can tell, señor," the *mestizo* replied reassuringly. "But then we have not seen her for some time. Your cousin, Señor Lobo, suspects she is being held captive in a small, windowless room up there in the attic." Mario pointed to an area just below the roof. "It is doubtless part of the servants' quarters. We would have broken into the house, señor, but at first there were too many guards, and the place was like a fortress. Then later we did not wish to risk Doña Aurora's life, and that of your unborn child as well, by such an act. For all we know, Don Juan is sitting in there right now with a gun pointed at her. We have not seen him since yesterday."

Salvador's throat closed with fear at that; and the more he thought about it, the more certain he became that Mario was right. It would be just like Juan to use Aurora as a shield—the cowardly cur!

"Come on," the visconde ordered, his face sick with worry. "*Vamanos!*"

THE day was so hot that Juan believed he would die. With his handkerchief he once more mopped his face and neck. Then he licked his parched lips and thought longingly of a cool drink as he squinted his eyes against the glare of the sun to get a better look at the terrain below. He had been sitting on the roof all morning, and so far he had seen nothing. But he did not dare to leave his precarious perch upon the red tiles. The last of his hirelings was dead, and Juan guessed that whatever was going to happen would occur today. Whoever was out there was coming to get him next—and soon. He was safe up on the roof, for from here, behind the cover of the protruding chimneys, he had a clear view of his entire surroundings. As long as he stayed where he was no one could sneak up on him, taking him unawares. Besides, his unknown assailant wouldn't expect him to be on the roof.

He wished he'd been able to get away, but he had not dared to leave the house, for fear that he would be attacked and murdered while trying to escape; and it had been impossible to obtain more men once word had gotten out about the fates of those who had served him.

If only he knew who was after him. It did not seem possible to him that Salvador alone could have killed all the guards. And his half brother was not brutal enough to have designed their excruciating deaths. César, the last to die, had been buried up to his neck in sand, and honey had been poured over his head. Red ants had eaten him alive.

Juan had heard tales of savage heathens committing such atrocities, but to think the deeds had been performed by a civilized man . . . No, that was just not Salvador's style; and the marqués shuddered with fright as he wondered again who was out there. If Juan must die, he wanted to go as quickly and painlessly as possible. He did not wish to suffer as he had tormented his captive.

Grimacing, he stared over at Aurora, huddled close beside one of the chimneys. She was petrified, the marqués knew. He need not worry about her trying to escape. Blind and pregnant, she could not traverse the precarious, slippery red tiles without aid. How she had screamed and wept when he'd dragged her up here, practically wrenching her arms off as he'd hauled her over the edge of the tiny cupola's wall on to the roof.

Then he had pushed her up against the chimney and hissed for her to stay put. Sensing she would stumble and fall to her death if she moved, Aurora had not stirred since.

Now she gave a helpless little moan of agony, for twinges of pain had started within her body; and they were growing worse with each passing minute. She feared she was going into premature labor.

"Shut up, you slut!" Juan spat nervously, tensing, for he was sure he had heard something. "Shut up!"

He fingered the carbine he held in his sweating palms. Though he had practiced endlessly loading and firing it, he still was not certain of his ability to use it. As most Spaniards did the marqués preferred the tempered steel of Toledo to a gun.

There! He had spied a movement in the courtyard below. He was sure of it! Quickly he raised the carbine and pulled the trigger. The shot went wild, reverberating crazily in the silence.

On slightly unsteady feet, for his ears were ringing again, and his eyes were blurring, Juan stood.

"Come out, you murdering bastard!" he shouted. "Come out, and show yourself! I know you're out there!" When there was no response he went on frenziedly. "Listen to me, whoever you are: I've got a woman up here." He yanked Aurora roughly to her feet and shoved her toward the edge of the roof. "She's blind and pregnant, and I'm going to kill her if you don't show yourself—and *pronto!*"

"Jesus Christ," Wolf whispered as his keen eyes finally homed in on the marqués. "He's on the roof—with your wife, Salvador."

"*Dios mío,*" the visconde gasped. "*Dios mío.*"

"I'm going to kill him. Now," Wolf declared, raising one of his pistols.

"No!" Salvador cried, knocking his cousin's revolver aside. "Damn you, Rafael! You might hit Aurora!"

"Not a chance," the gunslinger drawled grimly. "Not a chance."

"Goddamn you, Rafael!" the visconde swore again. "How can you be so certain of that? Do you never miss?"

"No, never," Wolf stated flatly.

"I don't care," Salvador uttered firmly. "I'm not going to risk Aurora's life on that. I'm going out there, and show myself."

"No!" Wolf spoke sharply, then, seeing the pain on his cousin's face, he continued more gently, "I'll go."

He was gone before the visconde could stop him. Salvador could do nothing but watch and wait and hope he wasn't going to have to shoot Juan himself in order to save his cousin's life, because the visconde was damned sure that his hand wasn't nearly as steady as Wolf's.

Up on the roof Juan peered down at the tall dark stranger now standing so boldly in the courtyard, his empty palms spread wide, his mouth grinning mockingly.

"Who are you?" the marqués queried, his voice rising as he stared at the man who had managed somehow to murder brutally all his hirelings. "Who are you?"

"Don't tell me that after all these long years you don't recognize me, Juan," Wolf taunted. "Your father, Don Manuel, would know me. But then I understand he isn't around anymore. Your half brother did us all a favor by ridding the world of that piece of garbage. I hope they buried him in a trash heap, though even that is more than he deserved."

"*Who are you?*" Juan asked again, shaking, his face red with anger at the insults being so jeeringly delivered to him about his dead father.

"Why, your cousin, of course. Do you not remember Don Rafael Bautista Delgados y Aguilar, Visconde Torreón, Juan? I am wounded, *mi primero*"—Wolf crossed his hands over his heart, as though stricken—"for I remember you."

"Rafael? Rafael?" Juan's voice was disbelieving. "No! It cannot be! It cannot be!"

"But I assure you it is."

"Keep him talking, cousin," Salvador murmured quietly from the dense gardens, where he was crouching behind Wolf. "I have a plan." The visconde turned to his young brother-in-law, who'd been standing by silently since they had crept up on the house, his dark eyes filled with apprehension. "Nicolas, turn Bribón loose, and tell him to go find Aurora. He's the only one who can get up on that roof from down here. Maybe he'll distract Juan long enough so he'll let go of Aurora. Then one of us can shoot the accursed serpent before he strikes!"

"Bribón," Nicolas commanded his pet as he removed the monkey's leash, "go find Aurora. Do you understand? Go find Aurora."

Then he pointed to the roof, and Bribón, with a little shriek, scampered off. Presently they saw him clambering up a vine that twined its way up one wall of the house. Once the monkey reached the roof, several things happened almost simultaneously, none of which Salvador had expected when he'd so desperately latched on to this rash plan.

Bribón, upon spying Aurora, instead of edging his way up to the girl in his usual manner, suddenly

squealed loudly and, bounding forward, flung himself
around her neck, causing her to stagger precariously.
She stumbled into Juan, knocking him off-balance; and
as the marqués, arms flailing, frantically held on to her
for support, he dropped his carbine. The weapon careened
off the roof, then clattered to the ground below,
discharging and sending Wolf rolling into the nearby
bushes for cover as he dodged the wildly ricocheting
bullet.

Then Aurora screamed, a high, thin, terrified wail
that pierced Salvador to his very core as he stood frozen
with horror and watched his beloved wife, Juan, and
the monkey fall.

Chapter Thirty-nine

THEY reached Juan first.

He was sprawled out on the earth, a short distance from the house. Somehow he was still alive, for he was groaning, obviously in tremendous pain. His eyes were glazing over with a red film, and Salvador did not know if his half brother recognized him or not.

"His back is broken," Wolf said as they raised up from their examination of the marqués's shattered body. "He won't live much longer—if he's lucky."

Juan must have comprehended the gunslinger's words, for he tried to rise, his head lolling pathetically as the attempt failed.

"End . . . it," he whispered hoarsely, his eyes closing. "End . . . it . . . now. Please."

It was probably the only time in his life the marqués had ever begged; and Salvador, despite everything his half brother had ever done to him, was moved to pity. Without a word he pulled the revolver at his waist and fired a single shot into Juan's head. The marqués jerked spasmodically for a moment, then lay still. Salvador tossed away his gun and began frantically to search for Aurora.

She was nowhere to be found. Not until they heard Bribón—who had managed to save himself by catching hold of a vine during the fall—chattering anxiously from above did they realize that Aurora lay upon a small balcony on the second story of the house. They rushed inside, Salvador's heart thudding louder than his boots as he raced up the staircase to his beloved's side.

She lay in a pool of fluid, but it was not blood; and the visconde was baffled as to the cause of the liquid, for he could find no serious injury upon his wife. The overgrown honeysuckle vine that had proven Bribón's salvation had also cushioned the blow of Aurora's body when she'd struck the balcony. She was alive and apparently unharmed except for some minor cuts and bruises. Still it was obvious that she was in great pain. Sobbing her name brokenly as he gathered her gently into his arms, Salvador carried her into the chamber that opened out onto the balcony and laid her down upon the bed within.

"*Querida,* oh, *querida,*" he murmured over and over. "Can you speak? How badly are you hurt—and where?"

At the sound of his voice Aurora, with an effort, lifted her head.

"Sal—Salvador?" she breathed.

"*Sí,* oh, *sí, muñeca mía.* I am here. No. Do not try to talk. You've had a terrible fall."

"I . . . know." Aurora paused and licked her parched lips. "But I'm—I'm only dazed and—and a little battered . . . I think. It's . . . the baby. Oh, Salvador. The baby . . . is coming."

"*Sangre de Cristo!*" Wolf swore softly, recognizing the symptoms from his own wife's pregnancy. "She's right. She's in labor! Mario, go to the hotel, quickly, and fetch my wife. Nicolas, run downstairs, set some water to boiling, and find as many clean cloths as you can. Salvador. *Salvador!*" Wolf suddenly grabbed his cousin by the shoulders and shook him roughly. "She's all right. Do you understand me? Aurora's all right! She's in labor. That's why she's in such agony. The baby is coming. Now!"

"But it's—it's too soon," the visconde stammered, bewildered, still overcome with shock.

"The baby doesn't know that, you fool!" Wolf snapped sharply, wondering if he were going to have to slap his cousin to shake him from his stunned, emotional state. "Now get hold of yourself. At once! Your wife needs you."

At that Salvador appeared to gather his wits, helping Wolf strip the sheets from the bed and tie them to the bedposts, so that Aurora would have something to hold on to when she needed it.

"Doña Aurora." Wolf spoke so tenderly that for a moment Salvador wondered if Storm had arrived, before he realized it was his cousin's voice talking so soothingly to the girl. "Doña Aurora, I am your husband's cousin," Wolf went on. "My name is Lobo. I know, from my own wife, Storm, how modest women are, so I don't want you to be embarrassed when I tell you I must get you out of these clothes that you're wearing. I want only to help you, as I did my own wife when our son was born. Will you think of me as family and allow me to do this? I will not look at you any more than is necessary, I promise."

"Of course, *el primero* of my husband."

Aurora managed to smile, though she blushed at the idea of a stranger removing her garments and gazing upon her naked form. Still he seemed so kind, so gentle, that she knew she could learn to love this man as much as Salvador did. The visconde himself pushed aside his feelings of jealousy that Wolf should look so upon Aurora. The gunslinger obviously knew what he was doing, and Salvador did not. He wrung his hands nervously as his wife's sweet face contorted once more as another sharp contraction ripped through her body.

"Pant, señora," Wolf ordered. "Pant! It will help to ease the pain. *Sí*, that's it. Now breathe. Breathe! *Sí*, it is better now, no?"

"*Sí*," Aurora replied as she gasped for air, her hands tightening on the bedsheets as deftly Wolf, with his knife, cut away her gown and undergarments. "How do you—how do you know so much about—about birthing babies?" she asked to take her mind off what he was doing.

"It is a long story, señora, one that Salvador will tell you someday, perhaps. Do you think you can get to your feet, Doña Aurora? It would help to lessen the shock of the contractions if you could walk about for a while."

"I—I don't know," Aurora replied as she felt her husband drape his shirt around her to cover her nakedness, there being no nightgown to be had.

"Try, Aurora," Salvador insisted as he buttoned the shirt. "If Raf—Lobo thinks it will aid you, then I am certain it will."

Supported by the two men, the girl managed to stand and to stumble weakly about the room. After a few turns she discovered to her surprise that the pain did indeed begin to recede somewhat. Still the strain of staying on her feet was almost more than Aurora could bear. She was so debilitated by her terrifying ordeal of the past several long weeks and so battered by her fall from the roof that she felt as though she were going to collapse any moment. Both Salvador and Wolf thought it was a miracle that she did not.

"And they say that women are the weaker sex," the visconde muttered aloud to himself as his wife leaned against him heavily.

"Don't you believe it," Wolf rejoined. "My Storm would brave the flames of hell and survive."

I would have braved even the flames of hell for the man I loved. . . .

The words that Aurora had spoken to him once long ago rang in Salvador's mind as he watched his wife grit her teeth against another onslaught of pain.

"Scream, señora. Scream, if you must," Wolf commanded softly.

But Aurora did not. Instead she closed her eyes tightly and staggered on.

Would I have been so courageous in light of all that she has endured? Salvador asked himself silently. *I think not. Oh, God, don't let her die. Please don't let her die. She has been through so much. . . .*

Aurora was grateful when Storm arrived at last, for there was something so vital and indomitable about Wolf's wife that Aurora seemed to draw strength from Storm's very presence.

"I bore my son Comanche fashion, squatting upon the prairie grass, my arms about a tree for support," Storm said. "But you, I think, would like to lie down now, Doña Aurora. Is that not so?"

"*Sí.*" The girl nodded tiredly, overcome by agony and exhaustion.

"*Enfin.* Then get into bed, for, if I'm not mistaken,

your time has nearly come. Nicolas! Where is that boy?"

"Here, señora."

"Ah, *bien*. You have the hot water and clean cloths. Wolf, you know what to do," Storm remarked as her husband began to sterilize his knife, with which he would cut the cord. She turned back to Aurora. "Now, señora. Push. Push!"

Aurora could restrain her cries no longer. She screamed and then screamed again as she strained and bore down, forcing the premature child from her womb. Her fingers released the bedsheets to clutch Salvador's hands so tightly he could feel them growing numb from lack of circulation. Still he did not withdraw them from his wife's grasp, feeling that in some way he was pouring strength from his body into her own.

Presently the baby's head appeared, crowned by a downy fluff of black hair.

"Again, señora. Push!" Storm ordered, then directed, "Aguila, come."

The visconde was reluctant to let go of Aurora, but nevertheless, he did as Storm instructed him, kneeling before his wife and cradling his hands to receive their child. Though she could not now touch him, Aurora understood what he was doing; and joy such as she had never known reverberated through her being.

"What is it, Salvador?" she queried weakly as at long last she felt the baby's slippery body slither from her own. "A boy or a girl?"

"A boy, *querida*. We have a fine, healthy son," he answered, his face filled with love and happiness as, after starting the child's lungs to breathing as Wolf had shown him, he placed the baby upon his wife's breast.

Marveling at the infant's smallness, Aurora hugged

her son close, her hands fluttering searchingly over his tiny form as gingerly she counted his fingers and toes to be certain he was perfect.

"Esteban," she said. "He shall be called Esteban, for your father, Salvador."

The visconde drew a sharp breath. How had she known that he had wished to name his son after the father he had never seen?

"Oh, *querida*," he whispered, then broke off abruptly as Aurora suddenly gasped, her face once more convulsed with pain. "What is it? What's wrong?" Salvador cried.

Everyone stared at Aurora, panic-stricken, for everything had been progressing so well they could not now understand what was happening to her. Then suddenly Wolf smiled.

"Twins!" he exclaimed. "There's another."

Moments later another small head made its appearance. This time the baby was a girl.

"Gitana, for your grandmother," Salvador stated softly as he pressed this child too to Aurora's breast.

Tears filled her sapphire-blue eyes at this. How like Salvador to remember her tender feelings for Abuela.

"How I love you, *mi corazón*," she murmured. "And now"—she sighed, yawning—"it has been a long day, and I would like to rest."

Before the visconde could speak further his wife was fast asleep.

"Is she going to be all right?" Salvador asked anxiously, startled.

"Of course." Storm smiled as gently she removed the twins from Aurora's arms and began to bathe and clothe them while Wolf disposed of the afterbirth and wiped off his knife. "She is simply exhausted, poor thing. Her abduction, her fall from the roof, her labor—all have been a terrible struggle for her. But she is strong, your Aurora. She needs time to heal and forget, but she will survive, I promise you."

"Oh, Storm. I hope you are right," the visconde uttered passionately, "for if I have not Aurora, then I have nothing at all."

Chapter Forty

Esplendor, Peru, 1852

THE great house built by Don Santiago Roque y Avilés so many centuries ago for his beloved Doña Arabela was nearly restored. It lacked only the huge solid gold bell to be complete, and this Salvador and Aurora planned to hang in the cupola, come sunrise.

It was a fitting time, they thought, for with Aurora's recovery the long dark nights of despair were behind them now; and a new day, a new beginning, was dawning on their horizon.

Somewhere in Mexico, on a farm called *Fin Terre*— Land's End—Storm and Wolf were putting their son Chance to bed. Down the vast Amazon River, Mario Nunes and his friend Bernardo, now the proud partners in their own trading company—thanks to the grateful Rodriquezes—paddled toward the manor, their dugout canoes carrying the Montalbáns and the Yerbabuenas to an eagerly awaited reunion with their children. A short distance away Lupe and Jim Rawlings stood on the front porch of their cabin, their arms entwined as they gazed out over the plantation. Out in the meadow, Nicolas taught the mischievous Bribón a new trick; and up- stairs, in the newly finished nursery, young Esteban and Gitana slept soundly in their cradles.

In the attic Salvador and Aurora were patiently clean- ing the angelus bell, getting it ready for tomorrow.

"My husband," the girl uttered quietly as she worked, "does it seem to you as though we belong here, at Esplendor, as though somehow we have always belonged here?"

"*Sí*," Salvador replied. "Now more than ever, since returning, do I feel it is so. You said once, *querida*, that you believed in a past life. Is it possible, do you think, that we loved long ago as Don Santiago and Doña Arabela? That our love was so strong it endured long after our tragic deaths to fulfill its destiny in these lives we now know?"

"*Sí*," Aurora answered, sighing. "In my heart I feel I am one with Arabela. Oh, look, Salvador. What is this? It feels like some sort of raised lettering. . . ."

"Let me see," the visconde said as he moved the oil lamp closer so it shone down upon the bell. "*Sí*, it is an inscription of some kind."

"What does it say?"

"I don't know. Give me your cloth, and let me polish away some of this dirt. Ah, there." Silently Salvador read the words engraved upon the angelus; then, still disbelieving, he turned to his wife. "Oh, Aurora," he murmured, his voice throbbing with emotion, "we have found the buried treasure of Esplendor."

"What?" she gasped.

"*Sí*, it was here all the time, written upon this bell. Listen!" Softly the visconde began to quote: " 'Love is the greatest treasure on earth, grander than gold and glory too: for riches are soon spent, and fame is but fleeting. Love alone is everlasting.' This was Don Santiago's fortune—his love for Doña Arabela. Love, Aurora! The most precious of golds, the brightest of glories; and it is ours, *muñeca mía*, now and for always."

Now and for always, Aurora thought again as, at sunrise, they hoisted the angelus bell to its proper place in the cupola. *Sí*, that is how long my love for Salvador will endure—and his for me. I am truly the most fortunate woman alive.

The sun stole slowly over the horizon, its shining rays sweeping across the blue-washed sky and striking the bell in a glittering array of glorious gold.

Gold?

Aurora blinked once, twice; and still the light kept growing brighter and brighter, filling her dark world with its luminescence.

My sight is coming back, she realized. After all this time my sight is coming back! She turned to her husband, seeing, for the first time since her accident, his handsome face, filled with love for her. I will not tell him yet, she thought, not yet, not until I am sure. Till then my beloved will be my eyes, as surely as he is my heart's desire.

Smiling down tenderly at Aurora, Salvador took her hands in his as together they pulled on the bell rope, and the angelus bell rang out joyously over the jungle, a song of love everlasting, sweet and strong and clear.

Author's Note

THERE are many awesome sights on earth—but none perhaps so compelling in its fashion as the Amazon jungle. This vast, tropical rain forest—and others like it—has stood for centuries, a life unto itself, so intricately interwoven that the death of a single species of bird can upset the jungle's delicate ecological balance.

The variety of life in the rain forest is endless. Over one hundred different species of trees have been cataloged in a half-square-mile area alone; some two thousand varieties of orchids flourish in the jungle; and over eight thousand species of insects have been classified.

The English naturalist Henry Walter Bates spent the years from 1848 to 1859 in the Amazon Basin, collecting 14,712 species of animals—the most extensive collection ever made—and taking copious notes on his observations. Unfortunately upon his return to Europe there was a fire on board his ship, and all of his priceless collection was lost. His book, however, *The Naturalist on the River Amazon*, originally published in two volumes in 1863, remains. It is considered a definitive work on the Amazon River.

Tragically, even as you read this note, the irreplaceable rain forests of the world are being systematically destroyed.

In Brazil alone more than twenty thousand prospectors and laborers have invaded portions of the jungle, mining for gold; legitimate lumber companies—as well as illegal loggers desecrating national parks, such as the Taï National Park in the Ivory Coast—are steadily slashing and burning acres and acres of rain forest regions; and oil companies are encroaching upon the virgin terrain. In 1980, much less than half of the jungle area was left in the Malay Peninsula alone.

No one is certain how important the rain forests are to our planet, but it is known that this wide-scale destruction is contributing to what scientists call the greenhouse effect, a global warming that may soon cause erratic changes in the world's climate—to say nothing of the thousands of species of plants and animals that are being irretrievably lost, some, sadly, even before they have been discovered.

For the reader who is interested in learning more about tropical rain forests, the author suggests *National Geographic,* Vol. 163, No. 1 (January 1983). This magazine contains two articles that are excellent: "Nature's Dwindling Treasures—Rain Forests," by Peter T. White, pp. 2–46; and "Teeming Life of a Rain Forest," by Carol and David Hughes, pp. 49–65. Additional sources may be found in the reader's public library. The television specials of Jacques Cousteau's travels along the Amazon River are especially thought provoking.

The author would like very much to thank the Neurological Surgery PA, in Wichita, Kansas, for its kind assistance in discussing with her the various types of injuries that may be incurred as the result of a trauma to the brain.

The author would also like to thank, once again, her dear friend and editor, Fredda Isaacson, whose fine, critical eye for plot development and detail helped to shape the structure of this novel.

REBECCA BRANDEWYNE